SOLDIER BOY

SOLDIER BOY

E. SCOTT JONES

ST. MARTIN'S PRESS NEW YORK

LIBRARY OF CONGRESS CATALOGING-IN-PUBLICATION DATA

Jones, E. Scott.
    Soldier boy / E. Scott Jones.
        p.   cm.
    "A Thomas Dunne book."
    ISBN 0-312-11895-3
    I. Title.
PS3560.04812S65   1995
813'.54–dc20   94-41109
                                                      CIP

First Edition: February 1995
10 9 8 7 6 5 4 3 2 1

ACKNOWLEDGMENTS

I owe gratitude to a number of people for this work

First and foremost, I thank my wife, Vicki, for putting up with a loner's loner.

I would especially like to thank my agent, George Wieser, who has been a real motivator throughout. I must also express thanks to Olga Wieser for her staunch support, and for being an avid fan in the process.

I would like to thank Tom Dunne at St. Martin's for undertaking this project. Pete Wolverton, my editor, was a big help. Thanks for the suggestions, Pete. Many thanks also to Judith McQuown for her excellent editing.

Thanks to Jim McGivney and special thanks to Robert C. Kerstann at the DEA. Without Rob's aggressive assistance I would have been at an extreme disadvantage concerning certain elements of my story. Thanks Rob. To the DEA as a whole, I must also express gratitude for the organization's openness and transparent lack of fear of those of us who write for a living.

Thanks to Art Anthony of the Georgia State Crime Lab for his forensics assistance.

Thanks to Ed Jones and Doreen Duncan for their editorial assistance.

Last but not least, I owe a great debt of gratitude, and much more, to Birdie Bomar for her unswerving support and devotion throughout the years.

E. Scott Jones, 1994

PART ONE

SHIMMERING THE MIRAGE

CHAPTER 1

They had him. Finally. The surveillance had been going on for weeks. They knew he was bent, but he'd been lying low for days and all they could do was wait. Now the waiting was over, he was on the move. With any luck, they were also about to house his contacts, which is what they were really after anyway. The cat-and-mouse charade had started just before lunch. That's when the target began clearing his path, moving from location to location, stopping here to browse, rushing there to catch a cab, all the while looking for the telltale signs that would indicate he was under scrutiny by the most feared law enforcement organization in the world.

The FBI surveillance team knew he had gone operational within minutes of his doing so. It takes a pro to know one, and they knew. The call went out and the Bureau mobilized. He would later admit that he hadn't the faintest scent; his instincts never flared; he thought he was in the clear. No wonder. Experienced agents had been called in from field offices all over the country in preparation for this exercise. They had been on twenty-four hour operational readiness augmented with daily briefings in small groups and dry-run deployments. The result was that the Bureau now had over three hundred agents, some ninety vehicles, five helicopters, and an assortment of fixed-wing aircraft arrayed against their target and his accomplices. They had also brought in the best surveillance controller in the business. Known affectionately as the Chess Master, not inventive but descriptive, he had the uncanny ability of being able to anticipate his opponent's moves and then counter them brilliantly with his own. All in all, it was, as the SAC—Special Agent in Charge—would later say when briefing the Senate Select Committee on Intelligence, a massive operation.

The first tidbit of information suggesting that Colonel Murdock was pitching for the other team came out of London. An obscure statement was overheard by an Indian woman who had been attired as one of Gandhi's faithful. The woman, as fate would have it, happened to have been sitting near a distinguished looking gentle-

3

man and his mysterious associate at a local eatery. The statement itself caused the gentleman, who was in reality a top GRU operative named Shevchenko and not really a gentleman, to glare at his associate for making it. It also caused an adrenaline surge in the Indian woman. She was not really Indian and, if asked, couldn't have told anyone too much about Gandhi or his mantras. A great deal of her studies over the past years had taken place at CIA headquarters in McLean, Virginia. Thus, when the gentleman's associate, clad in faded Levi's and a brown bomber jacket, remarked with a cocky grin that American payloads were about as secret as the royal family's romances, the woman took note and duly passed the information to the station chief, who immediately cabled Washington under a *critic* designation, or highest priority.

In and of itself, the statement might have been harmless. Considering the identity of the two participants in the conversation, however, it served in some measure to spark the beginnings of a discreet investigation within the corridors of the American intelligence community. The investigation heated up rapidly when, several weeks later, the Russians arrogantly charged top members of the U.S. disarmament team with infringing upon the unwritten law of double standards. In the interim, Russian strategic activity had been in full swing and was scaring hell out of Western intelligence agencies the world over. The United States decided turnabout was fair play, and it was becoming painfully obvious to those in the know that America's new sub-rosa policy of retrofitting and redeployment of previously earmarked-for-destruction nuclear warheads was a de facto progression that had become a dripping faucet.

And so the search began in earnest. Leaks were discreetly checked, verified, and backtracked. Who had access? Travel itineraries were finely combed. Of those who had access, whose vetting was not current? Disinformation was thrown into the pond. Where did it surface? And finally the hammer had fallen. Seven months later Colonel Murdock had been declared the nefarious winner in an arduous but extremely secretive mole hunt. All they had to do now was catch him in the act.

The dead drop was just off the road in a secluded stretch of woods in Fairfax County outside of Washington. Although it was no more than an hour-and-a-half's drive from the Pentagon, which is where he worked in A-2, or Air Force Intelligence, it took Colonel

Murdock roughly six-and-a-half hours to make the trip. His last stop had been Dulles Airport. That had given the Chess Master momentary heart palpitations until the watchers confirmed that Murdock was there only to pick up a gray Ford Taurus, which he was now in the process of parking near a clump of trees just off of the pavement. Within moments of his departing Dulles the FBI had ascertained that the car had been rented from Alamo the previous day by a gentleman named Tweed. The transaction had been secured with a Visa card issued by Chemical Bank, expiration date December of the following year. The FBI knew that the card would have been returned to its elements by now, and none of the agents harbored any naive aspirations of successfully tracking an apparition who once called himself Tweed.

The sun was drifting lazily toward the west, abandoning the Virginian countryside to the first assault of the late-afternoon shadows when Murdock got out of the car. As luck would have it, the FBI guessed right in this part of the operation. Murdock had been in the box all day. No matter which way he went—east, west, up, whatever—federal agents had him surrounded. On those occasions when it was necessary to get close, the agent involved was pulled out of the lineup immediately after the target resumed his surreptitious journey and was relegated to driving the backup cars or assisting with communication and coordination. The quarry was never presented with the same face twice. It had all gone very smoothly, like clockwork, but when the Taurus eased onto a lonely stretch of road some twenty miles back, the Chess Master's heart palpitations returned. An experienced team is almost impossible to beat in the city or other populated areas, but the advantage shifts to the target when the environment becomes isolated, as it was now. After all, only he knew where he was going. Any tails would have to show themselves in order to stay close.

The lead surveillance cars, well ahead of Murdock, had begun peeling off one by one onto roads that might be accessed by the trailing target. Each was receiving instructions from the Chess Master, who was in direct communication with the choppers and other tag vehicles that were passing Murdock head-on in the opposite direction. The helicopters were equipped with ultrapowerful scopes and thermal imaging capability so a visual could be maintained from a safe distance at all times. Along with outlying vehicles, they were also responsible for detecting any enemy countersurveillance which might be on station. There had been none so far. All communications for the operation were assigned a special frequency which was not authorized for use by the FCC. The Bureau knew, however, that the Russians would be scanning and retrieving signal after signal from active-repeater ferret satellites, attempting to pick up any modulations which might warn them that their own operation was in jeopardy. So while the formidable ocean of antennae atop the Russian embassy at Mount Alto continuously probed the airwaves, the FBI had been prepared and was returning serve with overhead slams. Floating high above the clouds and pulverizing the Russian embassy through a barrage of selective jamming pips was an AWACS with a crew who knew nothing about the operation or why they were doing what they were doing, but who nevertheless were getting a great deal of satisfaction out of doing it. As the Chess Master had told the SAC earlier that morning, everything was covered. The Master himself was trailing the whole affair in an elaborate van, the inside of which would have been considered a technological mecca by any electronics or radio enthusiast. Studying his computerized grid map for maybe two seconds, the Chess Master had directed seven of the lead cars—which were only several minutes ahead of their quarry—onto a particularly long, winding road he felt had potential. Not surprisingly, it turned out to be a good move. It was the same road where Murdock had just parked the Taurus. Each of the seven cars, nowhere in sight now, had been filled with five agents. All but the driver were attired in camouflage fatigues and sported assault weapons, headsets, face paint, and provisions. It was here that the FBI caught a break.

The agents in the seven cars had been well trained and were well rehearsed. Confirmation had come over their radios that the target had in fact taken this route and was unknowingly in pursuit. Several kilometers down the road the first car slowed and pulled over. The other six cars sped past. As the first vehicle glided along the pavement, the doors suddenly flew open and out leapt the four agents clothed in camouflage. They hit the ground rolling and then vanished into the woods. The remaining agent stomped on the accelerator and raced away. This same process was repeated by the other six cars, but these deployments were not random. The driver of each vehicle was responsible for establishing the origin of tactical deployment, and he had to make a snap decision based on what he was able to observe of the scenery flying by him at fifty miles per hour. Each deployment was calculated to position the agents in an area where a meet or a drop would most likely take place.

It was the driver of the fourth vehicle who hit the nail on the head. When Murdock stepped out of the car, eight eyes and four rifles were covering him from concealment.

Judging by the thickness of the brown manila envelope the traitor was carrying in his left hand, Special Agent Callahan thought privately that Solomon got it right when he said there was a time for every purpose or a purpose for every time, or something like that, and since the cross hairs were centered squarely on the bridge of Murdock's nose, which was no more than twenty paces from Callahan's position, he figured that this was one of those times when the Bible ought to be interpreted literally and squeezing off a couple of quick rounds would fulfill prophecy. However, he held his latent tendencies in check and watched as the traitor moved into a group of pines and placed the envelope inside the furrow of a hollow stump.

Although walking rapidly, Murdock hadn't retreated more than ten paces before he was on the ground. He would later confess that he couldn't remember how his nose had been broken, what with all the shouting and screeching of tires and the speed with which everything had happened. The official report of the incident would also concur that the broken nose must remain one of those unsolved mysteries since Callahan, the first to reach Murdock, couldn't seem to piece together the exact sequence of events. Everything had happened rather quickly for him, too.

Murdock had been whisked away, but his trip was neither boring nor completely painless. Was he supposed to signal someone that the drop had been made successfully, he was asked as he rode prone in the floor of the van with his arms and legs shackled. "No," he told them. The van must have hit a particularly nasty bump at that point because the timing coincided with the abrupt movement of a combat boot and sharp pains in his ribs. Was he sure? Yes. There is always a signal, he was told as another bump was encountered. "Not this time," he lamented, wondering if the van had any shock absorbers at all. When was the pickup to occur? He didn't know. What did his contact look like? What kind of vehicle would he be driving? He didn't know. It turned out to be a long, very bumpy ride for the colonel.

The various surveillance teams had been put in place immediately after being reorganized and juggled by the Chess Master, just as a general might deploy his troops before a major battle. Callahan and his force had been joined by eight additional agents with camouflage gear who were quickly informed by Callahan that they could deploy wherever they liked just as long as no one took a position closer to the drop than he. The Taurus had been removed and the entire area policed quickly but methodically—almost to the point of sterilization—to make sure that nothing appeared out of the ordinary. The only complaint that a group such as the Sierra Club might have had was the fact that a Coca-Cola can had been left by the side of the road near the base of a large pine. It was lying there before Murdock ever showed up, so the sweepers, after determining that it was empty, left it alone. If they knew that a man who sometimes called himself Tweed had been standing in that very spot polishing off a Coke about an hour earlier, the significance wouldn't have escaped them.

The waiting game began.

Although the FBI is a patient lot, that particular virtue wasn't tested in this operation. The twelve agents in concealment simultaneously heard the metallic voice of the Chess Master in their headsets; "Possible suspect moving toward you . . . one male . . . Caucasian . . . red Ford Ranger . . . ETA four minutes." Daylight was fading quickly now. Callahan, a perfectionist at heart, sighted in on the Coke can to adjust himself to the contrast. The wind was barely stirring. He measured the shadows creeping along the ground, played the scope back and forth, and scanned the positions of the other agents to make sure none of them had fudged in order to get closer to the drop than he. Johnson's pushing it, he thought. If there had been time, he would have moved Agent Johnson back a bit. Johnson was only about ten feet to his left and behind, and he knew Johnson could run like a wide receiver. "ETA three minutes." Something about the can began to bother him. What was it? Why were his instincts suddenly manufacturing butterflies? He moved the cross hairs slowly over the can, painting every centimeter with his vision, as if something would suddenly leap out and enlighten him. There was an anomaly there somewhere, but he couldn't put his finger on it. "ETA one minute." Uh-oh!

"Everybody stay put!" Callahan blurted into his mouthpiece as he dove out of his position and launched his body toward the can. The Ranger was just rounding the bend, giving the driver a clear view of the drop site. Callaghan slithered on his stomach and tore the can out of a wedge of two exposed roots from a large pine. He scrambled backward furiously, but it was too late to try for his former position so he planted himself just ten feet away from the drop inside a clump of bramble bushes. His camouflage would have to do the rest.

This one was different than Murdock, Callahan observed as the man stepped lightly out of the Ranger. Murdock had displayed that worried look which reflected the persona of a man who had been under extreme pressure for a long time. A look that all traitors get, he thought. But this one had a different demeanor altogether. There was a self-assuredness about him, a sense of purpose, and not the slightest trace of guilt. Either an illegal or a staff officer of the KGB or GRU, Callahan judged. He hoped he was an illegal. Otherwise he probably had diplomatic immunity and all they would be able to do is deport the SOD.

Callahan and the others watched anxiously as the man strode to the spot where the Coca-Cola can had rested just moments earlier. He bent down quickly and inspected the immediate surroundings. In an almost gingerly fashion, the stranger rubbed his hands over the wedge, as if to make sure it really existed, then stood up and headed for the hollow stump where Murdock had placed the envelope. At that instant, Callahan knew a rather large party would be thrown in his honor by over three hundred FBI agents and their wives. He might even get an "attaboy" from the Director himself.

The man reached in and extracted the envelope. He had no way of knowing that at this very moment the genuine documents were being analyzed by American intelligence and the package he now had in his possession was a dummy, placed there immediately after Murdock was grabbed. Had he bothered to open the envelope and peer inside he would have discovered his predicament straight away. As it was, it only took a few more seconds for him to get an education. Callahan broke his own record for stopping a man in his tracks. As the man lay flat on his back with Callahan on top of him and eleven other agents hanging on to some part of his anatomy, Callahan glared down on him and said, "We are from the FBI, and *you, maggot,* are under arrest for espionage!" Special Agent Larry F. Callahan had been waiting ten years for the opportunity to perform that particular rendition for a spy.

CHAPTER 2

"Passport, bitte," bellowed the Frankfurt customs officer. Jack Calumet handed it to him, along with his declaration card. *"Haben Sie etwas zu verzollen?"*

"Nein." And yes, old boy, a weary Calumet thought, I'm an American who can speak German, and if I had anything to declare I would have put it on the card. His passport was returned and he was waved through.

If ever there was an enigma within an enigma, Jack Calumet was it. In fact, had the existence of life on other planets ever been confirmed, few people would be accused of referring to him as an Earthling even though he claimed Mississippi as his birthplace. In many ways he was wise beyond his forty years, in others he had a sprightly, boyish quality about him which, on plenty of occasions, caused his friends to think he tended to tilt a bit too much, at least for their tastes, toward that stage of adolescence more commonly found in their twenty-year-old sons. Or, in some cases even, their teenagers, because if Jack Calumet was anything, he was an eternal prankster, and often at times when being the recipient of one of his comedic feats was most inconvenient. In spite of that and his many other oddities, such as his cavalier attitude about his dress, or lack of it, some would say, because he was a person who could feel comfortable at a black-tie dinner party clad only in his blue jeans, T-shirt, and Reeboks—not the ones he jogged in—and nobody would quite know what to make of "that guy over there dressed like a stinking bum," staunchly refusing to master their own jealousies since the "bum" could outcommunicate them on practically any subject; in spite of *all* that, everyone who really knew him liked him. It was difficult not to, even when expending a great deal of effort to that extent, because he had this strangely energetic, Pollyannaish way about him. The fact is, and most women would tell you so, Jack Calumet was simply irrepressible.

Perhaps his life-style had as much as anything to do with it. Calumet, and most of the men who knew him would attest to this part, was fiercely intelligent, inordinately perceptive, and an hombre who possessed the instincts of a nomadic lion. He always tried to get along with everybody and most of the time he succeeded at it, but on those elusive occasions when a person, or an entire group of persons, whatever the case, appeared incapable, or maybe just downright indisposed, of grasping the higher essence of his more charming and endearing qualities, he went on his merry way and gave it nary a second thought, for Jack Calumet, in addition to being a prankster, was a loner at heart. He had to be. As a double agent operating between the Americans and the Russians, he could ill afford to make a mistake, and his ability to juggle personas the way a short-order cook flipped pancakes was a prime requisite for his survival. He knew the Russians had him pegged as a double who was motivated solely by money. He also knew that the Americans, in clandestine contrast, counted him as one of their own, a loyal double motivated strictly by patriotism. He knew all of that, and he felt good inside whenever he thought about it—which was a lot these days, considering his present state—because the Russians had him figured wrong. Jack Calumet was an American patriot through and through, and now that Soviet Russia was once again united, he was engaged in a desperate, secret war that was being waged against the echelons of Moscow Center at full throttle.

Dressed in his faded Levi's and brown bomber jacket, Calumet took the long stroll through the terminal, finally reaching the overhead walkway that connected to the Frankfurt Airport Sheraton. "Careful, Jack, careful," he whispered to himself. He was unable to identify the Russian or American surveillants. He knew they would be watching him, confirming his arrival, but to select them out of a thousand faces was impossible, especially since they wouldn't have sent anybody he could recognize. The Russians had, in fact, sent a man to pick him up and tether him to his final destination, which the Russian presumed would be the Sheraton. After Calumet checked in, the Russian's job would be done. The Americans, on the other hand, had sent four men and two women. Their job was not so much to watch Calumet, but rather to look after him. Since the Murdock affair, the CIA was playing it safe by assuming that Calumet might be in danger. Loyal doubles had gone missing more than a few times in the past. The CIA was determined not to let it happen again.

Two incidents might have led the Russians to the conclusion that Jack Calumet was working for the Americans all along. One was the careless statement he had made in front of Major-General Shevchenko about American payloads some eight months earlier in London. The other was a blown agent named Murdock in an operation in which Calumet had participated. Having met with a GRU operative assigned to the Russian embassy in Washington, Calumet had been supplied with a Visa card and other documents identifying him as a man named Tweed. The Russians had had him under constant surveillance the entire three days he was in the United States, and they were certain he had made no contact with the Americans. Furthermore, although Jack was aware that the Russians had an extremely good source who was supplying them with information about American nuclear capability, he never knew the identity of the asset or that the asset happened to be an American colonel in Air Force intelligence. Nor was he enlightened as to why he was asked to rent a gray Ford Taurus and leave the keys over the left front wheel, or why he was supposed to place a Coca-Cola can between the exposed roots of a pine tree. Still, the operation had exploded in their faces and one of their Illegals had been captured. The lights would be burning round the clock in GRU headquarters, known to insiders as the Aquarium, while a task force poured over every detail of Murdock's tenure as a Russian spy in an effort to define damage assessment. At the very least, the Russians would have to begin wondering by now if Jack Calumet wasn't bad luck.

Jack checked into the Sheraton and went to his room immediately. He was tired after the overnight flight and wanted to grab a nap. He threw his bag on the stand, his clothes on the floor, and climbed between the sheets. Two hours later the phone rang. He picked it up. "Outside your door, two minutes," was all the voice said before the line went dead. He splashed water on his face, put on his pants, and waited. The soft knock was barely audible. Calumet opened the door and picked up the single folded piece of paper lying on the carpet. The hallway was empty. Latching the door and stepping back into the room he opened the paper. What he read sent tingles up his spine.

Shevchenko executed. Suggest you come in.

"Nuts!" was his immediate reaction, and he said it out loud. But then he began to analyze the message.

Jack knew that the GRU—Russian military intelligence—was a dragon that was treacherous indeed. With a virtual budget estimated by some to be tens of times larger than the budget of the KGB, the GRU was directly responsible for some of the Soviet Union's most celebrated scientific achievements. A great many of those achievements, however, came about not because of any exhaustive research, but rather by virtue of the fact that the GRU was very likely the world's foremost expert in the art of pilfering state-of-the-art technology from America and other scientifically advanced nations. In any case, it wasn't their acumen in the field of technology that had Calumet worried. He was much more concerned with GRU executive agents who had completed Spetsnaz training at the Frunze or Military-Diplomatic Academies and who were extremely adept at *mokrie dela,* or assassination. If the KGB had been the sword and shield of the party, then the GRU was the dragon who came forth to ravage and spew its fire.

Why was Shevchenko executed? He had to chew on that one. Did it mean that they were on to him? Was Shevchenko killed because he hadn't diagnosed Calumet for what he really was? Or was he killed because the GRU needed its pound of flesh for a compromised operation? That was possible. Shevchenko hadn't been running Murdock, but he had been running the GRU Resident in Washington who was running Murdock. Still, Jack reflected, the premise was a little thin. It didn't really make sense. True, the operation was blown, but it had been extremely successful for over a year. It had given the Russians, who were playing catch-up, valuable information about America's strategic deployment, targeting, and delivery capabilities. If anything, it would seem that promotions would be alighting upon the shoulders of those involved in the Murdock operation.

"Shevchenko executed," Calumet whispered to himself. The mere fact that he gave voice to it brought forth revelation. Jack knew he could rationalize it from now on, get twenty opinions on the subject, hammer it out and turn it over, but there really wasn't any question—he was blown. His instincts pronounced judgment as soon as he said it. "Shevchenko executed." He took the note into the bathroom and lit it with the complementary matches resting in the ashtray. The ashes fell into the toilet and he flushed them, waiting until the commode finished gurgling to make sure all the residue had disappeared. He rested his hands on the vanity and gazed into the mirror. He didn't look forty. More like thirty-five, he thought. And he was still in excellent physical shape. He was proud of that. At six feet, one hundred and seventy-five pounds, a full head of brown hair complemented by blue eyes and a mustache, he had received his share of sideways glances from the ladies, although that didn't excite him any longer. He was engaged to Diane Shylock, and she was still waiting for him back in Georgia. *Shevchenko executed.* He knew, after Murdock, that his situation would become a bit more dicey, albeit he certainly hadn't expected Shevchenko to be the victim. If anything, he thought, *he* was the one who would become the attempted victim, not the Russian. *Shevchenko executed.* Why? He couldn't read it, not even begin to read it, and in any event, that wasn't bothering him anywhere near as much as the second part of the message.

Suggest you come in.

Suggest? What the Sam Hill did that mean? Was it an order in disguise? Was it one of those implicit commands that a captain might deliver to a subordinate, such as, "Don't you think the men ought to move that latrine fifty feet west, lieutenant?" Or did it mean that they weren't ordering him in because they wanted him to remain in place as a double, but they wanted it to be his decision? In other words, it was very dangerous at this point and no one would think less of him if he begged off, but in reality they were hoping he'd stay out in the cold. He was too tired to work out all the permutations. Besides, he thought, maybe they had no idea themselves and were just leaving it all up to him. Maybe *they* didn't have a good read on this one, although he knew that as soon as the first two analysts in the Intelligence Directorate got into it a minimum of ten foolproof, policy-making conclusions would be drawn.

Jack picked up the phone and ordered room service. Lying back on the bed with his hands clasped behind his head, he began to think it through. Would this be the end of his spy career, or the new beginning? The first Cold War was over, although there were those who said that it had never really ended; it just continued at a lesser pace for a time. When the Berlin Wall came down and communism collapsed throughout the Eastern Bloc, there was a universal belief that mankind had the ability, after all, to sail forward through history with a steady rudder. Calumet hoped it would last, but he and others of his ilk never really thought it would. Gorbachev had pioneered a grandiose beginning, and Yeltsin had made a valiant stand to preserve it, but in the end the roots of the Bolsheviks had been entrenched too deeply, and just as a plant needs water and sunlight to survive and to prevent itself from being strangled by the ever-vigilant weeds, Russia didn't have the internal resources nor the aid she needed from a world of nations struggling under the weight of a beleaguered global economy. So the monster of totalitarianism, passing itself off as the savior yet again, raised its head and roared. The Cold War was back, only this time it was twice the demon that it had been in the first go-round. And the truth was, Calumet didn't want to miss it.

Did he really have any choice at this point? If he was blown and he stayed in the game, it would all come to a head one way or the other very quickly. Either the GRU would try to kill him or, much less likely, they would try to play him back.

Suggest you come in.

The words rumbled around in his head. In the first place, he wasn't even on the roster. He never had been. Years ago, when he had been working for a multinational corporation, the GRU had tried to suborn him in order to obtain industrial secrets. Calumet played along, but not before contacting old friends and associates who were in the arms trade and who happened to be contract agents for the CIA. His friends, in turn, passed him to Langley and the game began. He was a natural. He was also very careful. His name never appeared on the CIA payroll directly, and his bank accounts never varied outside the bounds of any visible means of support. Nevertheless, he had made a good living. As time progressed, he was able to work himself in deeper and deeper, convincing the Russians that he was a valuable source of information. In the Russians' view, Calumet had garnered quite a nest of sources within the American defense industry. All it took was money—

money for him and money for the people he claimed he had to pay. The Russians did a lot of their shopping through him, and he almost always delivered. To the GRU's way of thinking, Jack Calumet was an agent of influence extraordinaire. The CIA, in order to enhance his reputation, from time to time had provided him with very good product which they were willing to sacrifice in the hopes of a bigger payoff down the road. They weren't disappointed. Jack Calumet became one of the CIA's most prolific doubles ever. He also became, as most doubles do, one of the CIA's biggest secrets. Only a handful of people within the agency knew who he was. The FBI and other intelligence organs had never heard of him.

He thought back to his first consummation with the GRU. He was already proficient with weapons and skilled in the martial arts when he became a double. The first meet had been covered by the CIA who, by all rights, should have handed off to the FBI since it was on American soil. However, they decided to keep it in-house under the auspices of Executive Order 12333, and it was then that they discovered just what a racehorse they had in Jack Calumet. He showed up at the meet with information that could have been found in any library, but that was the GRU's modus operandi: ask for something innocuous at first, and then slowly reel them in. A Major Filatov had asked Calumet to hand over the information. Calumet wanted to see the money first. Filatov, very junior at the time, had explained that before he could be paid, Jack had to prove to him that the requested documents were bona fide, and furthermore, that Jack would have to sign a receipt for the money. Calumet exploded into action so fast that even the CIA watchers were caught off guard. He had put Filatov on the ground and snatched the envelope containing the money in less than a second. Standing over the Russian, it was Calumet who did the explaining. He told Filatov that if they wanted to buy secrets in the future he would be happy to oblige them, but he would be paid upon delivery on each occasion, and they could take their receipts and shove them up their collective derrieres. If they didn't like it, then don't contact him anymore. Period. And he threw the information packet onto the chest of Filatov and walked away.

At first the CIA had been furious with him, and Calumet, not one to be intimidated, told them he didn't give a good damn. If he played the game, he was going to play by his own rules, and that meant that he wasn't about to become some puppet whose strings got pulled one way by the Russians and the other way by the Americans. If he played the game, he told them, he was going to play it as a starter, not as a bench warmer. The CIA responded by informing him that, as far as they were concerned, he was through—the game was over. They didn't need any half-baked prima donnas mucking up their operations. But then three months later the GRU came calling again in the suave personality of a man named Shevchenko. They wanted a meet in Vienna. They wanted to spend a week with Calumet and get to know him a bit better. They wanted to determine if he could, in fact, be of value to them. Jack notified the CIA and quickly discovered what a forgiving bunch the gang at Langley could be. Their earlier disappointment had turned into jubilation. The real game began.

Was this the place and time that it would all end? Would he play it safe and go back home to settle down—really settle down—and get on with his life?

Jack needed to move. Suddenly the room had become stifling. He finished the coffee and pastry delivered by room service. Climbing off the bed, he retrieved his swimming suit from his luggage. He placed the suit and several other items in a small carryall bag and then went downstairs to the basement of the Sheraton where there was an indoor pool and sauna. The place was a miniature country club. It featured a small bar and stocked assorted chips, peanuts, and other light eateries. More substantial meals could be ordered directly from the kitchen by phone. He took a leisurely swim, picked up an *Orangensaft* from the bar, and spread himself out on one of the lounge chairs by the pool. A mother with two young children—roughly seven or eight, Calumet guessed—were the only other patrons affording themselves of the hotel's exercise facilities this morning. They had arrived sometime during his swim. The children were now finding a great deal of amusement in splashing each other and rollicking around their mother, who was standing in the shallow end and doing her best to keep her hair from getting wet. Calumet caught her look when she smiled at him. She shrugged, as if to say, "Kids, what can you do?" Except, he thought, she would have said it in German since that was the language being frivolously bandied about by the trio. He returned the smile and then interested himself in an article in *Der Spiegel*.

He was about halfway down the second page when he saw her approach. *"Entschuldigen Sie mich, mein Herr. Haben Sie Feuer?"* The cigarette was beckoning from her lips. Jack casually observed the woman. A fleeting thought caused him to speculate about how many conversations had been ignited by cigarettes over the years. He wondered if they had any statistics on that one. She was standing there with a coquettish grin and dripping on the tile in a modest one-piece bathing suit which didn't do her figure justice. No wedding ring, but that didn't mean anything in Europe. He noticed the faintest trace of stretch marks on her thighs and decided they could probably be attributed to the two children.

"Natürlich." Jack smiled and reached into his bag with his left hand while his smile and his eyes continued to hold the woman. After fumbling around for a couple of seconds, his hand reappeared with a pack of complementary matches. He plucked one out and lit her cigarette.

"Vielen Dank," she said politely, but the smile was missing this time. Then, without warning, she sat down on the edge of his lounge chair, nudging his feet slightly to the side. Calumet immediately wondered if she was one of those liberated women who felt a need to reaffirm her equality, or was she possibly something else?

She switched to English. "Did you get the note?" The accent was present, but not heavy.

He wasn't giving anything away. "Pardon me?"

"Shevchenko executed," she whispered. The smile returned.

Jack studied her eyes and watched her body language. She hadn't taken a pull off the cigarette since he lit it for her. "Who sent you?" he asked.

"Robert." She finally took a drag and exhaled sideways, her gaze meeting Calumet's. "He wants to know your agenda," she continued, and she struggled with the word, "agenda," pronouncing the first "a" as an umlaut. It forced her to draw out the syllables. She flipped some misbehaved strands of hair over her shoulders, as if to correct for it, but a few blond wisps had refused to make the leap and settled back on her chest.

So there it was. Relaxing by a pool in Germany, Calumet was suddenly being forced to make a career decision by a young German mother who was somehow involved in the business of American espionage. Where did they get all these people, he wondered? It never ceased to amaze him. Had he more time to think it through, his decision might have been different, but sitting here in a miniature health club with a Company surrogate demanding his verdict, there was something degrading about playing it safe. Besides, hadn't he always chosen the hard paths and left the smooth highways to others? Anyone who knew Jack Calumet knew better than to tell him that something couldn't be done. That would be tantamount to building another *Titanic* and pronouncing to the world that it couldn't be sunk. Maybe that was the one characteristic that made him what he was, that defined him ultimately, that fatefully cast him as an agent provocateur and set his course as surely as if it had been drawn on a map. Maybe the psychologists at Langley knew that, and that's why they had only *suggested* he come in. Whatever the rhyme and reason, anger swelled in Calumet as he stared into the woman's blue eyes. It was a nuclear anger, controlled but potentially violent, and it was evident in his tone. "I'm meeting Filatov tonight and I don't want any interference. You tell Robert that's my agenda."

"Robert wants you to come in."

"That's not what the note said." Calumet watched her closely for a reaction. Whatever he was looking for didn't materialize. Her demeanor remained completely even.

"He said you wouldn't." She finally took another drag and began looking around for an ashtray, but seemed to give up on it when it was obvious that there wasn't one nearby. "He wants a meet right away."

"Where?" Calumet was amused by the cigarette ash. A proper German would never think of flicking it on the tile, and it had grown to caterpillar size. He knew she wouldn't dare interrupt the conversation for it.

"Goethe Haus. You are to arrive at precisely one o'clock and stroll among the exhibits. If you haven't been contacted within twenty minutes, you will clear your path and arrive at Senckenberg Museum at three-thirty. Again, you will wait twenty minutes. If you aren't contacted by then, it means that you are under surveillance." She hesitated slightly, as if she didn't want to give him what was lingering on her tongue, possibly because she had sensed his anger.

Calumet was like a statue, mentally trying to coax her into submission. Finally she spit it out: "Robert says if that happens, he is bringing you in whether you like it or not."

His eyes were cold only for a moment, then he felt her discomfort and the beginnings of a pleasant grin began to frame his lips. "I'll be there," Calumet said as he stood up. He slipped an ashtray out from under his bag and handed it to her, his grin transformed into a warm smile now, and a tad curious why she didn't ask him how he knew. "But you tell Robert," he continued, "that I'm keeping my appointment with Filatov." He slung the bag over his shoulder and took three steps before turning back. "Surveillance or not," he snapped, and he emphasized it with a wink as he pivoted again and left.

*

Calumet arrived in that section of the city known as Alt Sachsenhausen at 12:57. He nosed around Grosser Hirschgraben Strasse until 12:59. Goethe Haus, though badly damaged in World War II, had been fully restored and attracted tourists the year round. It was adjoined by the Goethe Museum. At precisely 1:00, Jack the tourist paid his three Deutsche Marks and went inside. He had taken the *U-bahn,* changing often, switching directions, and hopping into various taxis—sometimes just to ride around the block—in order to shake any Russian tails. He thought he was clean, but one never knew for sure. The determination of that fact would be made by Robert and his team, who had been watching the ingress and egress to the museum for the past thirty minutes. Calumet knew they were watching him now as he ambled casually from room to room pretending to be interested in classical German literature. He was careful not to look at his watch. He estimated it took about seventeen minutes for Robert to show himself. Robert had just sort of materialized by his side. Neither acknowledged the other's presence.

"You're blown. Cancel the meet with Filatov." Robert was silver haired and aristocratic in bearing. Jack had known him for six years and he hadn't aged a day. Jack put him at about fifty-five, but he could have been forty or seventy. There was just no way to tell.

"You've been on the horn to the Aquarium, have you?"

"Give it up, Jack. Shevchenko recruited you, Shevchenko ran you, Shevchenko's dead. A dumdum in the back of the skull. Figure it out."

That's just what I've been trying to do, Calumet thought to himself. "Is that an order?"

"Yes!" Robert said it a little too quickly, and with a tad too much emphasis.

"In the six years I've known you, Robert, that's the first time you've ever lied to me." And then Calumet knew that whatever was going on, it was ratcheting up quickly. He wondered whether Robert had the answer.

Robert looked at Jack and shook his head, as if to say, "You just won't learn, will you? You're always looking a gift horse in the mouth." There was a trace of resignation in his voice when he finally answered. "The DDO said it's to be your decision. I happen to disagree."

Robert is a stand-up guy, Jack thought. He had been a career operations officer with the CIA for God only knew how long, and yet he was willing to throw it all away with a little white lie in order to protect his agent. A real gem. Calumet wanted to thank him for his concern, but it wouldn't work here. To admit that he was moved by Robert's effort would somehow jinx the camaraderie that had been built up between them over the years. "Why do you think the Deputy Directory for Operations is so concerned about my civil rights all of a sudden?" he asked instead.

Robert seemed to mull that one over for a moment before answering. Finally he said, "I wish I knew, Jack. I wish I knew." Calumet wished he knew, too, and still wondered if he really did. "Look," Robert continued, "I don't know what's going on, but this is the first time I can remember a decision of this nature being left open-ended. It's suicide, and it's obvious."

"It may be suicide, but it sure isn't obvious," Calumet responded. "Whatever it is." They both began to saunter slowly through the various rooms and exhibits, carefully avoiding the few people who were in the museum to enrich their cultural appetites. Calumet speculated privately on how many of them worked for Robert. At least two, maybe three, he figured. Not more. Robert liked to finesse.

"You've had a good run, Jack. Come in. I've got friends in the States who can set you up nicely." It was bordering on a plea, Jack thought.

Calumet turned and looked him in the eye. "Robert, do you know something you're not telling me?"

If it weren't for the circumstances, Robert would have been affronted. Instead, he adopted a fatherly approach and put his hand on Jack's shoulder. Another first. "Jack," he said, "the reason I want you to come in is because I *don't* know something I'm not telling you." He removed his hand and they continued their stroll.

Easing through the rooms and artifacts of Goethe's existence, they were presented with the various displays of the author's accomplishments. Such works as *Goetz von Berlichingen, Werthers Leiden, Aus meinem Leben,* and so on, had secured Goethe's place in history as Germany's greatest eighteenth-century writer. They had both been here before, but on each visit the gothic rooms seemed to charge the atmosphere with nostalgia.

"I think I'll play out the hand," Jack said suddenly.

"What about Diane?" Robert shot back. He wasn't going to let it go without a fight. Calumet stopped, the slightest flash of anger visible in his pupils. Robert turned and faced him. "That's right, son. What about her?" His voice carried a challenge.

"That's none of your business."

Obstacles were just objectives in disguise as far as Robert was concerned. "You've been engaged, what, two years now? How much time have you spent with her in the last two years?" Calumet began to move away, but Robert grabbed him firmly by the arm, holding him in place. "Listen, Jack"—his voice lecturing now, "you can't go on being the Lone Ranger forever. You can't continue to traipse around the globe and single-handedly save the world from totalitarianism. It can't go on interminably." And then he softened his voice. "You deserve better than that, Jack. You owe it to yourself. Come in from the cold, son. It's the smart thing to do. It's the *right* thing to do." Robert was a master of smooth; he could incite and defuse all in the same breath. The moment of challenge passed and he released Jack's arm.

They continued their stroll in silence for a bit. "Somebody is trying to play me, Robert," Calumet said after an interlude. "I have to know why. It's that simple."

"That's just in your mind, Jack, an intellectual distraction. Demons playing on your curiosity. You can walk away from all of this right here, right now, and never look back." He paused slightly before adding, "If you've the mental fortitude, that is." His eyes glanced sideways at Calumet to record the reaction.

"You mean just drop it all? Go back to the States and live happily ever after? Is that about it?"

"Something like that."

"Yeah, well I've never really cared much for chiropractors. Sorry."

Robert didn't answer. He knew Calumet was waiting for him to take the bait, waiting for him to ask Jack to unravel the mystery for him, so he decided to up the ante with silence instead.

The wily old coyote, Calumet thought; he isn't biting. "I'd be looking over my shoulder for the rest of my life," he finally explained. "You know . . . neck strain."

"Yes, I think I can keep up with you on that one, Jack." Robert was one of those people who could smart off and make it sound like a compliment. "But you're wrong. We'd publish your legend, make sure the right people knew the nature of your charter from the very beginning. Moscow Center would understand that you were hands-off. You'd be out of it for good unless they were prepared for payback."

"And you can guarantee it? You can guarantee that I'd never have to worry about a dumdum with my name on it? Absolutely guarantee it?" Try that one on, he thought.

Robert nonchalantly studied a manuscript as he spoke, "Maybe you should have been an accountant, Jack. No variables in that particular occupation, just numbers with a nice, neat solution at the bottom of each column."

" 'Variable' is the operative word, Robert. Too many of them. I like to tie down the sails. No loose strings. That's my motivation in this affair."

"Don't con me. *I* know what motivates an agent." His eyes returned from the manuscript and focused on Calumet. "The truth of the matter is, you don't want the game to end. You think you need the action to somehow measure your self-worth." Robert shook his head. "It's time to grow up, Jack."

That stung a little. "Okay, Dr. Freud, let's just cut to the chase. For your information, I knew I was blown the second I read the

note. It's so obvious it's not even funny. So why is Langley leaving
me on the ropes? Why is the decision being made in the field and
not at the desk?"

"That's exactly my point, Jack. We *don't* know, do we? That's
why the smart move is to pull out. Now."

"And you're not in the least bit curious?"

"Sure, I'm curious, but I'm not curious enough to send you into
a meat grinder."

They'd been standing in one spot, unaware of it. The realization
suddenly dawned upon them, and it was as if an unseen force
caused them to begin moving in unison. Both knew that their time
was about up. It wouldn't do to press the clock much longer.

Calumet took the reins. "You know, Robert, my old man flew
B-17s in World War II. Friends of mine served in Vietnam. Nobody ever gave them their pick of battles."

"No," Robert interjected, "but they had a fighting chance in
those battles. You may not."

"Whatever this is about," Calumet continued, his voice suddenly acquiring a very serious tone, almost surreal, "I'm not vain
enough to think that's it's all about me. Why this is an open-ended
charter is not within your purview or mine to understand at this
point, but it must be important or the boundaries would have been
defined. Maybe you understand what it's like being a double,
maybe you don't. Maybe it's a little harder on the emotions than it
appears, you know? Maybe sometimes we wonder if what we're
doing is really accomplishing anything." Calumet paused and took
a deep breath, as if he was refreshing himself and at the same time
preparing to deliver the final blow. "Well, this is my moment in the
sun. This is my moment to define that little piece of history that will
mark me as an American who served his country and didn't flinch
when he saw the whites of their eyes."

"Introspection can be deadly to an agent," Robert answered.
"You're on the edge, Jack. You've served your country already,
and you've served it well. Very well. To have doubts about that
makes you susceptible to taking unwarranted risks. The mind begins to say, 'I've got to do better,' when in fact you've been doing
more than has been asked of you all along. It's time to lock it down,
Jack. It's time to come in."

As they were entering another room, Calumet suddenly stopped and faced Robert. His voice was even and cool. There was no mistaking his intention. "Tonight's match will not be postponed. My game, my call. Think what you like."

Robert knew Jack Calumet as well as anyone. He knew him better than his mother knew him. And he knew by his demeanor and by the tone of his voice that Calumet was determined to walk into the lion's den and that no power on earth could talk him out of it. "Where's the meet with Filatov, and at what time?" he asked.

"They want to turn me over a few times in Römerberg Square near Nikolaikirche. I'm to arrive at ten past ten and give them a half-hour. Fallback is Eiserner Steg, the bridge, at oh-one-hundred."

"I have a feeling they'll pass on Römerberg Square," said Robert, eyebrow raised. "My bet is that you won't meet Filatov, or whoever, until Eiserner Steg. They'll want you to think that you were trailing baggage in order to make you nervous. They'll probably tell you the surveillance was definitely American and that's why they didn't pick you up at Nikolaikirche. They'll want you to be confused so you'll willingly accompany them when they make that very suggestion to you at the bridge."

"I'm glad we agree on something." Jack smiled.

"Don't show for the first rendezvous. Hit the square at about twelve-forty. Make your way to the bridge via the Rententurm. Play it back on them. Tell them *you* tagged American or German surveillance—you're not sure—and that's why you didn't make the first meet. That gives you the leverage to stay cool and maintain the upper hand, so to speak."

"Right."

"Filatov got himself promoted, by the way. Major-General."

"Interesting." Calumet was grateful for the acknowledgment: It told him much more than simply what was on the face of it. It told him that the CIA had penetrated the GRU and had an asset who could feed them real-time intelligence. The fact that Robert had revealed Shevchenko's execution and Filatov's promotion meant that he had a great deal of trust and respect for Jack.

"Here." Robert shoved a 9-millimeter Beretta and an extra magazine into Calumet's hand. Both quickly disappeared into the bomber jacket.

"If I scratch my left ear with my left hand . . ." Jack left it hanging.

"Right," Robert acknowledged that he understood.

Calumet gave him a final nod, then turned and walked out.

Robert would give him a few minutes before making his own departure. In the meantime, he busied himself by examining the manuscript lying in a glass case before him. It was Goethe's *Faust*. "I wonder if there's any way to conjure up Mephistopheles," he whispered into the air.

CHAPTER 3

The solid black Lear jet touched down on the runway of Rhein-Main Air Base at about 9:00 P.M. A crescent moon posted watch in the sky. The plane taxied to a stop and the door opened. Five men jumped out and walked briskly over to two waiting jeeps. Each was carrying a very large black canvas bag. Although dressed in civilian clothes, they weren't civilians. All five had been involved in *direct action* operations in the Gulf and other not-so-public conflicts. The jeeps scooped them up and sped them over to two waiting cars concealed from prying eyes. After receiving their passengers, the two cars drove through the gate at Rhein-Main and headed into the city. A few moments later, the jet engines of the Lear roared to life as the plane disappeared into the German night.

*

Calumet had moved. He had never returned to his hotel from Goethe Haus. Instead, he had called a trusted contact, a middle-aged Jewish man known as Avriel, and had him collect his belongings and settle his bill at the Sheraton. Avriel may or may not have been employed by the Mossad, but he and Calumet were the same species and shared the same basic ideals. After some fuss with his directions—a fuss which caused him to make several wrong turns subsequent to his leaving the Sheraton and entering Frankfurt proper—Avriel had handed over Jack's belongings to Moshe near the intersection of Kurt-Schumacher-Strasse and Allerheiligen-strasse. Moshe, in turn, after some fuss with *his* directions as well, delivered Jack's belongings to him at the Hauptbahnhof and promptly left. There was no discussion and no exchange of gratuities. Calumet had done similar favors for Avriel and his friends in the past.

Jack liked the Palmenhof Hotel. Although modernized, its architecture was turn-of-the-century and had the atmosphere to match. Located in Frankfurt's west end, the hotel was reminiscent of old Germany and stood in contrast to the city itself, which was more or less just another industrial haven speckled with historical odds and ends. Jack supposed the rooms were nice, but he had never really seen one. Instead, his customary patronage landed him in one of the hotel's thirty-five apartments. The lodging was expensive, partly to cover the costs of the exquisite Bastei Restaurant and the excellent nouvelle menu that went with it, but for those who could afford it, payment was accepted in the form of most major credit cards. The best feature of the Palmenhof, however, at least as far as Calumet was concerned, was an assistant manager named Rudi. Rudi had been working his way up the hotel ladder for the past ten years and had hopes of opening his own establishment one day. He was miserly with his money and skimped constantly to save enough to launch his dream. When Jack Calumet was in town, Rudi's financial portfolio was considerably enhanced.

A phone call from Jack Calumet to Rudi initiated a process. Rudi, using a Diners Club card given him by Calumet, would register one of the apartments to a Herr and Frau Koeplin from Hamburg. The registration would also show that the couple was accompanied by their daughter, Renata. Upon completion of the registration, Rudi would place an assortment of women's and children's clothing in the closet of the apartment, along with other knickknacks typifying the presence of two such people. Then he would meet Calumet and give him the key. Consequently, anyone attempting to trace Jack Calumet through hotel registrations would be fighting a steep uphill battle. Even the maids would have to testify that the apartment was occupied by a family of three, though they may not have actually ever *seen* the family itself. The only potential weak link in the chain might be Rudi, but since his savings account was pumped up daily when Jack was there, it was very unlikely that he would blow the whistle, even if pressed. Not even Robert knew of this arrangement or of Rudi. The legendary Mitchell Livingston Werbell III, former OSS agent and counterterrorist, among other things, had once told Jack over three fingers of imported Scotch—straight up, no ice—"Best to stock your own pantry in this business," and Jack knew he wasn't referring to the Scotch.

It was 5:00 when Jack took possession of his new lodgings. He set his alarm for 10:00 and collapsed onto the bed fully clothed. He was exhausted.

*

Lewis Armbrister was planning a long evening in his office at Langley. He had arranged a meeting for heads of the Covert Action Staff and the Special Activities Operations staff at 4:00 P.M. which, coincidentally, was the same hour Calumet had set his alarm for six time zones to the east. The Deputy Director for Intelligence and several of his analysts were also in attendance. The meeting would last until Zephyr was heard from. Armbrister was the Deputy Director for Operations for the Central Intelligence Agency. He had cut his teeth as an operations officer in various capitals around the world, and had served as chief of station in Moscow, Rome, Paris, Berlin, and London. When the previous DDO had been appointed Deputy Director of Central Intelligence by the president, he had insisted that Armbrister take his place. There were no arguments. Most everybody liked and respected Armbrister.

Armbrister was able to define the balance of a DDO through three successive DCIs. In the past, if the DDO or his methodology was not admired by the Director of Central Intelligence, he was gone. In Armbrister's case, none of the three, including the current DCI, found any shortcomings in the man. However, that was about to change, if an operation that was soon due to take place in Frankfurt went awry. Few people knew about Calumet. Fewer still knew the complexity of the matter in which Calumet was embroiled. That included the DCI. Not even Robert, otherwise known as Zephyr, was privy to the big picture, and that was saying a great deal because Armbrister and Robert went back some thirty years together.

If Armbrister had to choose between telling the whole tale to Robert or the DCI, he would choose Robert. While the DCI had a general knowledge of Calumet as an asset, he neither knew Calumet's true identity nor the full ramifications of what was about to take place. At sixty-two, Armbrister had seen too many Church Committees and too many Admiral Turners. He would pull out his officers and his agents, his entire team, and would then resign himself before jeopardizing the lives of his people by trusting their legends to a political appointee. As far as Armbrister was concerned, political appointees could be trusted only as far as a Senate subcommittee hearing, and nobody would want to repeat the words he'd use to describe one of those. Not that he didn't believe in the right of the American people to know that their tax dollars were being spent wisely. Ultimately, the American people were what he and his soldiers were fighting for. What Armbrister couldn't abide was the mountain of hypocrisy that engulfed the House and the Senate. In his view, they were managing to screw up the lives of the American people more than the Russians ever could. The truth was, in his view, men and women such as himself had a responsibility to do their jobs with the highest regard for honesty and integrity. Somehow he couldn't envision the words "honesty" and "integrity" in the same sentence with House or Senate. He couldn't reconcile the fact that the men and women of the CIA were honorable, and the body of the Senate and House, as a whole, was not. In short, he would rather die than risk betraying his people to a clan of intellectual egomaniacs who were about as skilled at keeping secrets as compulsive gamblers were at keeping chips.

"Where do we stand, Phil?" Armbrister asked his head of special operations. There were nine people seated around the oblong conference table.

"Our team arrived in Frankfurt about an hour ago. Zephyr cabled their arrival."

"This team," Armbrister rejoined, "what's the makeup?"

"Five men, all Delta Force. Opconned to us from DIA. Or sheep-dipped, as they say. Anyway, all have actual combat experience in covert operations. All have been trained in surveillance and countersurveillance tactics. Three of the five are fluent in German, the other two in Russian. They've worked together several times before." Phil Jenkins paused and cleared his throat. His mannerism indicated that he had something else to add, but wasn't really quite sure how to put it. His first attempt was rather weak. "I, uh, well—"

"Hell," bellowed Jake Watkins, a Texan who headed Covert Action Staff, "I thought I was going to a Clandestine Services meeting but I must have made a wrong turn somewhere and ended up at a Stammerers Anonymous Convention instead!" There was a chorus of laughter around the table. He and Jenkins were best of friends, and they showed it by needling each other whenever the opportunity arose. Watkins leaned over and patted Jenkins on the arm as he added, "Just say it straight out, son, same way John Wayne used to do it." That one received a few more chuckles before the room returned to silence.

"What is it, Phil?" Armbrister asked.

"Well, my man was talking to the pilot after the boys had loaded their gear."

"Yes, go on."

"It, uh, it seems that a couple members of the team were carrying M-79s."

"Roasted Bolshevik!" Watkins blared. "Looks like Zephyr and his crowd are gonna fry some Russians with grenade launchers if they get half a chance! Hot damn! I'd say we're in for a potential helluva ride, Lewis!" Only this time he was serious.

"Whose idea was that?" Armbrister wanted to know.

"It wasn't mine," Jenkins said. "They must have made that decision on their own initiative." Phil Jenkins didn't really believe that. The way he had it figured, Robert had talked to the DIA after Jenkins had set it up, but he wasn't about to place the blame on Robert because he, too, had a great deal of respect for the wily operations officer.

"Does the BND have any knowledge of this team?" asked Jason Strong, the Deputy Director for Intelligence and Lewis Armbrister's counterpart in the chain of command.

"No," Armbrister replied, "we're keeping the German service completely in the dark on this one."

"It's gonna be about as dark as the equator in a sun storm if they start popping those M-79s," Watkins offered.

"I'd say that puts the onus on our man Excalibur," Strong pointed out. "How good is he?"

Armbrister was glad to hear Strong refer to Calumet as "our man." He wasn't sure the DDI was committed to the concept. Both Calumet and Robert would be designated strictly by their cryptonyms in this room. Not all of those present knew Robert's true identity, and fewer still, including the DDI, knew Calumet.

Armbrister answered, "Excalibur is, in some ways, an unpredictable element. He's certainly no soldier when it comes to taking orders, but everyone in this room knows how valuable he's been in the past. He's impetuous and susceptible to a loose-cannon mentality. That's why we've committed Zephyr full time to running him. If anyone can control him, Zephyr can."

"That being the case," Strong rejoined, "was it wise to leave him in?" It wasn't a challenge, merely a friendly but unmistakable inquisition. If something went wrong, he would be on record as having asked the right questions.

"We have to take the good with the bad," Armbrister replied. "Excalibur has been able to penetrate the GRU where most others have failed. The Aquarium has been giving him their shopping list, he passes it to us, and we know exactly where they're vulnerable. It's almost as good as having an asset on site at Khodinka." The DDO was referring to the geographical location of GRU headquarters—which was located at the old Khodinka Airfield in Moscow. "Excalibur's had them eating out of his hand for—" He was about to say "six years," but caught himself. "Excalibur's had them eating out of his hand, period!" he backtracked instead. He smiled and a few of the older spymasters around the table chuckled.

"And you left the decision entirely up to him?" Strong continued the inquisition. "It was your decision to let *him* make the decision to stay in place? Just so I have all the facts, you understand." Jason grinned, but secretly was peeved that he had never been entrusted with the full details of Calumet's legend, and he was letting Armbrister know it.

"That's right," Armbrister replied. "And just for the record," he continued, directing his smile toward the DDI, "Zephyr's intent was to bring him in." That settles that, he thought. If something *did* go wrong, at least his old friend Robert would be off the hook now.

"Takes balls to go through with it," Watkins interjected. "Knowing that Shevchenko has been executed, yet he's still willing to play the hand? If you ask me, Excalibur's got himself a real pair of stones." Besides Armbrister, Watkins and Jenkins were the only other people in the room who knew Calumet's true identity.

"Big *brass* stones, I'd say." All heads turned to a demurely smiling Susan Weinroth, the only female represented at the meeting. "We have reams of open cases where our doubles have disappeared without trace in the past," she continued. She was more or less bland in appearance, but her analytical abilities were stunning.

Furthermore, she reported to Strong—the DDI—and she wasn't the least bit shy about contradicting him or voicing her own opinions. In his defense, he was a fair man and wouldn't hold it against her.

"You have a point?" Jenkins asked.

"She always has a point," Strong replied, an affectionate snicker on his lips.

"Brass stones, huh?" Watkins darted in again. "It's a good thing Excalibur's not present, young lady. Otherwise he'd have a good case against you for sexual harassment!"

"From what I've heard about *your* dichotomous sexual proclivities," Susan retorted, "he'd have a much better case against *you!*" She had barely finished the sentence before the entire room broke out in raucous laughter. Watkins was the loudest of them all. He could take a joke.

The DDI turned serious. "Do we have a presidential finding on this operation?" Presidential findings were formal authorizations necessary for conducting covert operations.

"No," the DDO answered. That was it. Their eyes met. It was the moment of truth for Lewis Armbrister.

After what seemed an eternal consideration, Strong said, "What the hell." A smile spread across his face. "You only go around once." Whatever tension might have existed in the room was immediately dispelled. It was now, literally, a team effort.

"What was your point, Miss Weinroth?" Jenkins asked. "Other than proving that my friend Jake has an affinity for filet of Reebok, that is." Another round of chortles bounced across the room.

"Our counterterrorism unit has confirmed that the Russians have been stepping up their interaction with various factions within western Europe. Specifically, a number of GRU and KGB officers have been directly involved in the supply of ordnance to these factions over the last several months. While I haven't been privy to any conversations which Lewis and the mysterious Mr. Zephyr might have had in past weeks"—she smiled for deflection—"it would seem that Zephyr is aware of the potential firepower aligned against him and has taken prudent measures to safeguard his operation."

"Miss Weinroth," Armbrister said, "Jason has been good enough to require your attendance here today. I understand you've been briefed and brought up to date on the bona fides?"

"She knows as much as I do," Strong stated sarcastically.

Armbrister grinned at the DDI. "Maybe I owe you one, Jason," he said. "Drink later?"

"Ask me that again in a few hours," Jason replied. "We may have to discuss it on the way to Bolivia or somewhere equally appalling."

Ain't it the truth, Armbrister thought. He wondered whether the DDI fancied himself as Butch or Sundance.

"Yes," Susan answered. "I'm up to date."

"What is your assessment of Major-General Georgi Filatov?" Armbrister queried.

"He's a White Russian, deep roots in the Communist Party. Radical purity is paramount in his mental process. He is anti-Jewish, anti-West, and antisocial. Unless, of course, he's conversing with his own species. In that case he's a climber, a high flier, although never as a result of his own imagination. He lives by the party line, chapter and verse. Our overall assessment is that he's rigid in his beliefs and is virtually incapable of improvisation. If it's not in the manual or he hasn't rehearsed it, he'll check with superiors before taking any action. We feel that the result of this is an inferiority complex. He'll look for means to elevate his status. His ego is a viable target."

"Are you saying he can be turned?" Armbrister asked, somewhat incredulously.

"No, sir. I'm saying that by aligning oneself with him in conversation, he is susceptible to deceitful persuasion and calculated flattery. I don't think he is capable of being turned overtly."

"And what about Excalibur?" Armbrister pressed on. "How do you assess him?"

"As you know," Susan continued, "I've only had access to bits and pieces of his operational activities. However, he appears to be the antithesis of Filatov. He's obviously instinctive, resourceful, high-strung, capable, and apparently very intelligent. That's quite a mix. As you mentioned, he is also capable of improvisation and is prone to charting his own course on the spur of the moment. He will obey orders as long as he perceives those orders to be in line with his own views. If not, well, I wouldn't give odds on his conforming. Having said that, another factor that must be entered into the equation is Excalibur's assessment of the individual giving the orders. If he feels that the individual in question—in this case

Zephyr—is on equal footing with him intellectually, he may obey an
order even if he disagrees with it."

"And now down to brass tacks." Armbrister said. "How will he
and Filatov—if in fact, Filatov is the one who shows tonight—get
along?"

"Lewis," the indomitable Susan Weinroth said, "tonight's meet
will either become one of the slickest covert battles in intelligence
history, or Georgi Filatov, to borrow your phrase, will be eating out
of Excalibur's hand."

"And which do you think that might be, Miss Weinroth?"

She looked him right in the eye. "It's blatantly obvious that Excalibur is blown. I think the Russians are going to try to kidnap him.
Failing that, they'll try to kill him."

"I agree," Jason said. "What other motive could they possibly
have?" he speculated. "Now that they know he's a double there'd
be no percentage, no earthly reason, to try to play him back."

Yes there would, Armbrister thought. They'll have the mother of
all reasons if Excalibur can pull it off.

*

It was 10:00 P.M. in Frankfurt and Calumet was hungry, but he
wouldn't eat. The mind was a bit sharper on an empty stomach, the
senses a whit more keen. And the reflexes were faster. To say that
Calumet was afraid would be inaccurate, but the churning that was
going on inside his soul was different from anything he had ever
experienced. In a way, he had been preparing for this moment all of
his life. He was about to enter the deadliest of games. What had
gone before was relatively routine. A meet here, a drop there, all
culminating in monetary payoffs and slaps on the back. Some inher-
ent risks, yes, and the constant emotional strain of being a double,
of living a double life, but no great danger. Tonight would be different. Tonight would test the mettle of the man within.

Is that what defines courage ultimately, he wondered? Knowing
that you're about to enter harm's way with an open invitation to
back out, yet marching onto the field of battle regardless? Was it
partly a macho thing? Possibly. He would allow for that particular
intrusion, at least to a degree, especially if he was going to be honest
with himself. And it was partly a matter of curiosity as well, he
reflected. An inner need to just *know*. Why was he still in sanction?
Why hadn't they pulled him? He knew that the men and women he

represented at the CIA were not the warlocks and witches of popular myth who disdainfully used people with reckless abandon and
malicious disregard. No, he reflected, the men and women of the
CIA, in general, were people with deep pools in their souls. People
who knew the exorbitant price of shed blood. At least that was the
impression he had gotten from the few he knew and worked with.
In spite of his considerable independence and his lack of respect for
authority, Calumet had an abiding trust, a deep-rooted belief in the
faithfulness of the Roberts and Armbristers of this world. Were
they the types of people who could wantonly waste lives the way
some people wasted food? Could they easily destroy a man with
just the casual stroke of a pen as they seriously debated about
whether to have the roast or the veal for dinner? Not in his opinion,
Jack thought, although he had never met Armbrister, but Robert
respected the man, and that was good enough for him.

No, he decided, the DDO had a reason. Why Armbrister chose
not to share that reason with Robert or with him was anybody's
guess, but it must be something vital. Maybe he would be able to
peel back the curtains of the veil, at least partially, in his meet with
Filatov later that evening. Maybe Filatov would baptize him with
enlightenment and understanding. Maybe, he thought, I'll even
make it out of this thing alive.

With such notions dominating his mind, it was not surprising
that he began making preparations to let Diane know that he loved
her deeply and that this was something that just had to be done. At
first he thought of calling her and having a very long, very solemn
conversation, but quickly changed his mind. For one thing, he'd be
violating his tradecraft. He knew better than that. He also knew
that if he made such a call, she'd somehow conclude he had gone
astray and was therefore doing penance for it. No, the call was a
bad idea. Then it came to him: he'd write her a letter. Yes, that
would do it. He'd had written only four or five lines before his
emotions began to give way to his inner resolve. That was how it
often went with him: at times he would let his emotions gain the
upper hand, but eventually, building slowly at first from some deep
recess within, he would regain control of his biorhythm. Suddenly
his instinct for survival would leap to the surface and dominate his
soul. His focus and professional alacrity returned instantly, as if he
were snapping out of a dream, and his attitude underwent a rapid

transformation. In a flash his mood changed from melancholy to *Catch me if you can!*

"Screw it." He rose and crumpled the paper, then burned it and flushed it down the commode. He turned and saw his own eyes reflected in the mirror, suddenly defiant. "I *always* come home." That's exactly what he had told Diane before his departure. He would leave it at that.

He dressed in a specially woven black turtleneck. The inside collar was fitted with thin but very tensile plastic—his throat would not suffer the trauma of anybody's garrote. His Reeboks were also black. He used adhesive tape to secure a stiletto to the inside sleeve of his left forearm. He swatted the air several times, testing it. It felt right. He rounded out his attire with blue jeans and his brown bomber jacket. The Beretta went into the right pocket of the bomber jacket, one round grooved and chambered. There was no need to cock the hammer; it was double-action, and the safety was off.

The time was 10:20. Calumet began his run.

*

The April sky was calm and clear. In contrast, Jack was anxious; he wanted to get on with it, but the professional inside him maintained control. He stuck to his tradecraft, playing it to the letter. He took the *U-bahn* to various points in Frankfurt and contributed to the financial security of ambitious cabbies. It was all second nature to him. It was part of the game, and just as he had done a thousand times before, he was clearing his path, taking every possible precaution to ensure that he wasn't being surveilled. Especially by the BND. Things could get nasty rather quickly if Germany's version of the CIA ended up in the middle of this operation, and they had been suspicious of him for several years now. It would be different if he was operating under official or even commercial cover, but he wasn't. He was odd man out. He was a double who was so far under that only a handful of people knew the real score. Robert had once warned him, "Remember, Jack, your life is like that of a lion in the midst of wolves. Stay balanced at all times. They won't attack as long as they think you're strong, but if you falter you're dead."

Calumet moved into Römerberg Square at about 12:40, as instructed. Robert and his team would pick him up here and put him in the glass. From now on, every move he made would be monitored. Jack knew that this part of the operation was the trickiest part for his controller. Not only did Robert and his crew have to keep an eye on him, they also had to make sure that the Russians didn't know they were there, and it was a sure bet that Filatov would have a countersurveillance squad on station to fend for just such an occurrence. The stakes were very high. Both teams would be fielding the first string tonight.

Calumet strolled south past Nikolaikirche and made his way toward Opernplatz. He was doing more than just killing time. By moving through the narrow streets and byways around the square, he was giving Robert and his team the opportunity to identify members of the Russian countersurveillance squad. Of course, it could backfire. The Russians could end up identifying Robert's team instead, but that was a calculated risk, one that had to be taken. In any event, Jack figured that Robert had the advantage. He knew exactly when Calumet was going to show and from which direction he would be coming. The Russians didn't. Furthermore, Robert and Jack knew each other's patterns. If Calumet walked down a narrow alley that had several offshoots, Robert would be willing to lose sight of him for a few minutes, knowing that he would surface at such-and-such a location shortly thereafter. The Russians would be forced to keep a tighter rein, thus exposing themselves. In essence, Jack and Robert were in tune with each other. Calumet knew when and where to make his moves in order to give Robert's team the optimum advantage. He and Robert had rehearsed it many times before.

At 12:55, he had done all he could do. He began to saunter toward Eiserner Steg and his meet with Filatov. He would be a little late, but he had planned to be.

Jack walked back to the Fountain of Justitia in the center of the square. From there, he headed over to the Rententurm, one of the city's medieval gates, and passed through. He found himself on the bank of the River Main. The great iron footbridge known as Eiserner Steg was in view. So was Filatov. The Russian was standing at the midpoint of Eiserner Steg, his hands in the pockets of his overcoat. So far so good, Calumet thought. Robert and his team had been able to maintain their cover, otherwise Filatov would have been gone. Jack was unable to spot anyone else who might be watching, but he knew a rather sizable audience was in tow for this meet. He approached Filatov.

"It's been a long time, Georgi," Calumet began. They had seen each other only once since their first encounter six years earlier. "Where's Shevchenko?" Jack edged himself in so his back was against an iron girder. Filatov was standing directly in front of him. Jack had a view of both ends of the bridge plus, as far as the darkness would allow, of the main streets running parallel to the river. He, too, had his hands in his pockets. His right hand was gripped firmly around the Beretta, which was pointing directly at Georgi Filatov's abdomen.

"Ah," Filatov smiled, "I'm pleased to inform you that Comrade Shevchenko has been promoted. He will be working in headquarters from now on. I'm afraid I'm to be your contact now." He put on a false expression to lighten the mood. "I certainly hope that will not present any inconvenience for you, Jack."

"No, I think we can work through any past differences," Calumet smiled. "I *was* a little curious when I was told in Washington that I would be meeting *you* tonight instead of Shevchenko." It was common for GRU officers to pass themselves off as KGB. Such was the case with Shevchenko and Filatov. Both had presented themselves to Jack as KGB. The way their story went, Shevchenko had been a colonel in the KGB instead of a major-general in the GRU. Calumet saw no use in pretending to be any the wiser. "So, Alexander is a general in the KGB now?" he asked. "That *is* the next rung on the ladder, isn't it?"

"Yes," Filatov answered with his ever-present smile. "I'm afraid our friend is forever bound to endless administrative duties now." He removed his hands from his pockets. They were empty, but the significance of the gesture wasn't lost on Calumet. It was a signal and he knew it. Here it comes, he thought. "Jack," Filatov continued, "we have a little problem."

"Everybody's got problems these days, Georgi." Calumet's eyes began to rove, but not in any perceptible manner. Rather, his peripheral vision went on instantaneous red alert. "Sign of the times, I'd say."

"Yes," Filatov agreed, "but our particular problem is quite complicated. For instance, why didn't you come to Nikolaikirche, as scheduled?"

"I think I was under surveillance, either by the Americans or the Germans. I'm not sure. Anyway, I thought it best to play it safe." As Robert had surmised, the admission caught Filatov flat-footed and had taken an arrow out of his quiver. The surveillance ruse was a trap the Russian had planned to spring, but Calumet had preempted him and didn't appear to be the least bit concerned about it.

Filatov required a moment to collect his thoughts. "Quite so, quite so," the newly promoted major-general finally remarked, "but that is neither here nor there, as you Americans are fond of saying." Calumet wanted to wipe that fawning smile off his face. Something about Filatov grated on him. "Instead, we are concerned about a matter of much greater importance," Filatov continued. "We think you are in a position to do our cause a great service, Jack."

"As long as you're in a position to pay me a great deal of money, I'll be happy to do whatever I can," Calumet answered as he returned the Russian's smile.

Filatov laughed. "Yes, we've always been willing to pay you for your very able dispensations, Jack." The smile vanished then. "But as I mentioned," he continued, "our problem is very complex. We feel that this is a problem you can help us with. However, this assumption, in turn, has led us to another very disturbing situation."

"What disturbing situation would that be?" Jack asked. And then he saw the first shape emerge from the shadows on the other side of the bridge. It was moving slowly along the riverbank toward Eiserner Steg.

"You touched upon it yourself, Jack. We monitored your arrival at the airport this morning. Our people have confirmed that you were under surveillance by the CIA."

"So? That's my problem, Georgi, not yours. I'm not worried about it. They have to catch me in violation of some law before they can do anything about it." What a game, he thought; Filatov was going to play the surveillance ruse after all. The shadow was near the base of the bridge now, holding its position.

"Ah, but it *is* our problem, Jack. You see, we have painted great horizons for you. If all goes according to our design, you will make more money than you ever dreamed. The operation we will be undertaking will be a windfall if we're successful. A windfall for you and a windfall for us. But we need *you* to make it work, and therein lies our problem." Filatov wore his best salesman's face. "You see, Jack, you will be of no use to us if you are under suspicion by the CIA."

"Then why are we still talking, Georgi? Since your people confirmed that I was being followed by the CIA this morning, one would have to assume that I'm already under suspicion. Why pursue it any further?" Two more shadows emerged from the darkness and took up positions on the opposite side of Eiserner Steg, Calumet noticed. So far, that made a total of three—four counting Filatov. Every fiber of his being was primed. His hand squeezed the Beretta for reassurance. However it turned out, he wasn't going down alone. If things got physical, he would take Filatov with him. Maybe one or two of the others as well.

"That's where we can help you, Jack," the Russian answered. He did a quick survey to make sure his assets were in place before continuing. "We feel that this morning's action by the CIA was preliminary. Merely a probe, if you will. You have traveled considerably between the United States and Europe in the past year, and you have no verifiable source of income. It is only natural that the intelligence services would therefore take a slight interest in you. Perhaps they feel that you may be involved in the drug trade, or even terrorism. They have no evidence, but they want to be sure. It is our assessment that this probing will continue as long as you maintain your current life-style."

"Sounds logical," Calumet played along. "How can you help me?"

"I can't go into detail here, Jack, but basically we want to set you up in a legitimate enterprise. At least it would appear to be legitimate, and we would make sure that it was able to withstand the scrutiny of your FBI or CIA. In reality, however, this enterprise would represent our specific interests, and at the same time it would make you a multimillionaire. How does that sound?"

"In theory, it sounds like a dream come true." Calumet answered the question, but his mind was on a black Mercedes sedan that had just materialized in the night some fifty meters down the street. It was rolling very, very slowly toward Eiserner Steg.

"Oh, I can assure you, my friend, it's more than a theory." It was obvious to Calumet that Filatov was nervous now. "Unfortunately," the Russian continued, "it will take quite a while to properly establish the foundation. There is much work that needs to be done, and a great deal of learning on your part. We want to take you to a safe location where your training can be conducted without interference."

Robert had been right. They were offering him the opportunity to go willingly. "Where is this place, and how long will it take?" Calumet asked. He knew the showdown was fast approaching. Whatever was going to happen would happen soon. It's all in the timing, he thought. Just stay loose.

"Oh, it's not far from here, actually," Filatov replied. It was one of the worst lies Calumet had ever heard. The Russian managed a weak smile as he added, "The duration depends on how fast you learn, Jack."

"Well, you've certainly got my attention, Georgi, and I'm definitely interested. I'll tell you what. You pass me the location of this place and I'll meet you there, whenever you say. Okay?"

"It's better if you come with us now, Jack." All pretense had vanished. Major-General Georgi Filatov was giving an order.

"Actually, I'll make my own way, pal."

"I'm afraid you don't have any choice, *pal!*" Filatov said menacingly. He nodded toward his assets on both ends of the bridge. The three GRU officers began to converge upon them from opposite directions. Calumet had no doubt that at least one of them was carrying a needle. The car came to a halt near the base of Eiserner Steg.

"Listen to me very carefully, Filatov," Calumet said coolly. Externally he was ice water; internally he was about to jump out of his skin. "That Kevlar vest you're wearing under your coat won't do you any good. I have a nine-millimeter Beretta pointed at your heart, and it's loaded with Teflon-coated rounds. You tell them to back off. Now. Otherwise you're going down." To emphasize his point, Calumet cocked the hammer. The atmosphere was so tense that it sounded like a crack of thunder.

Filatov assumed that Calumet would have a gun. He had planned for it by wearing the vest, but now he had just been informed that he was up against Teflon-coated ammunition. Was the American bluffing? Then he remembered their first meet six years earlier when Calumet had bested him. For the first time tonight, Filatov's confidence began to wane. "If you kill me, they will kill you." He nodded toward his assets, who were still approaching. "Be sensible, Jack."

"Tell them to back the hell off, Filatov! Now!"

"Listen to me, Jack—"

"I'm counting to three. So help me God, Filatov, I'll pull the trigger!"

Calumet got to two before Filatov gave the signal to withdraw. The three GRU officers reluctantly moved back to the base of the bridge. There were several moments when nobody knew what to do, so they all just stood there in silence. None of the players—including Jack—realized that the three GRU officers had only been about four or five steps away from having their heads disintegrated. Additionally, if one of the doors of the Mercedes had opened suddenly, the sedan would have been incinerated instantly by an M-79 grenade launcher. Calumet knew Robert was covering him, but he had no idea with what. He would have been pleasantly surprised.

Up to this point, Filatov had been doing most of the acting. Now it was Excalibur's turn. "Would you care to tell me why, after a six-year relationship, the KGB suddenly decides it's necessary to kidnap me?" Calumet asked the GRU major-general. "What the *hell* is going on, Georgi?"

It was obvious that Filatov was still confused, unsure what to do next. "Would you mind uncocking that gun, Jack?" was all he could think to say.

"The only way this gun is going to get uncocked, Georgi, is if I pull the trigger." Calumet was in control now and he knew it. He was determined to turn the screws. "I'm waiting, Georgi. What's going on? Is it a personal matter between the two of us because of what happened the first time we met? Huh? Come on, Georgi, what's the deal?"

Filatov sighed. "No, it's not a personal matter. I happen to like you, Jack," the Russian lied. "As I explained, we have a very complicated problem." He was beginning to recover now. Every operative has a fallback legend, and his was beginning to crystallize. "We weren't really going to kidnap you, Jack. We just wanted to talk for a while."

As was often the case with Calumet, a crazy idea entered his mind. Maybe I'm the one who ought to be doing the kidnapping, he thought. Maybe I ought to kidnap this lying Russian double-dealer right now and take him someplace and sweat him. He actually began to formulate a plan of action before he came back to reality.

"You want to talk, then talk," Calumet challenged.

This wasn't working out the way Filatov had planned it. He had planned to have Calumet under the needle before he questioned him. He had planned to have complete control and oodles of time so he could hammer and chisel piece by piece. Regrettably, the major-general hated to admit, that scenario wasn't going to be played tonight. He would have to improvise. Clandestine meets couldn't last forever, and he was at a disadvantage because he dare not pose frontal interrogatories which would zero in on the heart of the matter. That would give too much away. Too much of the puzzle would be revealed. A sober individual would be able to deduce too much from the nature of the inquiries. No, Filatov thought, he had to tread very, very carefully now.

"Jack," the Russian finally replied, "we really do have something big planned, something for which you've been considered. You are our top candidate, in fact. And believe me, my friend, no harm would have befallen you had you accompanied us. You've been too valuable to our cause over the years. We certainly don't want to upset a prosperous relationship. I'm sure you can see the logic in that." Filatov's smile returned. He paused just long enough to let his particular version of Russian hospitality sink in. "Are you still interested in working with us, Jack?" The GRU officer had thrown out the bait; now he felt he needed to regain some measure of control, so he presented a false ultimatum. "Because if you're not we can shake hands and depart on friendly terms right now."

Calumet didn't mind ceding a little control. He was batting a thousand with Filatov so far, and he was confident he could always take it back whenever he needed to. "I'm interested in making money, Georgi. If the KGB is still solvent"–Jack smiled–"I'm still interested in working with you."

Filatov laughed heartily. The three assets on each end of the bridge hadn't moved. "I've always admired you, Jack," the Russian lied. "I remember our first meeting"—he laughed again—"and I must be honest with you, my friend. I strongly advised against using you. My ego was bruised. I was very angry. Fortunately, however, Aleksandr Shevchenko, my superior, overruled me. He decided to handle you himself, and the rest, as you Americans say, is history."

Calumet waited him out, expressionless. Had he really wanted to grasp at straws, he could have asked the Russian why he hadn't used the word "comrade" when referring to Shevchenko, but Jack already knew the answer to that. Something else began to pique his interest, though. This was the second time Filatov had made a point of mentioning American colloquialisms. His tone on both accounts had carried just the slightest tinge of jealousy. It was intangible, really, but Calumet began to know his opponent. The Russian's inferiority complex was showing signs of struggling to the surface. *This is a man,* Calumet discerned, *who is elevated by the decline of others. He's race conscious. Maybe I can use it.*

Filatov must have realized that it was still his turn. "You and Aleksandr got to know each other very well over the years, didn't you, Jack? You became friends?"

Calumet's pulse quickened. He couldn't put his finger on it. He couldn't describe it, but something in the Russian's question ignited his instincts. He gambled. "We had a working relationship, but I don't think it would be accurate to say that we were ever friends, Georgi."

"No? Hmm. I would have thought that all the time the two of you spent together would have automatically ingratiated some sort of mutual friendship. Not so?"

"Nope. Afraid not, Georgi. I hung around with Shevchenko only as long as I had to. And only *when* I had to," he added. He was on autopilot now, his answers being driven by his sixth sense.

Filatov seemed unsure about how to proceed. It took him a moment to align his tack. "I suppose Aleksandr was always pleasant to work with, though. He was never moody or overly anxious, I mean. Would that not be a fair statement, Jack?"

Why was Filatov asking him about a dead man? The answer felt very near, but Calumet couldn't pin it down. "Yes, I guess that would be an accurate assessment," he replied.

"Never? At any point during your association with him, Aleksandr never seemed unduly worried or upset?"

Filatov was driving hard. Too hard, and Calumet sensed it. He was beginning to form a hypothesis. It sent shock waves through his soul as he suddenly realized that the Aquarium, in fact, did not know that he was an agent provocateur. Their focus seemed to be centered not on him, but on Shevchenko, whom they had already executed. But why? Why didn't they know that Jack Calumet was really a CIA double? If they didn't know, what was the purpose of the attempted kidnapping? And then he remembered. Three years ago. With the exception of their initial engagement, that was the only other time he had ever met Filatov. Calumet had delivered a package to Shevchenko. A month later Filatov had asked for a meet. He just wanted to confirm the contents of the package, he told Jack. There had been a minor problem with the diplomatic bag, Filatov had explained. Not to worry, he reassured the American. The meet took thirty minutes and they said good-bye.

Suddenly Calumet understood. *It can't be!* He almost said it out loud. The revelation stunned him. Major-General Aleksandr Shevchenko had been turned! At some point, the Americans had compromised him! Shevchenko hadn't known that Calumet was a loyal double, so he or the CIA, for some odd reason, had doctored the information in the package he had been given. The GRU had been able to determine from the meet with Filatov that the documents Calumet had delivered to Aleksandr were not the same documents that Aleksandr had passed along to them.

But who tipped them off in the first place? The Aquarium must have had another source. A source independent of Calumet. When they compared the intelligence from Shevchenko's package with the intelligence from their other source, the numbers didn't add up. So whose numbers were correct? It obviously took them several years to track it down. Murdock must have been the deciding factor. Murdock's intelligence must have corroborated the Aquarium's first source, and the two of them together must have contradicted Shevchenko's intelligence, ultimately exposing him. Murdock's betrayal of America got Shevchenko killed for Shevchenko's betrayal of Russia. Talk about poetic justice, Calumet thought. Did Shevchenko ever find out, or ever suspect, that Calumet had been working for the CIA all along? No. If he knew, they would have sweated it out of him in Moscow before they killed him, and Filatov wouldn't be asking these questions. Filatov had been sent only to explore the *possibility* of Calumet's complicity. They weren't sure.

Calumet suddenly understood that Langley and Khodinka were staging this competition on a much grander scale than either he or Filatov could have imagined. Filatov was just a gofer, dispatched by the Aquarium to nail down a potential loose end. If Shevchenko had been working for the CIA, Jack wondered, then why play the two of us together? Why hadn't they pulled me out when Shevchenko had been turned? There could be only one answer: Shevchenko was a sacrifice. And that scared the hell out of Calumet. If they were willing to sacrifice Shevchenko, then that meant there were much bigger fish to fry, and it was now obvious that Armbrister was using Calumet as the bait. He was being thrown into a pond full of sharks in order to find out which ones would start circling. He now knew why Armbrister had only *suggested* he come in. Armbrister was making a run at the grand slam, and he needed Calumet's panache and expertise to get there. All Calumet had to do was sell his innocence to Filatov.

It was a struggle to keep his voice from quivering as he answered the Russian, "I don't ever remember Shevchenko being out of character, Georgi." Then he frowned, as if he had an afterthought. "There *was* one incident that concerned me, though. But it's probably not important."

"No, no," Filatov slobbered. "You could never waste my time, Jack. Please, what was it?"

"You remember about three years ago, when we last met?"

"Yes, of course."

"Well, I have to tell you, Georgi, I was kind of worried. Shevchenko *did* act a little strange after that." Calumet knew everything hinged upon his ability to force Filatov to identify with him. Filatov would be reporting back to the Aquarium on his assessment of Calumet's participation, if any, in Shevchenko's treason, and it was crucial that Calumet appear to be something he wasn't. His perception of Filatov made him think that his best bet would be the white-supremacist approach. He explained, "I mean, after you had asked me to confirm the contents of that package, I got suspicious and began to wonder if Shevchenko wasn't about to try to screw me out of my money, just like certain minorities do in America. I don't know if I should tell you this, but I never trusted Shevchenko after that."

Filatov loved it. He suddenly felt simpatico. "Jack," he replied with a softer smile this time, "I know how it must have seemed. I would have thought the same thing if I had been in your shoes. Believe me, you are too valuable for us to be taking ridiculous chances like that." Georgi Filatov really began to warm to the conversation now, "I never knew you felt so strongly about the purity of the races. You know, we have similar problems in Russia."

"Really? Well, I'll tell you a little secret, Georgi. There are people in my country who are going to solve those problems one of these days."

Filatov laughed. "You should see how the certain minorities are faring in Russia, now that the proper government is back in power. You would be able to appreciate it, I think."

Calumet had had enough. He had gone as far as he could go with this thread before letting his anger show. He despised racism and he despised racists like Filatov. Perhaps that's why Filatov grated on him. Jack had seen the effects of racial hatred up close. He had seen the mangled bodies of people who weren't the right color or the right race. That's why it was very difficult for him to make the statements he'd just made. In any case, his ploy had obviously achieved the desired effect so there was no need to linger. He decided to bring the conversation back on track. "Georgi, what was this kidnapping about tonight? I knew when I was told to meet *you* instead of Shevchenko that something was up. That's why I brought the gun." Supply a reason for everything, Robert had once told him. They may not believe it, but repetition has a way of turning mirages into raging rivers.

"Jack, as I told you, it was not really a kidnapping. Quite confidentially, we feel that Aleksandr has been under a great deal of stress lately. He's not been himself. That's why we've given him a desk job. However, we have to trace backward and make sure that his diminished mental faculties over the past several months have not, how shall we say, caused us any undue concern. As a result, we merely wanted to have a long chat with you in order to aid us with our investigation of this matter."

"And what about this business enterprise you mentioned? Was that just a ruse?"

"Yes and no, Jack."

"What does that mean?"

Filatov didn't know the answer to that one himself. He still wasn't sure where to go from here. "Well, I will be in touch with my superiors," he floundered. "I'm sure that we'll want to talk to you again. Now that we've got it all straightened out, why don't you come be our guest until I hear back from Moscow?"

This ought to be interesting, Calumet thought. "Be your guest where, Georgi?"

"Moscow, perhaps."

"No, thanks. Why don't we meet in Berlin?" Calumet suggested Berlin because he knew the Russians would feel comfortable there. Although East Germany per se was no longer in existence, they still had a number of assets in place and they were familiar with the lay of the land.

"Berlin would be reasonable," Filatov answered. "Can you be there in three days?"

"Yes," Calumet replied. That was too easy. The scumbag is still going to try to take me, he thought. "I'll meet you at the usual places at the usual times. You *do* have that information, don't you?"

"Of course." Filatov wasn't lying this time.

"Here's what we're going to do, Georgi," Calumet ordered. "You signal the car. Tell them to move out. Tell your two men there to walk along the riverbank until they're out of sight. Then you and I are going to walk off this bridge and into the square."

"Jack—" Filatov protested.

"That's the way it's going to be, Georgi. Let's not spoil this valuable relationship we've been discussing, okay?" Calumet made his pocket bulge in order to emphasize the point.

Filatov felt he had no choice at this juncture. Besides, he thought, if worse comes to worst, we'll have another crack at Calumet in Berlin. He was confident that Calumet's hands were clean in regard to the traitor Shevchenko. In his view, Calumet didn't have the makings of a real intelligence operative. All Calumet was interested in doing was making money. He was just another typical American capitalist. And anyway, the documents Calumet had given Shevchenko three years ago had been authentic. Filatov had confirmed

E. SCOTT JONES   49

it himself. They had been doctored while in Shevchenko's possession. That was almost proof enough right there, he thought. He would be happy to report back to the Aquarium that *his* agent, Jack Calumet, was legitimate. After all, he—Major-General Georgi Filatov—would be the one running Calumet from now on, and receiving all the credit for it as well. Filatov gave the signal. The car and the men moved out.

Calumet walked directly behind the Russian. When they got to the foot of the bridge, he asked, "Where are your chase cars, Georgi?"

"One on the other side of the bridge, down the road. Jack, this isn't necessary."

"What about *this* side of the bridge, Georgi? You have another chase car up your sleeve?"

"No, Jack. Please. This *isn't* necessary."

Calumet nudged him onto the street, saying nothing. He was still jumpy. He forced Filatov to walk with him all the way into the square and into its shadows. "I'll see you in Berlin, Georgi," he said when he was sure he had a clear stretch. "Three days!" Then, like an ancient conjured-up apparition, Jack Calumet vanished into the medieval darkness of Alt Sachsenhausen.

Robert and his team dispersed. The five men from Delta Force would go to a safe house. Robert would clear the rest of his group and then head over to the consulate to cable Armbrister. All he would be able to tell the DDO at this stage is what he had witnessed. Only after debriefing Calumet later in the morning would he have anything tangible to report. In about thirty minutes, when he heard from Robert, Armbrister would be able to take solace in the fact that Calumet had walked away from the meet alive and that no violence had occurred. When he finally heard the whole tale, however, he would be jubilant.

Excalibur had pulled it off!

CHAPTER 4

Paris wasn't the most expeditious route to Amsterdam from Frankfurt, but that's the route Calumet took. Robert had warned him that Langley's sources within the BND confirmed what the two of them already suspected. The Germans were beginning to take an interest in him in an effort to determine why a Mr. Jack Calumet had, of late, been making so many sojourns to their fine land without seeming to have any related business concerns. His first appearance in their computers came two years earlier when the BND, mysteriously, received a photograph from an anonymous source depicting Calumet and a celebrated underworld figure sustaining an animated but friendly conversation next to a kiosk in Zurich. Obviously, he needed a buffer. A straight shot from Frankfurt to Berlin would have kept Calumet on German turf, thus inviting the BND— or challenging them, depending on how they viewed it—to place him under surveillance. He and Robert decided it would be best for him to lose them, if only for a couple of days, so Calumet flew to Amsterdam via Paris. In the meantime, the CIA pleaded interagency cooperation with the DEA, who in turn chatted up the BND and pleaded operational precedence, claiming that they too were keeping their eye on a Mr. Jack Calumet, and could the Germans please stay out of it since the gentleman in question was American. The Germans wanted to know, *bitte,* was the gentleman in question suspected of any terrorist activities? No, the DEA assured them, only drugs. Then he's all yours, the BND replied, if drugs is all it is. Thank you very much, the DEA told the BND, and to the CIA, you owe us one. History would eventually record the anonymous passing of the photograph as one of the more brilliant gambits fostered by Lewis Armbrister in the early stages of the operation.

Robert had flown directly to Washington after debriefing Calumet. To say that he had been incensed would be a mild understatement, although his perception was that the DDO had purposely withheld his motives so Robert's heart would be in it when he attempted to prevent Calumet from attending the meet with Filatov.

Nevertheless, Armbrister had sorely tested their friendship on this point. Robert made a big performance out of it when he finally confronted him face to face. Armbrister, for his part, had explained to Robert it was imperative that the decision be made by Calumet absent the influence of patriotism. In his words, "Robert, we are about to mount the most ambitious operation ever assayed against the Aquarium. Its successful outcome requires an agent—a little soldier boy—who is daring enough to march into hell without knowing why, and who is clever enough to steal from the devil himself once he gets there. Only a rogue like Excalibur can pull it off. And only an old sorcerer like you can run him. Sit down, old friend . . ." Armbrister talked for more than an hour. After Robert had heard the DDO's confession, they shook hands and Robert flew to Amsterdam. His parting shot was, "To hell with coach; I'm riding up front. Clear it for me, old friend."

Calumet had checked into the Hotel Ambassade and found that his favorite room was available. The room itself was actually beneath the sidewalk of the main thoroughfare, a narrow strip of road called Herengracht running parallel to the canal. His main attraction to the room was the fact that it could be entered only from the street, not through the hotel lobby. A narrow flight of concrete steps ran from the sidewalk down to the door. This arrangement offered less security, but Calumet didn't have to pass any clerks on those occasions when his forays propelled him into the city at strange hours of the night, if there was such a thing as a strange hour in Amsterdam. He registered under his own name, left his clothes for the laundry service, and then caught a taxi back to Schiphol Airport. He'd made a phone call from Paris on his way to Amsterdam. Satisfied with the outcome of the call, he now bought a one-way ticket on Sabena Airlines, tendering cash, and caught the next flight to Brussels. The German passport Jack Calumet presented to the Flemish customs agent had his own face, but the name was something altogether different.

Upon his arrival at Zaventem Airport in the Belgian capital, Calumet climbed aboard the first train bound for Gare Centrale, or Central Station. The train ride lasted about fifteen minutes. He disembarked and bought a ten-trip ticket for the trams. Changing trams several times, he finally ended up at Gare du Midi where he barely had five minutes to spare. His contact, an old Flemish gentleman known to him as Paul De Boeck, picked him up outside the station and they engaged in small talk until they reached the outskirts of Beersel, actually between Beersel and Halle, which is where De Boeck claimed he lived, although Calumet doubted that the modest wood-and-stone edifice was his principal residence.

"What can I do for you, Jack?" De Boeck asked after they had settled into two russet-covered chairs in a small room filled with bookshelves and a few antique lamps. There was a fireplace along the front wall, currently empty and swept clean, and two heavy beam rafters across the ceiling. The windows were obscured by dark green draperies with cream-colored linings and topped off with an art nouveau floral pattern. When looking at them from the outside, one would be presented with a view of gothic security grills bored into the stone. The cottage itself was set back from the main road, hemmed in by a squadron of conifers.

"I need three sets. Two German, one American," Calumet replied. "And I need some hardware."

"I presume you want all of this in a hurry?"

"Yesterday."

De Boeck's eyes were framed by wire-rimmed glasses which he removed and began to polish with the hem of his maroon cardigan. "What kind of hardware?" he asked.

"Nine millimeter, preferably Beretta, and a twenty-two long rifle, same manufacturer. Teflon coat for the nine. Stingers for the twenty-two. And two extra mags for each. Oh, and an ankle holster for the twenty-two, if you happen to have one."

"Hmm," De Boeck intoned. "Shouldn't be a problem. Let me check." He got up and left the room. Calumet guessed him to be about seventy, and was certain he had been involved in equally as many wars and police actions over the course of his adult life. There was talk that in his younger days he had been a member of Belgium's white army, otherwise known as the underground, who in World War II had aided the British immensely during the Allied eviction of the Nazis. Jack had been given his name by mutual friends in the arms trade and had done business with the cabalistic Belgian on several occasions in the past six years. Their relationship was one of mutual respect, and neither delved into personal niceties. The Belgian had never asked Calumet why he needed his special services; he simply accepted the fact that Calumet was a player who had been introduced through the appropriate channels. Jack had no doubt that the Belgian could be trusted. He was from the old school.

De Boeck returned a moment later. He was accompanied by a younger man in his late twenties or early thirties who was painted in a black muscle shirt and drab green parachute pants. He appeared to be big enough and fit enough to wrestle grizzly bears. And probably would, Jack thought, given half the chance.

"We can accommodate you," De Boeck said. He made no introductions. This was one of those environments, Jack knew, where it was safer to conduct pointed inquiries into the particulars of a man's wife or girlfriend than it was to ask him for his name. De Boeck pulled a pad and pencil from the pocket of his cardigan and began to figure, his spectacles dangling precariously on the end of his nose. "Normally, for you," he said after a minute, "the price would be two thousand five hundred American for each set, plus an additional fifteen hundred for the weapons and ammunition. Because you were a friend of my late friend, Werbell, I give you a break in his honor."

"I appreciate that," Jack said, and he did. "How much of a break?" he added.

"I give you each set for two thousand. And one thousand for the other. That is a total of seven thousand American. Is there any problem with that?"

"None."

"Then let us begin." De Boeck motioned him down a darkened hallway and into another room. It was laden with camera equipment, klieg lights, a stool, a white screen for a backdrop, and a huge L-shaped table which took up space along two walls. The table supported an array of guises, cosmetics, and other accessories that would rival a small Hollywood special-effects studio. "How will you want to appear?" De Boeck asked.

"Just like I am," Jack replied, "except for the clothes." He knew the closet, which could really be considered more of a small room, contained a vast assortment of apparel, including wings, shoes, ties, belts, and other specialties of the Belgian's peculiar trade. He stepped inside and chose three oxford shirts and two ties, all rather conservative in appearance. The gorilla watched his every move.

"You have a mechanic hidden around here somewhere?" Jack

asked the Belgian as he changed, purposely avoiding the gorilla's eyes. Calumet was familiar with all the little things that incited wild animals to provocation.

"Of course. The best in Europe!"

Jack handed him a sheet of paper. "This contains the information you need. Your man might want to begin."

De Boeck handed the paper to the gorilla, who disappeared for a minute and then returned. Calumet took his proper place on the stool and De Boeck snapped off ten or fifteen pictures with a Polaroid. After all the photos had been properly cropped, Calumet chose those he wanted and De Boeck once again gave them to the gorilla. The gorilla took them to the mechanic, who was busy forging three sets of passports, driver's licenses, and credit cards. The final product, Jack knew, would appear genuine because De Boeck, in some mysterious way, always managed to put his hands on such things as virgin passports and other official artifacts that could be used to create ersatz identifications. These fabricated identities, known in the trade as *light legends,* had come in handy for Calumet in the past, but they were not designed to beat a thorough inquiry. A thorough inquiry would reveal that they had never been officially recorded. Rather, their purpose was to beat customs agents at checkpoints. An experienced customs agent, Calumet knew, could handle a passport and determine if it was a fake unless the job was very, very professional. The most renowned method was to hold the passport in a vertical position and ascertain upon which page it fell open to of its own accord. This process, when repeated three or four times, would usually reveal a counterfeit because it would always fall open to the same page, implying either faulty paper, minute scrapes where text might have been altered, or too much pressure exerted in a particular spot during the forgery, all of which would most probably crimp it slightly. It would not be visible to the naked eye, but it would exist nevertheless. Genuine passports, on the other hand, properly forged, made this type of inspection unlikely to succeed. There were other dupes employed by customs agents as well, but *backstopping*—the one foolproof method of acquiring an identity that would stand up under the most rigorous of investigations—unfortunately could not be provided by De Boeck. The Belgian had the clout to obtain genuine passports, but he apparently didn't have the clout to introduce a legend for each one and have it registered

with the corresponding government. Thus, his mechanic was working with blanks. At any rate, Jack thought, today's purchase would
satisfy his requirements since he planned to use the legends only in
an emergency, and he had traveled to Belgium more for the weapons than the passports anyway.

They retired to the front room to wait, joined—naturally—by the
gorilla, who took a seat on an overstuffed couch not too far from
Calumet. For the next three hours, Jack listened to De Boeck talk
about the world's problems, mostly offering his own supremely fac-
ile remedies which were devoid of any penetrating analysis.
The Belgian was certainly no politician. All they ever got out of the
gorilla was an assenting nod on four or five conversational
pieces, which, as Calumet remembered it, had something to do
with violence.

The mechanic finally emerged from some inner sanctum with his
masterpieces. The gorilla went to another room and returned with
the weapons and ammunition. He handed them to Calumet after
Calumet produced seven thousand-dollar bills and handed them to
De Boeck. All was complete. De Boeck drove Calumet back to
Brussels with the gorilla sitting in the backseat this time. Along the
way, Jack hoped an annoying itch didn't suddenly manifest itself in
an inconvenient spot, like somewhere near one of the two weapons
on his person. The gorilla was an opportunist in such matters, he
surmised, and likely to misconstrue any number of innocent actions
as a threat to his employer. Finally they arrived at Gare du Midi,
uttered the obligatory parting encomium, and went their separate
ways. In all the time they'd been together, Calumet had never
heard the gorilla utter a single word. De Boeck trained his animals
well, he thought.

Calumet arrived at Midi just in time to catch the 4:10 train,
which would put him in Amsterdam at a few minutes past 7:00. He
couldn't fly back due to his cargo, so he purchased a first-class ticket
and boarded the train. His meet with Robert wasn't scheduled until
the next day and he needed to catch up on some sleep. After the
three-hour journey he made an early night of it and turned in, but
not before placing a call to Diane and making sure the home front
was still intact. He told her he was bored and hoped to conclude his
business as soon as possible. She wanted to believe him, so she did.
Before he placed the call, he had inspected the phone, the bed, and

other aspects of his room just to make sure nobody had conceived any lugubrious schemes concerning his fate. Regimen wasn't his strong suit, but that's one he never missed.

*

Gerhard Scheller decided the American would be an easy mark. He appeared to be fit, but also young and not very well traveled. Gerhard gave a sophomoric nod to his two accomplices: Kiri, who was to be his hand-off man, and Luther, a big, muscled oaf who would become involved only if something went wrong, which had happened only once during Gerhard's four-year tenure as a professional pickpocket. The American was standing in line at the *Wechselstube* in the central train station, more commonly known as Berlin am Zoo. Gerhard knew it would be easiest to hit him now, while he was stationary, before he changed his money.

Kiri started slowly from the other side while Gerhard moved in quickly. His hands were very deft and imbued with blinding speed. Gerhard's right hand had never moved more smoothly in his life, he thought, but the sensation was more shock than reality. A split second before his fingers found the wallet inside the rear pocket of the American's jeans, his ears discerned a perceptible crack in the air and a numbness that he couldn't quite understand began spreading across his right forearm. Kiri, he noticed in a detached sort of way, had veered off, making room for the oaf to come in and settle affairs. The oaf wasn't really sure how to account for the sequence of events himself, however, as he suddenly found the ceiling of the old train station very intriguing, although somewhat miasmic due to the constellation of bright little stars that appeared to be interfering with his clear view. By the time anybody could really fathom what had taken place, the American had vanished. Gerhard and his mates, not being of a civic-minded nature, rushed away from the scene to find a doctor, and the incident, for all practical purposes, was closed.

Thus, while Calumet was waking from a pleasant slumber in Amsterdam, the last member of the five-man Delta team had just arrived in Berlin. He would make his way to the address he had been given before leaving Frankfurt and join the others, who had already effected the journey. All had traveled independently and by separate routes.

*

Calumet treated himself to a leisurely breakfast and arrived at the safe house, which was located on the outskirts of Amsterdam past the museum quarter and Vondel Park, at noon. Robert was waiting for him, appearing weary. Several other individuals, some of whom Calumet recognized, were also present. Jack knew Robert had stationed additional people outside. They would monitor the surrounding area to make sure no directional surveillance was being applied, or if it was, to warn them. At any rate, soft music was being piped throughout the house, and the room in which Jack and Robert finally seated themselves—an inner room with no windows—had been soundproofed. Calumet had left the weapons and passports at his hotel, locked in his suitcase. He didn't want Robert to know about them—not because he didn't trust his handler, but because Robert really didn't have a need to know. In Jack's mind, it was that simple.

"You get any answers?" Calumet asked.

"You should have canceled the meet with Filatov, Jack," Robert said. There was no emotion in his voice, and although obviously very tired, his eyes reflected an intensity that commanded the entire room. Jack got the message. This meeting was going to be all business.

"Maybe I should have been an accountant," Calumet retorted, attempting to needle his controller for the statement he had made at Goethe Haus. Fine, he thought, let's spar.

Robert ignored the challenge. "What I'm about to tell you, Jack, doesn't leave this room. Understood?"

Calumet couldn't believe his ears. The qualifier was completely unnecessary, and Robert knew it. Why was he making such a statement? "C'mon, Robert! Who do you think you're talking to?"

"I'm talking to a maverick who had better shape up—right now—or you're out. Got it?"

I see, Jack thought. He's going for total control. He had never witnessed this sort of ferocity in the aristocratic Robert before. Something big was happening, and it excited him. "Well, I *was* planning to take notes and write a book about it," Calumet shrugged, his tone offhanded, "but if you feel that way, sure, I can keep a secret!"

Robert gave him a withering glare, holding it several moments before answering. "We think the Aquarium may believe that you've been a loyal double all along," he finally remarked.

If Robert's chastisement had any effect, it was impossible to tell from Calumet's demeanor. "I don't think so," he replied. "I can read that imbecile Filatov like a cheap novel, and I can assure you he swallowed my legend hook, line, and sinker."

"I didn't say Filatov." Robert's eyes locked with Calumet's. "I said the Aquarium."

Whoa, Jack thought. He knew better than to state the obvious. Filatov was GRU—he worked for the Aquarium—so naturally Jack would assume that they were one and the same in the context of this conversation, but Robert was implying something different. "You're not about to tell me that our friend Georgi has been compromised, too, are you? Because if you are, I *want* out. Whichever side has a screw-up like Filatov working for them deserves to lose."

"No," Robert replied. "Filatov is theirs. Always has been and always will be. As you say, we don't want him. I'm afraid it's a bit more complicated than that."

"I see," Jack said, even though he didn't. "Well, since I really don't have anything planned for the rest of the afternoon, I'd be more than happy to sit here and let you explain it to me. Fair enough?"

In spite of his weariness, Robert smiled at Calumet's flair. He had never known anyone quite so unflappable. Most anybody else would be seeking to regain some measure of approval after having been verbally dressed down by their controller, but not Calumet. As far as Robert knew, Calumet was probably working on his next wisecrack.

"We have been engaged in a very delicate subterfuge with the Aquarium for some years now," the operations officer began. "I don't think anyone can actually pinpoint its origin, but perhaps it could be traced back to a particular date during Gorbachev's regime." Calumet noticed that his voice had suddenly taken on a faraway resonance, as though Robert was suddenly lost in memories of ancient times. "It's an operation," Robert continued, "that seems to have just evolved of its own accord, like spontaneous combustion—Poof!—as if it had no strategist to set it in motion. Ever hear of anything so strange?" But Robert wasn't looking for an answer.

He galloped on. "We didn't begin to get wind of it until well into Yeltsin's tenure. Even then there were only a very few isolated bits of information which hinted ever so slightly at its existence."

What are you talking about? Calumet thought. Robert must have read his mind. "It is necessary for you to understand our strategy back then, Jack. You see, our objectives during those days had changed somewhat. We began to focus on political intelligence more than in the past. We knew there still existed within the infrastructure of the defunct Soviet government a core of hard-liners who were diametrically opposed to the events which were taking place throughout the eastern world. As a result, we retargeted our intelligence efforts—ELINT, COMINT, HUMINT, the works—in order to specifically keep abreast of the hard-liners. We wanted to know if they had the ability to carry out an overthrow and, if so, under what circumstances. In addition, we stepped up our penetration efforts, believing we had an unprecedented opportunity to breach the inner membranes of Moscow Center. Our recruitment endeavors doubled. We prepared for contingency after contingency, hashing out every scenario, playing it this way, playing it that way, and then rehashing it again until we were blue in the face. We thought everything had been well accounted for, but we were wrong, because another very clever, very arcane operation was underway in the bowels of an old adversary. It was an operation about which we had no inkling, but one in which we are still suffering from today. While we were enjoying a great deal of success on the one hand, especially with regard to a particular penetration effort, we were losing our shirt on the other. Have you ever heard me mention the name Nishka before?"

"No," Calumet appeared puzzled. "Who is she?"

"Not a she," Robert corrected, "a he. Nishka is our *glavni vrag,* as the Russians would say—our main enemy. Most of what we know about him is very sketchy. There is speculation, more rumor than fact actually, that Nishka heads up an entirely new, secret directorate within the GRU. This directorate, if it exists—and we now believe it to be so—doesn't even have a designation, or if it does, we don't know what it is. We're fairly certain it was formed during Gorbachev's regime, and its charter, back then anyway, was to galvanize a core of elite GRU and KGB officers who met and operated independently of any governmentally sanctioned sponsorships."

"To what purpose?"

"That very question confounded us initially," Robert continued. "Until the coup. Then we were able to begin to piece it together. Prior to the coup, we weren't sure of anything. As I mentioned, we thought we had all the bases covered. We didn't think that an operation of that magnitude could be blooming right under our noses without our knowledge of it. We've since conducted a postmortem, but looking back on it now, I'm not sure we could have done anything differently. You see, we talked to KGB and GRU officers in droves during Gorbachev's and Yeltsin's regimes, and every now and then one of them would mention Nishka and the secret directorate, but they could confirm nothing. Not one of them had so much as even a scintilla of circumstantial evidence, much less any *hard* evidence. It was all scuttlebutt. Well, we didn't take it lightly, we probed. 'Where were Nishka and his gang headquartered?' we asked. No one knew. 'What is the purpose of this secret directorate?' we wanted to know. Again, nothing. 'Well, how did *you* hear about it then?' we queried. 'From Colonel Anatoli Yuri Markelov,' one would answer. 'Then where is Colonel Markelov now?' we pressed. 'He's dead,' they would tell us. 'A very unfortunate accident.' And on and on it went. Basically the same story every time, just different players. Anyone who seemed to know something tangible, like Markelov, disappeared from the face of the earth. We even pressed a loyal KGB officer, Colonel Golovatenko was his name, and I mean loyal to Yeltsin—he would not consent to work for us—to use his own resources to check into the disposition of Nishka and this secret directorate. We were able to convince him that it was in Yeltsin's best interest to do so, which it was. Well, the next thing we knew, Colonel Golovatenko had hanged himself in Lefortovo."

Robert stood up and stretched, then sat back down and poured himself a glass of water from a pitcher resting on a bare coffee table. Besides the two chairs in which they were sitting, it was the only other parcel of furniture in the room.

"Back up a minute," Calumet said. "Who is Nishka? How did you know who he was?"

"That comes later, Jack. Let me do this my way." Robert smiled, but his tone went further, as if he wanted to add "for once" to the end of his sentence.

"Okay," Jack consented. "So what were you able to piece together?"

"Well, for one thing, we were able to determine why this secret directorate was formed in the first place. At least we're pretty sure. It became evident early on that Gorbachev was taking a gargantuan gamble in his dealings with the Reagan administration and with his own policies inside the Soviet Union. Winds of change were blowing in every direction. It was readily apparent—to some, anyway—that the old order was about to undergo a drastic transformation. The warning signs were blinking like beacons in the night. The riots in Romania. The Berlin Wall. The labor unions in Poland. And later, the demonstrations in Moscow. As the Republicans were so fond of saying, democracy was breaking out all over the world. Nishka, more than anyone else, saw it coming. As a result, he took active measures—not just to safeguard the old establishment, but to ride out the sudden wave of hysteria that was beginning to run rampant throughout the eastern bloc. He's a demon, that one, a real wizard. He knew the numbers wouldn't add up economically. The United States, Japan, Europe—we were all suffering from our own economic maladies. We were having trouble paying our own bills, much less anybody else's. In a nutshell, democracy was undercapitalized, and Nishka knew it."

"I think I see what you're driving at," Jack said, "but—"

Robert held up his palm, motioning Calumet to remain quiet. For all his patience, Robert had his own docket now, and he wasn't going to allow himself to be sidetracked. He proceeded. "So Nishka formed his secret directorate. Why? Nishka knew the GRU and KGB were both accountable to the governing body currently in sanction. At one point it was Gorbachev's government; another time it was Yeltsin's. Neither of the two intelligence services could operate without—in Gorbachev's case—Politburo authorization or—in Yeltsin's case—parliamentary authorization. In other words, the KGB and GRU needed a license from whatever regime was in power. Well, Nishka saw the inconsistency of that relationship given the ever-changing state of affairs within Russia. He saw how Russia's entire intelligence effort could be paralyzed by the shifting tides of political change, how years of strategy could suddenly be swept away by Center's inability to function due to a sudden lack of direction, and he couldn't abide it. There existed no official mechanism that was properly suited to accommodate his own solution for the welfare of Mother Russia. In effect, therefore, Nishka became a law unto himself. He literally sprang up overnight, without warning. One day he was just Nishka—servant of the Rodina, the next he was Nishka the power broker—self-appointed protector of old Dzherzhinsky's resting soul.

"The change was catastrophic. Whereas before Nishka was at the mercy of governmental whims, now he suddenly required no man's blessing. He would run his ops and counter ops any way he damned well pleased. He was beholden to no one. His secret directorate was initially composed primarily of hard-liners from the Soviet military-industrial complex and from the GRU and KGB. Not the same cadre, by the way, that bungled the attempt when Yeltsin made his triumphant stand. Nishka knew it was too early then, and he wasn't ready to expose his hand. No, sir. *Wait,* he told his people. *The time will come,* he assured them. *Not a hint,* the devilishly cunning Nishka commanded.

"The penalty for breathing even a word of Nishka and his secret directorate was instant death. So where was he? Where was this directorate? Possibly it had no physical location, as such. Perhaps the location was merely an abstract and existed only in the sheer force and energy of Nishka himself. We may never know. Wherever it was though, Nishka was there, under very deep, spinning his strategies and crafting his clandestine spears. He was never at a loss for direction. Nishka knew how to keep the pressure on. He had at his disposal an armada of exchequers and unconscious agents— politicians and others who were doing his bidding without even realizing that it was Nishka who was the driving force behind the scenes. It was Nishka who arranged the political obstacles to democratic reforms, passing them through several layers of esteemed policy makers and Generals until they ended up as voluble objections on the Parliament floor. It was Nishka who staged the pro-Communist demonstrations that swept the country like a plague, somewhat reminiscent of Lenin's day. Nishka the inciter. Nishka the mover and shaker of the country. Never in the open, though. Nishka was too clever for that; he kept himself insulated at all times. He knew how to play both ends against the middle, feeding his cover stories to one group, brandishing his half-truths to another. The argument could be made that he single-handedly kept the Russian government off balance while simultaneously spreading his own venom and playing on the fears of the Russian people."

Robert sighed just then, as if his weariness was overcoming him, but the light in his eyes continued to burn brightly, fueling his passion. "In the midst of it all, though," he continued, "we feel Nishka had another agenda as well. An extremely bold and ambitious agenda. On one front, he was striving assiduously to preserve agent networks and operations which had been in place before the downfall. In *his* mind, it was all a matter of timing; democratic reforms would eventually fail–he would see to that–and when they did, the Soviets would have to hit the ground running. Nishka wanted to be ready. He would put the word out to residencies across the globe, *Lie low. Wait.* And so his assets became sleepers, biding their time until they heard from the maestro. But there was another prong to Nishka's Machiavellian strategy–a second front, if you will. Maintaining his assets and operations wasn't good enough for him. Oh, no. You see, Nishka also saw this period as a great window of opportunity. He knew that personal and political sentimentalities would begin to develop in the West. Individuals who, for any number of reasons, would feel sympathetic to Russia's doleful plight. After all, the Russian people were struggling to bury seventy-five years of Communist oppression. There were plenty of decent tenants in the world, tenants of means, who were willing to take pity and lend a hand. Nishka predicted that, too, so he launched his own campaign of subornation and penetration. He knew our flanks would be exposed. While we were attempting to penetrate Moscow Center, lulled by a false sense of security, Nishka was attempting– successfully, I might add–to penetrate Washington. It was a brilliant strategy, really. To conceive of anything so bold, let alone manage it, took a man of tremendous resource. Nishka is such a man. In fact, the only one who really suspected Nishka all along, who actually *knew* the danger that Nishka represented, was Lewis Armbrister. Armbrister discovered that Nishka had gone underground–I'll explain that to you in a bit–and he knew that if Nishka had gone underground, it was logical to assume that he had done so for a very good reason. As a result, the DDO began to take measures himself, far-reaching measures, measures that ultimately involved one Jack Calumet and Aleksandr Shevchenko, among others. That is how you came to be embroiled in this very complicated affair."

"Then I was right about Shevchenko." Jack indicated he understood. "He had been turned and eventually sacrificed, correct?"

"We bought Shevchenko in the early days of Yeltsin's Administration," Robert took up again. "He was preparing a nest egg for himself and planning to put the secret war behind him. He was hitching his wagon to the new world order, he told us. How he was initially recruited is unimportant, but at first we couldn't be sure if he was genuine or merely a provocateur. At any rate, his defection presented us with a curious puzzle. We suddenly had a bent GRU officer teamed with one of our own doubles. What to do? Well, that's when Armbrister hit upon the beginnings of a very nifty scheme concerning you and Aleksandr. Up to that point we had been feeding you carefully sanitized intelligence which, of course, you were passing along directly to the Russians through a then-loyal Shevchenko. When Shevchenko entered the picture as a Russian double, however, our own strategy took a sharp turn. Instead of delivering sanitized intelligence, we began to give you raw, genuine product. Hot stuff. Of course, you had no way of knowing this. In effect, you had become for us an unconscious agent with regard to this particular phase of the operation. After you handed off to Shevchenko, we exchanged the package you had given him with a sanitized package, which he then passed along to the Aquarium. The objective here was twofold: one, to enhance your credibility as a Russian agent; and two, to sacrifice Shevchenko if our worst fears were confirmed."

"What worst fears?"

"I'm coming to that. Shevchenko, you see, would have to assume that you belonged to the Russians since we were forcing an exchange of documents before he passed them back to Moscow. In effect, we were telling Aleksandr that we knew you were a traitor. The way the DDO envisioned the ploy, it really didn't matter whether Shevchenko was a genuine double or a Soviet provocateur. Either way, your legend would remain intact."

"What was the necessity?" Jack asked. "If Shevchenko was ours, why hold him out as a potential sacrifice? Why not try to move me along to another contact instead? And why not use Shevchenko himself as a source of information that only an insider such as he would be privy to?"

"That goes back to Nishka," Robert replied. "In the first place, we didn't feel that Shevchenko could tell us much that we didn't already know. His usefulness as a penetration agent was therefore not considered to be critical. We had a much greater concern. For some time now, Armbrister has felt that Nishka has had his own deep penetration agent highly placed within American intelligence. At first, it was more suspicion than fact, but there were subtle patterns, haphazard leaks that couldn't be traced. To our initial consternation, it was an acutely frustrating exercise because it appeared that these leaks would sprout intermittently from different arenas—strategic intelligence this month, tactical the next, sometimes even highly sensitive political doctrine, and then nothing for days on end. We couldn't get a handle on it. If our worst fears were confirmed, we theorized, we knew that Nishka would be able to put two and two together. Any intelligence he received from you and other American assets could be corroborated or disavowed by this deep penetration agent. Our first step, therefore, was to confirm whether or not this penetration agent actually existed. Well, Shevchenko was the proof. He was the final curtain. When Shevchenko was blown, we knew. And that, in fact, *did* confirm our worst fears: namely, that this penetration agent, whom we now believe is being run by Nishka, has unparalleled access."

"What about Murdock?" Calumet pressed. "Where does he fit in?"

"Admittedly, Murdock was a surprise. In our view, he was simply a Russian sacrifice—or, more accurately, a Nishka sacrifice, in much the same way that Shevchenko was an American sacrifice."

"In other words," Jack rationalized, "Nishka surmised we were beginning to suspect American intelligence had been penetrated, so he gave up Murdock, thus hoping to pacify us in order to protect his other source?"

"Partly, yes," Robert answered, "but this whole internecine affair is even more convoluted than that. You see, Nishka also suspects—he doesn't know, in our view—but he suspects, that *we* also have a deep penetration agent within Russian intelligence. It is our assessment that Nishka believes we sacrificed Shevchenko for the same reasons he sacrificed Murdock: to protect *our* penetration agent. However—and this may be our saving grace—there is one other reason we feel Nishka may believe we sacrificed Shevchenko." Robert let that sink in, inviting comment.

"Okay," Jack replied, "I'll bite. What was the other reason?"

"To protect you."

"I don't think so," Jack said. "That would mean that Nishka thinks I'm a double. On the contrary, I would be willing to bet the farm that Filatov bought my story. As far as I'm concerned, Georgi Filatov is reporting back to the Aquarium that Jack Calumet has been suborned."

"That's where you're wrong, Jack. You see, Nishka knows Filatov isn't all that talented. He purposely sent Filatov to that meet knowing that he—Nishka—couldn't lose. You yourself said that Filatov was a screw-up. Didn't that make you wonder?"

"No," Jack said. "You've lost me."

"Look," Robert explained, "if Filatov had been successful in kidnapping you and putting you under the needle, Nishka would now have one set of answers. He would know all that you know, which is really not very much. On the other hand, Nishka knew that even though Filatov isn't the brightest operative in the world, his proficiency is certainly above that of any amateur. Therefore, if Filatov was incapable of pulling off a simple kidnapping, it would tell Nishka something else: it would tell Nishka that he was probably dealing with a professional, not an amateur, although he still can't be one hundred percent certain. Is it beginning to make sense?"

"Not a bit. I still don't know where we're headed."

Robert smiled. "Keep in mind, Jack, that we weren't dormant during Russia's tumultuous period, either. We were also preparing for the possibility that the hard-liners would one day regain their exalted position. Remember I told you Filatov had been promoted?"

"Yes, of course."

"Well, we knew about his promotion before Filatov himself knew it."

The revelation was poignant, Calumet thought. He wondered why Robert was exposing such sensitive information. Sure, he knew they had an agent inside the Aquarium, but he didn't know they had one that expensive. "You have an asset buried that deeply?"

"Yes, and he has tremendous potential. That's the crux of this entire affair. You see, Jack, the real fear—for us and for Moscow—is that one of these two penetration agents, either ours or theirs, will expose the other. The trick is to get there first. Considering the belligerence between our two sides, the stakes are enormous. This is the beginning of what leads us into the reasons for your involvement. It is our belief that Nishka *wanted* Filatov to fail in his endeavor to take you—I may tell you why in a moment. After all, any of Filatov's assets could have attempted to drill you once it was obvious you weren't going to go willingly."

Robert paused again, knowing that the lull would give weight to his next statement. "We're on the verge of diving into some pretty murky water here, Jack. Do you want to continue?"

"Is this the commitment point or something?" Jack asked. He knew what his controller was saying. Robert was offering him an out, and Calumet was aware that he had already been told too much for an agent who was about to be sent back into the field, especially since there was the strong potential of his being captured. With his knowledge of an American deep-penetration agent, Langley couldn't afford to have him captured. Alive, anyway.

"Let's just call it stage one."

"Like I said," Jack replied, "I haven't got anything else on for the day."

Robert leaned back and got comfortable. Jack could tell he was going into another story. "It's still classified," the operations officer began, "but about fifteen years ago we found out the hard way that our consulate in Istanbul had been penetrated. I won't go into great detail because it's immaterial at this point, but the salient facts are singularly enlightening. After Langley discovered the penetration, they dispatched Lewis Armbrister to Istanbul to attempt to levy a playback operation against the Soviets. The operation was a moderate success, but a great deal of damage had already been done. Eventually, both sides rolled up their nets and moved on to other ploys. The interplay between the two sides, however, or maybe I should say the interplay between the two individuals on the two sides, was a drama of no little proportion. Lewis Armbrister found himself engaged in a monumental battle of wit and will with a young Soviet GRU colonel named Vladimir Nikolaevich Tertishnikov."

"Nishka," Calumet said.

"Correct," Robert nodded. "Nishka. No one knows how the nickname came about. Perhaps it's a combination of Nikolaevich Tertishnikov. In any case, Armbrister and Nishka have been keeping tabs on each other ever since. At last report, Nishka had climbed to the rank of colonel-general and had attained the position of First Deputy Chief of the GRU. He held that position until just before the end of Gorbachev's regime. Then he vanished. That's when Armbrister knew."

Just then a red light above the door began flashing. Robert told Calumet to sit tight while he left the room. He came back several minutes later. Calumet thought he detected anger, but Robert had an all-weather expression.

"Any problem?" Jack asked after Robert sat back down.

"No," Robert responded, but without conviction. "No, no problem."

"Really?" Calumet wondered. "Hmm." He filed it away for a later time. "You said Nishka vanished. Why do we think he's involved now? Do we know where he is?"

"Yes. After the coup he surfaced again inside the Aquarium. We don't know what his official relationship is now—they have a new First Deputy Chief—but we are certain that Nishka is back in the game, evidently with some kind of license, and calling his own shots."

"I see," Jack pondered. "And therein lies the rationale that Nishka is, in fact, heading up a new, secret directorate, since he apparently has no official status. Right?"

"That's the way we read it," Robert agreed. "Especially in light of all the other facts I've just been telling you about."

"This Nishka sounds like quite a guy," Calumet observed wryly.

"Jack, we've done everything we could possibly think of to maintain your cover," Robert said. "You should understand that certain actions have been taken over the past several years—actions which you are not aware of—that we hope will throw Nishka off your scent."

"What kind of actions?" Calumet interrupted.

"However," Robert continued, choosing not to hear Calumet's question, "Nishka is extremely slippery, extremely crafty, and he won't be fooled for long. Penetration is his specialty. He's forgotten more about the subject than most will ever know. We are left, therefore, with two possibilities: one, Nishka knows you belong to us; or two, he doesn't know. It's really that simple. If he doesn't know, he definitely suspects. Of that you can be certain."

"What actions, Robert?" Although Calumet was able to hear and digest all Robert was saying, he was still hung up on that one particular point. He'd had his own suspicions for a while anyway.

Again Robert chose not to hear him. "If we accept the second premise—that Nishka isn't positive about your agent status—then we have to face the fact that Nishka thinks you are now a CIA target. After all, it would be naïve to think that we could have run Shevchenko for several years without knowing about a traitor who was selling information to him. Nishka has to be asking himself why we haven't arrested you by now. He will be very curious to see how you are handled now that Shevchenko is out of the loop. That's why we believe he wanted you to walk away safely from that meet with Filatov. In essence, both sides were hoping you could pull it off. Our fervent desire now is that Nishka will be led to believe that we are endeavoring to run you as an unconscious agent in order to expose his network."

"That doesn't seem to make sense," Calumet interjected. He knew he wasn't going to get an answer to his earlier question until Robert spit the bit, so he acquiesced. "What are you driving at?"

"I'm driving at symmetry," Robert answered cryptically.

"Symmetry?"

"Yes. You see, Jack, on one side of the coin, Nishka suspects we have a deep-penetration agent within Russian intelligence. On the other side of this same coin, we suspect Nishka has a deep-penetration agent within American intelligence. Symmetry."

"Don't be so coy, Robert. What are you saying?"

Robert leveled his gaze at Calumet. "I'm saying that you are going to be the proverbial straw that breaks the camel's back. We are going to attempt to play you into the middle to smoke out Khodinka's man. Nishka is going to attempt to play you back to smoke out our man."

Uh-oh, Jack thought, and wondered if maybe he *should* have canceled the meet with Filatov.

CHAPTER 5

As Ralph Cromwell stepped out of his car and began walking toward his elaborate suite of offices, he suddenly realized how wonderful he felt for a Monday morning. He paused a moment just to take it all in. It was the beginning of May and pristine clouds were etched in idle swirls across a clarion sky drenched in sunshine. Flowers were in bloom everywhere. The warm temperature was reflected by the city's omnipresent force of blue-collar workers clad in short-sleeved shirts or no shirts at all. They seemed to set the tempo for every metropolis in the world as they bustled about their tasks, peculiarly unaware that even the customary traces of big-city smog had deigned to take a brief hiatus this morning. All in all, an exquisite day, Ralph thought; a very beautiful day. He was so charged with energy that he appeared to have a slight jiggle in his stride, causing him to bob up and down like a buoy as he shuffled through the doors of the Paragon General building in Omaha, Nebraska. After all this time, he gloated, he was finally being summoned to participate in a uniquely important exercise. Since making his political biases known to the right people four years earlier, he had been wondering if the opportunity would ever materialize, but it finally had. Ralph Cromwell smiled inwardly. Yes, it was a splendid day, he thought.

The man had rung his doorbell at 9:00 P.M. on Tuesday of the previous week. It was fortunate for Cromwell that his wife had been at her monthly bridge club and not at home; there was less explaining to do that way. His visitor was evidently one of those individuals invested with the rare quality of good timing, Ralph guessed.

The man didn't stay long. Not long at all, really. Just long enough to chat for a few moments and to give Cromwell a set of papers sealed in a blank envelope. "Won't you step in and have a seat?" Cromwell had pleaded after unearthing the nature of the stranger's visit.

"No, I really can't," the stranger had replied, "but thank you so very much for asking."

"Then how about a cup of coffee, or a drink?" Cromwell had begged.

"You are too gracious," the man had said, "but no, I really mustn't tarry." The stranger remained only long enough to issue instructions and to force Cromwell to memorize a contact number. "Call me immediately when the information arrives," he had said, and although Ralph was completely oblivious to it, the genteel quality had suddenly been dislodged from the stranger's voice at that point.

"Of course," Cromwell had told him. "Without the slightest hesitation. It will be my distinct pleasure." A dog to its master.

Ralph Cromwell ruminated with great expectation as he entered his office. Today, he thought, will be the day that I become a real spy! He could hardly wait. The information he had requested should arrive in the morning post. If those blasted nurses were any good, it would have arrived last Friday, he kept telling himself—especially since he had overnighted the request. That had put a slight damper on his mood for the weekend, but it was all behind him now. Anticipation made it impossible for him to concentrate on his work, forcing him to make innumerable trips to the water cooler, the head, and anywhere else his flightiness carried him. It was an extremely rare moment that found him at his desk when the mail clerk finally *did* show up. According to Cromwell's astute observation, the hour was 10:33 and 42 seconds, give or take a tick.

His was the first parcel on the stack. A big manila package from a Dr. Zekeman in Atlanta, Georgia. Ralph Cromwell was ecstatic. He had requested and finally received the complete medical records of somebody named Jack Calumet. These were times, he knew, when it was necessary for doctors to maintain the utmost propriety in their behavior, and few people were ever able to obtain medical records without a battalion of good reasons; but as a CLU employed by Paragon General Insurance, Ralph Cromwell was legally able to do such things on a daily basis. All he required was a proper consent form with the patient's valid signature. The man who had knocked on his door less than a week ago had provided him with that, along with a completed application as an added bonus just to make sure all the bases were covered.

In this case, the nurses made no attempt to contact a Mr. Jack Calumet to inform him that an insurance company was interested in reading his tea leaves, but if any of the nurses had made such a call to Calumet's residence in Atlanta, they would have heard the phone pick up on the first ring, and Nishka's man—his wiretaps in place and posing as the patient in question—would have verified that Jack Calumet did indeed fill out an application with a representative from Paragon General Insurance company. When targeting the unsuspecting, electronic intercepts were still one of the best rackets going.

Cromwell had been reciting the contact number to himself at least thirty times every day. Now that his package had arrived, he could put it to good use. He was so excited that his hands trembled as he picked up the phone, dialed, and waited for an answer. When he heard the voice say, "This is Sherman," Ralph mumbled that he evidently had the wrong number and hung up. He waited exactly twenty minutes, as previously instructed, then left his desk and carried the unopened package downstairs and out the front door. This time the stranger wasn't so pleasant. He simply exchanged his small envelope containing $1,500 for Cromwell's large package containing Jack Calumet's medical records. Then he disappeared. Still, his abruptness hadn't fazed Ralph Cromwell in the least. Cromwell was so enraptured with the covert nature of his efforts that he wouldn't have been able to recognize a volcanic eruption had he been standing at the core, much less the solemn demeanor of a Russian illegal. Little did he know that his career as a foreign spy was to last a mere six days. The Russian would not see fit to contact him again before he was arrested by the FBI some months later.

The stranger carried the package to the airport and boarded the first available flight, ultimately arriving at Dulles International in Washington, D.C. At Dulles he entered the men's room and placed the satchel containing Calumet's medical records on the vanity so he could wash his hands. The young man who appeared a moment later and began to utilize the adjacent sink asked the stranger if he had just flown in from Miami. The stranger replied, no, he had just come in from Atlanta, not Miami. The young man nodded, picked up the satchel, and left. The stranger's job was done.

The satchel was whisked immediately to the Russian embassy at Mount Alto and placed in the diplomatic bag. The diplomatic bag was then flown directly to Sheremetyevo whereupon it was spirited with great haste to Khodinka Field, thus reaching its final destination just after midnight Moscow time. Nishka was in his office at the Aquarium when it arrived.

*

Thousands of miles away, Lewis Armbrister was locked in a furious spasm of concentration as he sat at his mahogany desk and studied the surveillance photographs of Cromwell exchanging goodies with the stranger. His source at the post office in Atlanta had alerted him that a request for Calumet's medical records was being forwarded by Paragon General Insurance. All mail having the remotest connection to Jack Calumet had been flagged, including that of Calumet's doctor, so it was simply a matter of tracing backward. The DDO immediately dispatched a team to Omaha to follow the package once it arrived. Having been alerted a second time by his source that the records were on the return trip to Paragon General, Armbrister's surveillance team had been able to capture the handoff on film, then had been successful in following the stranger all the way to Dulles. A rough looking biker type standing at the urinal—in reality, a member of the CIA's Office of Security—had witnessed the young man remove the satchel from the vanity and leave. The young man was later identified as a GRU major posing as a trade representative working out of the Russian embassy in Washington. After tailing the GRU major and the satchel to Mount Alto, the surveillance team finally dispersed. There had been no attempt to follow the satchel further; Lewis Armbrister knew where it was headed.

The DDO set the photos down, then leaned back in his leather chair and propped his feet on the desk. He clasped his hands behind his head and closed his eyes. Beyond his door the faint sound of clerical work could be discerned above muted conversations and idle chitchat, but Armbrister tuned everything out. Suddenly Jack Calumet's image appeared amorphously before him, forlorn and haunting, as if in a dream. Armbrister focused on the image, its imprimatur instantly becoming his own talisman somehow, and he wondered if the image's troubled soul would one day forgive him for what was about to be. As if in answer, the image suddenly dissipated, leaving only darkness.

"It begins," the DDO whispered softly, and since he was a praying man, he began to murmur a silent prayer.

*

The five men from Delta Force had christened themselves Team Interceptor.

They were initially led to believe that they were being sent to Frankfurt to participate in a turnkey operation—a simple in-and-out—thus, the idea of a team name had never entered their minds. However, now that they had been told the operation was open-ended they felt they needed a name, and since nobody else saw fit to assign them one, they made up their own.

The entire process had been quite complicated. At first there had been a considerable argument about which name to use. Soldiers are nothing if not superstitious, and the wrong nom de guerre, in their view, could jinx them, possibly screwing up their timing, enthusiasm, proficiency, and heaven only knew what else; whereas the right one could elicit great feats of heroism, bravado, and just downright good soldiering. It was really more of an attitude stimulant than anything else. As a consequence, they felt they had to have a name, but not just *any* name; it had to play. So they argued quite heatedly about the fifteen or twenty rubrics that had been proffered at one time or another by each of the five members. After about an hour they finally got it narrowed down to Team Interceptor and Team Terminator. At that point a secret ballot was introduced into the fracas and Team Interceptor came out on top, but the skirmish hadn't ended there. The two who had opted for Team Terminator realized it was imperative to cover all the angles when involving themselves in such a solemn undertaking, so they accused their buddy who was collecting the ballots of cheating. That opened a whole new can of worms and very nearly derailed their splendid representation of the democratic process at its finest, but in the end they collected themselves and decided to conduct an open vote with each member rattling off his choice in succession. Team Interceptor won that one, too.

After the name was settled, Team Interceptor got down to business. They dressed in dark civilian clothing and wore black windbreakers over their shirts. The pockets of the windbreakers were stuffed with a pair of black gloves and a ski mask. Underneath, shoulder holsters held 9-millimeter 226 Sigsauers and contained two additional slots which were occupied by fully loaded magazines. Each member also carried at least one backup weapon. At 10:30 P.M. Team Interceptor left the Berlin safe house and made their separate ways to Kurfürstendamm Strasse, otherwise known to Berliners as the Ku'damm.

The designation the soldiers had chosen for their team was a perfect match for the mission they were about to undertake.

*

Sold in bricks, each weighed 2.2 pounds, or one kilogram. Eighty-five percent pure heroin. Johann Leider was down to his last brick. He was unloading it tonight for a cool $55,000, which would net him roughly $40,000 after he subtracted his incidental expenses. Just several years earlier he had barely been able to make ends meet as a mechanic in the fabled worker's paradise of old East Germany, but when the wall came down all of that changed. The crude and ill-mannered Stasi—or Secret Police—were no longer lurking behind every corner. As a result, Johann's financial woes were a thing of the past because the heroin business in Berlin was brisk these days, especially for mid-level dealers like himself.

It was also deadly.

For years, most of the heroin consumed in Europe originated in the poppy fields of Southwest Asia and came up through the infamous Balkan route. Johann had no way of knowing it, but his particular brick had been cultivated in the Nangahar province of Afghanistan—second only to Burma as the world's largest producer of illicit opium—and had been carried by mule to Kabul, where it was then placed aboard a bus and trucked through Jalalabad over the Khyber Pass and into Landi Kotal and Peshawar. From there it was offloaded and taken to a crude laboratory for processing into morphine base and heroin. After processing, the opium-turned-heroin made its way into Iran and then on to the transshipment country of Turkey where it was ensconced aboard a bonded TIR truck. The TIR truck, short for Transport International Routier, was not typically subject to customs inspections, so it snaked its way unmolested up through the Balkan route, passing from Turkey into

Bulgaria, Romania, and Hungary without so much as a sniff. Along the way, each stop had lightened the load as the cargo was divided and dispersed to courier after courier until ultimately the poison had branched out and descended like a plague upon most of Europe's major cities.

And that was just one shipment.

As if the overworked, outmanned, and outgunned DEA didn't have enough to worry about in their interdiction efforts, the Southwest Asian heroin market in Europe—much to the chagrin of Johann and other continental mid-level dealers—had recently begun to receive a concerted challenge from poppy growers in the Southeast Asian country of Burma, which produced and shipped more of the contagion than any other nation in the world. Until recently, however, Europe had never really been their primary target, but that was changing. The West Africans, principally the Nigerians, had staked their own claim to narcotics trafficking and were smuggling Burmese heroin into Europe and the United States in enormous quantities. Through its Heroin Signature Program, which utilizes forensic chemical analysis to link a specific heroin sample with its geographic source area, the DEA had been able to determine from seizures at Europe's major points of entry that Chang Chi Fu a.k.a. Khun Sa, via the Nigerian network, was expanding his horizons.

Khun Sa, undisputed leader of the insurgent Shan United Army in Burma, had been dominating the production of opium in the Shan state and the export of refined heroin to the West for years. The DEA knew about him, but short of sending in a rather sizable paramilitary force to take him out, there seemed to be little anybody could do to stop him. As if aware of his apparent invulnerability, it was rumored that the warlord had deigned to make a brazen offer to the Drug Enforcement Administration which—in his view— would aid the crime fighters enormously in their interdiction efforts. Namely, pay him $75 million and he would quit shipping his heroin to the United States, just like that. In response, one DEA agent was heard to have remarked, "Sure, no problem! Tell the slimebag to personally drop by our office in Rangoon and pick it up!"

Buying Khun Sa's heroin relatively cheaply from sources in India, the Lagos-based Nigerian networks had established a trafficking, distribution, and money-laundering consortium which had been turning whirlwind profits. Their success in smuggling the white powder into the United States and other parts of the world, including Europe, was overwhelming and could be attributed in part to a close-knit society which was ordered primarily along historical tribal ties. This arrangement satiated the old African chiefs for a time, but soon they began to grasp the principles of free enterprise more firmly and realized that they had been failing to capitalize on the street-value income of their product thanks to mid-level dealers like Johann. As a result, the Nigerians decided to set up their own distribution rings in most of Europe's major cities and thus move in on the local competition in a big way. That meant violence.

Like distant drumbeats in the Congo, word of the Nigerian power play was spreading rapidly throughout Europe. It was no mystery, therefore, when Johann—his ear alertly to the ground—had been able to perceive in a general sort of way that nefarious undercurrents were surging through his own dark world with chilling ramifications, and although not his custom, this night he decided to bring a gun and a friend with him to the evening's exchange. Neither would save his life, but it didn't matter. This night Johann's salvation would come in the guise of another guardian angel and would convince the mid-level drug dealer beyond any doubt that, even for a lowlife like himself, there was a God after all.

*

Believing that God was just an invention of man—but also alluding to the possibility that his own hero, Stalin, might have been a devil—the Luciferian Nishka sat at his desk engrossed in Calumet's medical records. He was primarily concerned with the last three years, and he peered intently at the dates alongside each entry. He was perturbed that the nurses had remitted only a copy package—he would much rather have had the original—but he would overcome that small problem if the medical records revealed what he suspected. The only light in his office came from a bright desk lamp that poured its luster in a circle over the pages.

He went through each entry, making notes from time to time on a yellow legal pad made in America. As he worked methodically through word after word, sentence after sentence, a pattern began to develop. He noticed that roughly two-and-a-half years earlier Calumet began having frequent occurrences of postnasal drip:

October 25—Patient exhibits recurring runny nose. Mucus membrane linings slightly erythematous.
January 3—Mucus membrane linings of entire nasal cavity erythematous with foci of damaged mucosa. Blames it on allergies and pollen.

There were numerous other entries of a similar nature, and as his mind sifted and digested them, Nishka's own temperature began to rise. The report didn't come right out and say it, but it was clear: Jack Calumet, at least according to his medical records, had a co-caine habit. Interesting, but not necessarily surprising. The wizened spymaster continued to read slowly through the doctor's remarks until he came to a particularly intriguing entry:

July 7—Patient received complete physical. EKG interpretation evidences car-diac ventricular irritability manifested by runs of multiple premature beats. Dis-turbing changes in the ST-T segments suggesting coronary insufficiency.

Nishka slammed the papers down and pressed a buzzer on his desk. There was a firm knock on the door before it opened abruptly and an aide with the rank of colonel entered. He saluted smartly, marched quickly to the front of his superior's desk, and snapped to attention.

Nishka scooped up the medical records. Without so much as an upward glance, he shoved them at the aide. "Take these to forensics. I want a duplicate package resembling the originals as closely as possible within twenty-four hours."

The colonel saluted once again, then snatched the package off the desk and left.

After hearing the soft click of the door, Nishka leaned back in his antique Victorian chair and steepled his fingertips together, holding them steadily before his bright obsidian eyes. Had anyone been there to observe him, they would have noticed that his gaze was strangely translucent, almost hypnotic. In some unfathomable, mystical way, they were eyes which presented an accurate introduction to the nether recesses of his draconian soul.

Suddenly the light from his lamp flickered ever so slightly, caus-ing a momentary blackout in the room, but Nishka didn't notice. His concentration had been captivated by a mysterious titillation from somewhere deep within, like a mistress with a spell, and so intense was its allure that it held his senses at bay and compelled him to pursue its own subtle enticement. Except for an almost imperceptible, sinister smile that began to glissade slowly across his lips, one would have thought the iniquitous figure sitting there so quietly was an ancient statue frozen in time. In a way, the posture was apropos of the man.

Nishka had been agonizingly patient for the last five years. He had been able to weather the temporary dissolution of his beloved Communist government with a stoic resolve. While most of the world had their heads buried in the sand like ostriches, believing foolishly that totalitarianism had been banished forever, he had worked demonically night and day behind the scenes to right a capsized regime floundering in the turbulent waves of ineffective politics. For five years he had battled his enemies, both at home and abroad, with a tenacity rarely found in the spirit of men. He had calculated his gambits and measured his moves scrupulously, like a tournament chess champion, constantly pressing the attack from a seemingly indefensible position until, as sure as the morning follows the evening, he had caught the Americans off guard. The intelligence elite in the United States thought *they* had had the upper hand all along, but they were wrong. Little did the strategists at Langley know that it was by his *own* design, Nishka reminisced—not Lewis Armbrister's—that recent events had guided the life of Jack Calumet unswervingly into the Russian's lurid domain of move and countermove.

Yes, the old wizard pondered, broadening his sinister smile, Lewis Armbrister wasn't the only one who had been able to make the mirage shimmer. The DDO of the CIA was in for a prodigious surprise when he discovered that the clandestine course he was charting for his agent had already been laid out by Nishka himself. If he was right, Nishka conjectured, Armbrister would ultimately be destroyed by the cunning and savagery of the pitfall that had been set before him. Oh, how he would love to see the DDO's face when he found out. He would prove once and for all that he—*Nishka*—was the master of subornation and penetration.

And yet, in the back of his mind Nishka felt a twinge of foreboding. Armbrister was a savvy operations officer in his own right, the Russian admitted, and to underestimate him would be foolish. Although events were transpiring just as he had planned, there was still one variable in the equation that remained undefined, and it concerned him.

Jack Calumet was still a mystery. Was the American really what he appeared to be? Just another Western opportunist with above-average intelligence and a devil-may-care attitude? Was he simply another capitalist mercenary who was willing to dance his treacherous dance on a tightrope between Moscow and Washington and damn the consequences? Or was he a clever plant by that voodooist Armbrister? Nishka needed to know. They had made too much progress; the operation was too far along to allow for any miscalculations and thus compromise three years of deception and disinformation.

Nishka reflected upon the information just gleaned from Calumet's medical records. According to the records, Calumet could not survive the needle. A disturbing heart irregularity, brought on, no doubt, by moderate to heavy cocaine usage, was a testament to that fact. If the medical records were accurate, Nishka ruminated, it was a good thing Filatov had been unsuccessful in capturing the mysterious American spy. If Calumet had expired, that would have cut the legs out of his own ambitious operation.

That Calumet was a double was now no longer in question. Nishka knew that Calumet had been meeting with the CIA. That was an absolute. What he *didn't* know was whether Calumet had been meeting with the CIA merely on a subjective basis, or, more to the point, whenever his piggy bank had run dry—possibly to support his cocaine habit—in order to sell them tidbits of intelligence garnered from the Aquarium's shopping lists, or had he been giving them the whole kit and caboodle all along? The fact that Calumet had been passing legitimate intelligence to Shevchenko—Filatov had confirmed it—was a strong indication that the American was, in fact, just what he appeared to be: a gold digger and no more. Additionally, Calumet's involvement in the illicit narcotics scene apparently was a reality. Nishka's own source within the BND confirmed that the American had become an unwitting target of the Drug Enforcement Administration. On the surface, therefore, it was all very black and white. All the facts seemed to line up very nicely.

But something just didn't ring true, Nishka thought. The entire scenario was just a little too neat. Calumet was a slippery profiteer who had been managing to bilk the Russians and the Americans for the past six years without receiving so much as a scratch. A Teflon double agent with a coronary abnormality that would almost certainly erupt under the stress of torture or any type of chemical interrogation procedure. Coincidence? Maybe. But Nishka had learned long ago that there was no such thing as coincidence. Not in his business.

Other than the smile, he hadn't moved a muscle. Suddenly he lifted his chin and sniffed the air, as if he could detect the antiseptic smell of the doctor's office from whence Calumet's medical records had emanated, as if by transference the odor had somehow accompanied the medical records across the thousands of miles on their roundabout clandestine journey. How convenient that Jack Calumet had a disturbing heart condition. Convenient for Armbrister, anyway. Did the DDO have a hand in the makeup of those medical records? He wondered. No matter. He would soon lay his own hands on the originals, and then he would know. Meanwhile, he had to move very, very carefully.

He sniffed the air again. Yes. Possibly it was only his imagination, but he actually thought he could detect just the faintest trace of antiseptic wafting through the room. Just the faintest trace. But that wasn't all—there was something else in the air. It wasn't a physical odor, but surreal, as though his senses were being dominated by a slice of virtual reality. A distant aroma seemed to invade his memory in a surging wave of enlightenment just then, and the recognition alarmed him. It was the same instinctual scent he had detected fifteen years earlier in Istanbul. A paper trail had been tampered with in that operation, too.

Nishka suddenly jerked his head. His vacuous eyes peered intently in the direction of the Atlantic Ocean. His suspicion was growing, and his gaze tracked the familiar scent vicariously across the ocean's expanse, homing in on its owner.

"Lewis Armbrister," he hissed with great disdain, the serene silence of his office suddenly shattered, as if he were informing his own startled demons that he knew who was behind the ruse. And then he relaxed and mentally began to reconstruct the DDO's Byzantine playback strategy that he had employed some fifteen years ago in Turkey. Did history repeat itself? Would Armbrister make the mistake of duplicating a strategic move under analogous circumstances and thus expose his hand? Hmm. Perhaps by sifting through the methods and means of younger days, the principle of Achilles' vulnerable heel could be applied to a certain DDO in Washington. Yes, he thought. If there was a common thread running secretly between the operation then and the operation now, Nishka mused, he knew he would find it. It was just a matter of time. In the interim, he would manipulate Jack Calumet until the American was no longer needed.

Then, CIA agent or not, the Teflon double would die.

PART TWO

WHIPPING THE RACEHORSE

CHAPTER 6

Calumet was angry. And weary. He had caught the 2:10 train to Hanover, and from there the 6:50 to Berlin. After more than eight hours he began to see the familiar landmarks of the old Hohenzollern city and was thankful that the interminable journey was nearing an end. The train was due to arrive in Berlin at 10:50, about the same time the five members of Team Interceptor would hit the Ku'-damm.

Robert had warned him before leaving the safe house in Amsterdam, "Jack, you are about to march into a raging hell." Calumet thought the admonition was a bit melodramatic, but he nevertheless gave Robert the courtesy of at least thinking about it for five or six seconds before he departed. His conclusion was that Milton had probably illustrated the perfidious location better than anybody, and since Jack was not a person who was much given to the esoteric attributes of mankind, he let it go at that. It would not be long, however, before his cursory opinion of the subliminal theme began to undergo a radical transformation.

After crossing the border from Holland into Germany, Calumet had shown the same false passport to the German customs agent in Bad Bentheim that he had shown to the Flemish customs agent in Brussels. He had used it on only one or two occasions in the past and figured it was still clean, and he wanted to hold in reserve the three he had purchased from De Boeck. Although Robert had notified him that a deal had been struck with the Germans on his behalf, he saw no sense in rubbing his presence in their faces if he didn't have to, so he decided to make a technically illegal entry into their country. In fact, the particular passport he proffered *was* clean until a BND agent who was up to snuff on his names-and-faces list made the connection. The BND agent had accompanied the customs official on his rounds through the train's compartments at the checkpoint in Bad Bentheim, and his eyes mirrored a subtle recognition when his gaze fell upon Calumet.

Calumet perceived it when it happened. He was meticulous

about observing customs officials as closely as they observed him, especially when he was traveling on a light legend, so he had seen the glimmer of recognition in the BND agent's eyes. In some countries that single morsel of foreknowledge could mean the difference between life and death. In this country, however, since Germany and the United States were on friendly terms, life and death would not be an issue, but the weapons and the other illegal passports he was harboring would be. As a result, Jack began to prepare himself for action. Under no circumstances was he going to allow himself to be searched. Period. He would let them make the first move, though.

Fortunately for everyone concerned, the BND agent in this case was no rookie and had had a bit of seasoning. Instead of provoking a showdown, he crowded the customs official by looking over his shoulder and inspecting the passport. Calumet could see the wheels turning in his head as he memorized the pertinent information on the page containing the photo.

"Sehr gut!" the BND agent had said when he was finished. In addition to being a disengaging remark, it was also a signal for the customs official to hand the passport back to Calumet, which he did. *"Danke schön!"* the BND man added politely, but the smile and the eye contact lingered a moment longer than was really necessary.

After the train pulled out of Bad Bentheim and resumed its trek toward Hanover, Calumet made his way to the lavatory and spent fifteen minutes ripping the pages out of the passport, burning each one, and then flushing them down the toilet, which deposited its refuse on the tracks beneath the rolling train. Then he threw the cover of the passport itself out the window. He similarly destroyed and discarded all other matching identification. Having accomplished those tasks, he dropped his pants and removed his genuine American passport from a nylon money belt and placed it in the pocket of his bomber jacket for easy access. He knew the BND agent would be reporting the encounter. Jack could only hope that the BND remembered the deal Robert had told him about. In the unlikely event that they didn't, however, and German officials decided to wait for him in Hanover or somewhere in between, he would vehemently deny that he had ever used any passport other than the one issued to him in America, which he was now prepared to present if anybody asked.

The entire episode had not been a good omen, Calumet concluded. Robert never did tell him what "actions" had been taken to throw Nishka off his scent, but Jack was beginning to suspect the nature of some of those "actions." In his view, they served merely to exacerbate the tenor of his already-precarious standing in the operation, and he was angry about the premise of deception and Robert's intransigence concerning the facts.

"This is insane!" he had charged Robert when the operations officer ignored his inquiries on the matter.

Does Robert think I'm some kind of mongoloid? Calumet certainly wasn't naïve, and he knew the BND would not be haunting him simply because he'd made numerous trips to their country over the past several years without seeming to have any legitimate business concerns. There had to be another reason. He didn't know what that reason was, but he was positive it was directly related to the "actions" Robert had made reference to so obliquely.

Thanks to Robert and that dimwit Armbrister, Calumet thought to himself as he stared vacantly out the window of the moving train, I not only have to worry about some Russian fairy named Nishka, but now I have to play hide-and-seek with the omnipresent BND as well. *Great!* At least he didn't tell Robert about his procurements from De Boeck, he rationalized. The way things were going, the schmuck would have probably tried to confiscate them.

Of course, Robert hadn't been in the best of moods either, he noted. The operations officer later admitted that the flashing red light above the door had augured bad news. Another loyal American double, "much like you, Jack" Robert had pointed out, attended a meet with his GRU contacts in Ankara and never came back. His body was later discovered in a gutter just outside Ulus, the city's old section. He had been drugged and badly tortured. The murder was bad enough in and of itself, but discarding the body in such a supercilious manner was something else altogether. It seemed as if the Russians were taking their potshots in the open, and they didn't care if Langley knew about it or not. In fact, the Russians were sending a message. They were saying to Langley, "Every double you run at us will wind up like this one." As far as the Russians were concerned, it was evidently open season on doubles.

Calumet initially wondered why Robert was disclosing all the details, but then he found out. The double in question had been someone Calumet had been friends with. Several years earlier Robert had asked Jack to broker some intelligence through Conrad Thurman, an American living in Ankara. Calumet subsequently attended a meet in Paris with Conrad, Conrad's Turkish wife, and their little girl. Jack fell in love with the entire family right away. They were first-class people, and their daughter was precious. Afterward, they met on and off for a period of three years in various locations, Conrad always traveling with his family for cover. Their friendship grew with each meet, but they were also professionals. Conrad never learned Jack's real name, and Jack never learned his. Until now, that is. Now Conrad's wife was without a husband and their daughter was fatherless. Upon discovering the truth, rather than drawing back, Calumet fixed his resolve and became more determined than ever before. There had been no need to murder Conrad. The Russians could have held him and then later traded him. They didn't have to torture and kill him. But Moscow Center had become insatiably brutal of late. *Okay, you murdering psychopaths, I'm putting you on notice.* If there was any way, Jack concluded as the lights of Berlin glimmered in the distance, his anger boiling, he would make the masochists pay.

The train roared into Berlin am Zoo on schedule. Calumet was standing by the exit and jumped onto the platform as soon as the door opened. Although it was second nature for him to begin trolling for surveillance immediately, this time he didn't bother. He planned on checking into the Kempinski under his own name, so if anybody was really determined to find him, they would. Anyway, the Russians already knew he would be staying in that particular hotel, as did the Americans. Of course, they might want to confirm it. Thus, for all he knew, the CIA, GRU, BND, KGB, and maybe even a few others were lining up behind him this very minute as he strolled toward one of the train station's exits. Though he had informed no one of his exact itinerary, all of them possibly had static surveillants in the terminal to pick up him or anybody else they might consider to be interesting. Shucks, he thought, if the British and the French happened to be represented this evening, we could probably put together a toes-to-the-wall poker game. His ego most likely would have been a bit deflated if he knew that, in fact, nobody was on hand to observe his arrival this night. He was completely alone.

Although the Bristol Hotel Kempinski, located in the heart of the city on Kurfürstendamm Strasse, was only a ten- or fifteen-minute stroll from the train station, Calumet preferred not to be out in the open, so he took the short taxi ride over. There were plenty of rooms available. He registered quickly and was given a single on the fourth floor.

As he walked away from the registration desk, he felt an eerie, tingling sensation on the back of his neck, causing his hackles to rise. His sixth sense seemed to be alerting him that suddenly he was being watched. The perception was so powerful that he turned around abruptly when he entered the elevator to survey the lobby, but no one was there. Maybe I'm just being paranoid, he thought.

He dumped his luggage in the room and briefly considered a shower, but decided against it. His rendezvous was in an hour, and he needed all of that time and then some, he calculated, in order to clear his path. He quickly checked his weapons and, as he had done in Frankfurt, he taped a stiletto to the inside of his left forearm. Although his meet was to be nonhostile, butterflies were churning in his stomach, forewarning him that something wasn't right.

Deal or no deal, he was beginning to feel that the BND had suddenly become a giant albatross around his neck.

*

Rick Rossetti walked back across the Ku'damm opposite the Kempinski. He had been perched in the shadows outside the hotel when Calumet arrived, and he hung around for several minutes to make things look normal just in case the Russians were watching for watchers like himself. He also wanted to see who, if anybody, came out after Calumet went in. As far as he could tell, Calumet was clean. Then again, as the leader of Team Interceptor, Rossetti was under orders. He had been told explicitly by Robert that, from now on, the surveillance was to be loose. Very loose. They could not afford to take any untoward risks at this stage of the game. As a result, Rossetti never witnessed the pair of eyes inside the hotel that had mysteriously jump-started Calumet's instincts.

He walked down the Ku'damm until he reached an old green Volkswagen van parked on a side street. He climbed into the passenger side and the van pulled away. His four teammates, or—as he liked to call them—his four partners in crime, were in the back. Up front, in the driver's seat, was a man whom they all knew simply as Steve.

Steve, Rossetti had been told, was a DO—or case officer—who, until recently, had been locked away in the basement of CIA headquarters for a two-year stint in the Counternarcotics Center. Having been reassigned to Berlin just three months ago, his arrival in Germany hadn't gone over well with the Chief of Station. The COS had been told in no uncertain terms by Lewis Armbrister that Steve would be reporting directly to Langley, thus bypassing normal channels. Therefore, if the COS had any impassioned questions concerning Steve's activities, get on the horn and ask Armbrister, he'd been instructed. But leave Steve alone.

From the outset of his arrival in Berlin, Steve had been a dynamo in action. He had immersed himself in intelligence culled from the DEA and the BND regarding Berlin's drug tableau. With an approach reminiscent of a blitzkrieg offensive, he had gotten to know who the players were and where they played. He had reconnoitered location after location, conducted discreet surveillance on mid-level drug dealers and their cohorts, and traversed Berlin and outlying areas tirelessly to familiarize himself with every nook and cranny of the city's ashen haunts. Thus, as he steered the van containing Team Interceptor toward their secluded destination, it would be fair to say that few people—even Berliners—knew the old Prussian canton as well as Steve did.

The DO drove them west on the Ku'damm and then south on Clayallee, toward the American consulate, but pulled up short when they reached Königin-Luise Strasse and the eastern edge of Grunewald Park. When the van came to a halt, he checked the roadway in both directions for traffic. Nothing. Turning, he waved a thumbs-up at the commandos. "I'll see you panty waists on the other side," he remarked. "Try not to screw it up."

"Get a life, Breeze," Rossetti smiled.

With that, the van's side door suddenly slammed open and Team Interceptor piled out. They moved noiselessly into the park's canopy and deployed. As Steve applied pressure to the accelerator, the vintage auto groaned and faded into the night while a three-quarter moon observed them from above.

*

Calumet walked quickly through the doors of the Kempinski and out onto the Ku'damm. He felt pumped. His adrenaline was high. He stood on the corner a moment, mentally trying to work out his route, when suddenly the same strange, tingling sensation caressed the nape of his neck.

Good operatives have good instincts. *Great* operatives have a sixth sense. Calumet's sixth sense had always been true to him, and it was warning him now. The old adage came back to him: "I know I'm paranoid, but am I paranoid enough?" He had had similar experiences before, and he'd handled them with aplomb, but this time it was different. There was something obscenely malevolent about the premonition this time, and it spooked him.

And then it was gone. Just like that. Before he could even attempt to isolate it, it had vanished. And that *really* spooked him, because he was certain it wasn't a false alarm. Not twice in the space of twenty minutes. No way. There was a dragon in the land, and it had the power to become invisible.

"Idiot Armbrister!" Calumet said sotto voce. He had to blame his circumstances on *somebody*. "And screw you too, Robert," he added, just to make sure his karma came full circle. Then he moved.

He worked his way over to the *U-bahn,* took the first car and rode it to the first stop, surfaced on the street above, and not able to immediately find a taxi, retraced his steps back down and caught another train. His strategy was backtrack and speed. Only a first-rate, well-staffed team would be able to maintain surveillance at the pace he was working. And if they weren't well staffed, he would be able to isolate them and sort them out. As always, such action seemed to lighten his spirits. In this case, his instincts told him he was clean. He was confident he hadn't grown a tail, but nevertheless he continued to move. While he worked, the old movie title, *Planes, Trains, and Automobiles,* played in his head, like a bad song that won't go away. Finally, forty-five minutes later, his third cab deposited him on the shoulder of Pückler Strasse near the Grunewaldsee.

Robert had disclosed to him in Amsterdam, "You will meet a DO who will provide you with a weapon and will brief you on the current roster of known Russian assets in Berlin. We will try to maintain surveillance contact in your meets with Filatov, but we won't be able to cover you as closely as before."

When the taxi disappeared from view, Calumet began walking into the darkness toward the lake. The whole thing felt wrong.

*

Johann Leider was of the same mind. He suddenly felt very uneasy himself. The friend he had brought with him was supposed to be concealed in the trees, covering him, not standing just twenty paces away in a small clearing by the lake. Johann squeezed the brick cached underneath his jacket and fingered the pistol in his waistband.

"Was ist los?" he asked.

His friend made no attempt to answer. Instead, a tall black man materialized out of the shadows behind him. He cradled an Uzi in his arms and pointed it at Johann.

"You have something for us, I believe," the Nigerian stated in German, his voice lilting in the resonance of his African accent.

Johann was debating whether or not to go for his own gun or run, but the decision was made for him as four more Nigerians suddenly emerged from the trees and encircled him. All were gripping automatic weapons. Johann gulped.

*

Rossetti didn't like it. This was supposed to be a simple rip-off: no fuss, no mess, and no one gets hurt. Right. He counted eleven Nigerians altogether. Five in the clearing and six more posted around the perimeter. And those were only the ones he was sure about. There could be more. Great! The Nigerians weren't even supposed to be here. They could abort, but that would leave Calumet exposed. No, they had to see this one through, Nigerians or not. Well, no matter. As far as Rossetti and his team were concerned, the exercise had suddenly become just another tactical operation, albeit a bit more complicated now. They'd all seen action before; they'd all worked together as a unit, trained as a unit, and they knew what to do. They had been in position before anyone else had arrived, and surprise was on their side. From this point, years of training took over and the soldiers lifted their skills to a much higher plane. They were operating on pure instinct now. Don't think, execute. Who dares, wins.

Rossetti began to circle toward Calumet.

*

Calumet sensed it rather than saw it. Movement. Noise. Instinctively, he crouched quickly and drew the Beretta. His hands worked the slide and he chambered a round as silently as possible. Cover. He needed cover. He began to move toward a clump of shrubs and then froze. To his left, not more than thirty feet away, a tall shadow loomed large behind a tree. Farther on, in the clearing, he could make out Johann, Johann's friend, and the five Nigerians. Whoa! he thought. I've stumbled into a bloody drug deal. Was he in the right place? He began to wonder.

Then all hell broke loose.

CHAPTER 7

Perhaps the only smart thing Johann ever did in his entire life was dive to the ground and roll into the bushes when the first shot erupted violently in the trees to his left. He lay there, his hands over his head, his face in the dirt, whimpering over and over again, *"Bitte Gott, bitte Gott, bitte Gott . . ."* Please God.

One of the Nigerian sentries had apprehended Rossetti's movement when the commando began to circle toward Calumet's position. Jerry Kramer, covering Rossetti, saw the Nigerian wheel around to fire. The Nigerian never made it. Kramer, from sixty feet, "double tapped" the sentry, which is to say, he smoked the sentry with two rapid shots from his Sigsauer, placing both projectiles within an inch of each other in the Nigerian's chest.

Had they been amateurs, or maybe even regular army, the remaining members of Team Interceptor might have hesitated momentarily after hearing the shots, placing themselves in the unenviable position of setting up as a reaction force instead of an assault force. Or they might have cocked their heads and looked in the direction of the gunfire, attempting to determine what had happened. Or, possibly, they might have hit the ground and just plain panicked. *If* they were amateurs or regular army, that is.

But the lads from Team Interceptor were not amateurs. Nor were they regular army. They were consummate professionals, and they had been through this drill before. Prior to the eruption of Kramer's Sigsauer, each member, as he lay motionless in the dark observing the drug scene unfolding before him, had instinctively picked out a primary and a secondary target. There was no fore-thought; it was automatic. Thus, when the first shot rang out, the soldiers immediately lit up the night with muzzle flashes, taking out those targets. Seven Nigerians were dead before the others even knew they were in a fight. An eighth went down as he figured it out. That left three. Somehow they were able to retreat into a thicket of trees.

Calumet saw the muzzle flash of Kramer's weapon a millisecond before he heard it. By the time the sound reached his ears, he was flat on the ground, his own gun extended and pointing in the direc-tion of the Nigerian sentry he had spotted. At first, assuming natu-rally that he was in danger, he considered dropping the sentry, but hesitated, knowing that firing his own weapon would betray his position. As far as he could tell, nobody was even aware that he was in the neighborhood. Besides, he didn't know whom he would be killing, and that bothered him. It didn't matter. The problem be-came academic very quickly. While still attempting to work it out, he saw the sentry's body jerk suddenly, and then collapse. Witness-ing that, along with an assortment of scattered muzzle flashes, he actually whispered, "What the . . . ?"

And then Grunewald Park erupted into a full-fledged firefight.

The three remaining Nigerians began firing wildly, uncontrolla-bly. Johann's friend was perforated from his left shoulder all the way down his torso to the right femur. A fragmentation grenade couldn't have done much worse had he thrown himself on top of it. It made for a gruesome sight. One paramedic would later vomit when he turned him over and noticed that the body was beginning to come apart at the waist. Fortunately, he was the only casualty the panicked drug lords managed to inflict, even though they were lay-ing down a withering fire with their Uzis.

After a few moments, the Nigerians collected themselves and began firing their weapons in controlled bursts in the general direc-tion of the muzzle flashes they had seen, but without success. After quickly eliminating their primary and secondary targets, the com-mandos had rolled and moved. The Nigerians didn't know it, but their bullets were striking thin air.

The traffickers rapidly expended their 30-round magazines and were forced to reload. The lull, which the commandos knew must come, presented the Americans with the opportunity they were waiting for. Kramer and another member of Team Interceptor, each now well concealed and well protected behind a different tree, decided to do the drug barons a favor and offer them a target. Both began firing alternately into the thicket where the Africans had sought refuge. Neither was really attempting to hit anything; they were merely acting as decoys while Rossetti and the other two commandos circled for position. A classic ruse. As expected, the Nigerians fell for it and returned fire, the muzzle flashes of their Uzis blazing a trail right back to their doorstep. "Like taking candy from a baby," was how Kramer would later characterize it.

Suddenly one of the Nigerians broke cover and began racing toward Calumet. Calumet, believing his position had not yet been compromised, nevertheless felt he had no choice. As far as he was concerned, the charging figure, whoever he was, would quickly discover Calumet's presence, and since he was toting a machine gun—and obviously very willing to use it—he had to be taken out. Calumet drew a bead on him. He was waiting for the figure to get closer before he pulled the trigger, but he never got the chance. Suddenly the Nigerian went crashing down as two loud reports detonated simultaneously from his own rear flank. *Move!*

Calumet rolled into a 180-degree pivot and brought his Beretta to bear. Not ten feet away, frozen in a combat crouch, was a man dressed in a black windbreaker and ski mask. Had the man's weapon been pointing at him Calumet would have fired, but the weapon was pointing past him, into the trees.

"Take a hike, ace!" the man shouted. *"Now!"*

"Stuff it!" Calumet retorted. "Who are—"

A lethal burst screamed out of the trees and raked the ground between them. Both men immediately rolled and fired two shots in the direction of the burst, then rolled again. There were a few fleeting seconds of eerie calm. Then the thicket sheltering the remaining two Nigerians lit up in a fierce exchange of automatic and semiautomatic weapons fire. Though they were unable to see exactly what was happening, it was nevertheless possible for Calumet and Rossetti to discern the situation by the sound of the discharges. An Uzi and a Sigsauer produce a different noise and a different rhythm, so both men—about twenty feet apart—just lay there, watching, waiting, listening. In this case, the exchange was very brief, and then, rather abruptly, it was all over. The last four shots they heard had come from the Sigsauers. A triturated haze hovered just above the ground. Then Grunewald Park fell silent.

There is a certain release—a spiritual release, some would say—that human beings undergo after surviving a life-threatening experience. Such was the case with Calumet and the members of Team Interceptor. For the moment, nobody moved. They were all caught up in the exhilaration of simply being alive. As for Johann, he was still eating dirt, afraid to raise his head.

Presently, a low whistle pierced the silence, followed quickly by three others. Rossetti completed the circuit with his own shrill whistle, indicating that Team Interceptor was fully accounted for. Then the inevitable clamor of police sirens began to filter into the park.

Turning toward Calumet, Rossetti repeated, "I told you to clear out, slick!" But his eyes must have been playing tricks on him in the moonlight. He removed his mask for a clearer view and shook his head, as if attempting to shake off the puzzled expression painted on his face, but to no avail.

Calumet was gone.

*

Steve had witnessed the entire affair. He had even managed to bang off a few pictures. The last several frames he snapped were of Calumet's back as the Teflon double sprinted into the night. Although the pictures would be a bit hazy due to the darkness and the infrared film, the bomber jacket stood out nicely. Things couldn't have gone one whit better, Steve thought.

He jumped in the van, flashed his lights, and stomped on the accelerator. The vehicle careened around a curve and blazed a hundred yards down the road before he hit the brakes, causing the van to skid until it grudgingly came to a halt on the shoulder of Pückler Strasse. Team Interceptor dove through the sliding door and the van peeled away. They beat the Berlin Polizei by about thirty seconds.

"Did you get it?" Steve asked after they were into the city and well clear of Grunewald Park.

"Pull over," Rossetti ordered.

"What?"

"Pull over!"

Steve glanced sideways at Rossetti, but did as the commando requested. He slowed and the van finally came to a stop. Rossetti opened his door. As he was climbing down, he said to Steve, "Outside."

Steve complied and they both walked several yards up the street. "What is it?" Steve asked.

It was all Rossetti could do to keep himself from decking the DO. "Eleven scumbag drug traffickers staging a rip-off," he intoned. His voice was low and even, but the undercurrents were raging. *"Our* rip-off. Clean and simple, supposedly. Well, it wasn't clean and simple. There were eleven players with Uzis. Eleven players that I didn't know anything about. I don't know what your orders were, but I'm getting ready to tell you something, pal." Rossetti moved nose to nose. "Don't you *ever* send me and my team into another situation like that without coming clean on the details up front. *Capisce?"*

Not backing down, but nevertheless pleasantly, Steve said, "I didn't know about the hijackers. If I had, I would have told you. Period."

Their eyes were locked and they remained that way for a moment. Finally Rossetti became satisfied—the DO was telling him the truth. "Well, next time, do your homework better," the commando said. He backed off a pace.

"Look," Steve explained, "the buyer was a CI. A cooperating individual the DEA turned a while back. *He* was the one who was supposed to show up—not the other crowd. No doubt the hijackers either offed him and ripped off his bankroll, or they provided him with their own product. Whatever the case, they were here to take out the competition, plain and simple. No way to foresee something like that without having an asset inside. Judging by the color of their skin, I'd say they were probably Nigerians. And if they *were* Nigerians, that lot is primarily reared from tribal clans and the gang members culled from brothers, cousins, nephews, nieces, et cetera. In case you're not aware, you don't infiltrate tribal gangs, you're born into them. So that's that." Steve shifted his weight and, to let Rossetti know that he wasn't intimidated, stepped a bit closer. "Now," he continued, "did you get it?"

"Yeah," Rossetti sighed. "We got it."

Steve nodded and they climbed back into the van. Kramer was inspecting Johann's confiscated brick as the vehicle puttered away. He hefted it up and down in his hand, an expression of consternation on his face, as though he was attempting to determine whether a kilo was really equivalent to 2.2 pounds. Or something like that.

Steve glanced at him in the rearview mirror and smiled. Although not fully briefed on all the particulars, he knew—in the grand scheme of things—that Lewis Armbrister had just employed another gambit.

Now it was Nishka's turn.

*

If I had any brains, I'd pull out right now, Calumet thought to himself as he stripped off his clothes and rotated the shower's faucet. Right this minute. Catch the first plane back to Atlanta and find another profession. Maybe even become an accountant or something.

He set the Beretta on the vanity, within arm's reach, and stepped beneath the rushing water. At 3:00 in the morning he certainly wasn't expecting the maids or room service or anybody else to come knocking, but he jammed a chair under the doorknob of the door to his room just in case. After all, it was certain that the Kempinski's maids and staff weren't the *only* people who had access to the hotel's elegant accommodations. Any service worth its salt would have in their possession a master key to most any well-known hotel in the city, and some not so well known. You never knew when a guest's room might need tossing.

Calumet had been forced to jog two miles out of Grunewald Park before locating a taxi. It took him another hour to ensure that he wasn't being pursued, then he hit a crowded bar off the Ku'damm and treated himself to a couple of *Weissbiers* before retiring to the Kempinski. Whatever his sixth sense had detected when he left the hotel earlier in the evening had been absent upon his return. Apparently, however, his sixth sense wasn't infallible, because the same pair of eyes, quite by accident, had caught a glimpse of him as he was entering the late-hour drinking establishment. The unknown watcher followed him in and took a small table across the murky interior of the Ratskeller. The figure just sat there quietly, nursing a Stoli, and observed Calumet discreetly the whole time he was inside.

There were only two possibilities, Jack reflected as he toweled off and lay on the bed. Either Armbrister and Robert set me up, or the location for the meet had unfortunately been compromised simply by bad luck. And the DO I was supposed to rendezvous with spotted the trouble and aborted. But who was the guy in the ski mask? And who were the others? Whoever they were, they were definitely American. The masked man's lingo came straight off an angry Brooklyn street. DEA? No, not in ski masks. Hmm. Must have been some kind of setup then. But why? He fell asleep thinking about it, the Beretta firmly attached to his right hand.

The phone blew him awake at 7:30. He almost shot it. On purpose. American phones were bad enough, he figured, but European phones assaulted you. Before it could attack him again, he decided to spare the inanimate intruder and picked up the receiver.

"*Ja,*" Jack said, choosing for the moment to be German.

"Alexanderplatz. *Zwei Uhr,*" the familiar voice said, then hung up.

Jack replaced the receiver and glanced at his watch. So Filatov wanted him to show up at Alexanderplatz at 2:00. No problem, he thought, and wondered suspiciously why the numbskull couldn't have waited a couple of hours to make the call instead of rousing him at such an indecent hour. He went back to sleep concluding *everything* was a conspiracy these days.

Calumet trod downstairs at 11:30 and sauntered into the Kempinski's attractive restaurant on the corner of Kurfürstendamm Strasse. He took a seat and ordered a light meal along with *"ein Cola mit voll Glas Eis."* Specifying a glass full of ice seemed to be a perpetual ritual for Americans in Europe, and in the event anyone had been trying to guess his nationality as he walked in, the statement removed all doubt. Not that it mattered. The only person who was interested in him was one of Robert's DOs, and he was not able to acquire a table anywhere close to Calumet due to the lunch crowd, so he milled about outside pretending to window-shop. After about ten minutes, Calumet made him. *I hope that joker doesn't try to make contact with me now that he's managed to stand out like a sore thumb,* he thought. The DO apparently read Jack's mind and left.

After paying his lunch tab, Calumet walked back into the Kempi and made like he was going to his room, but before reaching the elevators he turned abruptly and mimicked a person who had suddenly forgotten something. Ah, yes. Seeming to remember, he walked briskly down the length of the hotel's lobby and out a side exit. Then he ran like mad for the *U-bahn.*

Perhaps it happened to Calumet a little quicker than happened to others. Perhaps the unusually rapid transformation could be attributed to Calumet's razor intelligence and his uncanny perspicacity. Or, in light of the stress he had been under in recent months, maybe it was due—in part, anyway—to his indelible penchant for self-preservation, for taking the short straw and beating all the odds, but whatever it was that brought it on, it was compelling and inviolable. The undercover syndrome was moving in on his soul.

Not that he lost his identity exactly, or his patriotism. He was too grounded for that. Such issues were fundamental down to his depths, and elemental within him, and precepts such as those would never be up for grabs where he was concerned. But the sheer necessity—no, the sheer *lifeblood*—of an undercover operative dictated that you didn't climb out onto somebody else's limb, especially when *they* were holding the saw. Right now, Jack felt he was on Armbrister's limb, and Armbrister—or Robert—held the saw.

It wasn't that Calumet was distrustful of Robert or the DDO; basically, he trusted them both. It's just that he trusted himself *more.* Why Armbrister had baited him with the BND was anybody's guess, but baited him he had. Of that, Jack was certain. And Robert was in on it. Sure, their intentions no doubt had been honorable, but that didn't find any purchase in Calumet. He knew he had to walk this wire on his own, without a net, fight this little piece of the Cold War in a foreign land by himself, and good intentions, to his way of thinking, weren't going to save him if things got nasty. Plus, if the truth be told, Calumet thought he had been treated just a tad unfairly. There was no reason he could think of why he shouldn't have been told what "actions" had been taken by Armbrister or Robert or whoever else was meddling in his affairs. No good reason whatsoever. *Well, two can play at that game,* he concluded. As a result, he took the decision to attend the meet at Alexanderplatz without cover. To that end, he was now in the process of clearing his path—not to evade the Russians or the BND, but the Americans. *Maybe the schmucks will think twice about playing me into a stacked deck like the BND without filling me in on the details next time,* his sly mind whispered.

As far as Armbrister was concerned, Calumet's was a fateful decision. Had Armbrister and the analysts at Langley known that these thoughts were coursing through their agent's imagination like pistons in a race car, they would have pulled him out and shut him down. By the time they got news of it and began to realize what was happening, however, it would be too late.

CHAPTER 8

"He just boarded the *U-bahn*. Appears to be heading toward location Sierra," the metallic voice rattled over Steve's hand-held radio. The van was parked near the Brandenburg Gate, Steve in the driver's seat, Rossetti next to him on the passenger side, and Robert in the back. Sierra was their designated code name for the Berlin Zoo, just in case any eavesdroppers were homing in on their frequency.

Steve depressed the send button twice in succession but didn't utter a word. The almost imperceptible squelch would be enough to acknowledge receipt of the transmission. Calumet, their quarry, had been tailed to Friedrichstrasse. He was ostensibly tracking backward, in the direction he had come from, toward the Ku'-damm.

Jack stood near the door of his train compartment, waiting, watching, listening. If he was right, two surveillants had climbed aboard. One was farther up in the next cabin, standing by a window, the other sitting in a seat just a few feet away pretending to read a magazine. They didn't know it, but Calumet was about to ruin their day. As he heard the familiar hiss and saw the doors of the train's car sliding together, Calumet launched his body without warning through the shrinking aperture, barely in time. Any hint of finesse was now gone. He was running, and he knew they knew it. He began walking briskly toward the stairs that would take him up to Friedrichstrasse.

"Belay that!" Steve's radio crackled again. "He just jumped ship, right before the train departed. He's running up to the street. I'm in pursuit."

"I've got him," another voice said as Calumet surfaced onto

Friedrichstrasse. Obviously, Robert's team had the contingencies covered, but, suddenly the other voice became concerned. "Wait a minute!"

Calumet hit the sidewalk, took two steps, noticed a vacant cab across the way, then abruptly wheeled around and began skipping back down the stairs. A man in an alpaca jacket with a camera case around his neck and, barely noticeable, a hearing aid with a wire attached to it, was climbing past him in the opposite direction. The fact that Calumet had caught him in the act of suddenly averting his gaze confirmed it. Gotcha!

"Uh-oh!" The first voice spoke into the camera case. "He just came back down. Brushed right past me. I think he made me."

"I'm on him," the other voice crackled, taking the stairs downward in pursuit. "Hold on!" he added a moment later. "He's turned around *again* and is now heading back topside. He made me, too. I'm sure of it!"

Calumet dashed across the street as he surfaced and nearly gave the cabbie, who had been reading a copy of *Die Zeitung,* a heart attack when he jerked open the door and barged into the passenger seat. *"Gerade aus!"* Jack blurted, and simultaneously flashed a 100-Mark note. *"Mach schnell!"*

The cabbie, his calculator-brain computing furiously, took one look at the 100-Mark note, one look at Calumet—"just to be sure he wasn't *verrückt,"* he would later brag to his friends when he regaled them with his tale of the afternoon's adventure—dropped his copy of *Die Zeitung,* and then planted the accelerator in the floorboard, as if he were now an extension of Calumet's will.

"Target just dove into a cab," the first voice announced.

At that point, a nondescript car pulled away from the curb and took off discreetly after the taxi. "We've got him," a voice from the car said calmly. "Zulu Two-two, he's heading toward you. Pick him up when he reaches your corner. We'll go around and try to leapfrog him." The taxi never reached Zulu Two-two's corner. They had traveled 300 yards when the cab screeched to a halt suddenly and Calumet flew out of the door. *"Hold on!"* the voice from the tail car proclaimed. "He's back on foot and sprinting into the crowds. He knows who we are, yet he's trying to burn us. I'm going after him!"

He knows who we are, yet he's trying to burn us! The words pounded in

Robert's temples. What was Calumet up to? What was his game? Why hadn't he left word of the meeting place as he was supposed to have done? A simple note in his shaving kit to be collected by one of Robert's men as soon as Calumet had departed the Kempi. The DO had returned empty-handed. There had been no note. Had Calumet forgotten? Not like him at all.

The truth was, Jack's *instincts* were dictating the game at this point. It wasn't that he was vengeful or egocentric, although his ego certainly came into play. No, Calumet had a feeling about this meet. He had a feeling that *this* meet, extraordinarily important, to be sure, was nevertheless safe. There would be little danger. But he also felt that the Russians would make sure the entire area around Alexanderplatz was blanketed, especially since the location was in old East Berlin. Any of Robert's team, no matter how inconspicuous they strove to remain, would somehow be blown. If he could *beat* them, he rationalized, the Russians could *detect* them; it was that simple. He suspected the Russians would be dusting the mothballs off ancient assets for this rendezvous—men and women who had been dormant for years. A banal old man sitting by the water fountain. A young lady pushing a pram. A longhair just standing there and looking like an idiot. Anybody and everybody.

"Not this time, Robert, old friend," Jack uttered to himself as he lay flat on the backseat of yet another cab, pretending to be slightly ill. "I have to go this one alone."

"I think I've lost him," Steve's radio declared.

Robert plucked the radio out of the DO's hand. "Has anybody got him?" he inquired. No answer.

Steve shot a discerning look at Rossetti, but Rossetti seemed to be in his own world, ensnared for the moment by a saturnine inspection of his fingernails. A thousand miles away. In reality, it was the commando's style of keeping his distance, of not being too familiar. Though not privy to all the details, he knew what was going on; could see it as plain as day. The operation in the park the night before confirmed it.

They were whipping the racehorse, validating his legend. From an academic standpoint, that was fine. It made sense to a professor. When you read about it in a case history it worked, but as an agent actually *experiencing* it, feeling that the world was closing in on you and squeezing you like a vise, feeling like you were trapped inside a looking glass with the hounds at the gate scratching to get in, certain that every stranger's glance was a harpoon, every slamming door the harbinger of inevitable imprisonment as the hordes came to collect you, when you were under so deep that the world became a kaleidoscope, its days a blur, you felt betrayed and alone and all of these other things and more, when you were an agent, like you were locked into a limbo, and it was all too real. In a similar way, Rossetti had been there himself.

When he and his team had implemented a night HALO behind Iraqi lines to run reconnaissance, they had essentially encroached upon the scorpion's nest as a swarm upon the horizon, swooping in apocalyptically, deathly, but without the benefit of tactical support due to the secrecy of their mission. When they ran into a SCUD sight and took it out, and then, in the aftermath, had been chased and hunted relentlessly for five days by reinforced elements of the vaunted Republican Guard, they'd survived virtually as a result of their own cunning and bravery, like leopards forced off the kill, fighting, moving, hiding, but without TacAir and without a reaction force waiting in the wings. They knew what to expect going in, but that didn't diminish their apprehension. They had deployed under the umbrella of the most powerful military armada ever assembled in one location, and yet the very nature of their mandate precluded them from its aegis. And now he was *here,* in another foreign country, witnessing the same sort of scenario but on a different battlefield and with a different set of players.

In an inchoate sort of way, he could identify. He had noted with interest Calumet's skillful handling of Filatov at Eiserner Steg in Frankfurt. He had witnessed the agent's coolness under fire at Grunewald Park. He had been impressed—a veritable exception where Rossetti was concerned—by Calumet's ability to seemingly just vanish from the point of action in the park the night before. He had recorded all of these things, and they were emblazoned upon his mind. In essence, the commando was being drawn by an elusive symbiosis as he watched another type of soldier run the solitary gauntlet, deftly balancing the reciprocity between the home office and the internecine lair of captains who wanted to bleed the world, and like it or not, Rossetti was beginning to admire Jack Calumet.

For him, that was rare, because Rick Rossetti was a man who leased his admiration like a banker, and he let you know up front that he reserved the right to take it back anytime he damn well pleased. To that end, he offered an unusual compliment: "You won't pick him up again until he wants to be found," the commando stated bluntly to no one in particular.

"No, we won't," Robert agreed. He spoke into the radio, "Let him go. Come on in."

"I guess you'll be reporting this as an unauthorized contact?" Steve timidly concluded, looking back at Robert.

In one of his rare moments of visible emotion, Robert glared at the DO and seethed, "You let *me* worry about the reporting. Understood?" It wasn't really a question, but Steve nodded and turned back to face the windshield.

Unauthorized contact.

The phrase was akin to leprosy. American agents who initiated contact with the enemy without authorization from their controllers, or handlers, were in violation of their contracts, if they had one. If they didn't have a contract, they were usually in violation of honesty and good judgment at best, treason at worst. Calumet was pushing the envelope. The note he was supposed to have left in his shaving kit would have sufficed, but he didn't leave a note. Not in his shaving kit, not in any of his other luggage, not anywhere within his entire bloody room. And, to add insult to injury, he had just broken away from his own surveillance team. On purpose.

An hour later Robert was on a secure line to Armbrister. Armbrister was infuriated with Calumet. Robert wiggled a hard sell. "Only a rogue like Excalibur can pull it off, you said," he reminded the DDO. "You have to expect aberrations with him."

"I expect you to *control* him," Armbrister answered.

"The kind of control you want—it doesn't exist with Excalibur. You want that kind of control, either get another agent or get another controller," Robert challenged.

There was silence on the line for a moment. Finally Armbrister said, "What's his scheme, Robert? What's he up to?"

Robert consigned his own rationalizations to the DDO, highlighting the soft points and glossing over the more perilous articles of contention. At one juncture in the conversation Armbrister remarked that it might be wise to pull Calumet out and bring him in. It would delay the operation, but eventually they could run it from another angle with another operative. That could take a year or two or three to set up, Robert told him. Can we afford it? Not really, Armbrister conceded, but *no* deal is better than a bad deal. After about twenty minutes Robert had fired all his rounds. Take it or leave it, was basically how he closed the sale. Armbrister didn't buy it exactly, but he accepted it.

This time.

*

Calumet stood casually against the building and inspected his surroundings. Satisfied, he crossed Spandauer Strasse and began to stroll toward Marienkirche on the lower end of Alexanderplatz. Past the church he could see the massive TV tower which seemed, in the days of old East Berlin, to rise like a gargoyle from the land and wield an oppressive, barren scepter over the showcase of communism in Europe. As far as he could tell, the appearance of this section of the city hadn't changed much. No matter how many times he came here, the old feelings of slinking and operating in the DDR stayed with him. To him, this part of the city was always drab and cold.

Jack walked slowly along the square in front of Marienkirche. Presently a young couple strolled up. The woman spoke. "Comrade Filatov will meet you in the old building off Waisenstrasse." She smiled for everyone to see; then the two of them moved on.

Calumet was familiar with the location. He had met Shevchenko there on numerous occasions in the past. Shevchenko. He still couldn't get over it. Shevchenko had been turned, and Jack had never had the slightest inclination. He never suspected. And now the Russian was dead.

Jack took twenty minutes to arrive at the dilapidated old building, knowing that the Russians had a countersurveillance team in place, observing him and anybody else who might be following along. The building still bore the scars of World War II, as did many of the edifices in Eastern Germany. The Communists never got around to aesthetics it seemed, at least not in the territories. The building would have been condemned had it stood in any large city within the United States, but here in Berlin it was just another problem that nobody had thus far seen fit to tackle. It was surrounded by a small courtyard scattered with rubble.

Calumet made his way into the courtyard quietly and cautiously, staying next to the walls. There was no sign of life. He assumed the countersurveillance would remain outside. He moved four or five steps, paused, observed, listened, even sniffed, then moved again. He tried to peer through a boarded-up dormer, but the shadows of the interior were impenetrable. "Figures," he whispered. He knew he was still being watched. He could feel it. The blackened windows of the surrounding buildings, most of them also in disrepair, could contain armies. The atmosphere suddenly became very eerie and he realized that at this pace it would take him another five minutes to get inside . . . unless he talked himself out of the whole affair, that is. Sometimes *too* much caution could make a man lose his nerve and run.

"Screw it," he decided, shedding his paranoia and appreciating the fact that he would already be dead by now if that was their pleasure. Leaping nimbly away from the wall, he walked down the alley and through the door, his feet crunching the gravel loudly as he went.

Filatov and another man dressed in an obviously expensive suit stepped out of the shadows and moved into a shaft of sunlight poking through a set of windows on the far wall. Filatov greeted him coolly. "Hello, Jack."

"Georgi." Jack nodded. He moved into their space, his hands in the pockets of his bomber jacket, his right one clenched around the Beretta. He noticed, or rather sensed, the presence of three other men in the building. One moved into the doorway, guarding the entrance—or blocking his exit, he wasn't sure which.

"Jack," Filatov said, "allow me to introduce Comrade Vartan-yan."

Neither Vartanyan nor Calumet offered his hand. Vartanyan said, *"Andrei* Vartanyan," and followed it casually with the slightest nod. His eyes, obsidian in color and flecked with gray, retained a singular intensity. They bore into Calumet with such aggression that he felt he was under attack.

Upon seeing the man, and then hearing him speak, Calumet instantly commanded all of his senses to full attention. Vartanyan was in a different league altogether. Filatov was a cakewalk, but this one was a searing bed of coals. Jack met his gaze. "I suppose you're KGB, too?" he said with the merest curiosity.

"GRU," Vartanyan corrected. "Colonel."

He's coming straight at me, Jack decided. No bluff, no fuss; head-on, like a steamroller.

And then Vartanyan asked, "Are you CIA?"

"I'm pure magic," Calumet volleyed and lobbed a devious grin over the net.

This response elicited no reaction whatsoever from Vartanyan. Keeping his eyes on Calumet, measuring him, Vartanyan spoke to Filatov, "Thank you, Major-General. That will be all."

Filatov hesitated slightly, as if he wanted to say something to Calumet, like "nice working with you" or some such balderdash, but thought better of it and walked out of the building. Calumet was fascinated with the brief exchange. There could be no doubt that Vartanyan, although outranked by Filatov, was absolutely in charge. A tall man, six-foot-three, lean and spare with thick, dark hair, sharp features and strikingly handsome, his demeanor was austere, forbidding. Roughly forty years old and powerfully built, Jack observed. Not the kind of man you would want to face off with if you could avoid it.

The fact that Vartanyan referred to Filatov as a major-general was interesting. A probe, Calumet judged. He apparently wanted to see how Calumet would react to it since Filatov had been passing himself off as a colonel in the KGB.

Jack chose to satisfy the Russian's curiosity. "Major-General?" he questioned.

"Jack," Vartanyan said, and suddenly he appeared to soften; the change in personality was astonishing. Suddenly he seemed to exude a vigorous, magnetic charisma. "I'm afraid our friend has been playing games with you," the Russian disclosed. "Georgi Filatov is GRU, not KGB. Some people—on *both* sides—" he paused for effect, studying Calumet and implying something ominous—"feel it's necessary," he then continued, "to employ these useless deceptions. Why? It's beyond me, but there you are." Vartanyan consummated his explanation with a smile, revealing perfect teeth.

Let's just test the waters, Calumet thought. "And what about Shevchenko? Same deception?"

Nothing in the eyes. Vartanyan offered no perceptible reaction to the mention of Shevchenko's name. "Yes," he smiled again, a disarming smile, "I'm afraid so."

Calumet turned up the heat. "Tell Aleksandr I said hello next time you see him."

"Haven't you heard?" Vartanyan, his eyes fixed on Calumet, reached slowly into his jacket and extracted a silver cigarette case. He snapped it open and held it out for Jack's perusal. "Cigarette?"

"No, thanks," Jack said. "Heard what?"

The Russian selected a cigarette for himself and lit it nonchalantly with the case's built-in lighter. "Aleksandr Shevchenko has been executed," he stated matter-of-factly. He formed his lips into a funnel and exhaled sideways, as though he had just commented on the weather.

As far as Calumet was concerned, the operation just went ballistic. The admission meant that the Russians were either telling him they already knew he was a double, or they were setting him up to become one. Either way, they had to know *something* since Shevchenko had been turned and later exposed, but the fact that they were admitting to the execution was crucial. Whatever the rationale, it seemed they were on the verge of positioning him in order to go for the jugular, and he now had no illusions as to their assessment of his capacity as an agent.

What worried Calumet, however, is how much they *did* know. Did they know that he was a double at all? If they did, they might not know that he was a *loyal* double, but they would still be under the assumption, if they thought he was a *legitimate* double, that he had had contact in some measure with the CIA. If so, to what extent? He couldn't corner that one exactly, but he was sure the Aquarium was convinced he was more than just a man with secrets to sell, especially since they were willing to disclose what had happened to Shevchenko. Or could they possibly think that he was simply an information broker and nothing more? Which way to go? Instincts. Calumet was forced to reach down and try to locate them because they appeared to have abandoned him at this moment, leaving the conundrum intact. Unsuccessful in his search, he quickly decided to play it smart and assume they already knew he was a double. That way, he would have an out. They wouldn't be able to trip him up if they were somehow able to produce surveillance photographs depicting him smack in the middle of a sub-rosa prayer meeting with two or three notables from Langley. And they probably *could* produce such photographs, the bozos. Thus, if he was right in his analysis, they already knew that he was *some* kind of double; they just weren't sure whose. Not yet. *He won't be fooled for long,* Robert had said, referring to Nishka. *Penetration is his specialty.*

"What?" Calumet pretended shock. "Shevchenko executed? By whom? And what for?"

Vartanyan held his cigarette the American way. He took a drag, biding his time while he evaluated Calumet. Finally he answered. "By us," he stated simply. No justification, no explanation. He wanted Calumet to work for it.

Calumet wasn't playing. He waited the Russian out in silence.

A thin smile took shape on Vartanyan's mouth as he contemplated the American. Calumet had just told him something—he had just told him he was no fool. Vartanyan was fully aware that Jack had asked *two* questions, not one. Vartanyan chose to answer only one, however, in order to record the American's reaction. But Calumet offered no reaction. He was still waiting for the answer to his second question, and he wasn't going to be baited into asking it a second time. No, Vartanyan deliberated, this American is no fool; this American is a player, and that's exactly what we're after. Good.

"Shevchenko made a very serious error," the Russian finally explained. "He began selling his wares to the CIA several years ago."

The disclosure was another bombshell. In Vartanyan's view, if Jack was really working for the Americans, then Shevchenko's treason would not concern him in the least. As a matter of fact, he would already know about it. On the other hand, if he was really what he portrayed himself as—a mercenary double—then the statement should scare the living daylights out of him. It would mean that more than likely the CIA was aware of his activities and that he was therefore on the verge of being compromised and probably arrested.

Your play, comrade, Vartanyan thought.

In his younger days, when he chased women, Calumet had developed the ability to make his countenance fall, as though he was bitterly disappointed. He usually performed this feat in order to persuade a woman to take pity on him, especially if the evening wasn't working out the way he had planned. The strategy wasn't infallible because the woman didn't always see fit to take pity on him, but she always felt sorry for him. He employed this same tactic now. "Oh, no!" he proclaimed. "If that's true, then they know about *me*."

Vartanyan had been dispatched by Nishka directly, and he was observing Calumet very closely, attempting to read every layer of the man's thoughts and translate his body language. If he's lying, the Russian speculated, he's very, very good. The Russian didn't know the half of it.

"You're going to have to assist me with this," Calumet stated further, looking worried.

"Then let's be honest with each other, my friend," Vartanyan returned. "Have *you* ever sold information to the CIA before? Like a few of our shopping lists, for instance?"

"What in the world are you talking about?" Calumet did not want to appear to be too clever. He knew that he was eventually going to have to come clean on the question, but if he made the Russian work for it, it might—it just might—force Vartanyan to think that Calumet wasn't quite flush on his intelligence logic.

But Vartanyan wasn't playing, either. He dropped his cigarette, crushed it with the heel of his shoe, and then folded his arms. His eyes were like lacquered marble.

"Look," Jack spoke after a moment, "the CIA approached me a year or so ago. Somehow they knew I was meeting with Russian intelligence. They even said they had photographs."

"A year ago?" Vartanyan quipped sarcastically.

Good, Jack thought. He thinks I'm trying to wiggle out of it. "Well, it might have been two years, or something like that. I'm not good with dates."

"Please continue," the Russian remarked, evidently skeptical.

"Initially, I denied everything. I told them I could meet with whomever I wanted to and it was none of their damned business. That was true, they said, but treason was a different matter, and they began to lean on me. They accused me of selling secrets to the Russians. I told them they were crazy. If they had any proof, I told them, then produce it. Show me the photographs, I demanded. Well, they didn't have any photographs. They didn't have any proof. As a result, I knew I was safe for the time being, but I also knew that I was on thin ice and that I was going to have to work something out in the future. That's basically all there was to my first contact with them. They left a number for me to call if I thought of anything else."

"And so you thought of something else?" Vartanyan seemed amused. If Calumet was legitimate, he thought, Langley unquestionably had the proof. And the photographs. Jack Calumet was merely a puppet on a string who knew nothing about the magnitude of the operation in which he was involved. After the defection, the CIA couldn't afford to arrest him. Not if they wanted to feed Moscow their reams of disinformation. After all, Langley's newfound agent, Aleksandr Shevchenko, had to have a source. Otherwise their operation wouldn't stand up and work for them. It *wouldn't* make sense to Calumet, Vartanyan conjectured—not if he was telling the truth—but it makes sense to us. Langley learned about Calumet after Shevchenko turned, and they had been running him as an unconscious agent ever since, playing him back.

"Yes, several things. For one, I refused to meet with Shevchenko for several months after that."

That much was true, Vartanyan conceded. There had been a dry spell for a time where Calumet and Shevchenko were concerned. So Calumet was running scared? Let's see where he's taking this, the Russian said to himself.

"However," Jack continued, "I knew I had to mollify the CIA. I knew they were suspicious that I'd traded with the Russians in the past; they just didn't have any specifics. So I worked a deal with them. I told them that Shevchenko had, in fact, asked me to procure secrets for him, but that so far I had declined to do so. They seemed to buy that. Then I told them I would be happy to deliver Shevchenko's shopping list to them in the future in exchange for immunity and, of course, a fee. That's what they wanted, they said, and they went for it. What they never knew, though, was that I was actually acquiring and then passing along the material requested in those shopping lists. Plus, they were never aware—I thought—of all the times Shevchenko and I met. But now you're telling me that Shevchenko was working for the CIA all along." Jack paused and imitated a controlled panic. He knew he was performing for more than just the integrity of the operation at this point; he was performing for his life. If Vartanyan harbored the slightest suspicion that Calumet was a plant, there was no way Jack would walk away from this meet in one piece.

Vartanyan. Completely unforeseen. The one variable he hadn't counted on was a different Russian handler; he'd counted on Filatov. He could manage Filatov. Filatov was a stroll in the park, but not Vartanyan. Vartanyan knew how to touch the tiger. He now regretted not having backup and berated himself for it. *Real smart, Jack. Brilliant.* "If that's true," he concluded with a pronounced suggestion of alarm, "then Washington knows that I've been passing secrets back to Moscow all along."

Vartanyan wasn't ready to throw any lifelines. He remained stolid, impassive. Let him keep talking, the Russian patiently decided.

"Did Moscow actually receive the intelligence I was forwarding?" Calumet asked, as though he were an ingenue where such matters were concerned.

For all Jack could tell, the Russian did not hear the question. He just stood there, absorbed in contemplation. After what seemed an eternity, he came alive. "We're aware of your efforts," Vartanyan said, sidestepping the inquiry. He removed the cigarette case again.

Calumet's fingers tightened around the Beretta. The cigarette case made him extremely nervous.

"Did the CIA tell you how they got onto you?" Vartanyan asked, already knowing the answer. "I mean, if they were accusing you of selling secrets, then surely they must have attempted to impress you with their circumstantial evidence, even if they really didn't have any." He removed a cigarette and lit it with the case's lighter, then deftly snapped the case shut. The case remained in his hand.

Calumet shifted his weight, stealing a few inches to the side. The case was a distraction, and it worried him. Maybe Vartanyan is doing it on purpose, to retard my concentration. That was one thing he couldn't afford to lose at this point. The Russian was pushing him into dangerous water. If his ad-libs weren't on the money, Jack realized he would soon be wearing his *own* case—about seven feet long.

"They told me nothing at first," Jack said. "Not until I began to trade with them. I challenged them when they first accused me, telling them that if they had any proof to lay it on me. They couldn't, so I knew they were bluffing." Try to tell the same story over and over, Robert had instructed. Just use different wording.

Vartanyan helped him along. "But they knew you were meeting with Shevchenko?"

"Yes, I guess they knew that."

"You guess?" *Tell me how they knew, Mr. Calumet, and I'll tell you whether you'll live or die today.*

"Well, come to think of it"—Calumet prayed he was on the right track—*"I* may be the one who volunteered the identity of Shevchenko." He knew he had rung a bell with that response. The Russian's body language, a subtle forward movement of the head, implied that the words had met with a familiar recognition.

In Vartanyan's mind, it was the only answer that would work. The CIA would never have volunteered Shevchenko—not to a traitor—so the information would have had to have come from Calumet.

"How so?" Vartanyan asked.

"You have to understand, Andrei," Jack's campaign took form swiftly, as though it suddenly sprang from nowhere, and he finally felt he was hitting his stride as he spoke, "I was between a rock and a hard place. When those goons from Langley showed up, I was scared. After all, I *was* selling secrets to Shevchenko. When they accused me of treason, I thought I was through; I thought they had me. At that point, I was waiting for them to roll out the projector and show me how I had just earned a lifetime reservation in a federal pen. They can be pretty persuasive, you know."

"I'm sure they can," Vartanyan sympathized cleverly. "It must have given you quite a start."

"Quite," Calumet said. "Anyway, even though I thought I was jailbait, I decided I was going to admit nothing. You never know what a good lawyer can accomplish, especially if they haven't obtained a confession. So I played hardball with them. I told them they must be getting too much fertilizer in their diet. They leaned on me a little at that point, but the bottom line is, I challenged them to put up or shut up. They couldn't put up, so I walked."

"Did they get physical?" Vartanyan wanted to know.

"A bit," Calumet fabricated. "Nothing serious. A few blows to the body, nothing facial. I decked one of the weasels, though." He figured that would be a nice touch. It was in line with what he had done to Filatov at their first meet.

"Good for you!" Vartanyan congratulated him.

"Damn straight!"

The Russian smiled and gestured for Calumet to continue, but Calumet suddenly seemed to be stuck on the swivel of the moment. His mannerism indicated he was eminently proud of the fact that he had popped a CIA man, as if that was the crux of the entire affair, as if that single, audacious attainment should suffice as the fait accompli of all justification. A barroom, backwater mentality. Vartanyan thought, *he's either the shrewdest operator I've ever laid eyes on, or he's going to be perfect for what we have planned.*

Calumet was in sync. He knew Vartanyan was angling for the logic of his interplay between Shevchenko and the CIA. In fact, that was the Russian's primal question. Calumet chose to forget the question, however, so that the Russian's suspicions would not be aroused by Jack's ability to focus on the intelligence aspect of the conversation. If he forged ahead and simply expounded the matter, thereby attempting to justify his legend, the Russian would pick up on it. Calumet would appear to be too eager. In essence, it could sign his death warrant, and he knew it.

"I believe you said you might inadvertently have been the one who originally identified Shevchenko to the CIA," Vartanyan remarked, attempting to steer the conversation back on course. And then, to Calumet's immense relief, he put the cigarette case back in his pocket.

"Oh, yeah. Well, I had to assume that they were onto me at that point, so I decided the best defense was an offense. I knew that if I kept up my current activities they would catch me sooner or later. Sure, I could have just quit, but the money was too good, and procuring the information Shevchenko wanted was too easy. That's when I called the number they had given me and arranged a deal. I really didn't know what I was getting myself into. They grilled me back and forth for hours—the same things, it seemed, over and over. I don't remember at exactly what point in the interrogation it came up, but when they got around to asking me about my Russian contacts, that's when I told them about Shevchenko. I mean, in my view they already knew about him anyway. Otherwise, how would they have got onto me in the first place?"

"Indeed," Vartanyan commented. "What was their reaction

when you told them about Shevchenko? Did they voice any insights about him? Any tidbits of information they might have
vouchsafed in regard to Aleksandr that you can remember?"

Why did he refer to him as "Aleksandr"? Jack knew he had to be
extremely careful here. Appearing thoughtful, he said, "No, I don't
think so. Of course, they wouldn't have told me anything about
him anyway, especially if he belonged to them. You know that." As
a matter of fact, Jack recalled, they really *didn't* inform me of Shevchenko's status as a double. Sometimes it was difficult even for *him*
to remember when he was telling the truth or lying.

"No, I don't suppose they would have shared their insights on
that matter," Vartanyan said reflectively. "So after your initial
meeting with them—the interrogation, as you refer to it—what was
the procedure? How were you contacted?"

No way! He's pushing too hard. He wants it all. Calumet wasn't
prepared for an in-depth treatise on his relations with Langley. He
was hoping that Armbrister's gambit of protecting his legend after
Shevchenko had been turned would suffice, especially since Filatov
had provided ample proof by confirming the contents of that package some three years earlier. "They didn't contact me," Jack said.
"I contacted them."

"How?"

Calumet determined it would be wise to try to circumvent this
line of questioning. Not only might he be forced to compromise
minor intelligence matters, but there was too much room for error
on the whole. They could know something he didn't know they
knew, and then toss it back at him, ultimately discovering him in a
lie. After all, Armbrister suspected that Nishka had managed to
place a deep-penetration agent inside American intelligence. Who
knew how far his tentacles reached? Besides, Jack calculated, he
had to draw the line somewhere; otherwise they would have him
reciting his entire biography.

"Nothing personal, Andrei, but that's none of your business. I've
always refused to acquaint the CIA with my tradecraft concerning
Moscow, and I'm not going to reveal my tradecraft to you as it
relates to Washington. That's my stock in trade; that's how I earn
my money."

Vartanyan smiled. "I never take these things personally, Jack, and I certainly hope you don't, either, because you are not leaving this building until I have the answers I'm after." He had spoken with no malice, no bitterness in his voice, just smooth and natural, like a Dodge City sheriff.

"Really?" Calumet acted amazed. He knew the Russian was aware of his Beretta. Only a fool wouldn't be, and Vartanyan was no fool. Robert had once told him that in order to take a man's temperature, you sometimes had to pressure him until he boiled. Maybe it was time to take Vartanyan's temperature.

"At least that blockhead Filatov was wearing a vest," Jack told the Russian. "You're not. It might interest you to know that I'll drop you like nobody's business before those pussies over there can stop me." He nodded toward the three GRU officers.

"Maybe you're that good," Vartanyan said casually. There was no fear in his eyes, no anger. "Maybe you're not. Either way, though, you'll still be dead. Those *pussies,* as you called them, are all first-class, veteran Spetsnaz officers. I wouldn't bet against them."

"Like American Express," Calumet smirked. "And you don't ever leave home without them, right?" As far as he could discern, Vartanyan hadn't been affected in the slightest by his verbal jabs. The mercury hadn't budged. This Russian was very cool. When you have your back against the wall, he had heard Robert say, throw everything you have onto the table; risk it all. They might belly up and take you on, but most of them will crumble. "Personally," Jack continued, "I was never such a pantywaist that I needed baby-sitters."

Vartanyan smiled, seemingly bored with the repartee. "Well, we all have our idiosyncrasies, my friend. At any rate, you really *are* in an extremely tenuous position, you know. Are you really *that* anxious to face death, Jack?"

"I figure my odds of walking out of here alive are pretty slim regardless," Calumet said insouciantly.

"Ah! You disappoint me, Jack. Why in the world would you even consider something so puerile?"

"Well, perhaps you've missed the locker-room parleys of late, Andrei, but Filatov and I had a little misunderstanding in Frankfurt a few days ago."

Vartanyan laughed heartily, and even his laugh emitted an infectious, seductive charm. "Filatov!" he exclaimed. "Now *there's* something we can agree on. He is most certainly, as you so aptly put it, a blockhead, and he botched that whole affair."

In spite of himself, Calumet found he was actually beginning to like Vartanyan. The Russian's personality was effervescent. It seemed to influence—possibly even dominate—all within its realm. It was one of life's cruel paradoxes, Jack thought, but here he was in the middle of a showdown with his archenemy, yet he found himself attracted—and cussing himself all the way for it—to the charismatic presence of the man. He sensed a kindred soul.

Jack grinned, deciding to go along with the conspiracy against Filatov. "He botched it because I kept him from kidnapping me. That's what I'm talking about, Andrei."

"The kidnapping was Filatov's own design." Andrei laughed again. "His orders didn't encompass taking you hostage. He was merely there to determine if you had a hand in Shevchenko's defection. Unfortunately, Comrade Georgi foolishly thought he should drug and interrogate you in order to obtain that information."

He just might be telling the truth, Calumet thought. But that still didn't help him in his present situation. "So what's the purpose of *this* meet, then?" Calumet fished.

"Come now, Jack." Vartanyan was smiling. "You still haven't answered my question about how you made contact with the CIA."

So much for *that* tack, Calumet thought. "Andrei, I *did* answer your question; it just wasn't the answer you were looking for."

Vartanyan sighed and pulled out the cigarette case again. He opened it and displayed its contents to Calumet. "Sure you wouldn't care for one?"

"No, thanks. I'd probably pick the poisoned one," Calumet half-joked.

"Probably." Vartanyan laughed. He lit his own and put the case back in his pocket.

Calumet saw that the Russian was on the verge of speaking, and he knew that Vartanyan was not going to let the matter drop. He therefore decided to try to blunt the inquiry by appearing to give in, by scratching only the surface. "Look, Andrei," he began, "they gave me a number to call. At first the number was in Washington. After that, they supplied me with a local number in Atlanta since that's where I live. There's really nothing mysterious about it. I call the number and we set up the meet. Very plain and simple."

Jack was working the outside, hoping to keep the conversation aligned on general terms. Vartanyan, on the other hand, although obviously willing to appease Calumet and allow him to nibble from the perimeter, was eventually going to push and try to take the conversation inside, toward the details. Calumet's goal was to keep the Russian from penetrating too deeply.

"I see," Vartanyan observed wryly. "You would call them from your cozy little home in Atlanta when you had information to disclose—on those rare occasions when Aleksandr happened to be in the United States, I guess—and then you all, very professionally—since there's a communist behind every bush—clear your paths and meet in some dark location to exchange gifts. Is that about how it goes?"

"You could spin that same satire about yourselves, Andrei." Why did he say "Aleksandr" again?

"Yes, well, let's stop waltzing, shall we? What about Europe, Jack?" Vartanyan probed.

Jack suddenly knew he was in trouble. It might have been the resonance in Vartanyan's voice, or it might have been the fact that there was just the slightest narrowing of the Russian's eyes when he floated the inquiry, or it might have been a combination of the two, but suddenly Calumet felt he knew what Vartanyan was truly endeavoring to resolve.

And it chilled him to the bone.

CHAPTER 9

"Other matters require my immediate attention," Robert remarked. He was speaking directly to Rossetti. They were back at the safe house, along with the remainder of Team Interceptor and Steve Phillips. "Steve is in charge in my absence. Understood?"

Rossetti shrugged his shoulders. "Sure. I don't have any problem with that."

Robert smiled. "I didn't think you would. Just wanted to make sure the order of battle was properly defined." He motioned to Steve, who immediately disappeared through the front door, presumably to bring up the van. Robert had spoken to Rossetti in the DO's presence on purpose. He wanted Steve Phillips to know that he had just been vested with the authority to control Team Interceptor. And he wanted Rossetti to know that Steve Phillips knew. Turning back to Rossetti, the spymaster said, "I'm afraid you boys are going to have to remain here in quarantine, so to speak. I don't want you on the streets except for operational matters. Do you have a problem with that?"

Rossetti shook his head. *How many times have I heard this before?* He'd been on a zillion missions or more in his life, and every one, it seemed, had been preceded by some sort of isolation. *We special forces people can be entrusted with covert ops, but we can't be trusted to walk down the street and buy a hamburger beforehand. I get it. We'd probably spill the whole mission to the first person we came across, right? Sure. It makes sense to me.* Nevertheless, he had some opinions of his own.

"I don't like what happened in the park, Robert," the commando stated simply. "I told Steve; now I'm telling you." His tone suggested no threat, no challenge, but he left no room for argument, either. "Next time somebody better have their head screwed on tighter," he added. He shifted his weight nonchalantly, but his eyes were steady. "If my attitude is a problem, feel free to replace me." Though bold, his tender wasn't a bluff. Rick Rossetti never bluffed. No, his offer was fortified with absolute conviction, absolute truth. And the truth was, Rossetti didn't care anymore. It wasn't surprising.

Rick Rossetti's military record read like a *Rambo* screenplay. He had completed the rugged Airborne and Ranger schools early on, graduated first in his class from the Special Forces Qualification course a bit later, and then served with the Green Berets and a host of other elite organizations before ultimately being scooped up under the umbrella of the U.S. Special Operations Command, formulated in 1987, and thereafter assigned directly to Range 19, a.k.a. Delta Force. Delta Force was the capstone of his career, the way he saw it. He'd gone in on the ground in Panama, through the air in the Gulf, by the sea in Grenada, and every which way on several occasions in Beirut—more than he'd like to remember, actually—and in between he had shotgunned a slew of operations that never made the news. But now he was getting tired. Really tired. In short, Major Richard A. Rossetti had had enough. He'd done it all and seen it all. It was time to move on.

Robert refrained from smiling, though with difficulty. He saw similarities between Rossetti and Calumet and wondered what would happen if the two of them ever got together. Calumet was more high-strung and probably smarter, but Rossetti had his own strengths. "Rick Rossetti," his commanding officer once remarked, "has an eye for deflection like nobody's business." And Robert knew what he meant. Rossetti was a tactician extraordinaire. He was literally the one person on earth you wouldn't want to run in to in a dark alley. If Calumet and Rossetti ever had to go up against each other, Robert surmised, he wasn't sure whom he'd bet on. Rossetti was unquestionably more skilled in the arts of war, but Jack Calumet was no slouch, and he had a weird light about him, difficult to describe and somehow mysterious, as if his persona cast forth an impenetrable, unsearchable aura. Calumet, in other words, was the ultimate survivor. The ultimate denizen of the jungle. It would be a tough call.

"I don't like what happened in the park, either," Robert confessed. "It was an honest mistake, Rick. Let's just forget about it and move on, shall we?"

Rossetti had heard that type of answer before. A passing conciliation, a smoothing over. And yet Robert seemed sincere. The spymaster appeared genuine, and Rossetti, in spite of all he'd seen, hadn't seen that one too often, not from the shakers and movers. "It's forgotten," he agreed.

Robert slapped him on the shoulder, as if to say, "That's the team spirit," and Rossetti had seen that one too; but again, with Robert it seemed to go over well. Anybody else might have found themselves on the floor suddenly. Such a gesture, for instance, was something Steve Phillips definitely should not try. Not on Major Richard A. Rossetti. Not now. When Rossetti was younger, maybe, but not now. At thirty-eight years of age, Major Richard A. Rossetti had seen it all.

*

Backpedaling quickly, Calumet said, "I wasn't even thinking about Europe, Andrei. My mind was in the United States." To emphasize his own stupidity, Calumet tapped his forehead with the heel of his left hand, the right pocket of his bomber jacket, along with his Beretta, retaining the other. His finger was prepared to pull the trigger. "What exactly do you want to know about Europe?" he asked, fearing the answer.

"The debriefings," Andrei responded. "Tell me about the debriefings, Jack."

I was afraid of that, Calumet thought. *Is he bluffing? Does he really know about the debriefings, or is he fishing?*

"The CIA insisted on those," Calumet explained, rationalizing that a mixture of truth was better than getting caught in an outright lie. If he lied and got caught, he'd have no fallback; but if he told the truth—or at least the partial truth—he just might be able to turn it around to his advantage.

"Then why did you tell me it wasn't normal for the CIA to contact you?" Vartanyan accused like a schoolteacher. "You stated that you always contacted them. You certainly didn't ring up the embassy or the consulate and beg the CIA to please take time out to come and debrief you, did you?"

"Not exactly," Calumet answered nonchalantly. *When you feel cornered,* he thought, *don't act cornered. Don't be too eager to dig yourself out of the hole. Force the klutz to drag it out of you.*

"Would you care to explain that little oversight, please?" Vartanyan was dripping sarcasm.

"An oversight is all it was, Andrei. I told you, my mind was back in the United States. I didn't even make the connection about Europe."

Again, it was as though the Russian had suddenly been transported into another dimension. He remained absolutely quiescent, as though his body had been abruptly metamorphosed into a waxen figurine, his cold, lifeless eyes riveted on Calumet. Finally: "Yes, well, we all have mental lapses from time to time." Vartanyan spoke softly, his voice amazingly empathetic, his countenance suddenly reflecting a warm, almost amicable smile.

Jack thought, *this guy is a freaking chameleon. One moment he's a panther ready to pounce, the next he's a gentleman from Fleet Street.*

And then, just as quickly, the chameleon changed back into a panther, the smiling face turned to stone, the eyes intense, as though they were attempting to shoot an X ray. "Now, tell me about the debriefings, Jack."

"I told you. The CIA insisted on them." *If you want me to get specific, you get specific with me first,* Calumet projected.

Vartanyan initially seemed to resent that answer, then his facial expression changed into one of contemplation. The cigarette case emerged yet again and he went through all the gyrations necessary to get one of those lit before returning the silver container to his jacket. Having thus disposed of his epicurean needs, he then wrestled the conversation into a detour. "May I share a little thesis with you, Jack?" he asked in a rhetorical tone. "A little thesis about how it all worked? Between you and Shevchenko and the CIA, that is?"

"Certainly," Jack replied pleasantly, wondering why Vartanyan was opening the door a crack. It would have been much more difficult if the Russian had simply forced Calumet to speak a cappella, without the accompaniment of any material from Vartanyan. Vartanyan was going to give him something to rebuff, something to work from, a basis from which to spin his own tales. Vartanyan was too sharp, too much of an operator to commit a faux pas of such an elementary nature, yet he was about to do just that. What was his angle?

"Very well," the Russian said sententiously, his sarcasm dissipated. "At first it was all rather simple. Six years ago Aleksandr Shevchenko recruits you, taking over for the blockhead Filatov, and the two of you have a heart-to-heart in Vienna. It goes well. You convince Shevchenko that you can readily produce the type of information he is seeking. American defense material, specifically tactical material—you're not too swift on the strategic stuff, not at first, anyway, and the NATO goodies as well, not yet—and the two of you set up your schedules. When to meet, where to meet, how to meet, emergency contingencies, all of that. You'll have to forgive me if I leave out some minor detail here and there; it's been a while since I've listened to the tapes."

Calumet knew at the time that every word spoken between him and Shevchenko six years earlier had been recorded. An inane thought breezed through his mind just then, wondering if he should ask the Russian if he might obtain a copy of those tapes so he could keep his story straight, but he dismissed it quickly and focused on the Russian's words.

"So," Vartanyan continued, "Aleksandr gives you a small shopping list and some money—the money as per your own insistence, because you refuse to work without money up front and you refuse to sign receipts, a practice which we always require but make a very unusual exception for in your case—you leave Vienna, and then in a few short weeks you're back with the information. And very good information at that, I must say. It checked out, in case you didn't know."

Calumet wasn't sure whether the statement was an accusation or a compliment, but he decided to confront it either way. "Of course it checked out, Andrei. Who did you guys think you were dealing with? A second-stringer?"

"Oh," the Russian smiled sardonically, "I don't think any of us ever had you pegged as a second-stringer, Jack. Not since that first meet with Georgi Filatov."

"You got that right!" Calumet exclaimed, as though the Russian had come perilously close to offending his manhood.

"As time progressed," Vartanyan took up again, "we elevated the requirements of our intelligence tasking where you were concerned. We strove for more quality and quantity in our requests. To your credit, you rarely ever failed us. Of course, we paid you enormous sums. Much more than we paid the Walkers and Whitworths over all those years. In fact, I would dare say that you cost us possibly as much as ten times what we paid other agents. I'm not complaining, you understand, just noting the facts."

"A great deal of that money went to my sources," Calumet interrupted. "You know that, Andrei. That's how I was able to procure the intelligence you requested. My sources were taking dire risks by passing me all those secrets."

Vartanyan held up his hand. "As I said, I'm not complaining, although it might be interesting to have a look at your profit margins sometime." He smiled speciously.

"Speaking of profit margins, Andrei," Calumet snuck in, "did you ever consider the irony of the fact that your regime has been using capitalism to achieve totalitarianism? After all, you've been supporting free enterprise by paying people like me for secrets." Calumet flipped his own smile into the ring. Touché. "Just a thought," he remarked.

"We could discuss ideology for a thousand years and never arrive at consensus, Jack, but since you brought it up, I wonder if you've ever considered the irony of the fact that you've been helping us achieve totalitarianism due to the weakness of free enterprise and the greed that it instills."

"Number one," Jack rejoined, "ideologies don't instill greed; greed proceeds from the heart. Number two, when every soul in Russia has equal access to beluga caviar, or when Russian generals are willing to eat the same meat as the common people, or when Russian politicians are willing to buy goods from the same stores as the ordinary man, then you can talk to me about greed, my friend. Until then, I'd say your premise is basically bankrupt."

Calumet was gratified that the conversation had taken this fork. While his ideological disquisition would have certainly rebated his credibility in the eyes of someone like Filatov, he believed it would fortify his authenticity in Vartanyan's mind. In Vartanyan's mind, he would appear to be genuine. He would not be attempting to align his philosophy with the Russian's, thus striving to justify his legend; he would not be buttering him up.

"Yes, well," Vartanyan riposted, "perhaps you'll be kind enough to provide me with a list of countries you consider to be suitable when it's time to invoke your own defection . . . since Russia is obviously out of the question, that is. After all, we would not want to force you to live in a society which you obviously despise, now would we?"

"What makes you think I'm defecting anywhere?"

"Oh, I don't think you'll have much choice, Mr. Calumet." *If you're what you appear to be,* the Russian thought. "But let us return to my thesis."

"Sure," Jack agreed. And then, as an afterthought, "By the way, could I possibly get a copy of those tapes? You know, as a memento?" *So what?* he decided. *Everybody acts like an idiot at one time or another.*

Vartanyan shook his head in wonderment. Having spent two years at the United Nations in New York, the Russian not only spoke American English without an accent, but he was also familiar with the colloquialisms. *This guy is a piece of work,* he told himself. After recovering, he retook the soliloquy. "So, we paid you your money, and you delivered to us very indispensable intelligence. This luxurious romance continued nicely for roughly three years. A romance made in Heaven, you might say—at least between you and Aleksandr Shevchenko, that is. Comrade Filatov is another story."

More like a romance made anywhere but in Heaven, Calumet thought. A romance conceived in the hell of Khodinka, actually, and consummated in the Hades of subterfuge and dissimulation would probably be a more accurate illustration, he decided.

"About three years ago, however," Vartanyan continued, "our little romance began to show signs of strain. The mask began to crack, if you will. Surely you can speculate about that, can't you, Jack?"

"Loaded questions and riddles never much appealed to me, Andrei," Jack smiled. "Why don't you lay it out for me?"

"Indeed," Andrei pondered, his eyes frisking Calumet, as though he was engaged in the chimerical formality of sizing him for a fitting. Or a kill. "You see, Jack, about three years ago we found ourselves staring straight into the face of a very ugly coven, an extremely nasty intrigue." Again, there was the patient searching of his judicious eyes before moving on. "We suddenly found that the intelligence we were receiving from Shevchenko, vis-à-vis Jack Calumet, was suspect."

Of course, Jack meditated. *By then Shevchenko was ours. By then Shevchenko was a funnel for American disinformation and Armbrister was spinning his own webs, one of which was seeding my legend in the hopes of someday promoting me into the game as a penetration agent. All I have to do to bring the seedling to fruition is figure a way to get out of here alive.*

"I'm sure you can imagine how that concerned us, my friend," Vartanyan plied.

Calumet decided to take a stab. "How did you know the intelligence was suspect?"

Vartanyan's eyes squinted ever so slightly at the probe, his own mind questioning deeply from whence it originated. He chose to ignore the inquiry as he continued, "We suddenly had to determine who was peddling this poison. At first, Jack, we assumed it was coming from you. You were our top pick as the purveyor of American disinformation at that point—"

"I can understand that," Calumet interjected.

"In order to make sure, however," the Russian proceeded, "we sent Georgi Filatov to meet with you. His charter was to ascertain specifically what you had managed to purloin from your sources and, from there, what you then passed along to Aleksandr Shevchenko."

"But certainly by that time you must have nurtured some suspicion of Shevchenko, Andrei. Otherwise you wouldn't have risked exposure by setting up a meet between me and Filatov." *Would the Russian admit it,* Jack wondered.

"That's one interpretation," Vartanyan said noncommittally. "Or it could have just been that we were covering all the bases, couldn't it?" he asked rhetorically.

"Could be," Jack admitted. "Or it could have been that Georgi Filatov was just dying to see me again," he added mischievously.

Vartanyan grinned. "Don't give any odds on that one," the Russian counseled, flicking his spent cigarette into the gloom of the building's interior. Exhaling forcefully, he picked up the trail again, "Alas, I'm afraid, comrade Filatov confirmed what we at the Aquarium considered to be our worst nightmare. He confirmed that you had been passing us legitimate intelligence all along, and that our very own brother, Aleksandr Shevchenko, was bartering in treason."

There was a pregnant pause at that point and neither man spoke. In the distance, the sounds of the city could lightly be discerned, as though the traffic noises and sultry metropolitan intrusions had been compelled to make themselves known.

Finally Vartanyan resumed. "It would have been much simpler if it turned out that you, in fact, were the culprit, my friend."

"I can certainly understand that," Calumet consoled. "Having one of your own turn against you must be hard to bear. Not to mention the security considerations." He then decided it was time for a stroke of profundity. "I guess that means that after Shevchenko crossed over, he handed my package to the CIA and they, in turn, sanitized it, then handed it back to him before he passed it along to you?" He privately wondered, knowing what tightwads the Soviets could be, if the Russian was about to ask him for a refund for all those years.

"I believe that would be a safe assumption," Vartanyan danced, obviously unable to read Calumet's mind.

Vartanyan had thus far spit every hook Jack had fashioned, but Jack nevertheless cast again. "The only way you could be confident of that fact, Andrei, is if the Aquarium owned another source who could corroborate or disavow Shevchenko's doctrine." Calumet was peering intently at the Russian just then, his concentration focused, his gaze searching ardently for a telltale acknowledgment in the eyes, or some subtle mannerism, but Vartanyan was like petrified wood.

He's not ready to admit to the fact that the Aquarium is running their own deep-penetration agent, Jack resolved. This entire dialogue was shaping up to be a full-court press, he concluded, only he was chagrined that Vartanyan was the one who seemed to be doing all the pressing. Not that he had any choice, really. Vartanyan had brought the three assets with him—all GRU Spetsnaz aficionados, to hear him tell it—to cover his flanks; Jack had brought nothing but his Beretta and his wit.

"Then as far as Aleksandr Shevchenko is concerned," Calumet ventured, taking up the slack, "you've been wallowing in nothing but disinformation for three solid years? For three solid years, Aleksandr Shevchenko has been feeding you nothing but flimflam?" Calumet acted astonished.

Vartanyan shrugged nonchalantly, as if to announce, Why cry over spilt milk? But his smile seemed to reflect an inimical, mysterious approbation. It was a bizarre smile, one that Calumet had not witnessed in the Russian until now, and it proposed to Jack an aura of something inscrutable, something sere. And unmistakably, it conveyed to him a leprechaunian flash of insight—one of those baffling, unexplainable instances that somehow induces a mental transference without benefit of the spoken word.

Calumet would later remember this moment as significant; as an affirmation, in fact, of the devious skein into which this entire operation had inexplicably managed to become entwined, like a restive, legendary halcyon that suddenly appeared out of nowhere to magically calm the waves and nest itself upon tranquil seas, as if Lewis Armbrister and the Luciferian Nishka were so insidiously cunning that they had evolved into modern-day sorcerers and now wielded the power to conjure souls. Owing to the great revelator of hindsight, it would not be long before he would gaze back upon this enigmatic moment forlornly and utter to himself, *That's when I should have known!*

CHAPTER 10

"Does that concern you, Jack?" Once again Vartanyan seemed to be amused. "That Shevchenko was a traitor, I mean?"

"Sure it concerns me. If he belonged to Langley, then they unquestionably know all about my own sedition!" *This is where it gets interesting,* Jack thought.

"Possibly not," Vartanyan stated cryptically.

"What?"

"Possibly not. It *is* conceivable that the CIA does *not* know about your extracurricular activities, my friend."

This was a new twist, one that Calumet was completely unprepared for. It was almost as if Vartanyan was taking sides. Jack's side, to be exact. As if Vartanyan was carving a hole that Jack could steer an eighteen-wheeler through. The Russian was voicing a concession which would justify Calumet's station as an effective agent-in-place instead of a traitor on the run. What was the Russian driving at? Jack pondered. As is often the case in such cerebral exercises, the question itself suddenly seemed to father a complementary notion. Was Vartanyan attempting to stage an ambush? Was he watching to see if Calumet would swallow the bait, hook, line, and sinker, so he could then abruptly close the trap and thus seal Calumet's fate? Yes, possibly. Jack calculated it would be wise to play devil's advocate just in case.

"How can you say that, Andrei? If Shevchenko belonged to Langley, how can you even imagine that he would not have sold me to them?"

"Let's turn it around, Jack, shall we?" Vartanyan shifted his weight and glanced at his watch. Did the Russian have a schedule? Or was he merely timing the meet? Vartanyan nodded at one of the three GRU officers. The GRU officer returned the nod and marched hastily out of the building. "In your debriefings with the CIA," Vartanyan resumed, "debriefings which, for some reason, you conveniently failed to disclose to me, did the CIA ever tell you that Shevchenko was theirs? At any time, did they ever reveal to you that he belonged to them?"

"No," Jack replied. "They wouldn't have, of course. But certainly they talked at length with Shevchenko about his provenance of information, and it would be foolish to think that my name didn't surface during some of those conversations."

"True, but is it not possible that Shevchenko might have misled them about the type of information you were peddling?"

The question sent shudders through Calumet. He couldn't pin it down, but the feasibility of such a scheme met with a singular knowledge deep within. Though he felt it was somehow related to that mystical moment of gleaming insight, the details and the meaning of it all still eluded him.

"Andrei, I'm afraid you've left me back at the paddocks. I haven't got the slightest idea what you're talking about. What are you inferring?"

"I don't think I'm inferring anything, my friend. I'm merely speculating. You know as well as I do"—Calumet thought, now *there's* an inference at least—"that operatives hold cards up their sleeves. Chestnuts for a rainy day, if you will. Well, Aleksandr Shevchenko, whatever else he may have been, was a first-rate operative. Is it not possible, therefore, that he might have sanitized the intelligence procured by you before passing it along to Langley? Is it not possible that he provided only partial dockets of information—remnants of the whole, as it were—in order to retain a bartering advantage down the road? As I said, I'm only speculating."

No you're not, Calumet suddenly realized. *You're fishing.* Jack now knew why Vartanyan had changed direction earlier in the conversation. How true the old proverb, *Beware of wolves in sheep's clothing.* Vartanyan was still trawling for Jack's relationship between Shevchenko and the CIA. And the debriefings. The debriefings most of all, Jack surmised. All the Russian had done was change bait. In Vartanyan's mind, painting Calumet into a corner in the beginning had only forced the American to take the defensive. Perceiving correctly that pressing too hard would cause the rod to snap, the

Russian deftly switched tactics and began to favor the catch-the-fly-with-honey approach.

Careful, Jack, careful. Be very careful with this hombre. "I couldn't even begin to speculate on what Shevchenko did after he met with me," Jack crafted his reply. "All I know is that he presented me with his requests, I obtained the intelligence, and then he paid me. A simple wham-bam-thank-you-ma'am. For what it's worth, I can't imagine that Shevchenko was able to doctor the information I'd given him. That would take an enormous amount of scholarship, as you know. And the CIA would have been all over him during the debriefings in regard to the meets, grilling him about every minute detail." Calumet hated to use the word *debrief,* fearful that it would trigger Vartanyan's mental acquisition of the subject, but he wasn't in the habit of carrying a thesaurus with him so he just let it fly as a matter of natural course. He paused, then added facetiously, "As far as Shevchenko being a first-rate operative, well, he *did* ultimately get caught, didn't he?"

There was the faintest glimmer of anger in the Russian's eyes at that remark. It was the first time, Calumet noted, that Vartanyan's temperature had bubbled ever so slightly. *Why? Why that particular remark?*

Vartanyan composed himself, gratified that Calumet had taken the bait, and, smiling like a good friend, said, "So in the debriefings, particularly here in Europe, the CIA never admitted to the fact that Aleksandr was a double? And you never asked?" The Russian shook his head, as if such things were beyond him. "I mean, it seems to me that the Agency certainly would have portrayed Shevchenko to you in *some* kind of light, wouldn't they? As a Soviet provocateur, perhaps? Would they have portrayed Shevchenko to you as a Soviet provocateur, Jack? No," the Russian answered himself thoughtfully, "I doubt it." He shook his head again and grinned. "After all, it would be foolish to think that Langley would have admitted Shevchenko's treason to *you.* In Langley's view, you're a traitor in your own right, isn't that right, Jack?"

Calumet chose to interpret the question as rhetorical and remained silent.

"Are you, in fact, an American traitor, Mr. Calumet?"

"I'm a capitalist, Mr. Vartanyan, who doesn't happen to believe that any information I might toss your way is going to make one whit of difference in the balance of power or the overall scheme of things."

But Vartanyan seemed to have no use for that answer. "Ah! The lone wolf. A man without a country, then. Very interesting." The Russian cocked his head slightly, displaying a curious manner, as if he was revving his engine to take off down his own trail again. "Or possibly the CIA presented Shevchenko to you as a KGB operative whose goal was to simply pilfer the crown jewels of the American defense establishment? That theory is more logical, I think. Otherwise, how could you justify your worth to the American intelligence community? You would be of no use to them if they didn't make you think that you were snugly in the harness and towing the clandestine line, would you?" He paused briefly and then asked as an aside, "You never had any suspicions yourself that Aleksandr might have been turned, had you, Jack?"

Calumet perceived that this last question of the series mattered very much to the Russian. So *this* is the line of inquiry that Vartanyan has been pursuing all along, he thought. He saw that all of the Russian's previous interrogatories had merely been a clever setup, a gentle segue into what Vartanyan considered to be the heart of the matter. The Russian had walked a mile just to get around the corner.

Calumet apprehended the sheer brilliance of Vartanyan's ploy. At first Vartanyan had attempted to bully the information out of Calumet by pressuring him into a dilemma. Then, mysteriously, just as he was on the verge of forcing the issue about the debriefings, the Russian had pulled away and had started in with his "thesis." This was to set Jack at ease. Vartanyan had pushed him to the brink and then abruptly let him up. Vartanyan's motive was clear. The Russians desperately needed to determine whether or not Calumet belonged to the Americans or if he was in fact a bona fide free lance. In order to accomplish this objective, Vartanyan had taken the back door. By determining Calumet's level of knowledge in regard to Shevchenko, Vartanyan would be able to deduce how much Langley had been telling Jack along the way. Ergo, Vartanyan would be obtaining the information he had been looking for in the first place in regard to the debriefings, knowing full well that that's the only time Shevchenko would have ever been discussed. From Vartanyan's viewpoint, the real maneuver was to get Calumet to contradict himself. If that didn't happen, the chances were good that the American was a legitimate double and Nishka, Vartanyan's master, could play him back.

Very, very careful, Jack. His playback potential was the only reason he was still alive, and he knew it.

"None," Calumet replied. "I never had the slightest doubt that Shevchenko was anything other than the KGB officer he'd told me he was."

"Not even after you met with Filatov?" Vartanyan seemed amazed. "The fact that Filatov wanted to take inventory of the intelligence you delivered to Shevchenko didn't elicit at least *some* measure of suspicion?"

"No. As I explained to Georgi the other day, I honestly thought Shevchenko was about to try to scam me and beat me out of my money."

"If that's what you honestly thought," Vartanyan countered, "then you couldn't *honestly* think that Aleksandr was operating in an official capacity, could you? That would be completely irrational, wouldn't it? No, my friend, I think you would have had to assume at that point that Aleksandr, at the very least, had turned renegade. Isn't that so?"

"Andrei, I don't know what the hell you're pressing this for, but I didn't much care *what* kind of capacity Shevchenko was operating under. I'm just a simple man. I perform and I get paid. Period."

"Then let's talk about your performance, Jack," Vartanyan insisted. "After you made your bargain with the CIA, what was their charter where you were concerned? How did they want you to play Shevchenko?"

"It was very simple. After I met with Aleksandr and retrieved his shopping list, I was to present it to Langley. They would assemble a package for me, one which was obviously filled to the brim with disinformation, and I would then, in theory, arrange another meet and deliver that particular package to Shevchenko. In actuality, however, I procured *authentic* information from my own sources and delivered the real McCoy to Shevchenko instead." This was the brief he and Robert had rehearsed in Amsterdam. Langley, in fact—according to Robert anyway—had been providing raw intelligence to Calumet. Calumet never needed to meet with other sources since he was being supplied directly by the CIA. However, in order for his brief to stand up and work, in order for the Russians to buy it—it was necessary for him to invent the middlemen. Otherwise he'd be blown sky-high.

"And in your mind, the CIA never got wind of this? They never knew, as far as it goes, that you were actually dealing in the real McCoy?"

"No, of course not. But now that we've discovered that Shevchenko was compromised, I've obviously got a problem. In fact, why haven't they arrested me? Or do they know that Shevchenko has been executed?"

"Oh, I think we can safely assume that Langley is aware of Shevchenko's execution," Vartanyan stated confidently.

And how would you know that? Calumet wondered. *Is your own Russian penetration agent placed so highly that he can communicate back to Moscow what our American penetration agent has already communicated to Washington? Is this whole thing nothing but a revolving door, for Heaven's sake?*

The real fear, Robert had cautioned—*for us and for Moscow—is that one of these two penetration agents, either ours or theirs, will expose the other. The trick is to get there first.*

"I'm still curious, though," Vartanyan continued. "Langley had apparently prearranged to have you debriefed after delivering the goods to Aleksandr. True?"

"Yes." *Back to the blasted debriefings,* Jack thought.

"Where did these debriefings take place?"

"Mostly safe houses."

"Do you have the addresses?"

"Actually, they were all temporary. Or so I was told." Jack knew he was free of circumspection in this matter. Robert had assured him that all the safe houses Jack had graced with his presence in the past three years had been abandoned and new locations had been acquired specifically for this operation. *Show them pictures if you like,* Robert had said.

"But you could still find most of them?"

"Sure," Jack replied. "For a fee."

Vartanyan smiled wryly. "I think you may find yourself willing to forgo negotiations with us on certain issues before this is all over, my friend. You see, Jack, you may not know it yet, but you're going to need me."

"Maybe so," Jack admitted, awesomely aware that he just might be in. "But that doesn't mean that I'm going to bend over."

Vartanyan laughed. "I won't be asking you to bend over, Jack." Then the laugh ran out of steam and was immediately replaced by a stern, somber mien. "I'll just be asking you to jump through hoops."

Figuring he'd *been* jumping through hoops for the past six years, Calumet decided to make a grab for the Oscar. "So why do you think the CIA hasn't attempted to arrest me yet?"

"Perhaps," the Russian chameleon snarled menacingly, "it's because you've actually been working for the CIA all along, Mr. Jack Calumet."

Both men locked eyes. Calumet could smell a fishing expedition a mile away, and although Vartanyan was sharp, the statement he had just made reeked of chum.

"You know," Calumet said disdainfully, "this is getting old. Every time I talk to those screwballs from Langley, they accuse me of working for the Russians. Every time I talk to the Russians, you accuse me of working for Langley. Do the CIA and GRU teach some kind of course in this psychological crap?"

"Who is your contact with the CIA?"

I thought I was in. "A guy named Steve Phillips."

"Is that his real name?"

"How would I know? I would imagine it's only his work name."

"What's his position? Officially."

"Officially he's out of the State Department. Consular Affairs, I believe. In reality, I think he's just another DO."

"Where? Out of the embassy? Or one of the consulates?"

"No. Washington, I believe. He moves around."

"Describe him."

Robert had shown several pictures of Steve to Calumet before leaving Amsterdam and had briefed him on Steve's legend. The reasoning was simple. As far as anyone knew, Robert was very much a threat to Moscow. Moscow knew Robert by reputation—he was infamous where they were concerned—and they probably had a viable description of him as well, maybe even a picture or two, but if Nishka discovered that Robert was in fact Calumet's controller, the game would be up. Nishka, if possible, was more wary of Robert than he was of Armbrister.

"Steve," Jack replied, "is about six feet, brown hair, brown eyes, one-seventy-five, one-eighty." Both men knew Calumet had just described at least half of the male population in the solar system.

"And his age?" Vartanyan queried.

"Oh, I'd say late thirties, early forties."

Vartanyan made the cigarette case appear again.

Calumet tensed. A pencil pusher *might* chain-smoke, but not a field man. A field man would be too cautious of his wind to chain-smoke. No. Only a pencil pusher would chain-smoke, and Vartanyan was no pencil pusher. Jack conjectured that the Russian was manipulating the silver container like a yo-yo in order to inure Calumet to its presence. After a while, Jack would become used to it. By producing it often, the Russian probably figured it would eventually lose its menace. Uh-huh. *If that cigarette case discharges,* Jack decided, *so will my Beretta.*

Vartanyan extracted a cigarette, lit it, then returned the case to his pocket. In the meantime, the GRU officer who had departed a few moments earlier came back into the building. Vartanyan nodded to him and the man walked over to Calumet. He was holding a picture album, similar to the mug books which seemed to roost upon the hallowed desks of every police station in the world.

As the man opened the book and displayed the contents of what appeared to be passport photographs, Vartanyan said to Calumet, "Please identify Steve Phillips."

Calumet took his time. He was attempting to memorize—discreetly—as many faces as possible so he could advise Langley about the specific individuals who had had the bad fortune of making the Russian's hall-of-fame register.

After a moment, Jack shook his head. "No. Not this page."

The Russian turned to the next with the same result. Five minutes later Calumet had seen them all.

"He's not in here," Jack said.

"You're sure?"

"Positive."

"Do you recognize any of the others?"

Calumet thought he might have distinguished one or two faces from the lot, but replied, "No." He felt relieved that none of the people in the photographs were on Robert's team.

Vartanyan signaled the GRU officer, who retreated with the photo album.

"Let's discuss your future with the Aquarium, Jack," Vartanyan remarked.

I'm in! Jack concluded. "Let's not."

"What?"

"Let's get something straight right now, Andrei. I don't work for the Aquarium. I'm a solo act. Period."

Vartanyan saw no use in fencing with the American. If Jack Calumet was what he appeared to be, he would soon have no choice. The Teflon double might not know it yet, but he belonged to Vartanyan lock, stock, and barrel. *If* he was what he appeared to be. If not, he would just die a little sooner.

"Perhaps I misstated the premise, Jack." Vartanyan smiled. "To put it another way, let us discuss your entanglement—or perhaps I should say your *predicament*—with the CIA. Would that be acceptable?"

"The way I see it, Andrei, is that the Aquarium will want to keep me in the game. You'll want to continue to provide me with shopping lists—bogus lists this time—which I can then sell to Langley." At that point, it might have been the exaggerated lightness in the way he shifted his weight, or it might have been the meandering grin and the cocky tilt of his head, but Calumet suddenly appeared to be swimming in revelation. "On the other hand, if I'm misreading my tea leaves and that's not the case, then it's just dawned on me that I may be able to wiggle my way out of this thing with the CIA regardless. You see, I can always deny that I ever gave anything tangible to Shevchenko in the first place. My guess is that they'll play hell trying to prove anything against me, now that I've had time to think about it." As though he had learned about Shevchenko's treason only in the past ten minutes and had just finished sorting out all the ramifications.

"Will they, now?" Vartanyan seemed concerned. Calumet could suddenly take him or leave him. "What makes you think they don't have enough proof against you already? After all, Shevchenko, as you said, must have sold you to them."

"Sure," Jack replied confidently, his voice a suspicious decibel higher than normal, "but all they have is his word against mine. I made very sure that none of the meets between myself and Aleksandr were ever surveilled. Very sure!"

"They have the raw intelligence you delivered to Shevchenko," Vartanyan countered. "How do you propose to explain that, if it comes down to it?"

"Simple. I'll tell them I don't know what they're talking about. I'll tell them maybe Shevchenko had another source. I'll tell them they were nuts to trust a withering old defector in the first place. Like I said, I made very sure my meets with Aleksandr were not surveilled." Calumet suddenly felt inventive, inspired. "And if *that's* not good enough," he tacked on triumphantly, eyes agleam, "I'll tell the idiots I'm sitting on a ton of explosive information that will be delivered immediately by unknown sources to the wrong people if they even *think* about messing with me!"

"I see," Vartanyan mused. For a fleeting moment he appeared to appreciate the fire in Calumet's concentrated burst of fanaticism, as if this crazy American was the type of person who frequently indulged in private conversations with visiting aliens and truly *did* march to the beat of a distant drummer. *There's no telling what kind of stories we'd hear if we could put this guy under the needle,* Vartanyan thought, *but Nishka said, "No!"*

"You might be able to get away with it," the Russian added calmly, attempting to soothe Calumet's troubled demons, "you might not." He knew he needed Calumet for the time being. "In any case, you certainly don't want the aggravation though, do you? You don't want the suspicion of the entire American Intelligence community hanging around your neck like a millstone, I wouldn't think."

Calumet had staked his claim. He had defined the boundaries of his sovereign territory. Once he discerned that Vartanyan had accepted him as an agent-in-place, in the instant of that perceived recognition, he had moved quickly to prevent the Russian from owning him outright. *Give yourself as much room to maneuver as possible,* Robert had encouraged. Jack figured he and Vartanyan were now on level ground.

"I agree," Calumet said, his words abruptly rational, his presence of mind suddenly rescued from the land of delusion. "As long as Langley thinks I'm useful I won't be forced to endure their overt suspicion." He smiled, as if to announce that the two of them had come to terms. "So what did you have in mind, exactly?"

"I suppose, my friend," Vartanyan replied coolly, "you could say that what we have in mind is a bit of symmetry."

Calumet almost choked. For a moment he even thought he was only a second away from death. The play on words was uncanny. *I'm driving at symmetry,* Robert had hinted in Amsterdam. Surely, Jack thought, they couldn't have—No. *Stay cool, Jack.*

Calumet cleared his throat. "Symmetry?"

"Yes." Vartanyan was puzzled at Calumet's sudden discomfort. "For now, we want you to forget about your own sources altogether, Jack. We want to give you a shopping list which you will not, under any circumstances, present to anyone other than the CIA. Do you understand?"

"Sure," Jack replied. "You want me to throw a stack of disinformation at them." Then, because he was still agitated over the play on words, "What's that got to do with symmetry?"

"I would think that would have been obvious," Vartanyan remarked quizzically. "For the past three years, Langley has been receiving our legitimate shopping lists and feeding us nothing but disinformation due to Shevchenko's treason. Now we're going to return the favor by having you shovel it back. Symmetry."

"Oh," Calumet managed, still nursing a slight hangover from the savage déjà vu. "I see."

"This material we're providing to you, Jack, our bag of requests as it were, is going to be a bit over your head, I'm afraid." Vartanyan smiled. "If it's any consolation, it's over my head also. But don't let that concern you. All we want you to do is deliver it as per usual to your controller at the CIA—this Steve Phillips—and run with what they give you in return. How are you to contact him?"

"Actually," Jack replied, "he's supposed to be in Berlin. I met with him in Frankfurt after I met with Filatov and told him I was coming here."

Vartanyan was about to speak—it was obvious by the tightening of his vocal cords—but he suddenly censored himself. Taking a quick pull off his cigarette and then discarding it, he asked instead, "When can you set up a meet with him?"

He was about to ask me to lay out my operational game plan, Jack thought. *He wants to know the details of how my meets are arranged with the CIA.* Calumet also noticed that the Russian had smoked only one cigarette to the nub. The others had been abandoned after taking a mere two or three drags and then left to burn down along the way. *The little things can speak volumes,* Robert had lectured. *Pay attention to the little things.*

"Within the next couple of days." Calumet bought as much time as he calculated he could get away with.

Vartanyan nodded at his GRU accomplice once more. The accomplice walked over and handed Jack a manila package before retreating quickly. He obviously did not want to give Calumet any longer than necessary to record his face, although Calumet had done just that when the accomplice had been holding the picture album moments earlier. Calumet could swear the man was wearing a wig. The bushy mustache might have been false as well, he speculated. Outside of that, there was no further evidence of such things as telltale scars or other distinguishable markings. In fact, all Calumet could really say about the man was that he possessed a chancy pair of frigid blue eyes.

"What's in here?" Jack pointed to the package. "Is there anything I need to be briefed on?"

"As I said," Vartanyan postulated, "it's over your head." The deflective smile appeared again. "And mine. But if you really have to know, the enclosed shopping list contains questions about DEFSMAC and SIGINT capabilities, and encoding and decrypting telemetry data, that sort of information. See what I mean?"

"Yes. I guess you're right," Jack agreed. Shevchenko had asked him about the same thing years ago, before the Russian became a player for the CIA. Calumet knew that DEFSMAC, pronounced "deaf smack," and which stood for Defense Special Missile and Astronautics Center, functioned in part as the United States' early-warning nerve center. It was considered to be so secret that when Jack had mentioned it to Robert, Robert had told him to forget about it completely and never discuss it again. In return, Jack, though not broaching Robert's identity, relayed that very same message to Shevchenko. *My source told me to forget about it, Aleksandr,* Jack had told him. *My source said that type of intelligence was way too hot.*

And then Calumet suddenly understood what was happening.

This was a dry run. The Russians knew very well they weren't going to achieve any success on this pass from an informational standpoint. They weren't banking on being able to unearth the crown jewels by analyzing the disinformation Langley would toss back at them, as if they could reverse-engineer the intent behind the misleading intelligence. No. The Russians wanted to see how the CIA was going to react to Jack Calumet. Robert had foreseen it himself—*Nishka will be very curious to see how you are handled now that Shevchenko is out of the loop.*

Nishka was about to funnel some very heavy solicitations through Calumet. Heavy enough so that the CIA would be forced to play him back. Or drop him completely, and for good. After all, American intelligence would be driven into a compromise just to keep Jack in the game. The disinformation itself would reveal to the Russians what *didn't* work, thus narrowing the possibilities, even if ever so slightly, and the Americans would now have to think twice about chasing this clandestine rabbit. In their minds, the safe play would be to shut Calumet down.

But Calumet knew both sides were committed to dealing all the cards and betting on every tedious hand at this point. No question about it. Both sides were in this contest for the duration because both sides were after a mole. The GRU was after a man who must be lurking somewhere in the lofty corridors of the Russian military-industrial complex; the CIA, on the other hand, was after a person who, of necessity, had to be concealing himself in some obscure crevice situated turgidly in the epicenter of America's power elite. As Sherlock Holmes would have described it, "The game is afoot, Watson!" And what a game at that, Jack ruminated, noting the significance of Nishka's neoteric gambit. If the package handed him by Vartanyan merely contained information pertaining to tactical intelligence, or something less significant than DEFSMAC, that would be one thing, but the Russians were changing the game in a major way, and Nishka's intentions were clear—Moscow was raising the ante, thereby forcing Washington to belly up to the table or fold.

"Return to Alexanderplatz three days from now at the same time," Vartanyan said, breaking Calumet's reverie.

"I won't have anything by then. You know that."

"Yes, Jack, I know the CIA will not be able to fabricate a package in so short a space of time. However, I want a complete debriefing of your meeting with them."

"All right," Jack agreed. "Three days, same time, same place."

There was a moment of silence before Vartanyan remarked casually, "I hear there's a lot of money in the heroin business these days. Especially here in Germany."

Calumet suddenly wondered if Vartanyan was behind the mysterious presence that had activated his sixth sense at the Kempinski. He knew last night's operation had been set up by Langley somehow, but he didn't understand the reasoning or the methodology. Sure, it was true that he had been ushered smack into the middle of a drug deal in Grunewald Park. How was he supposed to know, however, that the poison in question had been heroin, if it *was* heroin. How did Vartanyan know? Did Vartanyan have a source in the BND? Of course. That's the only way he would have heard about the firefight because the morning's papers hadn't mentioned it. Somehow the BND was keeping the entire affair under wraps. But did Vartanyan have any idea that Jack had been anywhere near the park? If so, how? *No, he's only speculating. So Armbrister is validating my legend by making me out to be a mercenary who dabbles in anything and everything,* Jack deduced. *Including drugs.*

"I'm sure you hear a lot of things in your line of work, Andrei," Jack spoke noncommittally. He hadn't decided exactly how to play it.

"Yes, well, three days then," Vartanyan said. He was dismissing Calumet.

Calumet walked to the doorway and turned back. "Just out of curiosity, Andrei. If you're to be my handler now, how come Filatov came to Frankfurt? Why not you?"

Vartanyan gazed reflectively at Calumet, as if debating whether or not to answer. Finally he said, "I had some business in Ankara."

The vision of a mutilated loyal American double named Conrad Thurman lying in a gutter in Ankara flashed suddenly into Calumet's mind, along with Conrad's forsaken wife and daughter. Striving to remain composed, phlegmatic, he locked eyes with Vartanyan. For a fleeting instant it seemed as though the two men were fastened together in an ocular tug-of-war, facing each other like a raging wind, their demeanors stoic, their dispositions irreconcilable, the intractability of their souls transparent. A subtle communion passed between them at that moment, indefinable in words but whispering anyway and struggling to be heard. Without knowing what the other was thinking, both men had arrived at identical decisions. Each decided surely, when it was all over, that he would kill the other. For Vartanyan, the resolution was a challenge, a gauntlet to be lifted. For Calumet, it was a certain type of justice, a chivalrous justice maybe, or maybe not, but a justice nevertheless, and one that was to be administered according to Moscow rules. In any case, for both men, the operation—Operation Odyssey Robert had called it in Amsterdam—had suddenly become personal.

"Dah skorich vystry' ehché, tovarish," Calumet said. *See you later, comrade.* Then Jack Calumet pivoted and walked into the ramparts—too long embattled—of old East Berlin.

CHAPTER 11

Georgi Filatov stepped into his waiting car at Sheremetyevo. He was nervous. He had every right to be. What he had seen before leaving Berlin had almost caused him to faint. In fact, he would have collapsed right there on the spot had he not steadied himself by leaning against a wall. It took him a full five minutes to master his giddiness. Then he began to worry. What worried him most was why they hadn't trusted him with the shocking disclosure in the first place. Was he not a major-general in Russian military intelligence? Was he not sufficiently high up on the ladder to be privy to such matters? Yes, he admitted to himself, although what he'd seen *was* absolutely jolting.

What could Nishka possibly be up to?

His driver was different, he noticed. Not his usual driver. When he inquired about it, the new man told him his normal driver had been reassigned. Oh, Georgi said, that was understandable. Georgi was driven straight to Khodinka. Stepping out of his car at Khodinka, he was led into a hangar where, without preamble, he was shot once in the back of the head by a uniformed assailant, the weapon a Makarov. Moscow rules. His body was quickly removed and taken to an unmarked grave and buried. The burial itself was very simple—no eulogy, no ceremony, just six feet under in a pine box. Russia grew plenty of pines. No one ever saw or heard from Major-General Georgi Filatov again. In the end, Nishka hadn't even given him the courtesy of knowing why.

*

The note was in his shaving kit when he finally got back to his hotel room. Jack opened it and read it.

Tomorrow morning 11:00 A.M.

Good, Jack thought. He was tired. Not physically, but mentally. He had anticipated that Robert would be chomping at the bit by now, asking for an immediate meet, but not so. *Great, in fact,* he told himself. His powers of concentration required a rest, if only for a brief period. The respite was a welcome one. Knowing that he did not have to set out on an expedition to clear his path and cover his tail for this one evening, he suddenly felt refreshed. He was sure he was in no danger from the Russians. Not yet. They were determined to burrow down this tunnel to the next level, and Jack Calumet, for the time being, was their guide. But only for the time being. He knew there would come a day when they wouldn't need him anymore, or, he shuddered to think, he would be blown too early and the game would be up. In any case, whichever came first—one or the other—*then* he would be in danger.

After calling Diane, Calumet locked Vartanyan's package in his suitcase and scampered down to the pool and sauna in the basement of the hotel. As in Frankfurt's Sheraton, the Kempinski's health club was open not only to guests—for a fee, of course—but also retained memberships in the names of the more affluent patrons living in the city of Berlin and surrounding principalities. After a leisurely swim, he took a seat not quite poolside next to the cocktail bar, his back to the entrance. He was sipping his Orangensaft and ruminating about the day's events when suddenly his attention was drawn by possibly the most enchanting voice he had ever heard. And that was a magnificent feat considering the fact that the words sailed out in naturally accented Hochdeutsch. It was a voice, Calumet thought, that, even in a casual exchange, seemed to steal gracefully, passively into the heart, and innocently, as if it had conferred a summons before ever being pronounced.

"I'd like a mineral water, please," she said politely in German to the attendant.

Calumet glanced to his right and regarded her. The woman was stunning.

"Guten Tag," she smiled delicately at Jack, noticing his movement. Her hair cascaded past her shoulders, raven and lustrous. A faint hue of indigo stabbed all around its tresses like a flurry of tracers in a firefight as the sparkle of the club's lights quarreled with the motion of her head, and the diamond bracelet encircling her left wrist played elegantly against the backdrop of her black one-piece bathing suit. The suit itself was snug and very slick in appearance. It wrapped its vinyl fabric around her supple figure and hugged her like tights on an aerobics instructor.

"Hi," Jack replied in English, somewhat shyly, but returning the smile. His first assumption was a honey-trap. She had been sent to set him up. Or possibly she had been sent just to get to know him. Or maybe neither. Too hard to tell right off the bat. He dropped the smile, turned his head, and focused his interest on a magazine lying on the bar. *Let's just find out,* he thought. Calumet concluded that his shy response and his obvious disinterest would tell the tale. *If she pursues it,* he calculated, *she's been sent by somebody. Either that, or she just can't grapple with the notion of rejection. Or,* he also allowed, *she's one of those Europeans who are simply fascinated by Americans.*

"Here you are, Karola," the attendant said, handing her the drink. "Would you like me to put that on your tab?"

"Yes," Karola responded dulcetly. "Thank you, Hans." She carried her drink and her belongings to the far end of the pool and settled comfortably into a lounge chair.

So, Jack speculated. *Maybe none of the above.* The woman—about thirty-five, he observed—was obviously a regular. And she was merely being friendly, he concluded. Oh well. So much for conspiracy. He had another Orangensaft, read his magazine, and then returned to his room.

*

Rossetti was stalking the streets. *The hell with it,* he thought. Before this operation, he had been contemplating quitting the military anyway, and if they wanted to toss him because he wasn't going to walk the straight and narrow anymore, then so be it. After having been delivered to the safe house by Steve, he and Team Interceptor were under orders by Robert to sit tight and wait for further instructions, but Rossetti got antsy. "Tell them I went for a walk," he'd said amid his teammates' protestations. "If they don't like it, they can ship me home!"

That was almost two hours ago. As time progressed, he found himself gravitating slowly in the direction of the Kempi, being drawn like a magnet almost, as if he couldn't stay away. It was by happenstance that he witnessed from a distance Calumet's return to the hotel. He had been window-shopping in the vicinity and caught Calumet's arrival out of the corner of his eye. Then, moving in closer, discreetly, he noted the package under Calumet's arm and thought, *The rascal has actually done it!* Rossetti smiled. He decided to hang around for a while and see what developed.

*

After ensuring that everything in his room was in order and that nothing had been tampered with, Calumet hit the Ku'damm and sought a quiet place to enjoy his evening meal. However, as a person who was normally decisive in almost all that he did, his decision-making capabilities seemed to have escaped him this night. He couldn't quite make up his mind about what he was in the mood for. He wandered aimlessly up and down the street and its offshoots for thirty minutes or more searching for just the right spot, but to no avail. Finally the bachelor syndrome kicked in and he dutifully abandoned his quest outright. After all, he was an aficionado—somewhat rusty, maybe, but an aficionado nevertheless—of the nomadic, carefree life. The freedom of suddenly ditching a perturbing responsibility—such as eating, for instance—breathed new fire into his spirit and gave him a lift. As a result, he soundly convinced himself that he really wasn't in the mood for anything at all anyway. Whatever he ate, he rationalized, he would be full when he was finished regardless, so he fell into stride effortlessly and set off at a brisk pace for an old standby. Burger King was good enough, he concluded. He had a Whopper with cheese, pommes frites, and—since they owned Burger King—a Pepsi. "With a full cup of ice," he forewarned the server as a precaution against being treated like a European. "Not just one little cube."

Twilight was just beginning to descend on Berlin when Calumet strolled through the doors of Burger King and out on to the Ku'-damm. Walking back toward the Kempinski, he suddenly heard a shambling sound coming from around the corner, just down a side street. Deciding to investigate, he turned into the artery and immediately froze.

Karola? The woman from the Kempinski's health club was being assaulted by two rough-cut men in their late twenties, some thirty yards away. One was grabbing at her purse while the other attempted to restrain her arms. She was putting up a magnificent fight, scratching, flailing, biting . . . but not screaming.

Calumet pulled his pirate's grin, momentarily admiring the woman's brave, sturdy effort, then he launched into action, covering the distance like a charging lion. The first perpetrator barely had time to notice Calumet before Calumet spiraled into a roundhouse and hammered the man's chin with his left foot. One down. The other assailant released the woman swiftly and squared with Jack, but he never had a chance. As the assailant was mounting his stance, Calumet's elbow took him flat on the nose and then followed that blow with a knee to the groin. As the perpetrator was falling, Calumet delivered an additional chop to the left jaw, just for good measure. Two down; game, set, and match. Both men lay moaning on the sidewalk.

"Oh my!" Karola exclaimed, throwing her arms and practically her entire body around Calumet. Her English was heavily accented, making Jack that much more aware of her sexuality. "Thank you. Thank you," she blurted excitedly. And then she came to terms with the recognition. "You are the man from the pool? Yes?" The fear in her eyes was genuine, he thought. Or was it anger?

Calumet, with no little effort due to the woman's shaking and quivering, extricated himself from Karola's embrace and grabbed her elbow. "Let's get out of here!" he commanded. He pulled her gently as the two of them retreated from the scene toward the Ku'-damm.

*

Rossetti had sprinted down a parallel street, rounding the opposite corner just in time to see the two perpetrators lying on the pavement and Calumet walking away with the woman. Deducing what had transpired, he melted into the shadows and leaned casually against the railing of an old building, watching and waiting. A moment later his patience was rewarded.

A big man with a full head of blond hair and a bushy mustache which stood out even in the twilight emerged from an obscure doorway up the street. The two assailants, one dripping blood, the other crouching in pain, dragged themselves off the ground and approached him. Rossetti grabbed a handful of sunflower seeds out of the bag he was carrying and, popped a couple into his mouth. For all appearances, had anyone been there to observe him, he was just another local taking an evening stroll. Turning his attention back to the street, he noticed that there was obviously some kind of verbal altercation under way among the three men, evidenced by the fact that the two perpetrators were gesturing animatedly, as if they were outraged. This went on for fifteen or twenty seconds before the big blond man grabbed the larger assailant by the throat and shook him menacingly. His point made, the blond man then released the assailant and reached into his own pocket. His hand surfaced with a wad of money, which he shoved into the shirts of the assailants. They took the money and ran.

Interesting, Rossetti thought. He had just about made up his mind to follow the blond when a black Mercedes suddenly screeched around the corner and pulled up to the curb. The blond opened the rear door and out stepped a tall, handsome dark-haired man, a gentleman by all appearances, dressed impeccably. The two exchanged a few words and then the blond bounded into the rear seat. The dark-haired man, Andrei Vartanyan, was about to climb in behind him but paused. Placing his hand on top of the car door, he glanced around quickly, surveying his surroundings.

Vartanyan's eyes locked on Rossetti's form some fifty yards away. The commando was chomping on his sunflower seeds, coolly meeting the Russian's gaze. To act in any other manner would arouse suspicion. With the approaching darkness it was difficult for either of them to distinguish each other, but both men strained their eyes in an attempt to do just that. For Vartanyan, it was more of a knee-jerk reaction than anything else. The stranger could be standing in that particular spot for any number of reasons. After a moment, Vartanyan slid into his seat and the car roared away.

Rossetti popped another seed into his mouth. He pushed himself away from the railing, put the bag of sunflowers into his pocket, and then watched quietly as the Mercedes faded into the distance. After the car and its strange occupants had disappeared, Rossetti, his mind lingering long on the man whose stare he had just repelled, spoke crisply, the thin air his only audience. *"Nailed you to it, sucker!"* he said.

CHAPTER 12

Calumet led Karola into the nearest Ratskeller and, without asking her what she wanted, ordered Weissbier for the two of them. He knew Weissbier was much more potent than the regular brew, and he calculated it would calm her frayed nerves faster. Every man in the establishment did a double take as they entered. Karola was not only naturally beautiful, but she also, in spite of her ordeal, had a vibrant air about her. At the moment, she was wearing a white blouse stretched taught over her moderate but adequate breasts. The blouse adhered perfectly to her curves, as though it had been melted on. It was tucked neatly into a black miniskirt which provided an ample view of her long, slender legs. The combination only accentuated her allure. They took a corner table, seating themselves as far away from the other customers as possible.

Calumet grinned as they settled in. "Since those two bozos didn't get your purse, I'll let you pay for the drinks. Fair enough?"

"Well," Karola returned the grin, revealing perfect white teeth and pronouncing the *w* as a *v*, "you are certainly a cheap date, aren't you?" She hesitated just long enough to prevent Calumet from responding, then added with a flirtatious toss of the head, her hair sweeping perilously close to Calumet's face, "Or is that all you're going to cost me?"

Calumet smiled, his eyes full of confidence, his bearing commanding, his demeanor indicating a paternal superiority. Pretending callowness to the sexual innuendo, he stuck his hand across the table and said, "My name is Jack. What's a handshake go for in Berlin these days?"

"Yes," Karola replied, taking the proffered hand and simpering sweetly, "I know your name is Jack." An irresistible admission.

Calumet went for it. "How is that?"

"I asked Hans. After you left the pool."

"Ah!" Calumet exclaimed, as though it was that simple. Then he had an afterthought. "Hmm. I don't ever remember telling Hans my name." Jack appeared puzzled. He knew he had signed for his Orangensaft and that Hans would have seen his name on the bill, but he wanted to see how the woman would handle his feigned confusion. At the same time, he thought to himself, *Am I ever going to be able to relax? Am I forever doomed to move and countermove?*

Karola appeared unflappable. "You would have to ask Hans about that," she responded. Then, as if a dam had burst, tears began to stream down her face. "I don't know. Why are you confusing me? Those men . . ."

"Okay, okay," Jack consoled her. "Don't get upset. I was just curious."

"Perhaps you signed for your drink?" she quivered, still appearing shaken. "Maybe?"

Jack chuckled. "Yes, as a matter of fact I did," attempting to succor her. He abruptly decided to make a concerted effort to slack off and forget about the universe and all its implications for a while. This woman didn't appear to have anything to hide, and the odds were strong that she would not have admitted to inquiring about him if she was something other than the intended victim of two street punks. "So why did you ask about me, Karola?"

Calumet had known only a handful of people who could blush on demand. Karola's glow appeared to be genuine. "And how do you know *my* name?" she dodged coquettishly.

"I'm afraid Hans mentioned it at the pool," Jack smiled. "Remember?"

Karola laughed. It was an enticing laugh, Jack thought. Their drinks arrived and she paid for them, leaving the young woman who delivered them a warm smile and a Deutsch mark.

They talked through their first beer, and then another, each revealing shaded insights into their own personal lives. Calumet discovered that Karola was, in fact, thirty-five years old and lived in an upper-class dwelling in Potsdam. She had borne the oppression of East Germany throughout most of her life, but when the wall came down she'd managed to scrape together enough money for a few well-timed ventures and make profitable investments that were finally beginning to pay off. She talked for twenty minutes, and she went into elaborate detail about her financial escapades, so much so that Calumet wondered why. *A self-made woman,* he ultimately concluded after hearing her narrative, *proud of what she's accomplished.*

Calumet invented his own stories as needed. Mostly independently wealthy, he told her. Dabbled in big-ticket items back home, like Caterpillar tractors, and so on. He had to be careful when using the Caterpillar tractor legend. He told that one only to women. Calumet knew as much about Caterpillar tractors as he did about moon rocks. And he was known to play commodity futures from time to time, he admitted. At least that part was true. No, he told her when she asked, he knew nothing about the European markets. And he thought privately, *unless maybe we're talking about arms, young lady. If we're talking about arms, I know a little something about those markets.* But he wasn't about to come anywhere within a mile or two of that subject, not with this woman.

The music was going strong as the third round of drinks arrived and Calumet suddenly realized he was thoroughly enjoying himself. For the first time in months, he was immersing his emotions in revelry and languishing on the cushion of a pleasant atmosphere, intellectually drafting along in the company of a beautiful woman whom he was positive meant him no harm. The cozy Ratskeller exuded a smattering of Bavarian charm, even here in Berlin, and the crowd seemed robust, lively, but disinterested in the two of them. They laughed about the evening's earlier events as they bounced from topic to topic. When Karola asked him where he had learned to fight, Calumet intimated that he had simply been lucky. It must have been his extreme anger at seeing a woman abused. Naturally, this response only seemed to intensify his mystique, a phenomenon with which he was completely at ease and secretly relished.

Two hours passed and seemed like only minutes. They took turns pounding out their arias, each engendering patience while the other performed, each becoming more and more animated as the evening progressed, like impresarios who had been caged and suddenly set free, lively, famously, and sometimes even voracious in their levity.

"You must come to my home and let me prepare a proper meal for you sometime," Karola invited when the dialogue somehow slammed into an intermission. Jack had related the details of his earlier feast at Burger King, explaining to her that was why he had been in the vicinity when she was attacked.

"What makes you think you know how to cook?" Calumet toyed with her. "Especially anything I might actually *like!*"

She leaned forward, inches from his face. "I just *love* a challenge. Is that a challenge, Mr. Jack?"

Her scent stirred him. He reached up to her face with his left hand and brushed back a few wisps of hair. This was basically an elemental, involuntary reaction for Calumet. Whenever he felt his emotions were being influenced against his will, he subconsciously decided it was necessary to regain control, to ward off whatever sentient force happened to be assaulting him on a hormonal level. The movement of his hand to her face, the brushing back of her hair; these subtle motions all implied he could have his way, that he was not on the verge of succumbing. She, however, leaned her cheek affectionately into his hand, making the assault against his manliness a fierce one, raising the stakes. Their eyes swam together momentarily, and in that instance, in that moment, Calumet sensed something strangely, vaguely familiar about the woman; a familiarity in . . . what? He couldn't put his finger on it, but aside from her conspicuous sexuality there was a confidential aura about her, intangible yet making itself appreciated. In that moment, the force of her nature seemed to transmit something akin to one of those informal flashbacks which occur when the nostrils liberate a suggestive aroma from the passing wind, and Calumet was suddenly awash in its riddle. *If they ever find a way to harness sex and fit it onto MIRVs,* he thought, *nuclear devices would become obsolete.*

Jack leaned back and took a sip of beer, breaching the intimacy. Wiping his mouth with the back of his hand—and making a point of doing so like a sailor on shore leave—he said, "That's what I figured."

She giggled. "Figured what?"

Calumet's eyes were suddenly transformed into lasers, penetrating. He chose his words carefully. "That you were the Joan of Arc type. She was a woman who also got off on a good challenge." He was sending a message. His phraseology let her know that he wasn't embarrassed or intimidated by her sexual badinage.

Karola smiled demurely, acutely aware of his unbridled display of masculinity. A sudden chill shot through her veins, making her feel vulnerable, but she compensated for it by responding casually to his remark. "If I remember my history, the English put the poor girl in chains. You don't strike me as that type, Jack."

Jack chortled. "No, I'm afraid I'm not." He glanced at his watch. It was getting late, and anyway the moment seemed to have been tarnished as a result of their last exchange. Not that the hour really had anything to do with it, Calumet knew, but he was also beginning to feel a little guilty. He had been sitting here with this delightful, beautiful woman and having a time of it while Diane, his on-again-off-again true love, was presumably squandering her life away in Atlanta, waiting faithfully for him to come home. "Listen, Karola, I can't tell you how much I've enjoyed your presence this evening, but I really have to be going. Maybe I'll take you up on that meal someday. For now, may I walk you to the *U-bahn?* Or do you have a car?"

"Please," she said, putting her hand on his arm, gesturing for him to remain seated, "I feel so light right now, and happy. And I'm enjoying our conversation immensely. Stay and have another beer." And then she donned an irresistible smile. "Please?"

"I can't believe a woman as beautiful as you doesn't have a husband or a boyfriend. Or even twenty or thirty boyfriends."

"Haven't you heard that it's usually the prettiest women who stay home on Saturday nights?"

"Yeah, I've heard that," Calumet said skeptically. And then, more to himself than to her, "But not where I grew up, they didn't."

Karola laughed. "I'm sure that's true." Then her voice adopted a somber, almost sad intonation. "Jack, I hope I'm not being"—she struggled for the word in English but couldn't snag it—"*überheblich?*"

"Presumptuous," Calumet assisted.

"Yes. Presumptuous." And struggled again with its pronunciation. "I just want you to know that I like you very much. I'm not only grateful for what you've done, but I'm really enjoying your company this evening. As a friend. There's certainly no harm in that, I wouldn't think."

"No. No harm in that," Calumet agreed. "Actually, I hadn't assumed anything different, in case you were wondering. About your
being just a friend, I mean." He smiled deprecatingly. "The truth is,
Karola, I'm enjoying all of this myself. It's been a while since I've
kicked back." As if on cue, his own words acting as a catalyst and
causing him to face the realization of the strain he'd been under, his
deportment suddenly seemed to loosen at that point, releasing
weeks of regimen and pent-up inhibition in one fell swoop. "Why
not!" he sang out. "You win, pretty lady. One more drink."

So the discourse continued, first one drink, then another. They
rode the clock past midnight, she plying her charms and allure, at
times treading dangerously close to seductive overkill, he nibbling
at her enticements, attracted to her in every way, her feminine nu-
ances, her smell, her intellect, her body, but keeping his distance all
the same, refusing to be mastered by her potency, knowing that she
was a siren who could turn men on and off like a faucet. The crowd
thinned little by little until few remained, the two of them now conspicuous in their corner retreat.

It was after two when Calumet called a halt. Standing, he took
her by the arm and lifted her gently out of her chair. "Come on,
Karola. I'll take you home."

They found a taxi and climbed in. Karola gave the address, unaware that Calumet was fighting the effects of the alcohol so he
could remember it. She sat very close, her legs turned into him, her
hand on his thigh. They rode in silence for thirty minutes, finally
arriving at her house in the suburbs of Potsdam. It was a modest
home, obviously refurbished somewhere along the line, made of
wood and stone with a chimney.

As the cab pulled up, he opened the door and got out, holding it
for her, perceiving that she had planned to exit the vehicle on his
side. She quickly noticed that he left the door open after she
emerged from the cab, indicating that he was getting back in. And
he made no effort to reach for money to pay the driver.

She hugged him, saying, "Thank you, Jack. Thank you for what
you did for me. I hope we see each other again." And then she
kissed his lips lightly. He didn't pull away; he accepted it, and
maybe—at that point—would have accepted more, she thought. But
she stepped back.

Jack smiled. "You never know, Karola." He squeezed her hand

and eased back into the car. "Good night, fair maiden." He nodded
to the driver and the cab puttered away, him watching her through
the rear window as she took the steps to her front door, her hips
caroming back and forth, hitting all the angles.

Unlocking and opening the door, she entered, the only light a
dim lamp in the hallway. She saw him immediately, the image of his
outline blotting out a chair across the room, his cigarette barely
aglow.

"What are you doing here?" she asked, slightly startled.

"I knew that even *you* wouldn't be able to get him to come in
tonight. Not on the first encounter."

She closed the door and locked it. Walking toward him, unbut-
toning her blouse, she said, "It's just as well. It's you I'm in the
mood for right now."

Andrei Vartanyan stood and gathered her into his arms.

CHAPTER 13

For someone who was supposed to be operating undercover, Steve
Phillips was out and about early and making all kinds of mistakes in
relation to his clandestine tradecraft. It was bad enough that he'd
attended a diplomatic function the night before, breaking his *real*
cover for the first time since arriving in Berlin. He had bordered on
making a nuisance of himself at the wingding, flitting about and
introducing himself around—"Steve Phillips, American consulate,"
shooting his hand out like a spear—"over there on Clayallee, right
across from Truman Plaza," as if none of the other diplomats had
the faintest clue about where the Americans made their beds. Certainly all that was bad enough, but this morning he took it upon
himself to enter the American consulate on Clayallee by the front
gate at 9:00 A.M., making sure it was a solo affair all the way, meaning he was careful to enter when no one else was going through the
doors at the same moment—in case anybody was taking pictures,
you know—then came back out a half hour later only to set off aimlessly for a leisurely stroll across Truman Plaza, just shuffling along
slowly, essentially a snail's pace, apparently without a worry in the

world, sightseeing almost, as it were. Well, in a manner of speaking, not exactly. It must have dawned upon him that he had forgotten something because twenty minutes later, amazingly, he could be seen sauntering back across the square toward the consulate, once again entering by the front gate, but pausing at the steps this time to tie his shoe. Certainly in no hurry—*that* was obvious—whatever it was that must have slipped his mind. Dressed, uncharacteristically, in a Brooks Brothers suit, indelibly marking him as some sort of stuffy American official full of self-importance.

Perhaps the capstone of all his mistakes, though, perhaps his creme-de-la-creme of clandestine carelessness this day—so far anyway—was the fact that at about 10:30, Steve Phillips emerged from the consulate yet again, only to treat himself to a morning smoke right there on the sidewalk, the cars zipping by, and the strollers—the few that happened to be in the vicinity—brushing past, right out front, out there where the American consulate was framing the skyline, joking and carrying on with the German guards, as if they didn't have a job to do, what with terrorism and all. Feeling neighborly, he probably offered the guards a smoke as well, and maybe even introduced himself to them, too: *"Ich heisse* Steve. Steve Phillips,"* and rather loudly at that. Right out there in the open, acting like some kind of junior diplomat or something. When he finally walked back inside, he thought to himself, *Center surely has a line on me by now.*

*

Robert decided not to press the issue with Rossetti. He never asked the commando why he had chosen to disobey orders and disappear for three hours the evening before. Nor did Rossetti offer any explanation. The commando didn't want Robert to know that he had been shadowing Calumet. There was too much risk of exposure, and Robert would be furious about it, if he knew. As a result, for reasons he was not really sure of himself, he kept the entire matter of Calumet and the woman under wraps. In the end, he figured Calumet knew what he was getting himself into, and Rossetti trusted the agent's instincts. Besides, had the positions been reversed, Rossetti knew he would not have wanted any outside interference himself, not at this stage of the game.

Robert was waiting in the safe house when Calumet arrived. A different safe house than that of Team Interceptor. Robert had no intention of making Calumet aware of the team's existence.

Calumet came through the door looking like hell and feeling like hell. He rarely drank, but the night before, by his own calculations, he must have consumed eight or nine *Weissbiers*. Still, he was up with the sun this morning, knowing it was necessary for him to take special precautions in clearing his path before his meet with Robert. If the Russians spotted Robert, he might as well turn himself over to the marines and pray they could get him out safely. He left at 8:00, utilizing the full three hours to make sure he was clean before finally hoisting his feet up the steps and stumbling in.

"You look like hell," Robert confirmed it.

Calumet set Vartanyan's package on a table. "You got any Coca-Cola or something similar? You know, something carbonated?"

Robert nodded to one of his DOs, who disappeared into the kitchen. "What did you do last night?" he asked Calumet.

"I smoked some dope, shot some heroin, snorted four or five lines of coke. Things like that. What did *you* do last night?" He was incensed about the aborted meet in Grunewald Park and all its implications. He planned to have it out with his handler right here and now.

Robert refrained from smiling, though with some difficulty. One of his duties as handler was to continuously assess his agent's mental state. Whatever else Calumet might have been through, he conjectured, there was still plenty of fight left in him. A docile Calumet would be completely out of character, indicating something amiss, but that certainly wasn't the case at this point. *Good,* he thought.

"Tell me about that little fiasco in the park, Robert. And don't start in with me on how it was all a big mistake, I won't believe you."

The DO arrived with Calumet's Coke, which he attacked, guzzling most of it in one shot.

"Actually," Robert answered him, "that little fiasco in the park *was* a mistake. As I told you in Amsterdam, you were supposed to meet one of our men and go over all the details we discussed. Unfortunately, he stumbled onto the same situation as you when he showed up, so he hightailed it out of there, and properly so."

"Nuts." Calumet held his glass out for a refill, which the DO provided for him.

Robert shook his head, holding his hands out palms upward, as if this particular vein of dialogue was useless.

"Well I've got news for you, Robert. You and Armbrister both!" Calumet's tongue was sharp, angry. "You get the BND off my case, and you straighten all this crap out with whoever it is you knuckle-heads set me up with in the first place. Otherwise I'm taking a hike." Using the word, he suddenly remembered what Rossetti, the man with the ski mask, had said to him in the park, *Take a hike, pal.* "Oh, yeah! And who were those guys in the ski masks? Huh?"

"What are you talking about, Jack? What guys in ski masks?"

"You're not going to admit to a thing, are you, Robert?" Calumet was animated, his hands helping his mouth shape every word, his face red, partly from the anger and partly from the night before. "Fine. Keep your eyes on the damned airport then. Send every one of these guys in here out to Tegel or Tempelhof," referring to the other members of Robert's team. "If you look very carefully, you might see me on the next plane to the States."

Robert seemed thoughtful. His lips turned downward just then, frowning, as though he was suddenly concerned. "It's funny you should bring that up, Jack. The airport, I mean. Armbrister wants to pull you out anyway, in fact. Right now."

"What for?"

"He doesn't think you're up to it. Thinks maybe you're cracking."

"Armbrister is the one who's cracking. And maybe you too, Robert. I've been beating those GRU fairies all by myself for six years now. I don't need you and that desk-bound half-wit in Washington cooking up all kinds of crazy legends just to get me through this operation. I can get through this operation without any extracurricular assistance from someone who doesn't know squat about being undercover in the first place!" Then he turned to the DO and held his glass out again. "Just keep those Cokes coming until I tell you to stop. Okay?"

"Why did you beat my surveillance team yesterday?" Robert asked.

"Who were those clowns in the ski masks?" Quid pro quo.

"If you pull a stunt like that again, I won't be able to help you. It was all I could do to keep Armbrister from yanking you out of the lineup."

"Yeah? Well I've got something Armbrister can yank on."

"Let's go over your meet yesterday." Robert pointed to Vartanyan's package lying on the table. "Presumably, you were successful?"

"Presumably." Calumet was still intransigent.

"Did you meet with Filatov?"

"Yeah. At first."

"What does that mean?"

"It means I met with Filatov." Had it been anyone else, Calumet would have left his answer right there, hanging, but he and Robert had always shared a certain camaraderie, so he continued. "Then a real ringer took over and dismissed Filatov summarily. A guy by the name of Andrei Vartanyan. Colonel in the GRU. Or so he said. Very slick, very smart. And very cool."

"A tall man, dark hair? Handsome chap?"

"That's him."

Robert's demeanor took on a noticeable sobriety. "You've entered the dragon's lair, Jack. That's one brutal honcho, this Andrei Vartanyan. He goes by different names, as you can imagine, but he's infamous nevertheless. We've witnessed glimpses of him and his handiwork for years. He's Nishka's protégé, his right arm. We believe that this Vartanyan is responsible for the sadistic torture and barbarous death of our double in Ankara."

"He is," Calumet stated categorically, his eyes suddenly on fire, ready to explode.

Robert knew better than to question the validity of Calumet's information. However high-strung and unpredictable he might be, Calumet's intelligence had always been dead on the money. "Tell me about it," Robert said.

Calumet explained, then added. "For what it's worth, Robert, I'm going to even the score with that perverted assassin when this is all over."

Robert stared at Calumet, noting his agent's rectitude and tone of voice. He had never heard Jack say he was going to kill a man before. Standing there and witnessing Calumet's foreboding, even *he* felt a chill tingle down his spine. He asked, "You're going to kill a man because he said he was in Ankara when Conrad Thurman was killed?" Robert was probing, playing devil's advocate. He was concerned about his agent's motives. *Has this operation somehow become personal for Calumet?* he wondered.

"Conrad Thurman and his family were friends of mine, Robert. And don't give me any static about not having hard evidence that Vartanyan was involved. You just said yourself that you suspected Vartanyan."

Yes, Robert thought, *Odyssey has definitely become personal for him.* "Jack, listen," the controller sighed, his apprehension palpable. "I am truly sorry about what happened to Thurman. For what it's worth, we're looking after his family. We'll see that they want for nothing." He paused, inspecting Calumet. "Look, to be honest with you, Jack, I would also like to see Conrad's murderers brought to justice, probably just as much as you would in fact, but this operation is much more complex than you can possibly understand—"

"Then explain it to me," Calumet interrupted.

Robert suddenly became acerbic, stern, on the verge of losing his temper. "Let me tell you something, buster!" he exploded. "Neither myself nor Lewis Armbrister is engaged to this affair for the sake of one Jack Calumet. The national security of the United States and her vital interests are at stake here. You will be told what you need to know and nothing besides. Period! Is that clear?"

"Crystal!" Calumet snapped. He knew he had pushed too far.

"And you will do as you're told," Robert further asserted, "without forcing me to listen to your constant whining! Otherwise we'll be happy to put you on an airplane and fly you home ourselves. In handcuffs, if necessary. Got it?"

Calumet concluded that the best he could come away with on this exchange was no acknowledgment whatsoever. Even though he felt abused due to Robert's refusal to enlighten him on certain matters, he privately wanted to see this operation through to its conclusion. He remained silent, meeting Robert's gaze head-on.

"You are not to take any action against Vartanyan short of saving your own life. Understood?"

"Perfectly!" Then to the DO again; "I told you to keep those Cokes coming."

The DO glanced at Robert, who nodded, and quickly went after another refill.

"What's in the package?" Robert asked.

Seemingly unfazed by the dressing-down, Calumet went into complete detail about his meet with Vartanyan, carefully reconstructing the entire scenario with remarkable clarity. Robert rarely interrupted, asking only four or five questions throughout Calumet's lengthy discourse.

When Calumet was finished, Robert said, "You did well, Jack. Very well. Not many can hold their own against Vartanyan." Then his tone softened, becoming as friendly as he could manage without being sloppy. "That's why you were chosen for this operation, Jack. Armbrister felt you were one of the few people who could pull it off. If it's any consolation, I disagree. I think you're the *only* agent we've got that can see this thing through." He smiled.

Characteristically, Calumet said, "Spare me the pep talk, Robert. Where do we go from here?"

Robert pointed to Vartanyan's package lying on the table. He had been careful not to handle it. "Pick that up. You have another meet to attend."

Calumet handed his glass to the DO, then collected the package. "Well, are you going to make me try and guess it? Or do I *need* to know who I'm meeting? Presumably, I *will* have to know the location, if that's not asking too much. Or have you got a limo and a chauffeur waiting out front?"

"Jack, as I mentioned, this operation is much more complex than you can imagine. If you want to throw in the towel, nobody will blame you. I told you in Frankfurt that you've served your country very proudly for the past six years. *You* insisted on pursuing this. Remember?"

Calumet nodded.

"Contrivances have been fabricated—schemes, machinations, which you are not, *cannot*, be made aware of at this point. Perplexing intrigues, but very necessary. You can't possibly see it now, but there are viable reasons for all of the subterfuge. Very good reasons. This is not a simple matter of funneling disinformation to the Russians anymore. It goes much further than that."

"I know," Calumet said sourly. "You're after a mole."

"It goes even further than that, Jack."

And that single cryptic admission, perhaps, was the greatest adumbrate of the whole affair to date, Jack thought. Robert would allow nothing further, even when pressed. In fact, it appeared as though the controller regretted making the statement at all, but made it he had, and now Calumet was totally mystified. *Odyssey goes further than ferreting out a mole? What in blazes is going on?*

"Maybe you should go home to Diane, Jack," Robert advised. He said it sincerely.

"You know me better than that."

Robert frowned, his face dispirited. "Yes, unfortunately, I *do* know you better than that." He sighed. "My friend," and he put his hand on Calumet's shoulder, "it is unlikely that we'll meet again. For a while at least. From now on, your communications with us will be made through Steve. That's who you're meeting with today at four o'clock. In the *Tiergarten.* Near the *Grosser Stern,* but across the street, in the park. He'll make contact with you there. Give him the package. Play it out all the way, go through all the motions. You won't be tripped up in your debriefings with Vartanyan that way." Robert removed his hand, and for the first time since Calumet had known him, Robert seemed at a loss for words.

"Jack," the controller continued after a moment, "you can pull out at any time, no hard feelings and no loss of face. I want you to understand that. It's still your choice. But I also want you to understand that if you continue, you may be approaching the point of no return. Are you with me on this?"

"Sure."

"And . . ." Robert hesitated again, struggling with his emotions. "Well, just be careful. Okay?"

Calumet saw it in Robert's eyes. Unwanted betrayal. Sacrifice. As if his handler's eyes reflected the searching soul of Abraham crying out to God to spare his only son, knowing that if the grace failed to flow, it was by his own hand that Isaac would die. And, strangely, Calumet felt a twinge of sorrow, but not for himself. He felt Robert's guilt, and it made him uncomfortable.

"You worry like an old lady." Calumet's tone was upbeat, attempting to soothe.

Robert stuck out his hand. Calumet couldn't ever remember shaking hands with his controller, except possibly when they had first been introduced. Nevertheless, he accepted the proffered hand, tenuously at first, wondering why Robert was making the gesture, then firmly, and they shook.

Calumet walked to the door and turned around. "I'm still going to *do* that sadistic honcho when this is all over," he vowed, a final assertion of his own irrepressibility. Before Robert could respond, he quickly opened the door and disappeared, slamming it behind him.

CHAPTER 14

Steve Phillips was continuing to have a tough time of it. He'd done a lousy job of clearing his path. The Russians picked him up outside the American consulate and managed to stay with him all the way. By the time he arrived at the *Grosser Stern* for his rendezvous with Calumet, the Russians had the meet cold; telephoto, directional surveillance, the works. They even had a lip reader on station in case the directional fouled up or, for one reason or another, could not be applied.

Calumet was leaning against a tree, the package under his arm, when Steve approached.

Steve knew the Russians were watching and probably listening. He acted quickly to set the stage. "Well, you don't look much worse for the wear since three or four days ago in Frankfurt, Jack."

"Hi, Steve," Calumet responded, taking the hint, playing along. "I've got some hot stuff for you. It's going to cost you, though."

"What have you got, Jack?" Steve's manner seemed cold, wary.

"DEFSMAC. The Russians are interested in DEFSMAC."

"Oh? Did Filatov expound on it? The particulars of DEFSMAC, I mean?"

Good, Calumet thought. *He's opening it up for me, giving me latitude. The Russians, if they're watching, will be able to ascertain that I'm not compromising their players.* "No, Filatov made no reference to it, really. Just see what I could find out, he told me. Same as usual."

"Was anyone besides Filatov present at your meet?" A cursory debriefing.

"Nope. Just me and Georgi."

"Where did you meet?"

"Marx-Engels Platz." Anywhere but the truth, Calumet thought, knowing that Robert already had it all anyway.

"Did they ask you when you could deliver?"

"No, I told them it would be a while. I'm to remain in Berlin and wait for them to contact me. They'll reach me on a daily basis starting two days from now, until you give me something to fire back at them."

"Were you in Grunewald Park the other night?" Steve inquired suddenly, a touch of accusation in his voice.

"No," Calumet answered angrily, not acting. He was still indignant about Armbrister's fabrication of his legend and the debacle in the park. "Why?"

"Because if you're involved in drugs, Calumet, the CIA may not be able to step in and bail you out. There's too much heat coming out of Washington about drugs right now, national security considerations aside."

"I'm not involved in drugs," Calumet said testily. He knew Armbrister was up to something here, plying another strategy, but he couldn't figure out what.

"Well, if you are, you better lay low for a while. Those DEA people are a bunch of cowboys. We have very little influence with them these days. If they get onto you, don't look to us for assistance. Just a friendly warning."

Calumet was concerned. He wondered how far they were going to take this cockamamie legend, this beclouding ruse of his involvement in the drug trade, and why. To what purpose, exactly?

Suddenly Steve produced a thick envelope and handed it to him. "Your usual," he said, a conspiratorial gleam in his eye, sending a message, the first of many lifelines.

Calumet exchanged the package for the envelope.

"Just sit tight then," Steve said. "You're staying at the Kempi?"

"Yes."

"Fine. But in case you need to get in touch with me, call the American consulate and ask for me directly. You'll find a secure number and a list of fallbacks in the envelope. Just in case. In the meantime, I'll run with your package and get back to you as soon as possible."

Before Calumet could speak, Steve lit out, walking away rapidly.

Calumet remained for several minutes, discreetly counting his money. The envelope contained $10,000. A sum far too large. *What are they doing to me?* he wondered. *And why?*

*

Vartanyan cabled Nishka immediately after the tapes had been transcribed and translated into Russian. The originals were on their way to Moscow by special diplomatic courier. In the meantime, Nishka spoke with Vartanyan on a secure line.

"They're suspicious of him, Comrade Nishka. They are convinced he's involved in the drug trade."

"And what is your assessment, Andrei?"

"It could go either way with this one, comrade. I cannot read him. He's either the shrewdest creature I've ever laid eyes on, or he's merely a double who's gotten in too deeply. I just can't tell. Steve Phillips, his handler, is concerned about it, though. He pointedly admonished him."

So the Teflon double was about to incur a scratch? Nishka thought. *And that scratch was possibly going to come by the hands of his own people?* Nishka made a snap decision. "Watch out for him, Andrei. If he is really a target of the American DEA, protect him, keep him out of their way. Keep your ear to the ground with our German friends in the BND. I want him operational for the time being."

"Not to worry, comrade. I'll handle it."

"I know you will, Andrei. You always do."

*

"DEFSMAC? Are you sure it's DEFSMAC?" Armbrister asked anxiously, speaking to Robert over their own secure line.

"Positive."

"Perfect!" the DDO exclaimed. "Nishka has taken the bait, Robert. Now let's see if we can get him to swallow the hook. What about Rossetti?"

"Our psychologists might have hit the jackpot with Rossetti. His disenchantment with the military and all. He took off on his own yesterday. I'm almost positive he was keeping tabs on Calumet. He respects him."

"How do you read the risk at this point?"

"I'm not sure. I think, for the time being, we have to give Rossetti all the rope he wants."

"Well, keep a close eye on it, Robert. Cut him off if you have the slightest doubt."

"Lewis," Robert protested, "Rossetti may be the only one who can keep Calumet alive, depending. I've got to let him run."

"Like I said, Robert, if the integrity of Odyssey is at stake, cut him off. How is Calumet?"

"Like a cornered wolverine. He's hot."

"Yes, well, you know what I mean, Robert. Can he take the heat? Can he bear up? We've been friends for thirty years. Don't give me your feelings, old friend. We're at ground zero now. Can Calumet pull it off?"

"If anybody can handle it, Lewis, Calumet can."

"Then make it happen, Robert."

Robert's concern was evident in his hesitation.

"It's the only way, old friend," Armbrister confided. "You know that."

"Yes," Robert reluctantly agreed. "I know."

"Look," Armbrister said. "He went into this with his eyes open. It's his play, and he's a grown man."

Robert preserved the silence. *Maybe I'm too involved myself,* he thought.

"Do it," Armbrister commanded. "Set Calumet in motion."

"Okay," Robert sighed heavily. "Consider it done. And may God help him."

*

Calumet sauntered through the front doors of the Kempinski, tired, confused, angry, and yet committed. The hook was set in his own mouth, regardless of what might ultimately befall him. He knew he was the rueful scapegoat in a twisted operation he nevertheless found himself compelled to untangle, constrained to a mystery that must be unwound. And through it all, regardless, he felt strangely oppressed, enveloped by a sinister cloud of impending danger. He was wired, tuned in, yet his instincts were wreaking havoc with his paranoia.

Making his way to the elevators, Calumet suddenly detected that all-too-familiar prickly sensation on the back of his neck again. This time he made no effort to conceal his alarm. He whirled around with such frenzy that the concierge and other guests milling about were momentarily startled. And he saw—or thought he saw, in the dimness across the lobby—the bare leg and sandaled foot of a slender woman in a flowing white robe disappearing around the corner. He couldn't make out the face as it was already beyond the wall, but the hair, he thought, was dark. Very dark. Raven, in fact.

Ignoring the bystanders, who had obviously concluded by now that he was mental, he strode rapidly across the lobby. He turned the corner and froze, his heart beating loudly. But he was highly disappointed. The hallway was empty. And the prickly sensation had all but evaporated. Vanished.

As is often the case in life, it is the odd quirks which sometimes chart the course and steer the rudder, blindly redirecting the tributaries and byways that shape the events of human souls and, ultimately, history. Perhaps, could it ever be analyzed, it was this last little happenstance—the prickly sensation, the empty hallway—that circumscribed Calumet's orbit and forged his iron. And perhaps, if such abstruse slices of time could ever be recorded or set to print in a case history or a tome, the transcendental occurrence in the Bristol Hotel Kempinski this spring day might possibly go down as the defining moment of the entire operation, operation Odyssey, as it was rightfully known. Without a doubt, it was upon the fulcrum of this singular, mystical moment that Calumet turned the corner inside, his mind resolute, forming, plotting, conspiring, drafting an autonomous blueprint, unfleshed, and alighting upon an operational campaign completely of his own design. *The point of no return,* Robert had forewarned, hinting at its proximate arrival.

But Calumet was already there. He had, if not yet physically, mentally reached that point—his point of no return. Though unaware exactly of what was in store, he sensed its sullen flavor, its hot breath licking at his soul, and he closed with it, the battle joined. The Americans on one side, about to betray him—though he didn't really know that yet, hadn't fully come to terms with it yet, but the scent was on the wind, a delicate touch of thunder in its wake, rumbling around and tickling his instincts—the Russians on the other, each using him, playing him, pulling his strings, without regard it seemed, all for their own gain. Jack Calumet in the middle. And he suddenly thought of what Vartanyan had said, his enemy to be sure, and how unforgiving becomes the irony when a truth is spoken by the devil. *A man without a country,* the Russian had remarked. *How true,* Calumet pondered. *All of a sudden, how sad and how true.*

Calumet took the elevator down to the pool. "*Guten Tag,* Hans," he greeted.

"Herr Calumet," Hans smiled. "An *Orangensaft?*"

"No thanks, Hans. Have you seen Karola?"

"Hmm. No, not since yesterday." Then Hans adopted the locker-room mentality, remarking conspiratorially about her sybaritic qualities, but Calumet had no interest in that, not at the moment. He excused himself and departed.

If not Karola, who was it? he asked himself. *Or maybe she just didn't go to the pool.*

He ordered room service, and after it arrived, locked himself in his room, calling it a night. Two days until his next meet with Vartanyan, he reminded himself. *But tomorrow,* he thought, *tomorrow I will embark upon the fight of my life.*

CHAPTER 15

Jim Eldridge, the DEA's country attaché, left Bonn and arrived at the safe house in Berlin at 7:00 P.M. He had been ordered by the Administrator of Drug Enforcement in Washington to aid and assist to the fullest extent. Robert was waiting for him, cautiously optimistic that the attaché possessed the tact and skill to finesse the Mansfield Amendment with his German counterparts in the BND. Among other things, the Mansfield Amendment precluded the DEA from effecting arrests and interrogations on foreign soil. Their meeting lasted an hour.

*

The following morning Jack arose early and felt rejuvenated, the day's itinerary fresh upon his mind. But he had to move fast. His intuition was warning him, prodding him, whispering that he was racing the clock.

Ensuring that he wasn't being followed, he made his way to the Hotel Berlin on Lützowplatz and took a room. He let them imprint his credit card—his *real* credit card, the one which bore his own name—confiding that he planned to stay about a week, maybe longer. He then repeated this process with three other establishments, the Seehof on the Lietzensee in the residential area of Charlottenburg, the Achat in Spandau, and the Hotel am Zoo near the Hauptbahnhof. Along the way, he purchased toiletries and placed them in each room in order to make them look occupied. Not that he thought he was fooling anybody, really; he was just muddying the waters. If the DEA or the BND or anybody else ran him through their computers, they would be obligated to send someone to check out the locations in person, forcing them to expend time and manpower, spreading themselves thin. Still, that wasn't enough, Jack concluded.

To further complicate matters, Calumet left a German driving license in the dresser drawer of the room he had procured at the Achat. The license bore the name of Reiner Kästner, which was one of the light legends he had purchased from De Boeck in Brussels. If things got nasty and they decided to come after him the hard way, they just might assume he had forgotten the license in his haste to evade capture. In turn, that might lead them to believe that he was in possession of a matching passport and was now traveling under that particular alias. Of course, he wouldn't be. If it worked at all, it would throw them off his scent only for a short time, but that might make all the difference in the world. Other than the money he was forking out for the rooms, his cost was one burned identity. He now had only two left.

After completing these tasks, he located a travel agency off the Ku'damm and made reservations on the evening flight to Zürich. Again in his own name. Again another red herring. *Just keep them hopping,* he told himself. Then he located yet another travel agency and made reservations on the night flight to Paris, this time under the name of Reiner Kästner. Depending upon how far they carried this little charade, they could chase that ghost for a while. He smiled to himself when he remembered that even Robert knew nothing of his excursion to Brussels and his business with De Boeck.

Next, after changing some of the money given him by Steve, Jack went shopping. He purchased clothes and more toiletries, and then a suitcase which he filled with his new acquisitions. His shopping complete, he proceeded to a seedy hotel off the Ku'damm where he registered under the name of Karl Hahn. The name was just something he picked out of thin air. This particular hotel did not concern itself with the identity of its patrons. As long as they paid up front, that is, and agreed that it was unnecessary to complain about the amenities, or, more accurately, the lack of them. Calumet tendered cash in advance for two days, reasoning that he might have to move, and anyway, obtaining longer terms would only arouse suspicion due in large part to the caliber of the establishment's customary clientele. He deposited his suitcase in what could barely be considered an excuse for a room and left.

It was 3:00 when Calumet finally returned to the Kempi. He approached the hotel like a ranger on a jungle recon, but not really knowing why. He simply sensed peril as he neared, and the feeling of imminent danger galvanized his innate disposition for caution. He stood across the Ku'damm for a full twenty minutes, observing. Spotting nothing untoward, he then walked across the street and circled the hotel casually. Everything appeared to be in order. No undercover cars in the vicinity that he could tell. Then again, detecting undercover cars was such an inexact science that the exercise itself was practically useless, but you never knew when someone was going to be careless. Even a cop. He stood just around the corner for another ten minutes, noting specifically the bellhops marching in and out, loading and unloading luggage. Having committed their faces to memory over the past two days, he recognized them all. Not an impostor in the flock. And the thought suddenly struck him: *Why am I acting like a criminal?* His inner voice screaming back the answer: *Because they're about to set you up.* And his soul crying out, *Why? Did I do something wrong? Something I'm not aware of?*

Calumet entered the lobby of the Kempi warily. He took two steps inside before arresting himself on the spot, like a gunslinger swaggering into a saloon and spoiling for a fight. He slowly scanned the vestibule's ambit, evaluating everyone his eyes beheld. Satisfied all was as it should be, he walked to the elevator bank and waited, again panning the area. His concentration was so intense that the bell startled him when it finally sounded the lift's impending arrival. He entered, pressed the button to the fourth floor, and then watched the doors slide together, shutting off his view.

As the elevator began to chug away, the reservationist at the back desk turned and spoke into the office door behind him, "He just went up."

The young BND agent stepped out. Glancing at his watch, the rookie wondered, *Where are they?*

The DEA had earlier disclosed to the young agent's superiors that an informant they were cultivating had tipped them off to an American citizen staying at the Kempinski who might possibly be trafficking in heroin. However, the DEA persisted, they'd very much appreciate it if the BND would allow them to pursue their investigation sub-rosa, intimating that there were bigger fish to fry. Absolutely, the BND remarked, no problem. What can we do for you? Well, the DEA assured the Germans, we don't need any heavyweights for this one; not right now. Perhaps if the BND would be kind enough to provide a complementary official to assist them with their probable cause, the DEA sort of said, they might just take a quick peek inside the gentleman's room. This exercise, the DEA then rapidly propounded, owing to the sensitivities of German constitutional law, would simply be an endeavor to corroborate and substantiate the efficacy of our informant's information, you understand. Of course, the BND sympathized. We understand completely, though in reality the BND was a bit suspicious of the DEA's sudden good manners, not fully comprehending why these cowboys were actually asking permission to toss a room. At any rate, the deal had been arranged, and the young agent was now waiting for the DEA lads to show up, but they were late. Strangely. No matter, the young BND agent thought. He was about to make his first of three mistakes this day.

Taking the decision to handle this matter himself, without backup, he headed for the elevators.

*

Vartanyan was nervous. He had received the intelligence only an hour ago. He wasn't sure he would be in time. The blond GRU officer was stationed across the Ku'damm, leaning against an automobile, its engine running, while Vartanyan and three associates were farther down. They were hoarding a clear view of the Kempinski's facade, evaluating the scene. Vartanyan suddenly noticed two rugged-looking men climbing the steps to the Kempinski's entrance. Probably DEA. He nodded to two of his assets and they immediately began walking briskly toward the hotel, about fifty yards behind the Americans. Each carried a small radio concealed in his jacket. Vartanyan sent the other GRU officer around the side to cover one of the hotel's auxiliary exits.

The GRU spotter was already in the Kempi's lobby, scanning a newspaper. Unknown to him, however, he had arrived only seconds after the BND man disappeared into the elevator. He had no idea that the BND was already on the way up. Attempting to get a handle on the situation, he suddenly observed the DEA agents enter, and made them immediately. They gave themselves away by the hard look in their eyes, the inimitable awareness in their disposition, and the loose shirts. Too loose, almost. They took a position on the far side of the lobby, away from the elevators. *That's curious,* the GRU spotter thought. A moment later the two Russians entered, glancing quickly at the spotter, who gave them a most imperceptible shake of the head, more with his eyes than anything else. *Hold,* he was telling them. The two men strode to the sitting area and relaxed, as if they were waiting for a guest.

*

The first thing that caught Calumet's eye when he entered his room was the protrusion of his suitcase from the closet. He hadn't left it that way. And the chambermaids at the Kempinski wouldn't have left it that way, either. He kept the door slightly ajar, knowing he was about to make a fast exit.

The only thing Calumet wasn't sure of was what kind of drug it would be. He knew by now what was happening, could sense it effortlessly. Heroin, coke, hashish? Probably heroin, he thought, since that was the particular poison Vartanyan had questioned him about at Alexanderplatz, the Russian being fed, no doubt, by his own German source. Calumet wasn't even angry at this point. His instincts had been forewarning him all day, whispering to him that it was coming.

He opened the suitcase and there it was. Heroin. A brick.

He trod quickly to the window and peered outside. Had he given the scenery more than a cursory glance, or had he been looking for something other than police, he might have noticed Vartanyan, but he missed him. At first. Then he did a double take. *What in blazes is he doing here?* Jack thought. However, this was no time for speculation. He had to move. Fast. But he didn't; he entertained an impetuous notion instead.

"Screw it!" he said out loud. He ripped his jacket off, then his shirt, and then yanked his favorite garment out of his suitcase—the blue, green, and red flannel pullover which could be worn tucked in or out—donned it, then the jacket again. *No way the shysters are going to get my favorite shirt,* he thought, obviously a spy with an attitude.

That's when the door crashed open.

*

Rossetti and Kramer strode into the Kempinski. *Make sure he gets away,* Robert had ordered. The third and fourth members of Team Interceptor had taken positions outside, on the street, covering the action, waiting. They'd know when to move, if necessary. Neither was aware of Vartanyan, and Vartanyan wasn't aware of them. The fifth commando, Alex Yardley, was already on the fourth floor. He occupied the room across the hall from Calumet.

Rossetti and Kramer had been cooling their heels in the Kempinski Eck restaurant for most of the afternoon. They had seen the BND agent enter thirty minutes earlier, but quickly sized him up and decided Calumet could handle the young German without assistance when he arrived. If not, Yardley was nearby. Rossetti then *made* the blond GRU agent across the Ku-damm—the same one who had paid off the hoods—and Kramer had spotted the DEA agents and the two Russian GRU officers as they turned the corner and headed inside. Rossetti and Kramer had then paid their bill at the Eck and followed them in, fully aware that the DEA agents had no arrest authority here in Berlin, but nevertheless were concerned that the drug agents might forget about such trivialities if the situation became heated. The two commandos moved into the vicinity of the elevators and pretended to engage in conversation.

This sudden convergence of rough traders in the Kempinski's lobby might have alarmed the management in a smaller hotel, but the Kempinski's lobby was a sprawling affair, huge and always populated, so the presence of seven additional men went basically unnoticed by the staff and other guests. To the untrained eye, it was business as usual. However, as he stood there, poised, Rossetti was thinking to himself, *We may have to intervene against the Russians if they move against the DEA boys.* That worried him. Rick Rossetti wasn't about to allow fellow Americans to be harmed by Russian thugs, critical operation or not. *Then again,* he thought, noting the ruggedness of the DEA agents, *the Russians may be the ones who need the assistance.*

*

"Bundesnachrichtendienst! Halt!" the German shouted, his gun drawn and pointing at Calumet's chest. The second mistake the young BND agent made was extending his weapon, arms stretched out, so that it was within Calumet's reach. The third mistake was averting

his eyes momentarily when he heard the sound of an opening door across the hallway.

In the very instant that the German averted his eyes, Calumet sprang. He slammed the heel of his right hand into the cartilage of the BND agent's nose while simultaneously launching his left hand like a rocket and twisting the gun counterclockwise, tearing it from the German's grasp. The BND agent went down like a sack of potatoes. Calumet cocked his right hand instinctively, in preparation for a blow to the agent's temple, but arrested his motion. If delivered too hard, the blow could kill the man. Calumet just wanted him immobilized, unconscious. So he cold-cocked the agent with a right cross to the chin. The agent's lights went out completely.

Jack quickly kicked the door shut, and then wondered why he'd done it. He needed to go out, not remain locked inside. Possibly it was a subconscious reaction to the noise that had distracted the BND agent. An arcane thought passed through his mind just then, reminding him that in the movies the hero always discarded the gun. Stupid. Asinine. Calumet stuffed the BND agent's gun into his pants in the small of his back, underneath his jacket and shirt. He peered through the peephole in the door. Nothing—at least not as far as his restricted vision was able to discern.

Conducting a final survey of his room, Calumet eased the door open and stepped out. *The stairs or the elevator?* Then he noticed another man, young, fit, waiting by the lift. Calumet concluded that acting normal was his best course of action. He joined the man, strongly sensing that he was more than just a guest.

"Guten Tag," Yardley smiled.

No way! Calumet thought. *He may be speaking another language, but he's definitely American.* Had anyone asked him how he knew, Jack would have said he couldn't explain it; he could just tell. He nodded curtly in response to the man's greeting.

The elevator arrived and they entered, Calumet allowing Yardley to go first. Neither man spoke for most of the way down. The light rested upon the button designating the third floor, then the second.

Suddenly Jack nurtured a growing suspicion. He said casually, "That was quite a show you guys put on in Grunewald Park the other night."

Yardley acted the debutante. *"Bitte?"*

Calumet was pondering how to pursue it when the light flickered, illuminating the first-floor button. As the doors were just beginning to slide open, Yardley suddenly mastered his command of the English language. "Watch out for the woman, Jack," he said abruptly. Then he walked briskly away.

Calumet didn't immediately make the connection. *What woman?* He assumed the man was talking about a female BND agent who might possibly be waiting for him as he stepped out of the elevator. But as he entered the lobby, he saw quickly that there was no woman—not an *official* woman, anyway. Only men. Hard men. He noticed Rossetti and Kramer, though they had moved off a bit, and he certainly didn't know exactly who they were, albeit he knew they were *somebody*—somebody besides hotel guests; that much was evident. He also recognized the GRU crowd. They had been in Alexanderplatz the other day. And then he spotted the two DEA agents, far away, on the other side of the lobby. They were staring straight at him, and not as though he might have been a long-lost friend. Yardley glided up to the counter and began engaging the desk clerk in conversation.

Calumet had no time to stand there and try to figure it all out. He walked purposefully but unhurriedly toward the front doors. *If I wasn't a criminal before, I am now. I just assaulted a Federal German agent.*

Nobody else moved. The DEA agents just stood there, continuing to stare. Rossetti and Kramer maintained a discreet watch on the Russians, who were maintaining a discreet watch on the DEA. There was a perceptible tension in the air until Calumet effected his exit, disappearing quietly through the front entrance, gratefully causing all the players to breathe a little easier.

Then it happened. Suddenly pandemonium reigned as the elevator doors opened, revealing the bloodied face of the BND agent. The gruesome sight elicited a chorus of gasps and a few muffled screams from the truly innocent bystanders in the lobby.

Once outside, Calumet noted the blond GRU agent waving frantically, beckoning him to approach. Vartanyan, whom he had spotted earlier, was now nowhere in sight. Calumet briefly weighed his options. He reluctantly considered the undesirable: the fact that the blond Russian—the same GRU officer who had held the photo album for him—just might be his best bet at the moment. A cab was no good. They would trace him so fast it would make his head spin. And the *U-bahn* or *S-bahn* was too confining. The Germans could arrange to have people stationed at every stop within a matter of minutes. As far as Calumet was concerned, these conclusions pretty much narrowed his alternatives.

And then there was also the other consideration, one which made him shudder. By now Calumet had begun to glean a subtle shimmering of insight into Armbrister's scheme. Armbrister and Robert were purposely attempting to drive him into the arms of the Russians. They were orchestrating circumstances designed to force him into the only available avenue of safety, an avenue that led straight to Moscow, like Apaches driving a herd of stallions into an arroyo.

Suddenly Calumet became enraged. *Okay, boys, it's time to rock and roll. Set me up and won't tell me why? Fine! I'm going to turn this whole operation inside out!* He made up his mind to accommodate the blond GRU officer. That was the only acceptable alternative at this point. He'd just begun to walk rapidly across the Ku'damm when the sharp toot of a BMW horn almost caused him to jump out of his skin. He glanced to his left and saw Karola waving to him, a smile on her lips and mirrored sunglasses repelling the glare of the sun, as though she had just happened to be driving by, apparently oblivious to the undercurrents raging all around, completely separated from the activities of the BND, the DEA, and the spooks. Calumet suddenly felt very much relieved, knowing now that he wasn't going to be forced to accept the Russian's hospitality. He ran over to Karola's car, jerked the door open, and jumped in.

"Hello, Karola," Jack said serendipitously. "What's for dinner?"

PART THREE

CALUMET'S RUN

CHAPTER 16

The GRU spotter understood his orders. His AO—area of operation—was the hotel's interior. Once Calumet was outside, his responsibilities were concluded. He folded his newspaper under his arm and headed for the Kempinski Eck. The remaining two GRU officers would pretend to chat a moment longer, each glancing once or twice at his watch to show everybody that his appointment was late, and then leave. Rossetti and Kramer had dispersed within seconds of Calumet's departure.

As soon as the DEA agents saw the bloodied face of the BND man in the elevator, they started walking rapidly toward him. The BND agent rushed over to the front desk and began barking out orders. When the two DEA men came up his eyes shot daggers at them, as though he was accusing them, partly for being late and partly for his own stupidity. He would never know that the two men, although not comprehending why, were themselves under orders to make *sure* that they were late. In fact, they, like Rossetti and Kramer, had been cooling their heels in a small café off the Ku'-damm awaiting a telephone call before ever proceeding to the Kempinski in the first place. Furthermore, if their quarry got physical, they were correspondingly under orders to let the drug trafficker escape. It would have been a small consolation to the BND agent, but those orders didn't sit well with either one of them.

*

"Nice sunglasses, Karola," Calumet complimented her. "Drive. I'm trying to elude the bad guys."

The car was rolling before Calumet had finished his sentence, flowing with the traffic. "Are you kidnapping me?" she teased.

"Absolutely. I'm a Neanderthal at heart." He was working the side mirror furiously with his eyes.

"You're probably just running away from an angry husband," Karola continued, the glint in her pupils implying that she approved of such behavior, but her tone casual, as though she didn't really think he was running away from anything at all. She turned off the Ku'damm and headed toward Potsdam.

The turn was a welcome maneuver, advancing Calumet a small dose of relief. Yet he remained slightly disoriented. He still considered Potsdam enemy territory, seeing as how the Russians used to own it. "Nope. An angry wife," he countered. "Me and the husband had something going."

Karola laughed. "I know my men, Mr. Calumet, and I don't believe you." Her laugh regressed into a wide smile, the gloss on her lips, an understated shade of pink, inviting sinfulness. She leaned over and kissed his cheek, then added lightly, "I'm so glad I bumped into you."

He looked at her, a specter of uncertainty in his glance.

"I never felt I thanked you properly," she explained. "I shook all night thinking about what might have happened had you not come along."

"Kismet," Calumet said. "It's Kismet, Karola. You don't question that, you accept it. If it's good, that is. If it's bad, well, then you try to work something out." But as he spoke he was thinking about his two encounters with this sultry lady, and it made him wonder. *What are the odds that two virtually unattached coincidences would bring the two of us together in as many days? Watch out for the woman, Jack, the man had said. Did he mean Karola? How would he know, whoever he is?*

"Actually," Jack fished, "I tried to catch you in the lobby yesterday when I noticed you walking down the hallway, but I missed you." He watched her intently for a reaction.

"Yesterday? Hmm. No, I wasn't in Berlin at all yesterday."

If she's lying, it comes naturally to her. "Oh well, I thought it was you. Maybe it was Miss Germany instead. Or Miss Universe." He smiled. "That would certainly be an easy mistake to make." *Hans said he hadn't seen her, either.*

"Oh, my. Now I'll have to be sure to bring out the *good* bottle of wine tonight. *Such* a compliment deserves a proper reward." She batted her eyelashes in an exaggerated fashion, pouting playfully and acting the coquette.

"I'm definitely worth it."

"We'll see about that," she challenged.

They bantered back and forth for thirty minutes, sparring, laughing, joking. Calumet's eyes labored like a pinball machine the entire way, bouncing off the side mirror, the rear window, her, and even the car ashtray to see what kind of person, if any kind, might have hitched a ride with this fiery damsel, a damsel who had probably apportioned much more distress to the lives of men than she would ever need rescuing from. But the ashtray was factory clean.

They entered her home, she leading the way, blazing a path, Jack thought, which presented two forks, either freedom or bondage, and freedom only if you turned around and left this minute. He wondered how many souls had been lured into and seduced upon the web of her spidery domain—for a domain it was, very much evident in the decor, on the one hand plush, but also lived in and comfortable. Her furniture appeared to be arranged for hedonistic pleasures rather than magazine centerfolds, situated about the tenement so that there was space enough for one guest at a time, not more. A bookshelf lined an entire wall in the living room, stocked to the brim. That surprised him because he hadn't pegged her as a scholar, though she was certainly intelligent. No family pictures anywhere in sight, or pictures of friends. Calumet thought this unusual as well. But the colors were chipper and lively, as he expected, so he got that part right at least. And he just knew her bed had to have a canopy, but he was wrong again as she escorted him from room to room, showing off her housekeeping. The house defined her somewhat, if such a woman could ever be easily defined.

The kitchen itself was Americanized, with breakfast bar and a pair of stools, the high-backed kind with miniature Doric columns sprouting up from the seat and spiraling into the entablature. They settled on the stools after she opened the Moselle from Koblenz and insisted that it breathe a bit, her European ancestry commanding on this point, and their knees grazed each other's while they sipped from carved crystal goblets, the grazing itself mostly one-sided, her sensual inclinations taking charge on that one. She was into her first refill and getting close to her second when she momentarily got dismayed and asked him why he had barely lowered the watermark on his own glass, but found great encouragement when he replied with his grin that the night was still very young, and what about dinner, since she'd promised and he'd accepted. And he made her laugh by reminding her. But she harnessed her own power, too, and she made him long for its essence, tempting his soul—or some part of him, her raven hair dancing all around, impetuous, spontaneous, responding wildly to every delicate motion of her vitalized figure, the Scandinavian lips glistening upon every uttered word, and those that weren't uttered, only implied, and he thought of home, his girlfriend, and why the hell was he here. It all seemed so surreal. And then he remembered why, sharply, a wee nightmare forming out of nothing, a macabre replay of the Big Bang, suddenly self-propelling, growing stronger, like he was locked into a limbo, and the nightmare was *really* all too real. And somehow just beginning.

She prepared what she called a "Ukrainian cuisine," referring to it with so many syllables that he couldn't quite get a fix on what she said exactly, and didn't care to make her repeat it. Whatever she called it, it was heavy on the cabbage and sparsely populated with stewed beef, and surprisingly very good. He watched her intently as she sailed from pot to pan, delimiting her every move, albeit not sexually motivated in his observation, though it would have been extremely easy at this point to begin feeling sorry for himself and let the chips fall where they may. He had been betrayed by his own, and even though he realized it had been done for the greater good, *he* was still the one who was now being forced to live it, and Robert had been recalcitrant in his disclosures. For all Jack could fathom, he was being sacrificed, and he didn't even know why. Yes, it would be easy for him to take solace in the arms of this exquisite woman, regardless of how temporal her comfort might be.

But Calumet had something else in mind. Any woman as rapacious as this one, he figured, *had* to have demons tugging at her insides, and those kind were usually survivors, for whatever else might be gleaned from her biography, one thing was certain: she had survived Stalin's legacy and had emerged from a brutal East Berlin to take her place in the new order, and she was evidently doing well. Something told him he could use this woman.

They chaffed lightly through dinner, though she forced him to deflect a stray innuendo now and then, and his deflection, in turn, only forced *her* to try harder. There were also times, he noted—several of them, really—when she was able to coerce an acrobatic routine from her tongue, nimbly performed, but the overtures were not *too* brazen. He thought, *Sex . . . that's the only way she knows how to fight.* At any rate, with each passing moment, his suspicion of her grew.

He saw in her a hardness of spirit, a woman who not only had the power but the callousness to use people like a paring knife, carving their emotions into brittle little pieces, men especially, ensnaring them with the sheer magnetism of her physical perfection, then discarding them when she was finished and never giving it a second thought. He speculated that at some tragic crossroads in her life she had lost her innocence, all of it, and that somehow she had been spiritually reduced to such a state that redemption for her was forever unattainable. And the more she performed, the more he analyzed. He ultimately assessed the embodiment of her existence and concluded it was purely predatory, and that all she ever left in her wake was desolation, evident in the broken lives of those she'd suborned and inveigled through the narcosis of her sexual elixirs. In the end, he decided, she was nothing less than a grievous catastrophe, because through every morsel of cabbage and every sip of wine, her rapid-fire seductive arrows, rather than hitting their mark, provoked antipodal feelings in Jack Calumet, merely causing him to pity her that much more, and to think of her as a beggared vixen whose only reward in life would be a cold death and whatever material inducements she might manage to hang onto between now and then. A woman *full* of spirit, he judged, but without a soul.

He offered to help her with the plates, but she said no with a warm smile, and their voices fell silent for the first time all evening. He moved into the living room and grazed along the bookshelf, scanning the titles, briefly perusing a few, and was actually impressed by the array and depth of topics reflected in what was evidently a very diverse collection. At one point, he even came close to viewing her in a different light, as it were, and was on the verge of commenting about it, when suddenly the prickly sensation electrified his neck.

Again. Just as before. The same eerie feeling he had experienced in the hotel, and then later on the street, and he knew. Though highly suspicious before, at that moment Calumet knew. *Watch out for the woman, Jack!* The warning was well meant, but unnecessary. Calumet possessed something they couldn't teach in an academy: his sixth sense. Earlier it had alerted him to the danger, now it was revealing the source of that danger, shearing away the veil and showing him that the haunting apparition from the Kempinski had been Karola. In *his* mind, there was no doubt. He was positive now.

It all added up—the coincidental encounters, especially today, her timely arrival in front of the hotel, her carnal potency, her voracious sexual aggression, implied maybe, but aggression with intent to seduce nevertheless. Other than the obvious, he speculated—Why? And who was this woman, exactly? What drove her? *Know your enemy,* he thought.

How did Karola become entangled with Odyssey in the first place? Jack wondered, knowing now that she belonged to Vartanyan. Vartanyan hadn't hung around the Kempinski today simply as a spectator. Of that he was certain. Vartanyan had timed this woman perfectly. Was she former KGB? Or former Stasi, perhaps, now incarnate? The origins were always important, Jack knew. Had she, in the past, been one of the KGB's prizes from the First Chief Directorate, previously serviced by a Line N officer or run by an officer from Line PR in an effort to destabilize the west through Group Nord's Active Measures campaign, all in preparation for the time the wall came down so the faithful could one day stage their comeback? Or had she been trained in sabotage and terrorism at Balashikha with scores of other would-be heroes and then put on a shelf until her handlers, in their sagely nepotism, decided to activate her? Was she all of these things, maybe, and now on loan to Khodinka as just another piece to be moved across the squares, another pawn to be sacrificed in Nishka's assault on Odyssey? Whatever she was, the probability was high that she wasn't a Line officer herself; that particular function would appear to be incongruous with her status as a German businesswoman, with her legend, that is, if that's what they'd built for her, and he knew the Soviets spent years building their agents' legends. In the final analysis, that's probably what she was, he guessed: an agent whose legend had been carefully crafted in the deceptive bowels of Center's Directorate S, an agent provocateur, like himself. Yet there was still more, Jack inferred, *much* more. *Whatever* she was, he calculated, she was also human, and a woman at that, and the specificity was important to him because Calumet believed in the distinction. Not that one was better than the other, he surmised, just different, each possessing a unique nature, each responsive to dissimilar incitements, and the fact is, he worked a woman differently than he worked a man.

"So tell me about your family, Karola," he invited, turning suddenly and catching her in the act, her eyes boring into him.

"I have no family," she stated flatly, her voice filled with a trace of melancholy, the momentary flicker of grief seeming genuine.

"Well," he smirked, lightening the mood and, at the same time, tunneling, "someone as lovely as you could not possibly have been hatched, so there must have been a time when you were nothing but a pesky little girl with a father and a mother to disobey. *Nicht wahr?*"

He thought he noticed a glimmer of anger blitz across her eyes, the pupils narrowing rapidly, going in and out of focus like a shooting star, but recovering quickly, she smiled. "My mother is dead, and my father had left her long before. A dull story, I'm afraid." And then she reached for the wine, downing her half-full glass in the process, unmistakably a bracer to get her through the moment. She entered the living room and stood close.

Jack capitalized on the weakness. "When did she die? Was it due to natural causes?"

"Jack," she concocted a tear. "Please don't spoil the evening." It was a ploy he was sure she'd used a thousand times before. "Let's allow the past to *be* the past and live for the moment. Shall we?" She moved into him, her raven wisps attempting to caress his face but catching on his whiskers, modestly injecting her seductive venom.

Calumet stirred his own brew, though, for he had a different agenda. Choosing his words carefully, actually rehearsing them mentally first, he said, "I like to know who I'm making my bed with, Karola. Talk to me." Speaking softly then, and brushing a gentle kiss across her forehead, combing back her hair, he dared her, "Tell me all your secrets, mysterious lady." He pulled her gently as he sat on the chair. Playing the moment, she took a position on the floor, at his feet, and draped her arms over his legs, her breasts flattened on his thigh.

The reference to the bedroom and the kiss on the forehead reeled her in, confirming in *her* mind that he was putty in her hands now, her sensual snare having found its stranglehold, like so many men before him who had been taken in just the same manner. Knowing who he was, and what was expected of her by her lords, she dove in, completely oblivious to the certitude of his own proficiency in the art of deceit and to the fact that the ambush had already been sprung by him. Supposing she could make him feel sorry for her, enmeshing him inextricably, she began with a half-truth. "My mother was raped by Russian soldiers in World War II. Right here in Potsdam. Before they were able to finish with her, a young soldier—a Ukrainian—intervened, shooting his fellow soldiers on the spot. Naturally, my mother was very grateful. They became friends until he was transferred back to Russia. She never heard from him again." She paused, a curious vacancy in her eyes, waiting for feedback, almost Pavlovian, it appeared, as if she expected another question.

Nothing about the father, he thought. Something told him the stress lay with memories of the father—perhaps that tragic crossroads in her life. She seemed momentarily subservient, as though she had been in this spot before, abused possibly, if not physically, emotionally, and that could be just as savage, he reckoned. He studied her, her just sitting there, suddenly vulnerable, waiting for the next blow. *Maybe—deep down—she hates men.* And he detected a noticeable personality change. It seemed to have washed over her abruptly, taming her lusts. Professional that she was, Calumet perceived that she wanted to talk, that he had hit the right button, that she was in the mood to talk now, but perhaps required a tiny nudge. "Your mother must have been very pretty."

"A woman didn't have to be pretty to get raped in those days. A woman only had to be a woman. But yes, my mother was pretty. Very pretty, as you say. She was young herself, you know, and had everything to live for, in spite of the Holocaust." The word seemed to have triggered something. "And make no mistake, Jack, the Jews aren't the only race of people who went through the Holocaust. The people of Berlin endured a hell every bit as boorish as that of the death camps." There was a sudden fire in her eyes now, stoking her emotions.

Calumet had seen the titles on her bookshelf, among the bric-a-brac and the candles, books of Berlin and the war, and the horror.

She continued, spitting her words: "Berlin was in ruins in 1945. Families torn and shattered. A once-proud city now pillaged and plundered. A once-beautiful city now a desolation. Lives and homes incinerated from saturation bombing by the Allies . . ." Pausing momentarily, she appeared to be groping suddenly, searching for the end of her sentence, but finally conceding failure, having lost it forever, started a new one and reverted to German, *"Sie haben nie so gelebt!" You have never so lived.*

As if *she* had, he thought, quickly calculating that she wasn't even a gleam in her father's eye at that point, whoever her father was, but he didn't speak.

"Did you know, Jack, that by the end of the war, in 1945, over a billion cubic meters of rubble lay upon Berlin? Did you know that, Jack?"

Calumet shook his head, fascinated by her sudden fervor. She took her hands away from his legs, and he noticed it was the first time all night that she had declined to touch him.

"Yes," she continued. "One billion cubic meters of rubble and over one hundred thousand Berliners dead or maimed. More than one hundred thousand women and children, massacred by American and British bombs. That was Berlin's holocaust."

Not quite six million, Jack thought, but big deal, she was more or less in the ballpark if you notched it off in chunks of a hundred thousand and never made it past first-year math. Intrigued by her hidden passion, mystified by the implied political digression, he decided to open her up and drive in a wedge, already suspecting where it would make its mark. "Karola, the tragedy of every war is the innocent people. Whether they be in Berlin or Dresden or Pearl Harbor or anywhere else. But what you're alluding to is similar to blaming the cop for shooting the rapist. After all, we never would have been here in the first place had it not been for a monster named Hitler. What should we have done, Karola? Left him alone?"

"The bombing was unnecessary," she fired back, full of conviction. "Your people could have marched into Berlin like the Russians did."

Ah! A tiny bit of insight. The first evidence of brainwashing. Dutifully towing the party line, shackled to a million pounds of crap. The statement told Calumet a great deal, proving his instincts. The absence of family photographs, especially for a woman who chambered everything she owned right here in this house, had kindled his suspicion. Along with her voyeuristic nature—which in and of itself was symptomatic of a psychological canker, Jack maintained—the lack of any evidence of family ties hinted that she might be harboring emotional skeletons where such matters were concerned, hence his initial probe into the subject of her ancestry. Now he had to find out how it tied in with the Russians, Odyssey, and those devils, the Americans. If successful, he could use it against her. But he knew he couldn't argue with her about the bombing, although secretly he wanted to ask her how she figured the American, British, and French troops would have gotten to Berlin without it—and the Russians too, for that matter. And speaking of bombing, had she ever heard of *Lebensraum,* London, and Warsaw, just a thought, he wanted to say. Then again, she had typecast herself already. Her persona fit that of all the other fanatics, and although Calumet judged himself capable of debating with the best of them, he'd never finished first in an argument with a fanatic, mainly because even when he won they weren't aware of it and wouldn't admit it.

"So your mother and father suffered through the horror of the bombing, then?" Calumet prodded.

"Not my father," Karola quickly replied, without thinking. "Just my mother."

That's what I wanted to hear, Calumet thought. *Because your father is the real mystery, isn't he, Karola?* "Really? I don't understand. Where was your father?"

She suddenly appeared defiant, as though Calumet had tread on holy ground. "I never knew my father. My mother told me he was just some man she had a fling with after the war."

"Karola, you weren't born until ten or fifteen years after the war was already over." He put on his warmest smile for the next comment. "Unless you're invoking the woman's privilege of lying about your age."

"Jack"—she appeared troubled—"this is all very personal for me. I really don't wish to discuss it. Okay?" To get her point across, she leaned forward and hugged his knees, smiling widely, her overtones implying strongly: *Forget the conversation, just take me.*

Which he did. He lifted her onto his lap and kissed her passionately, his hand behind her head, grabbing a fistful of hair. She made the breathing sounds, heated, steamy, and he thought they might have even been genuine. He eased her head back and gazed into her eyes. Stroking her hair, he said softly, "When did your mother die, Karola?"

"Years ago," she replied, then kissed him back. "Forget about the past, Jack. Don't try to psychoanalyze me. Just enjoy me."

"Maybe I should leave. It *is* getting late."

"Aren't you staying here tonight? With me?" She acted surprised.

"I don't think that would be wise." He removed her arms from around his neck. "Can you give me a lift into town? Or should I call a cab?" With this remark, suddenly, he could see the wheels turning in her mind, calculating rapidly.

"I felt deserted when my mother died," she said morosely. "Don't make me feel that way now."

Calumet was tuned into her psyche. Karola's sudden rampage on the bombing of Berlin by the Allies, her focus upon the savagery of the war as it applied to one specific locale and not another, told him that she had personalized her mother's own horror of that time. This girl loved her mother. Jack suddenly appeared sympathetic. "I'm sure you *did* feel deserted when your mother died. Were you close?"

"Yes," she replied, the vacuous look surfacing again. "We were."

"Her death must have been a shock. How old were you?"

"Thirteen." Her demeanor changed abruptly once more, as if the memories were scaring up old demons and frightening her. "She was murdered in West Berlin."

Jack said nothing, perceiving that the floodgates were about to open of their own accord. He was right.

"She had crossed over in the morning to do some shopping," Karola continued. "The next I knew they were telling me that she had been stabbed in an attempted mugging. The body was returned, and a small funeral was held for me and a few of her friends. That was all, just me and a few of her friends. Nobody else came."

The revelation was significant, Jack thought. The *"nobody else"* referred to her father. "What about brothers and sisters?" he asked. "No brothers or sisters?"

"No."

Calumet held her close, gently rocking her, tears cascading down her face, none of them fabricated this time. He knew her wounds had been inflicted years ago and had never healed, merely festered, lying always just beneath the surface, in ambush, oozing whenever disrupted. "I'm so sorry, Karola. I didn't know. I wouldn't have pressed had I known." He kissed her cheeks, breathing warmly on her skin, the salty savor of the tears wetting his lips. Calumet was pretty sure he had it figured out now; had *her* figured out.

His tone compassionate, he asked, "When did your father finally show up to take you back to Russia?"

Jerking away suddenly, she demanded, "How did you know?"

Though this woman was accustomed to exercising control over her targets, she was also a woman very much controlled: controlled, Calumet knew, by Vartanyan and other masters. If they could control her, so could he, he judged. He threw the dice, seasoned with a pinch of voodoo. "Because I'm CIA, Karola, and I have powers which you can't even begin to comprehend."

*

The van was parked around the corner, out of sight. Calumet hadn't seen it when he and Karola arrived. Vartanyan yanked the earphones off and swiveled about to confront the older, distinguished-looking man sitting next to him, his face in shadow.

"Damn it!" Vartanyan exclaimed. "He's onto us! He knows who you are!"

"No," the man said calmly. "He doesn't. He's only speculating. You need to calm yourself, Andrei. I told you before that Jack Calumet is a sorcerer. If he was onto us, if he was aware that I was Karola's father, he would not be taking this tack with her. And I think I know him better than anyone. Don't you?"

CHAPTER 17

As far as the Germans were concerned, the underlying implications yet a mystery, Armbrister's gambit had run its course–Calumet had been set in motion. The Teflon double was now a wanted man in Berlin. A kilo of heroin and the assault of a German Federal agent placed him at the front of the queue on the BND's watch list. Armbrister knew it would not be necessary to use the photograph taken of him in Grunewald Park now. That particular card would have been played only if the BND presupposed insufficient grounds for targeting Jack Calumet as high priority. At this point, Jack Calumet's priority with the BND was beyond high; it was personal. One of their own was lying in hospital with a fractured nose and severely blackened eyes due to the location of the blow and the force of the percussion. Because of it, the BND was seething. They wanted Jack Calumet, and they wanted him badly.

*

In Atlanta, Diane Shylock had been placed under a close but discreet watch by a team from the CIA's Office of Security. She was shadowed around the clock by unseen protectors, and her house was presently under twenty-four-hour surveillance. Neither she nor her fiancé, Jack, was aware of it, but Armbrister had decided not to take any chances. Armbrister knew how slippery his operative could be, and if Calumet aggravated the Russians, or more specifically, Nishka, beyond what might be considered reasonable—and Calumet could easily do such a thing—it would not be unusual for Moscow Center to snatch Diane and attempt to leverage her against him in an effort to secure his cooperation. That was one variable Armbrister chose not to live with, so he ordered in the team.

Still, the decision had not been taken lightly. The gurus at Langley had deliberated upon the subject at great length before a verdict was finally reached. They weren't exactly sure how to play it. If the Russians knew that Calumet's girlfriend had been placed under the aegis of Langley's umbrella, how would they react to it? How would they read it? Many assessments had been bandied about, many analyses proffered. In the end, however, concern for her safety alone won the day. If the Russians tried to move in on Miss Shylock at this stage of the game, they would have a colossal mountain to ascend. In fact, some people might even say that Miss Shylock was now safer than the president himself since, in some circles, the CIA's Office of Security was regarded as potentially the most lethal and proficient security force on the planet.

One small footnote to this portion of the operation would later cause Armbrister to countenance a piratical grin. While setting up the surveillance umbrella, a slight hitch in the process developed when a pallid disagreement suddenly broke out between Armbrister's liaison from the Operations Directorate and the point man from the Office of Security, whose affiliation is chartered under the Administration Directorate. The phones were covered, of course, but the point man from the Office of Security wanted to penetrate the house and install audio equipment to make sure every single room was also bugged, including the bathrooms. As he'd remarked with a sly wink, "You never know." "That's true," the liaison agreed, returning the wink with pronounced exaggeration, and an unmistakable display of disapproval. But one thing he *did* know, he then stated sardonically, was how *some* technicians got their kicks, so he bluntly told the point man to go to hell. Case closed.

*

"You were just . . ." Karola lost the word again.

Calumet noticed that even though she was fluent in English, German, and probably Russian as well, she seemed inclined to bemire her sentences when she became excited.

Privy to her thoughts, he supplied the ending for her: "guessing."

"Yes," she nodded vigorously, "you were merely guessing."

"Assuming that's true, it would mean that I'm an excellent guesser, then, wouldn't it?" When she didn't respond right away, he continued. "What is your father's name?"

"*You're* the soothsayer," she retorted, giggling suddenly. "You tell me!"

Calumet couldn't help but laugh. *At least she didn't deny that he was still living.* "You never told me your last name."

"And you never asked. But it's not a state secret. My last name is Eichendorff."

Uh-huh. Her real name probably *is* a state secret, he thought. "So you adopted your mother's maiden name?"

"Yes." Her countenance dimmed again. She despised the past, but she knew she was expected to keep him here, expected to conquer him eventually, so she felt hemmed in, as though she had no choice. He had already threatened to leave once. And yet she had no idea that he was already way ahead of her, that she was completely out of her depth. She had never failed before—not with men—so in *her* mind it was only a matter of time before he succumbed. Still, in view of his cryptic admission, she felt obligated to ask her own questions now. She had known for some time that he was CIA, or a double anyway, but to let it go without comment would jeopardize her own clandestine cover. "What do you mean you're a CIA agent?" she asked.

Calumet knew *they* were listening. If not live, then tapes. But probably both, he conjectured. "That's not exactly accurate. I've been paid by the CIA for the past several years to supply them with certain information. However, I've also been paid by the Russians for the same reason."

"So you're a double agent? Isn't that what they call it?"

"Yes," Calumet smiled, unable to conceal his amusement. "That's more or less what they call it. What's your father's name."

"Is the CIA interested in my father?" she responded glibly.

Probably, he said to himself. "No. Just me. I'm curious. I'm fascinated by you, Karola. I'd just like to know. Or is *that* part a state secret?"

She laughed. "No. My father is dead. Some years ago. Heart failure. As you might have surmised, he was the Ukrainian who rescued my mother. His name was Sergei Petrovich Obinin."

"I see," Jack said. She had *that* act rehearsed perfectly, he realized. Her professional alacrity was shining through now, spinning off lies, her father conveniently dead so the matter could rest. False means, false timing, false name. Except he figured that the statement about her father being Ukrainian was probably true. You don't prepare bizarre Russian dishes unless you've learned the recipes firsthand or unless you've spent hours pouring through exotic cookbooks, and that's one type of book he hadn't noticed on the shelf. Even if he had, he had never marked her down as a frustrated gourmet.

Calumet's insides were churning. He felt, somehow, that he needed to control this woman, but he wasn't sure why exactly. Perhaps, he convinced himself, he might possibly be able to leverage her against Vartanyan down the road. Or maybe, knowing himself as he did, his determination was merely a rebellion against *her* attempt to control him, to suborn him, and it was therefore only natural for him to repel the assault. In any case, he simply could not pin down the reasoning, but his instincts propelled him onward. He desperately wanted to question her about Russia and her adjournment there, and where her father, the Ukrainian, had taken her when she was thirteen years old, but he must not allow her handlers to hear that part of his interrogation, he decided, so he filed it in the back of his mind as something to be attended to in the future. Besides, he knew he would have to wade through a legend a mile long before he was able to break her and get to the truth. That would take some time. No matter, though. If things worked out the way he planned, he would have plenty of time and plenty of opportunity to discover this girl's secrets.

Calumet glanced at his watch. It was past 11:00. He figured he had made them sweat long enough. "I need to use your phone," he told Karola.

*

Steve Phillips had run out of fingernails. He had chewed them down so efficiently that microscopic precision would be required to whittle away any more without cutting into the cuticle. Even Robert had calculated that Calumet, after his little escapade at the Kempinski, would be calling within the hour, but not so. Here it was, more than five hours later, and they hadn't heard zilch.

The safe house was situated in a suburban neighborhood. Inside, Rossetti and Kramer were in an adjoining room watching television. And laughing. That infuriated Steve, but he said nothing about it. Robert had departed several hours ago and had not yet returned. He confided that there were pressing matters which mandated his personal attention and he wasn't sure when he'd be back. So Steve was left to man the phone, even though, technically, he was slated as the only person who would answer it anyway.

The call would be routed through the consulate if the blasted thing ever rang. That's the number Calumet would dial, they knew, since that's the number that had been enclosed in the envelope Steve had given him. But where was he? Had the Russians kidnapped him? Were they exposing him to chemical interrogation at this very moment? Had he been netted by the BND? Were they holding him incommunicado? The possibilities were endless. Or was Jack Calumet just being himself? *Probably*, Steve thought. *That prima donna!*

Then the phone rang. Finally. Steve dropped a mangled soda straw and picked up the receiver. "Hello!"

"Did you miss me?"

"Where have you been? The city is crawling with heat."

"No joke."

Steve composed himself and went into the routine. "I warned you about the drugs, Calumet. The BND *and* the DEA are warm for your form, son."

"They'll get over it. Can the CIA intervene for me?"

"Not a chance. I told you those DEA honchos are nothing but cowboys. And there's also that little matter about a BND agent who at this very moment happens to be relaxing in a hospital with a severe headache. What did you do to him? He looks like a panda bear."

"Is he going to be okay?" That truly worried Calumet.

"Fortunately, yes. He's expected to recover fully. Where are you, Jack?"

"I'm over at the chancellor's castle. We're smoking Havanas and sipping cognac."

Steve hesitated for a split second. It took him that long to figure out that Calumet was cracking wise. As crazy as Calumet was, one never knew. "Okay, smart guy. Listen up, and listen good. *Wherever* you are, stay put. Lay low. Check back with me every day beginning day after tomorrow. I've passed your material up the ladder. We should have something for you in a few days. I'm not joking, Calumet. Stay under!" Steve hung up.

Later, after Steve briefed Robert on the phone call, and after Robert related his version of the day's occurrences to Armbrister, Armbrister would conclude that events were progressing nicely. His only concern was Calumet's volatility. In order for Odyssey to run smoothly, in order for the operation to really stand up and work, Calumet would not only have to be brave enough to remain in place, under very deep, but he would also have to be able to walk a very slippery tightrope. Precarious indeed. Armbrister's fervent desire was that Calumet be clever enough to elude the Germans, but not clever enough to do it without assistance—Russian assistance. In short, Armbrister wanted Calumet in Nishka's camp. He hoped desperately that the Russians would look after his racehorse and take him under their wing, because in order for Odyssey to succeed, a double agent had to be sacrificed. It was the only way. Moral considerations notwithstanding, the soldier boy must walk into hell alone. If he was somehow able to make it back out, well, then he would have to do it the same way . . . alone.

*

Calumet replaced the receiver. He was confident that Karola's phone lines were still set up on one of the old switch-banks. If the lines were on a modern bank they could trace the call instantaneously. It would not take fifteen or twenty seconds or however many seconds they counted them off in the movies. However, on an old bank—which is what hers was, he assumed—they wouldn't have his location at this point. Nevertheless, he decided not to take the chance.

"I need you to help me, Karola."

"Are you in trouble?" She almost seemed pleased.

"Sort of."

She laughed, throwing her arms around him tightly, and planted a sloppy kiss on his lips. Leaning back, she chortled enthusiastically. "Of course I'll help you. I just *knew* you had a dangerous side to you, Mr. Calumet."

"I'd like you to drive me somewhere," Jack said seriously.

"Now?" Her arms enveloped him and she began to kiss him passionately. When he responded in kind, she slid her hand slowly down his chest, then his stomach, and finally his crotch, teasing all the way. Finding her target, she made kneading, circular motions with fingers that could only be described as slender, powerful, and most definitely professional. It took about a second for his manliness to assert itself. He speculated privately that his hormonal feat might have been a world record. Her sexual charisma was absolutely awesome.

Calumet, however, was his own master, and in spite of what *some* women preferred to maintain, his penis did not dominate his thought patterns. Rarely missing an opportunity to exhibit his rapier wit, even in climactic situations, he gently pulled her hand away and said, "I'm afraid that's one mountain you're not going to climb, Karola. Not tonight anyway."

She suddenly appeared hurt, disappointed.

Jack added, "Later maybe, but not now. Okay?" He dispensed a rapscallion grin and pecked her on the lips. "Okay?"

Seemingly reassured, she smiled and replied, "Okay. Where are we going?"

"I have some personal items at another hotel off the Ku'damm which I need to retrieve. You can go in and get them for me. Then we'll come back here. How does that sound?"

"Another hotel? You devious man!" She donned her own treasonous grin. "That sounds *wunderbar!*"

"Great! Let's roll, Fräulein Eichendorff."

She giggled, secretly elated with the prospects of her success. They proceeded to her car.

*

The BND was swarming, as though the lid had been ripped off an angry beehive. Fortunately for Calumet, however, it had taken them approximately three hours to become effectively organized. They took care of their agent first, questioning him in detail, then met with the DEA. The meeting with the DEA had been a little coarse, especially since the DEA appeared to stall a bit, but the Germans, detecting the ploy, declined to play along and rapidly moved on. They formed a task force, and that meant that they meant business.

It wasn't a cakewalk, though. Their first effort, which took place almost immediately after the incident itself and before the task force had been organized, was slightly disheartening, mainly because they got their information secondhand from the local *Polizei*. After canvassing the area around the Kempinski, the local boys were slightly embarrassed due to the fact that they very nearly came up dry. All they were able to chalk up from their heavy-handed exercise was the supposition that someone fitting the description of Jack Calumet *might* have gotten into a white BMW, license unknown. How many white BMWs existed in Berlin and surrounding areas? How many men fit Calumet's description? However, the BND was a determined bunch and refused to be denied. After running Calumet through the computers and making phone calls, they came up with four locations: the three hotels in which he had previously registered, and the reservation he had made on the evening flight to Zurich in his own name. Once saddled with this information, they made progress quickly.

As one team was in the process of confirming that a Mr. Jack Calumet had never shown up for his flight to Zurich, another was lifting the German driving license out of the drawer at the Achat. That discovery caused a sudden flurry of excitement at headquarters. Just as Calumet had hoped, though, it muddied the waters slightly. A directive was issued immediately to all airports, train terminals, shipping terminals, and border posts, ordering them to be on the lookout for one Jack Calumet, a.k.a. Reiner Kästner. A facsimile of Jack Calumet's photograph accompanied each directive. Then, running the name of Reiner Kästner through their computers, they quickly discovered that he, too, had made reservations on a night flight, this time to Paris, but like the real Calumet, had never shown up. By 11:00 P.M., the aggregate of all these facts led the BND to one conclusion: Jack Calumet, a.k.a. Reiner Kästner, was still in Germany. Maybe even still in Berlin. With the help of the local police, they began showing Calumet's picture around, blanketing the Ku'damm and hitting every seedy hotel in existence. If he was in one of them, they knew it was just a matter of time.

The BND was licking their chops.

*

Secretly, Karola was impressed by Calumet's tradecraft. Or, more accurately perhaps, his coolness in implementing his tradecraft. A very hunted man, yet he was making all the right moves, not in a rush, not forcing it. She admired his bravado. He was doing exactly what the KGB had trained her to do.

Leaving Karola's house, Karola behind the wheel, Calumet insisted that they circle the block. Karola hesitated at first, wise to the fact that the van was parked just around the corner, but then quickly realized she had no choice and stepped lightly on the accelerator. She was greatly relieved when they completed the cycle and discovered only empty streets. The van had disappeared. It was nowhere in sight now, calming her appreciably. She knew Vartanyan was a great anticipator. So was her father, for that matter.

As they proceeded, Calumet noted favorably that the gas tank was three-quarters full, but he forced her to stop and top it off anyway. "Surveillance precaution," he explained, like he was revealing a military secret, pretending she didn't know the drill. Then they drove slowly toward Berlin. At various times Calumet ordered her to turn off onto a side street, park for a while, then resume the journey. Other than issuing orders, he never said a word. Neither did she, implying surreptitiously that she apparently *did* know the drill. As they snaked closer and closer to the city, but never too close, and usually just after a park-and-watch routine, he would instruct her to make a U-turn, his apprehension candid as his eyes darted everywhere all at once. Like a lion sniffing the kill. On other occasions he commanded her to detour without warning, and even forced her to run a red light a couple of times, both of them praying that there were no cops in the vicinity.

Then he did something that seemed utterly strange to her. He ordered her to drop him off momentarily. "Why?" she asked.

"I want you to drive back up the road, about four or five kilometers, then turn around and come back. I want to see if anyone goes after you."

"Jack . . . ," she said, reams of uncertainty in her voice.

"Don't worry," he reassured. "I'll be here."

After she was out of sight, Calumet walked over to a phone box and made a collect call to Belgium. He had barely concluded his business by the time her headlights loomed in the distance. She pulled up and he climbed in.

And then he shocked her. Frightened her. She didn't know it, but Calumet had made the decision long ago. Sometime during dinner probably, or thereabouts. Or maybe while he was studying her book titles and wondering how he could use her. At any rate, Calumet had made a decision that infuriate them all: Armbrister, Robert, Steve, Nishka, Vartanyan, Karola—thelot. A very unsociable resolution.

Somewhere along the line, Calumet decided it was time to take the BND out of the equation. Completely.

He grabbed her purse in one swift motion and placed it on the floor beneath his feet. Then he pulled the Beretta and cradled it in his lap. "Karola, Switzerland is a nice place to visit this time of year, don't you think?"

"Wh . . . Jack," she stammered. "No! I'm not going to Switzerland. Not tonight. We can't. We—We just can't!"

Calumet cocked the hammer and pointed the gun at her lovely chest. "My guess is that Andrei Vartanyan prefers his concubines healthy and whole, not splattered all over the interior of some automobile." Grinning wryly, his eyes teeming with threat, he added, "Wouldn't you agree, pretty lady?"

CHAPTER 18

George Menzel's appointment with Dr. Zekeman, Calumet's physician, was set. He entered the doctor's office, which was simply a house that had been converted, and reported directly to the matronly nurse at the front desk, informing her that he had arrived for his physical as previously scheduled. A physical was considered standard procedure when hiring a new physician, he'd been told. The matronly nurse greeted him with a starched frown and explained mechanically that it would probably be a while before the doctor could see him. This, she conceded, was on account of the vast multitude of doctorly chores the great man must attend to in pursuit of his reverent work. "Please be patient," she chanted as she ushered him into the waiting room with a wide sweep of the arm, as though she was waving back a curtain to award him a view of all the other worshipers who were sitting there obediently and behaving as they should.

"No problem," Menzel said, the wait was fine with him. In fact, it was perfect. George Menzel wanted to spend as much time as possible on the premises.

While inside, he made mental notes of the alarm system, the windows, the entrances, the exits, the rooms where the medical files were kept, the power box, and numerous other odds and ends. And the phone lines, just in case. But that was just the basics.

He also presented himself as the sprightly caricature of a time-lapse video. Had anyone noticed, which they didn't, they might have surmised that the man was plagued by weak kidneys since he found it necessary to use the facilities on more than a few occasions. Some might even have inferred that Mr. Menzel was a trifle loose in the cranium, seeing as how he actually got lost on the way back from one of his somatic expeditions and ended up roaming into forbidden territory—at least according to the nurse who reprimanded him for it. Even a rat would have been able to figure out the elaborate maze of a doctor's office by now, one would think.

But no one seemed to notice. At any rate, he wasn't able to make the switch right away. There was too much activity.

As Menzel was being examined, Zekeman, in casual doctor-patient conversation, asked him who his doctor had been before, and just out of curiosity, Zekeman further persisted, why was he in the process of changing physicians now? Menzel remarked that he had been living in Canada for the past several years and had just recently moved to Atlanta. Of course, it was all true. Menzel *had* been living in Canada for the past several years and *had* just recently moved to Atlanta. What he failed to mention, however, was *why,* exactly, he had just recently moved to Atlanta, and how he came to live in Canada in the first place. Dr. Zekeman would have found the tale quite fascinating had Menzel chosen to relate it, for George Menzel was not the man's real name, and the man was not Canadian. Nor was he American. George Menzel was a Soviet illegal, and he had been ordained by Nishka.

Prepared to wait decades and willing to expend massive resources in the waiting, the Soviets have continuously sought to embed illegals in the societies of foreign countries—most specifically, America. Of course, such undertakings can become unwieldy, are enormously difficult to maintain, and are consequently susceptible to failure. In fact, many more fail than succeed, but the Russians know that a single success can far outweigh the failures. A single success can reap untold dividends for the Soviets and wreak untold havoc upon the recondite infrastructure of the host country. A single success, therefore, is worth all the effort. George Menzel was just such a success, and the fact that Nishka was risking Menzel, elevating the agent's chances of exposure, spoke volumes concerning the spymaster's interest in Jack Calumet and likewise furnished a cogent testament to the Aquarium's stake in an operation called Odyssey.

George Menzel, whose given name was Valeri Kirillovich Sepelev, had been born in a small village near Tbilisi some fifty years earlier. It became apparent early on that he had a gift for languages, was a bright boy, and generally got along well with his peers. As a result, his teachers, knowing what was expected of them, passed his name up the line where the recruiters quickly took note. From that time on he was loosely supervised and secretly guided throughout his unobtrusive adolescence. Finally, at the age of twenty-three, five men showed up suddenly in Tbilisi one afternoon and questioned him ardently about his political views. In response, Valerie Kirillovich Sepelev quoted Marx and Lenin flawlessly and convinced his strange suitors that he was an enthusiastic zealot who was capable of upholding the faith, no matter what. Two months later he was summoned to Moscow. Would he be interested in a life of intelligence work? It would mean hardship, sacrifice, possibly even death. And, of course, since this is a weighty matter, they said, there's no rush for an answer. Take a few days to think about it, why don't you? No, he told them, he didn't need to think about it. He accepted on the spot. And thus began the clandestine career of Valeri Kirillovich Sepelev.

The first task in convoking Sepelev's future, after three solid years of training, that is, most of it taking place in and around Moscow, was to provide him with a legend, but not just any legend. The Soviets had compiled a macabre portfolio and were careful to invest Comrade Sepelev with a legend that would really fly. A foolproof legend, one that could withstand the gravest scrutiny. This was accomplished, as is the case with most legends, by a mixture of truth, lies, and a little forgery.

The real George Menzel had been a Nazi conscript, ensnared, like so many, by the Russian winter of '43. Along with many other German soldiers, he chose the relative warmth of a Soviet prison camp rather than a hideous, frozen death. Of course, his capitulation seemed only natural, given his circumstances, and oddly offered him a shred of hope for the future. In fact, had he lied to his Russian captors when they grilled him about his life before imprisonment, he might have survived his ordeal and seen his homeland again, but unfortunately, George Menzel told the truth. For George Menzel, the decision to live had not only been fateful, but truculently paradoxical.

At seventeen, Menzel was old enough to fight, but he was not a man. Not in the universal sense of the term. Had the times been kinder, and had the world been more hospitable, he might have overcome the emotional storms that have ravaged men and women for generations long forgotten, searing the souls of the young and old alike. But George Menzel was a tragedy himself, a calamity in motion, a piteous, brokenhearted boy. His parents had drowned in a boating accident when he was fifteen, and he had no brothers or sisters. He suddenly found himself without a star to steer by, foundering in a chaotic universe, and he discovered the facts of life quite brutally when he was told that his grandparents couldn't afford him or, if they could, wouldn't, so he was forced to try to conquer the world's horizons on his own. Thus, as the Führer's mania was sweeping the Sudetenland, he opted for the excitement of joining a cause more than an army, but saw the army as a stepping-stone to that cause, or as a gateway to religious consummation, perhaps. In any case, it was a filler for his confusion and bitter pain, so he signed up. Several years later, when he could bear the harsh temperatures of a vast and vacuous wasteland no longer, he surrendered with all the others. After that, he suffered the abuses of hard labor until the end of the war, and the abuses of interrogation as well, his body only a shadow of his former self, as if cast upon broken clay. But the greatest abuse suffered by the real George Menzel occurred on the last day of his life.

The cell doors clanked open early one morning and George Menzel's name was called. He was told he was going home. That spurious promise was perhaps the most inhumane of all his treatment, but at least he died with hope. Where he was ultimately taken he never knew, and the bullet that shattered the back of his skull he never heard. But he died instantly, and for all the tragedy that characterized George Menzel's existence, at least at that moment he thought he was going home. At any rate, a grisly maxim had been preserved: one life, one legend.

Armed with Menzel's legend, Sepelev journeyed to Dessau, a proxy of the Soviet Union at the time, situated in East Germany, and former hometown of the real George Menzel. He spent his time familiarizing himself with the area and dredging up old acquaintances who might have known him when he was a boy so as to validate his existence and ratify his return from the war, confiding all the while that he was looking for work. Soon he stumbled into a chance meeting with the owner of a small printing establishment and revealed that he was in dire straits, and did the man have an opening, even as a custodian perhaps? The man asked him why he was in his current predicament and why he was willing to accept such a menial job. His programming automatic at that point, Sepelev replied, "Because I don't wish to work for the bastard Communists!" The man hired him on the spot.

Sepelev spent two years in Dessau before his application for migration to the West was approved by his superiors. He was driven to Berlin by his KGB handlers. From there, Valeri Kirillovich Sepelev a.k.a. George Menzel slipped across the border at Checkpoint Charlie with all the right papers. He was one of the lucky few who were allowed to emigrate in those days. He soon journeyed to Frankfurt and found work in another printing business, his two years on the job in Dessau serving him well. He labored for four years in Frankfurt, traveling only twice to Bonn to meet surreptitiously with the KGB Illegals Resident. Soon after his second meeting with the Illegals Resident, as per his orders, Sepelev immigrated to Ottawa where he established his own printing business. He flourished in that occupation for ten years before ultimately being ordered to move to Atlanta. While it's true that he had become an agent of influence to some degree in Canada, establishing networks and so forth, his primary target had always been the United States. His future penetration of the United States was the cardinal reason for all his training. Now he had finally made it. Valeri Kirillovich Sepelev a.k.a. George Menzel was in America and embedded about as deeply as one could get.

Still, Nishka was gambling big by exposing Sepelev to Operation Odyssey. Too big, really. Then again, Armbrister had toyed with medical records in Istanbul, and the DDO never found out that the Russians were onto it, so Nishka was willing to take the risk. All he wanted from Menzel at this point was Calumet's original records, not a reproduction. If Menzel could accomplish that without being blown, fine. If not, that was okay, too. There were always other pawns.

While waiting for the nurse to administer the blood tests, which took place in the room next to the office containing the file cabinets, Menzel electronically activated the small incendiary device he had placed in the lavatory earlier. The distraction worked, he was able to slip quietly into the office next door and quickly exchange Nishka's reproduction for Calumet's originals. The light jacket he was wearing contained an opening in the lining and the medical records fit nicely. After completing his physical, Menzel left the premises immediately, promising to call for the results in a day or two. As far as the doctor's staff was concerned, the small fire in the wastebasket in the men's room would remain a mystery. The doctor himself, however, was not so sure.

After the nurses were gone and the office closed for the day, Zekeman dialed the special number he had been given by one of Armbrister's DOs. The telephone conversation itself was short. Had anyone been listening in, all they would have heard was Zekeman confirming a tennis date with an associate. The tennis match would actually take place, just in case. At any rate, the DO visited Zekeman at his home that evening and Zekeman handed him the tale of the day's events along with the medical records and other pertinent information regarding one George Menzel. When the DO reported all to Langley, Armbrister would be very pleased.

Whatever else might occur as a result of Operation Odyssey, one causal event would be conclusive: Valerie Kirillovich Sepelev a.k.a. George Menzel had been blown. It would be many years before he was arrested, however, as Armbrister would eventually turn him over to the FBI, and the FBI would stalk him mercilessly until they profiled every contact the poseur had ever known.

But for now, George Menzel had done his job. He had obtained Calumet's original medical records. They would soon be on their way to Moscow and an eagerly awaiting Nishka. Nishka was betting heavily that the forensics wouldn't match up.

Just like in Istanbul.

CHAPTER 19

All pretense had vanished. Karola was seething inside, and the anger was reflected in her fiery expression. They were headed south-southeast toward the Thüringen district. That's all Calumet was willing to reveal of their projected route at this stage.

"I don't have my passport," Karola informed him.

"Don't worry about it." The gun was resting in his lap.

"Are you going to force me to crash the border or something?"

"Or something. Don't worry about it."

"What about your meet with Andrei tomorrow?"

"He'll understand."

"Oh?" Karola smiled deviously. "Really?"

"Karola, you're much too pretty to worry about such heady details." It was a calculated insult. "You just concentrate on the driving and let me do the thinking. Okay, pretty lady?"

"Stop calling me that!" she exploded.

Calumet laughed. "Sure thing. I didn't mean to insult you, pretty lady."

She shot him a sideways glance. He thought, *if looks could kill.* "Andrei will be very upset," she said.

"Tough," Jack replied. "At the moment *I'm* very upset, and I wouldn't aggravate me if I were you. I've been known to display my very volatile nature from time to time. It can erupt without warning, you know."

She compressed her lips. She knew debate at this point was futile. Instead, her mind was spinning wildly in an attempt to figure out how to extricate herself from this madman.

"Understand something, Karola," Jack warned. "I'm in trouble. I'm on the run. I've got nothing to lose. You do as I say and you'll be back in Potsdam in a day or two. That I promise. On the other hand, if you cross me up, I'll kill you."

She was sure he meant it. It was in his eyes. "How did you put me together with Andrei?" she inquired.

"I told you, Karola, and it would behoove you to start believing me—I have powers which you can't even begin to comprehend." Calumet was running on the premise that Karola had been abused at some point in her tempestuous past. Her Pavlovian responses earlier, her almost subservient attitude when pushed about her father, led him to believe that she could be impressed and persuaded by mere puissance and force of will. He desperately hoped so. Karola, he surmised, might be able to provide him with a significant piece of this mysterious puzzle. He didn't have the time to try and sort it all out—not at the moment—but the fact that Vartanyan had thrown this woman at him engendered in Calumet a growing suspicion that there was more to Odyssey than he had been told. Although a miscued admission was as far as Robert would go, his controller had slipped up and hinted at it in the safe house, and now the Russians were coming at him gingerly instead of head-on, as was their custom.

"Andrei's powers are greater than yours, and he won't like this," Karola countered.

"If you don't behave yourself, you won't ever see Andrei again," Jack stated blandly. "I'd keep that in mind."

They traveled mostly in silence until they entered the outskirts of Jena. He was feeding her each location piecemeal, instructing her to drive from one town to the next. They had been heading in a southerly direction, but at Jena he ordered her to take the west fork toward Erfurt. Upon reaching the outskirts of Erfurt, he forced her to pull over on an obscure stretch of road. They sat for fifteen minutes, Calumet pensive the entire time. At one point she started to speak, but he cut her off. Finally they resumed. He ordered her to head due south again toward Nuremberg. Just after Nuremberg he forced her to pull over once more. This time they sat for forty minutes. It was a very long forty minutes for both of them. Again, Calumet refused to be drawn into conversation. They pulled out and headed for Munich just as dawn was beginning to break out over the eastern horizon.

At Ingolst Calumet instructed Karola to turn off the autobahn and take the road to Augsburg. Upon reaching Augsburg, they drove straight into the city. The traffic was moderately heavy due to the morning rush hour, but they proceeded to Hoher Weg in front of the cathedral. There Calumet spotted what he was looking for. Parked just down the street was a yellow minivan with a skull-and-crossbones bumper sticker. Calumet ordered Karola to pull alongside and roll down the window. He looked past her into the passenger side of the van and met the alert gaze of a younger man, probably in his early thirties, Calumet guessed. And not a typical German, either. He had hard eyes and curly brown hair, offset by almost-olive skin. Both men observed each other briefly, then Calumet nodded when he was sure the connection had been made. The van eased away from the curb and Calumet ordered Karola to follow.

The van headed southwest for about thirty minutes, finally reaching the outskirts of Krumbach. At Krumbach they drove another fifteen minutes before taking a long, winding road that meandered through a deciduous forest, the leaves just beginning to explode into full bloom. Along the way, hart's-tongue ferns poked out in jolts through a maze of conifers, seemingly in quest of recognition, and lush grasses mixed with more luxuriant vegetation, implying a richer, damper climate than the north. The entire panorama was thick with scrub oak and fir. All in all, there could be no mistake: this was Bavaria in springtime. The two vehicles ultimately broke into a wide, expansive clearing with well-hedged fields and a dirt road that appeared to be worn by centuries of wheels. An old stone house was set upon a tiny hill, the low curve of the forest behind it etching a backdrop, and a granite chimney was smoking, spiraling into the pristine morning sky. To the left, a large barn grew out of the landscape, but there was no sign of livestock. The cars swirled dust as they circled into a gravel drive in front of the house. Parking, Jack removed the keys from the ignition and he and Karola climbed out. Calumet locked the BMW and walked toward the van, leaving Karola standing by the car door.

"Jack Calumet?" the curly-haired man asked, sticking out his hand.

"Yes," Jack replied, accepting the shake.

"Gustav Taschner," the man disclosed softly, ensuring that only Calumet could hear. He glanced suspiciously at Karola. Keeping his eyes on her, he continued, "Our mutual friend in Belgium tells me you can be trusted. What exactly can I do for you?" The driver of the van had climbed out and was now standing alongside. He was a big man, oddly resembling De Boeck's gorilla, and Calumet began to wonder if such creatures were mandatory in this crazy business.

Calumet inclined his head toward Karola. "She could become difficult while we conduct our business."

"Take her into the house," Taschner told his gorilla. "Leave her with the girls."

"She's a professional," Calumet warned.

"So are Greta and Erna," Taschner replied. "Don't worry. She'll be fine."

"I want my purse," Karola demanded as the gorilla began to escort her into the house. She yanked her arm from his grasp. Snapping angrily, she looked back at Taschner and added, "And you should know, *Herr,* that you are assisting in the kidnapping of a German citizen. I'll overlook it if you release me right now."

Taschner laughed. "I see what you mean," he remarked to Calumet. He nodded at the gorilla.

"I want my damned purse!" Karola screamed as she yanked her arm again, but this time the gorilla's hold was too much for her.

Calumet and Taschner ambled over to the car. Calumet unlocked the door and grabbed the purse. He emptied its contents on the hood, then handed her the empty bag.

"Very funny!" she remarked caustically and threw it back in his face. The gorilla escorted her up a rickety set of wooden stairs while Greta held the door open at the top.

After the odd couple disappeared through the entrance, Calumet refilled the purse with its quondam contents. "I'll have to look these over later," he told Taschner. "In the meantime, I need to get across the border into Switzerland. Me and the girl." Then his eyes bored into the German. "The BND will be looking for me."

Gustav smiled. "Of course they will, my friend. Why else would you need me?"

Calumet returned the smile, relieved. De Boeck was good people, he thought. "Just making sure there's no misunderstanding," he explained.

"None," Taschner replied. "Obviously, we'll need to alter *your* appearance. What about the girl's? Is she also hunted?"

"No, just me." Calumet pulled his buccaneer's grin. "It's like she said—I'm kidnapping her."

Gustav laughed. "I'd say she's worth kidnapping. I wouldn't mind kidnapping her myself . . . er . . . when you're through with her, that is." Then he became serious. "You mentioned she's a professional. She's not BND, is she?"

"No," Jack assured. "She's probably former KGB. At the very least, she's an illegal."

"Ah!" Gustav exclaimed. "Then I have absolutely no problems with this affair. De Boeck hinted that you might be a spook."

"De Boeck doesn't know what I am," Calumet retorted. "Only that my money spends."

"And I shall not pry," Gustav said amicably, smiling. He did not wish to upset a client. "You've been driving all night?"

"Yes."

"Well, if you're not in a hurry, why don't we go inside and have breakfast. Then you and I can discuss our business afterward."

"Sounds good," Jack agreed. "But let's move the car out of sight first. They may have a description of it."

"Very well," Taschner responded. The gorilla—whose name, Calumet would later learn, was actually Manfred Sänger, and whose skin also had a curious olive hue to it—had reappeared. Calumet handed him the keys. Sänger drove the car into the barn while Jack and Gustav climbed the steps to the house.

"Nice place you have here," Jack remarked as Taschner held the door open for him.

Turning and looking over the land, Taschner replied, "Yes, it is. It will be a shame to get rid of it." He presented Calumet with a discerning smile. "But then, we move around a lot."

A real pro, Calumet thought, nodding in conspicuous approval. They went inside.

There was no foyer; they stepped abruptly into a sprawling, spacious room. The size was deceiving, especially if compared with the outside. The house did not look that big when contemplated from the front. Above, the ceiling was heavily rafted with great beams of blackened oak, aged enough so that the beams probably creaked in the wind, Calumet speculated. Along the far wall a dominating plate-glass window disclosed a view of the magnificent Bavarian forest rolling into the horizon. The tapestry was serene in the crisp morning air, and no doubt could have leapt onto a canvas and been dubbed a masterpiece. Immediately to their right, wooden stairs climbed steeply up to a loft, while the kitchen, off to one side, stood open. Below the loft, a granite fireplace with an oak mantelpiece centered itself on the wall next to the glass. The architecture was all Middle European and contrasted sharply with the modern furniture that was scattered about, presenting an incongruous appearance on the whole. And yet the place had atmosphere, Jack thought.

A long, lumbered table reposed just off of the kitchen where Karola, Greta, and Erna were enjoying a light breakfast of bread, rolls, and fruit juice. Jack and Gustav joined them. Calumet noted that Greta and Erna were seated either side of Karola. He was beginning to think there was more to Gustav and his crew than met the eye. The first thing that struck him was not Karola, whom he was sure would be a handful by now, but the two girls. The girls, although they could have passed easily for Germans, oddly did not seem to be German—at least according to Calumet's first impression. There was something about their deportment, in their eyes, maybe, friendly but aloof. They were professional to be sure, obvious in the way their gaze investigated him when he entered, and in the way their very presence seemed to quell Karola's demons, but he couldn't put his finger on the anomaly.

"You have interesting friends," Karola challenged Calumet.

"I certainly hope she's been behaving herself," Calumet said to Greta while nodding at Karola.

"She's been a perfect charm," Greta smiled.

"I won't cause you any trouble, Jack," Karola said sweetly, dripping sarcasm. "I'm planning to just sit back and enjoy our little adventure. After all, it's not every day that a girl gets kidnapped by revolutionaries. Isn't that what all of you are?"

Everybody laughed.

"Exactly," Gustav responded, smiling. "Revolutionaries who favor the Mark more than the cause."

They bantered back and forth for the next thirty minutes, Karola performing admirably, at times acting as though she were the hostess of the entire affair. Jack found it all quite amusing. Though tired, he carefully measured the interplay between Gustav and the two women. Gustav, he imagined, emerged from this strange clan as the first among equals rather than an outright dictator. Jack also sensed a team spirit in the trio, and was fascinated by the finesse and aplomb with which they handled Karola and her antics. They were all perfectly polite throughout the sortie, regardless of the tempo of the conversation. Calumet thought it was all very curious. As he continued to observe, saying little, his suspicion of Gustav's true charter grew with each passing moment, and soon he thought he had it figured out. Paul De Boeck had some interesting friends himself, Jack decided. If correct in his assumptions, he could not be in better hands.

After breakfast, Karola remained inside with Greta and Erna while Calumet and Taschner went into the barn. Sänger and a tall, lanky man were already inside. The lanky man was introduced as Lutz Heck—Gustav's mechanic. The barn itself had been converted for Gustav's special purposes. In addition to a forger's unique tools, there were boxes of weapons and ammunition lining one wall, partially concealed behind bales of hay, and Calumet noticed that the loft appeared to contain more of the same. All in all, a small arsenal.

Taschner handed Calumet an electric shaver. "The mustache should come off."

"Yeah," Jack replied, accepting the shaver. "I know."

While shaving, Taschner held a pair of glasses in front of his eyes. "Can you see through these?"

"A little blurry, but it's okay."

"Good," Taschner said. "They're 20–40. Not too thick, but if examined, at least they're genuine. What about your hair?"

"I'll just slick it back. That ought to be enough."

"Lutz?" Gustav was asking his mechanic for confirmation.

"Yes," Lutz replied. "It will work."

"Fine. Have you an identity in mind? And a nationality?"

"Austrian," Calumet responded. "For me and the girl."

"Try not to speak much German, then," Gustav cautioned. "You have an accent, you know."

"Yeah, I know, but I can fake it if pressed."

"Perhaps you should be British?"

Calumet mulled that one over for a second. "Okay, fine. I'll be British and she can be German. Will that work for you?"

"Yes, that should do quite nicely. What about the identities?"

"I think—for myself—" Calumet said in an exaggerated fashion, "I'll be Bond. James Bond."

Gustav and his friends broke out laughing.

"I've never been a Charlie before," Calumet continued. "Make it Charlie Wynne. Pick your own name for the girl."

Karola was brought in for photographs while the mechanic went to work on the documents, then taken back inside when her session was complete. Calumet and Gustav discussed planning and money.

"I'm light on cash," Calumet said. "Do you happen to have a Swiss account?"

"As a matter of fact, I do," Gustav replied.

"I can let you have a few thousand in cash and place the remainder in your account once we make it into Switzerland."

"That would be fine," Taschner smiled. "On the other hand, if you wish to conserve your cash, you may wait and wire the full amount to us once you get across."

"Very well," Calumet replied. "That's just what I'll do." This was *one* gift horse he had no intention of looking in the mouth. It was an unexpected gesture, and it confirmed his earlier hunches—Gustav and his merry band were more than just forgers and arms dealers. Gustav was an intelligence officer; Calumet was certain of it. An Israeli intelligence officer. Mossad.

It all made sense. What better way to keep tabs on the enemy than being an arms merchant for terrorists? What better way to know who was who in the internecine world of criminals than to be a forger who supplied phony legends to terrorist cells from one country to the next as they traipsed across the continent? *The devious chiselers,* Calumet thought in admiration. He smiled lightly to himself, envisioning the beauty of it all. *They don't really care whether I pay them or not. They figure I'm up against the Russians, so they're all for it. I owe you one, Paul De Boeck.*

"Let's discuss transportation," Jack said. "I can't take a chance on the BMW. Can you procure an automobile for us?"

"I *could,*" Gustav mused. He appeared to consider the problem, then said, "Maybe I have another solution, though."

"What's that?" Calumet asked suspiciously.

"Greta and I could drive you into Switzerland ourselves. I have some business to attend to in Zurich."

"If Karola causes problems at the border, I plan on making a run for it," Jack warned.

"No problem," Gustav answered. "You will be in the back of the van with her. Greta and I will be in the front. Just control her."

Jack thought it over briefly. "Okay," he finally agreed. "You've got a bargain. When can we leave?"

"As soon as Lutz is finished. Where are you going in Switzerland?"

"Shangri-La," Calumet smiled.

"Right," Gustav grinned back.

Calumet suddenly had an idea. "Do you have assets in Switzerland?"

"What do you mean, exactly?" Gustav asked, quickly alert.

"Let's cut the crap, Sabra," Calumet said mercurially. The term

Sabra referred to Israeli-born Jews. "Have you got assets who can set me up with a couple of safe houses in Switzerland?"

Overhearing the dialogue, Lutz suddenly lifted his head and looked at Gustav. Sänger did the same. They were not prepared for Calumet's keen burst of insight.

"Perhaps," Taschner replied, ignoring the assumption. "Where in Switzerland?"

"Wherever," Calumet stated. He was attempting to convey a message. Would Taschner assist him without making it official?

Taschner decided to take a gamble. "What is your status with the CIA?"

Calumet counted to ten before answering. He liked Taschner, but could he trust him? Yes, he concluded. His instincts told him to make the leap. "I'm under about as deep as you can get right now. I can't afford for any of this to make it into the official pipeline—Israeli, American, Russian, Martian, you name it."

"I have some people in Bern who do favors for us from time to time. They are not in any way connected to the government."

"Or the embassy?" Calumet probed.

"Or the embassy," Gustav assured him.

"Fine. In and around Bern. Two safe houses, virgin, and neither one located near the other. Can you set it up for me?"

"Consider it done," Gustav replied.

Calumet nodded his appreciation. These people were first-class.

They left at 3:00, Gustav and Greta sitting in front, Calumet and Karola squeezed together in the back, as planned. They crossed into Switzerland and arrived at St. Gallen about two hours later without incident. Karola had been no problem; she seemed resigned to her fate. In fact, Calumet had given her a choice before leaving.

"You're free to go, Karola," he'd said.

"What?"

"You're free to go. I don't need you anymore."

But Karola protested. "No, Jack. I've been a pain, I know, but I've changed my mind. I want to stay with you now," she had said. Calumet suspected that she had decided to play along for professional reasons. After all, her mission had been to get as close to him as possible. How much closer could she get to her target than being kidnapped by him? So the matter was settled. For the time being, anyway.

At St. Gallen they drove west to Zurich, where they were met by Ari and Inga.

"Adios," Calumet said to Gustav as he and Karola climbed into Ari's car. "I'll wire the money tomorrow. And thanks."

Gustav and Greta nodded their good-byes. Gustav had given Calumet his account number and the name of the bank, plus a contact number for future reference. Their business was concluded.

With Calumet and Karola aboard, Ari turned the car toward Bern.

CHAPTER 20

Other than outlining their prescribed agenda and discussing details, Ari and Inga spoke little during the drive to Bern. Karola slept on Calumet's shoulder the whole way, oblivious to the world. Calumet debated within himself about whether or not to let her sleep, knowing that she would have an edge if he allowed it, but in the end his humanity won out so he left her alone. They took the E17 from Zurich and arrived in Bern just as darkness was descending upon the medieval city.

Ari steered the car onto Bahnhofplatz in the center of town and parked outside the main station. Seconds later a man approached casually. Ari rolled down the window and spoke to him in Hebrew. After a few moments of quiet conversation, he cocked his head in Calumet's direction. "Everything is set," he informed him.

Jack nodded. He and Karola climbed out. The man introduced himself as Eitan. He began to explain the situation to Jack, but Jack cut him off, his eyes squinting almost imperceptibly in Karola's direction. Eitan understood. He led them to a waiting car. Calumet opened the back door and nodded for Karola to get in. When she was seated, he closed the door and faced Eitan.

"What have you got?" Calumet asked.

"Two safe houses, as requested," Eitan replied. He handed Calumet two keys—one for each habitation—and a note containing the addresses. "You plan to keep one location secret from the woman?" he asked.

"You got it," Calumet smiled. "Take us to the safe house in Worb, if you don't mind. This other location is in the city, not far from here. Right?"

"Right."

Eitan drove them to the quaint, historic suburb of Worb, arriving at the safe house in about twenty minutes. Calumet liked what he saw. The house was small and obscure. Eitan explained that it was customary for this particular domicile to accommodate renters, so the presence of two strangers should not attract any unwanted attention.

Calumet gave Eitan $500 in cash according to the arrangement he had made with Gustav, then he and Karola unlocked the door and went inside. The house was small but cozy, and nicely furnished. There was a living room with a couch and two recliners, a small fireplace, an open kitchen, and two bedrooms and a bath. But no telephone.

Karola saw that he was very tired and therefore decided to test his resolve. While standing together in the foyer, she flung her arms around his neck and kissed him.

"I'm sorry I gave you so much trouble," she whispered softly, saturating the statement with as much humility as it would bear.

She had a nice touch, Calumet thought, but he pushed her away gently. "Don't worry about it, Karola. I would have done the same." Smiling wearily, he added, "I need a contact number for Andrei."

Karola appeared startled. Recovering quickly she said, "I don't have a contact number for him. He always contacts me."

Calumet knew she was lying, but let it slide. He had another idea. "Oh? Oh, well. No problem. Listen, would you mind going into the kitchen and whipping up something light?"

Karola seemed pleased that he believed her. "Of course. In the meantime, why don't you get comfortable and relax? You must be exhausted."

"I am. And that's a good idea."

Karola glided into the kitchen while Calumet stretched out on a recliner in the living room. No wall separated the two chambers, which Calumet appreciated. It would be easier to keep an eye on her that way. He struggled to stay awake, making only a half-hearted effort to remain blandly alert while she flitted about.

"Soup?" she asked. "Will soup be all right?"

"Sure."

They sat at the small table in the kitchen and ate. Calumet wolfed down his portion in less than five minutes and felt rejuvenated from the nourishment. Standing, he said, "I have to go into town for a bit. You should try to get some sleep." He was interested to see how she would react, though he had already formed his own ideas.

"How long will you be gone?"

That's what I thought. What she really meant was—*How much time will I have before you return?* "Probably about an hour and a half, maybe two."

"You *are* coming back, aren't you?"

"But of course," Jack grinned. "Do you think I'd kidnap a prize like you and then leave you to the dogs?"

"I really don't know what to think about you, Jack. One moment you kiss me, the next you're threatening to kill me." He noticed she tried to appear hurt. "Anyway," she continued, "I'll probably relax in a hot bath while you're gone." Then, leaning into him, pressing her breasts against his chest and smiling devilishly, she added, "I might even still be in the tub when you get back."

Calumet kissed her lightly on the lips. "Save some hot water for me." Giving her his most reassuring smile, he turned and walked out, locking the door behind him.

Once outside, Calumet began striding the short distance to the train station. As he was leaving, he noticed the curtains in the front window stir. She was watching. He reached the station in about five minutes. Eitan was leaning against a pole near the track. Calumet noticed that although the man had probably seen his seventieth birthday come and go, he still appeared fit and lively. What hair he had left was sprinkled with gray, but his eyes and his demeanor were vibrant. The man had a lot of energy.

"She's all yours," Calumet told him.

Eitan nodded to three young men standing nearby. They set off in the direction of the safe house while Calumet and Eitan took the car and headed into Bern.

"I have to know something," Calumet said as they cruised along. "Are you Mossad? Or Aman?"

"Neither," Eitan answered without looking at him.

"But you were?"

Eitan turned his head and met Jack's penetrating gaze. "Yes, young man. I was."

"Mossad or Agaf Modiin?" Calumet asked, using the long form for Aman, or Israeli military Intelligence.

Eitan stared at him for an interminable few seconds, then answered, "Maybe both. Why?"

"Well, each service has always had its own personality, hasn't it? Maybe I'm trying to typecast you, old man." Jack smiled.

"You want maybe we should arm-wrestle sometime?" Eitan grinned. But the question was rhetorical. He continued, "Gustav asked me to keep this unofficial. Isn't that what you really want to know?" This time he was fishing for a response.

"Yes," Calumet admitted. "That's what I want to know. I want to know if the details of this whole setup are soaring into the airwaves from the Israeli embassy or being spirited away in the diplomatic bag by a fast plane. I hope not, because I desperately desire that all of this stay buried for the time being. In short, what I want is total autonomy. Is that what I've got?"

"Things were different in my day," Eitan digressed. "Communications were not so sophisticated, politics were not so pervasive in our services—not like they are today—and the rules were different. Today, there is no honor. In my years, we never put expediency above decency—not as a general principle. Sure, there were always critical exceptions and on occasion the odd bad apple; but for the most part, we had a code and we lived by it."

Oh, no, Calumet thought. He was extremely weary. *Another philosopher. Another one of King Arthur's Knights of the Round Table.*

"In my day," Eitan resumed, "we lived and died by our word." He shot a withering glare at Calumet. "I don't know what your game is, young man, but Gustav—his game I know. Gustav is a true warrior. For him, I do what he asks. He asked me to keep this unofficial, so I keep it unofficial. Understand?"

Thank God for King Arthur. "Yes," Jack replied, "I understand. Thank you."

"Your other safe house is not too far from the Bahnhof in an apartment we leased this afternoon. We were lucky. You should know, it took some doing to get the phone set up so quickly." He seemed to begrudge every word.

"Eitan," Jack's tone was thoughtful. For some strange reason he felt he had to justify himself to this man. "Obviously I can't tell you what my game is. If you want the truth"—he sighed heavily just then, the reality of his situation taking hold—"I'm not even sure myself at this point. But one thing I *can* tell you: I would fight to the death to keep the American flag from being trampled on. Do *you* understand?"

Eitan smiled. Nodding vigorously, he confided, "Now I know why Gustav trusted you. I can read it in you, just like Gustav must have read it. You're not sure yourself at this point?" He shook his head in wonderment. "You know something? You tell me you've got it all figured out, I know you're lying. You tell me you're not so sure, I know you're hurting inside. I know this. I've been there myself. I've gone through what you are going through right now. I know what it's like to be an agent operating on a need-to-know basis. Isn't that what you're doing? Operating on a need-to-know basis? Of course it is." He paused to make sure Calumet was hanging on every word. "They never give you credit, do they? They always think you don't need to know so much, right? And you want me to tell you something?" Nobody can dish out rhetorical questions like the Jews, Calumet thought. "Whatever the game is," the old spy continued, "you will work it out. I know people, and you will work it out, believe me."

"I always do," Calumet grinned, more to reassure himself than anything else. "I always do."

The old spy was enjoying the dialogue now, mostly his own, that is, in a sense reliving his greener days vicariously through Calumet. An agent on the run. Calumet wondered—had Eitan operated behind the lines in Egypt or Syria, posing as an Arab in the early days of Israel when they were struggling madly just to survive? Had he lived every single day with that special quiet terror in his mouth that only an undercover in a foreign country can truly understand? Who was this man? Did he have relatives who went into the camps and came out through the ovens? He was certainly within the age range, but he hadn't been there himself; that much was plain enough. The short-sleeved shirt he was wearing revealed that there were no tattoos on either arm, no number designating him as a survivor of the Holocaust. Whatever and whoever he was, though, he had come through it well and had aged gracefully in spite of it all. Ultimately, regardless of the whys and wherefores, Calumet concluded, Eitan was a good ally. A good man to know in a pinch. After all, he had been there himself, and apparently he understood.

Eitan dropped Calumet at the city safe house, saying he would be in touch with him in the morning. Calumet went inside. It was a one-bedroom affair, with a small kitchen and sitting room. He plopped down in a chair next to the phone. Lifting the receiver, he dialed the safe house in Berlin.

"Yeah!" Steve answered on the first ring.

"There's been a change of venue," Calumet said.

"What? What are you talking about?"

"I'm in Bern. If you want to continue this little action, you'd better get your carcass to Switzerland."

"You're *where?* Are you serious, Calumet? Listen to me—"

"I'll ring the Bern embassy tomorrow just before five," Calumet interrupted. "Be there, or Odyssey is finished." He hung up.

Next, he took out the note upon which he had scribbled Karola's phone number when he was browsing through her living room. He dialed the number. Vartanyan also answered on the first ring.

"How's it going, Andrei?"

"Who is this? Calumet?"

"In the flesh. I'm in Bern. Karola is safe. I'll meet you at the bear pits tomorrow at two o'clock. You owe me for our last meet. Bring the money or I'm history." He mashed the button with his finger and returned the receiver to its cradle.

Calumet briefly considered calling Diane, but chose not to take the chance. They probably had her surrounded by now. And he was too weary to go out and find another phone. As far as Karola was concerned, he was confident that Eitan's men were professionals and knew their jobs. They could keep tabs on her tonight; he would deal with her tomorrow. Thus, satisfied with the day's outcome and the succession of events, he went into the bedroom and collapsed. He was asleep in seconds.

*

Twenty minutes after Calumet left the safe house in Worb, Karola slipped out quietly and headed for the train station on foot. She was not aware of the three young men who shadowed her all the way. She immediately found a phone upon reaching the station and, like Calumet, called her home in Berlin. Andrei Vartanyan was waiting. She quickly explained everything and gave him the address of the safe house in Worb. Vartanyan probed her intuition concerning Calumet. Was he truly upset? Or was he acting? Has he made any verbal slipups? Has he committed any errors? No, Karola told him. Not that she could tell. He was on the edge, threatening to kill her, she said, but he must have been under extreme pressure to make those kind of threats because he is no killer by nature. Vartanyan agreed and then reassured her, "You've performed superbly, my dear. Stay close to him. We'll be there soon."

"Who is *we?*" Karola wanted to know.

"Me, my team."

"Is that all?"

Vartanyan hesitated momentarily. "No, Karola. Your father is coming along also. He's been worried about you."

Karola's voice suddenly deflated. "Sure he has."

Vartanyan knew how to gauge her, and he was not about to allow her to gain the upper hand by playing into her self-inflicted sympathy. "You will do as you're ordered, comrade. And that means that you will treat your father with the respect due any of your superiors. Understood?"

"Yes," Karola answered, her tone one of unfeigned resignation.

"Your father has performed brilliantly for our country. Without him, we would be lost in this operation. He is highly regarded by the most powerful men in Moscow. You would do well to keep that in mind, dear Karola."

Karola preserved the silence, not wishing to continue in the present vein.

"We'll be there in the morning about ten. You say Calumet is due back in the next hour or two?"

"Yes."

"Okay, my love. You know what to do. And I'm looking forward to seeing you. When this is all over, we'll take a trip somewhere."

"Oh, Andrei," she exclaimed gleefully. "Do you mean it?"

"Absolutely."

After ringing off, she walked hurriedly back to the safe house. She wanted to be there before Calumet returned. Not far away, one of Eitan's three surveillants stashed the tiny but extremely powerful pair of binoculars in his pocket. He was easily able to read the number she had dialed from the pay phone. He scribbled it down. Afterward, while the three shadows remained outside the safe house holding her under twenty-four-hour surveillance, Karola spent a good part of the night pacing the floor before she finally fell asleep. She had been looking forward to an evening with Calumet. There was something about him that intrigued her, that attracted her. She was highly disappointed when she finally realized that he wasn't coming back.

*

After Calumet had placed his calls, the lines and orbital repeaters began burning ferociously between Berlin and Bern, Berlin and Washington, and Berlin and Moscow. Nishka took it all in stride. In fact, he was pleased with the turn of events. Armbrister, on the other hand, was furious. And worried. It was evident in his conversation with Robert.

"It's not the way I wanted it to work out, Robert. Not exactly," Armbrister remonstrated.

"I told you not to underestimate him, Lewis."

"I'm not concerned so much by the fact that he was able to slip the Russians, the Germans, *and* us, but I'm concerned about what he said. It makes me wonder."

Robert said nothing. He would let the DDO sustain the tempo for now.

"Did he actually use the word? Did he actually say *Odyssey*, Robert?"

"That's what I'm told."

"That tears it! On an open line?"

Robert chose not to respond.

"Do you know what that means, Robert?"

Utter silence.

But Armbrister wasn't going to let it go this time. "Robert, I want an answer. Do you know what that means?"

"I think I know what *you* think it means, Lewis."

"Yeah? I'm sure you do. Well, I think it means one of two things, old friend. To use a code word like that—a defining code word—on an open line is absurd. Especially for someone as careful as Calumet. That was no Freudian slip, Robert. He said it on purpose. And I'll tell you what that means. It means that either that prima donna is in the process of switching sides, or he's already done it! If you want my opinion, I think Jack Calumet has made up his mind, Robert. He believes we've screwed him, and now he's going to even the score. He's cracked. The writing is on the wall, old friend. At the very best, Calumet has turned renegade! At the very worst, he's crossed over!"

Robert vouchsafed no opinion immediately, and his hush was deafening. In fact, if the truth be told, he was actually bordering on thinking the same thoughts as Armbrister. Why *did* Calumet use that word? he pondered.

CHAPTER 21

Although he slept soundly, Calumet was up at first light. He showered quickly. When he stepped out of the bathroom, he found Eitan sitting in the front room, waiting.

"You could get accidentally shot like that, old man," Calumet stated. He was angry with himself for not securing the door with a chair or something.

Eitan grinned. "At my age, everything in life is a gamble. Besides, I had a key, and you apparently believe that locks will keep out the ganevim."

"Ganevim?"

"Criminals, murderers."

"Yeah. Well, thanks for the Hebrew lesson. You ready to move?"

"Whenever you are, young man."

Calumet smiled. "Then let's get cracking, mate."

Eitan filled in the details for Calumet while they drove toward Worb. "She left the safe house about twenty minutes after you did last night. She walked to the train station and made a call to this location." He handed Calumet a slip of paper with Karola's phone number. "The call lasted approximately fifteen minutes. She subsequently returned to the safe house and finally switched off the lights at about three this morning. At last report, she's still inside and still asleep."

"Excellent!"

"Not really," Eitan rejected the praise. "My man was supposed to get close enough to overhear the conversation, but he concluded that she would make him if he did, so he held back."

"No problem," Jack replied. "I know whom she called, and I know what she said."

Eitan smiled. "I thought as much."

Calumet reached into his pocket and extracted $2,500 in cash. He handed the money to Eitan. "You've been a big help. Thanks."

Eitan accepted the money, then said, "Our agreement was only two thousand. You've overpaid me."

"Eitan," Calumet said philosophically, "you may be older than me, but hasn't anybody ever told you not to look a gift horse in the mouth?"

Eitan grinned. "As a matter of fact, I was trained to *always* look a gift horse in the mouth."

Calumet laughed. "Consider it a tip. I might wish to do business with you again in the future, and I want you to have pleasant thoughts of my patronage."

"Very well," Eitan replied. "I'll try to think good thoughts of my young American friend from now on."

"Good. While you're thinking," Calumet said, suddenly producing an additional $500, "can you procure another safe house and phone for me by this evening?"

Eitan stared at him for a moment. He was apparently beginning to appreciate Calumet's feral flair. "I suppose I could."

Calumet handed him the five hundred. "I'll need a contact number. I'll call you around four this afternoon."

Eitan nodded his assent and supplied the number. They pulled up just around the corner from the safe house in Worb. Eitan's man approached the car. "No change," he said. "She's still inside. And no lights, so we assume she's still asleep."

"Gather the boys," Eitan ordered. "We're all through here."

Calumet shook hands and got out. He waited until all three men had arrived and then watched his makeshift surveillance team disappear into the morning haze. He walked the short distance to the safe house and entered softly.

Finding Karola fast asleep, he shook her gently and half-whispered, "Karola, I'm home."

Karola turned over, blinking her eyes and suddenly realizing where she was. She smiled, her teeth bright, her lips bidding. She was wearing a sleek semitransparent blue negligee which had been in the closet. Calumet was almost overcome by her beauty, even without makeup. She was truly a ravishing creature, he thought. In fact, her sexual suggestiveness was vivid even when she wasn't trying.

"Where have you been?" she yawned. "What time is it?"

"It's about six-thirty. Sorry, sweetheart, but I thought I was under surveillance. I checked into a cheap hotel near the Bahnhof and then fell asleep."

"Climb in here with me, Jack," she said huskily. Her lips were open a crack, glistening, inviting, and the tip of her tongue was slightly cocked. She rose up on one elbow, exposing a portion of her left nipple. "I want you," she stated simply.

Calumet could tell she wasn't acting. She truly desired him at the moment. Correspondingly, he felt the same, but he knew better. "As much as I'd like to, I can't. Not right now. I have some errands to run first. Want to come along?"

"What kind of errands?" Obviously she was disappointed at being spurned yet again.

"You go back to sleep," Calumet said, standing. "I'll be back later."

"No!" She leaped out of bed. "Just give me a few minutes."

Calumet smiled. He had no intention of leaving without her, but thought it best if it was her idea. He knew she was under orders to stay with him.

They rode the train into Bern and ate a light breakfast of danish, coffee, and milk at the Bahnhof. Afterward, Calumet led her to the safe house he had slept in.

"What is this?" she asked, suddenly alert.

"Another safe house," Jack replied calmly, smiling. "This is where we're going to spend the night together."

"Oh!" she exclaimed, though it was evident that she was still a bit skeptical.

After they were inside, Calumet locked the door. Karola conducted a cursory inspection of the premises, then they both took a seat in the front room. Calumet pulled his chair very close, facing her.

"You didn't check into a hotel, did you?" she accused. "You slept here last night."

"Brilliant deduction, pretty lady." Calumet's tone was suddenly somber and slightly sinister. It sent chills through Karola and actually made her shudder.

"What's going on?" she asked, startled now. "What is this about?"

"You never finished the story about your father. You're going to do that now."

"The hell with you!" she shouted. She jumped up to leave.

Calumet forced her back into the chair. He let her keep her purse this time, as he had already made a thorough examination of the contents the previous day. "Don't fight me, Karola. You have no wins against me."

"Go ahead!" she spat. "Beat it out of me!"

"I'll leave those tactics to your Russian friends, if you please. I've got plenty of time, so we'll just sit here until you're ready to talk."

She compressed her lips, obviously attempting to communicate that she was the personification of patience. Calumet folded his arms and stared her bumptiously in the eyes.

"Do you have a cigarette?" she asked after a minute.

"Sure." He went to the kitchen and snatched a pack of Gitanes from the drawer. He gave her the pack, along with a box of wooden matches. An ashtray sat on an end table next to her chair. She extracted a cigarette and lit it.

"Why do you want to know about my father?" she blurted.

"Did he visit you often? Before your mother was killed, I mean?"

She held her peace for about twenty seconds, glaring maliciously. Then, finally concluding that the disclosure couldn't hurt, she answered, "No, not at first. Why?"

"Not at first," Calumet mused. "Hmm. But later, in the months or weeks preceding your mother's death, then the frequency of his visits increased. Right?"

"Maybe," she said. Almost like a little girl.

"Were you happy to see him then? When he began to visit more often?" He took the *maybe* as a *yes*.

"Sometimes. He always brought me things. Mostly the latest fashions." Her next statement came out of left field. "What girl wouldn't be enormously pleased with such gifts?"

"Indeed," Calumet smiled. *She felt guilty for being pleased! Interesting.* "What was your favorite gift of all?" he asked, suddenly cheerful.

She returned the smile, faintly, as though it came upon her against her will. "He brought me a black English riding outfit, with a white blouse and a leather riding crop. I always treasured that the most."

"Did he take you riding, then?" Calumet asked quickly.

"Yes. That's what I enjoyed the most about his visits."

"And what did you enjoy the least?"

She said nothing.

"Was it the arguments?" Calumet suddenly inquired. "Karola, tell me. Was it the arguments between your father and your mother?"

"Yes!" she screamed. "I want to leave."

Calumet inched forward and stroked her hair. "You're doing fine, Karola." He knew she had been badgered and broken before. The spiritual evidence was painfully transparent. In turn, this caused him to be at odds within himself. He realized he had to break her again, but he didn't like it. Not at all. However, he had a reason. If he could pinpoint her weakness and capitalize on it, he just might be able to compromise her sufficiently enough so that he could play her back against Vartanyan. It was a thankless task, but Calumet figured he would need every advantage he could muster and then some in order to make it back home. He decided to cause her a measure of discomfort.

"I'm afraid we're in for a long haul, Karola. This is probably going to take hours." That was not true, it was just a ruse, but making her think it—if he read her correctly—would cause her to speak voluminously in an attempt to speed the process along and get it over with. He had no doubt that she had given Vartanyan the address of the safe house in Worb and that Vartanyan and his team would be arriving at any time. She was probably expected to be there.

"Please," she begged, "I don't want to go through this. What do you want to know.

"What you don't understand, Karola," Calumet patronized her, "is that I'm trying to help you. I want you to admit what you've been burying deep inside yourself all these years. I want you to come clean. You'll feel better once it's all out in the open."

"What are you talking about? And what makes you think you can help me? That's obviously just a line."

"Oh?" Calumet said sardonically. "I don't believe you really think that, Karola. You see, all the others before me have merely used you. Including Andrei Vartanyan. I haven't. I haven't violated your soul by taking you to bed. Not that I haven't wanted to, believe me. But I care about you as a person, not as a sex object."

She suddenly seemed to soften at his implications, abruptly respectful of his prescient overtones. His explanation offered her ego an 'out,' and she needed the explanation because she wasn't accustomed to failure—not when it came to sex. "Is that really why you've refused to go to bed with me?"

"Absolutely! I genuinely like you, Karola."

"Well, what are you talking about, Jack? What is it that you think I'm hiding?"

He had her wondering now, her curiosity titillated, but it was too early in the process, Calumet knew, to take her into the depths. He needed to work her first, soften her resolve, guide her up and down the mountain, an emotional roller-coaster ride, before he went at her head-on. He decided to crash every barrier separately, one at a time, then quickly back off, allowing her a brief respite. Subsequently, after each upheaval, each of which he carefully orchestrated, he would then charge on to the next wall of resistance and smash it down without warning. To accomplish this, he initially took her back to her father's visits and concentrated on the happy days, his words soothing and pure. Sometimes he covered the same ground twice, or even three times, depending on what seemed to work. Then, like ripples in a pond, he submerged slowly into the depths, ever toward her perimeters, and forced her to remember those disagreeable occasions of her father's visits, which were many. She repelled at first, but grew weaker with each pass. Just as a person who sticks his hand in cold water, then in hot, and repeats the process for several minutes, soon finding himself incapable of telling the difference, Calumet was able to confuse her emotional sensitivities, and she became vexed at his instigations. She hated him one minute, laughed with him the next. And all the while he was driving for the pole. He wanted *all* the memories of her father stirring inside her when he sprang. At last, sensing that the time was ripe, sensing that the valley was now fertile, Calumet began to close the circle and move in for the kill.

"Let's step back briefly to your mother's death," he said sympathetically. *Here it goes.* "Your mother's death was no accident, and you know it."

"Yes it was!" she shouted vigorously, protesting too much. "And you're crazy. I told you she was the victim of an attempted mugging." The tears began to cascade, forging rivulets down her cheeks. "What are you trying to do to me?"

"That's just the official line, Karola. Oh, sure. I'm positive that's what it looked like to the West Berlin police—a simple mugging—but the whole thing was staged, wasn't it?"

"No! I don't know what you're talking about, and I want to leave. *Now!*"

"The fact is," Calumet continued, "it was a hit, pure and simple. Your father and mother had been arguing for months, or weeks maybe—the duration is not really important—because your father wanted to take you back to Russia and your mother would have no part of it. She knew what he would turn you into ultimately, and she fought against your emigration with all her might. And in the final analysis that's what got her killed, isn't it? Your father had your mother killed, Karola, and you've suspected or known it all along!"

The floodgates opened suddenly and she sobbed in great heaves, the crying punctuated with loud groans. Calumet held her tightly, his assumptions finally confirmed in her pain.

"I didn't know," she quivered, a fragile little girl. "I promise. I didn't know. Do you believe me, Jack?" Suddenly she was starving for approval.

"Yes," he soothed her. She had been living with the guilt all these years. Her ambivalent feelings toward her father, one moment loving him, the next distrusting him, was too much for her. Calumet speculated that the inconsistency went a long way in contributing to her voyeuristic nature. "But you suspected all along, didn't you?"

"Not at first," she sobbed. "But later, when I'd grown up and gotten to know my father better, that's when I began to suspect."

"And you never confronted him about it? Ever?"

She shook her head, fresh wails gushing out now, the tears flowing rivers.

"Under the circumstances, I don't think I could have either," Calumet consoled her. "That would have taken enormous reserves, and I don't think I would have been brave enough. I'm not sure anyone would. Does Andrei Vartanyan know your father?" It was possible that they knew each other, he supposed. He hoped so. The subject of Andrei Vartanyan was the crux of his entire assault. All he needed was the proper opening.

"Yes."

Perfect! "And how much of your own story does Vartanyan know, then?" If he was her handler, he would know a great deal, Calumet surmised.

"I imagine he knows quite a lot about me, though I don't think he suspects that my father had anything to do with my mother's death."

"I wouldn't make that assumption, Karola. Andrei Vartanyan is about as sharp as they come. My guess is that he knows *everything* and has simply decided to whitewash it. In exactly the same way as your father has whitewashed it." *If I can force her to equate Andrei Vartanyan with her father, I've got her.*

"No!" she retorted, suddenly defiant. "Andrei loves me!"

It was the only hope she could hang on to, he thought. The hope that somebody in her barren world truly cared about her. "Think about it, Karola. Andrei Vartanyan is your controller. It necessarily follows that he knows your entire case history. *Any* professional handler would have studied you backwards and forwards, and if Andrei Vartanyan is anything, he's a consummate professional. It is therefore only logical that he would know the truth about your mother."

The syllogism found purchase in Karola, and her demons seemed to struggle momentarily with the intuition. Still, she could not let go of the lie. The corresponding free-fall would probably destroy her. "If Andrei knows—which I'm not convinced that he does—then he hasn't informed me simply because he doesn't want to hurt me. I told you, he loves me."

"If he truly loves you, Karola, then why is he doing everything he can to get you into bed with me? I couldn't do that to a woman I loved. No way. I'll tell you why he's doing it. He's using you, and you know it."

"The state is more important than the individual," she chanted. The party rhetoric was her last line of defense.

"Not where I come from, lady. The state is made up of individuals, each individual precious, each possessing certain inalienable rights. Without the individual, there would *be* no state. And the fact is, the party dogma is just an excuse. An excuse to let the end justify the means. Andrei Vartanyan will ultimately discard you like an old suit when he is finished with you. After all, he actually *believes* that the state is more important than the individual. He *believes* that the individual should be sacrificed for the welfare of the state. In this case, that means you; you're the individual, and Vartanyan is using the machinations of Moscow to impersonate the state." Calumet decided to gamble. "I'll bet he even told you he'd do something very nice for you when this is all over, didn't he? A long vacation, perhaps? With plenty of wine, song, and romance? Something like that?"

Karola was rapidly coming to the conclusion that Jack Calumet *did* have powers which she couldn't even begin to comprehend. His insight was uncanny. She had no idea that he was merely following a logical progression of facts. He knew she and Vartanyan had spoken by telephone last night and that the Russian would have egged her on and encouraged her, made her feel good about herself, given her fuel to run on. Any competent handler would have done the same. The fact that Calumet had hit upon the presage of a vacation was simply the offshoot of his discernment of her character. What would engender fruits of pleasure in this woman? Wine, song, romance, of course. Those things were only natural in view of what she was. Besides, what else could it be? She was way beyond black English riding outfits with a white blouse and a leather riding crop. In fact, she was way beyond a lot of things.

"Who are you?" she asked, amazed at his mental prowess.

"I may be the only friend you have on this earth, Karola."

"Friends don't threaten to kill friends, Jack."

It was the first coherent point she'd made. "I did not know your situation then. Don't forget, I'm a hunted man. I knew you were working for the Russians, and they're certainly no friends of mine. As far as I was concerned, you were out to get me, just like all the others." *Maybe that will work,* he thought.

"What's changed?" she challenged.

"What's changed? The fact that you are being used just like I am. It's obvious. You're nothing but another sacrificial lamb, just like me. We're simpatico, Karola."

"You mean you don't have any ulterior motives?" Karola asked askance. "You want nothing from me?"

"I want nothing from you if you don't want to give it," Jack finessed. "I guess, most of all, I just wanted you to see the truth for what it is, and then not be afraid to confront it. Whatever happens, Karola, Andrei Vartanyan is not your friend. Lover maybe, but not your friend."

Karola did not respond immediately. Calumet could perceive that his seedling was taking root, that his inculcations were grabbing her thoughts and taking hold. Whatever the outcome of his interrogation, he had placed the stigma of doubt in her mind. She would never look upon Vartanyan in exactly the same way. She would never trust him fully, never again.

"What *do* you want from me, Jack?" she finally asked.

"What is your father's name?"

"Ha!" she laughed facetiously. "He has a thousand names. Which one would you like?"

"Why don't we start with his real one?" Calumet smiled.

"I have a better idea," she said deviously.

"What's that?"

"He and Andrei are arriving in Bern this morning. How would you like to meet him?"

Calumet was stunned. He was completely unprepared for the revelation. This was the first hint that her father was involved in Operation Odyssey. Calumet had never entertained the notion of her father's involvement. He figured her father was merely another bureaucrat serving in some supercilious capacity as some sort of intelligence officer for Moscow, but he'd had no suspicions whatsoever that the man was actually intertwined with his own operation. Who *is* her father? he suddenly wondered.

"Is your father Andrei's superior?" he asked, attempting to hide his incredulity.

"Yes," she replied glibly, enjoying the upper hand for a change. "My father is operationally in charge of whatever he and Andrei are currently involved in. It obviously has something to do with you."

Calumet took a deep breath. Here was a perfect opportunity to knock in a grand slam. If he could turn Karola, he would be in the catbird seat. Looking intently into her eyes and placing his hands on her shoulders, he asked, "Are you going to give away the location of this safe house, Karola? Are you going to tell them about this conversation?"

"If I say yes," she answered seriously, "are you going to hurt me?"

The way she said it almost broke him. He knew she'd been hurt before. In fact, was there ever a time when she wasn't hurt? Was there ever a time when she was at peace? He struggled to keep from wincing and cursed a forming tear silently. *No! Square it away, Jack. Stay focused.* He dug down and forced himself to remain hard-hearted. He took her into his arms and squeezed her tightly. Stroking her hair he said, "I'm not ever going to hurt you. Period." He pushed her gently away so he could gaze into her eyes again. "You've been hurt far too much in this life already, Karola." Appearing remorseful, he removed his hands and sat back. "I just thought you might feel that you owe it to your mother, that's all. I thought you might feel that any appeasement of Andrei Vartanyan and your father would dishonor her memory. Since they're both in this thing together, that is." *Make her think that her father and Vartanyan are both alike. Tie them together. And then get rid of her. Right now. Before she breaks my own no-good lying heart.* "You're free to go, Karola."

Whatever it was he said had found its mark. Silent tears made a sudden appearance on her cheeks. She dabbed at them quickly. "Are you coming with me?"

"No," Jack admitted, forcing a smile. "Not now, Karola. You go back and tell them that I'll meet Vartanyan at the bear pits as scheduled. I'm on a high wire, and you know it. I have to be extremely careful. You're familiar with this location now. If you want to see me later"—he extracted his key and gave it to her—"you can use this. If I'm not here, just wait for me." He kissed her. "You'd better be going. I would imagine they'll be arriving soon, won't they?"

She leaned over and hugged him warmly, genuinely. "Yes."

Walking to the door, they embraced once more and kissed, holding the pose for several moments. Calumet wanted the whole world to stop. He wanted what he knew he could never have, and in that instant he felt as though he was being overwhelmed with melancholy. But then Karola rescued him.

She pushed away from him suddenly, clutching him at arm's length. "Jack!" she said excitedly. "I've got money. Plenty of money. Let's run away from all of this. Just the two of us. The South Pacific or somewhere." Her eyes were dancing with anticipation.

Calumet had been fighting his attraction to her from day one, but he couldn't hold out any longer. Her nature had been gaining on him all along. He couldn't help himself. He grappled her to his body, squeezing her. She had gone from siren to ingenue on a whim. Just like that. She was free of her demons suddenly, and she seemed so innocent, so childishly vulnerable. She had suddenly become hopelessly irresistible in her nouveau purity. Jack's heart was pounding, and he was sure she could feel it beating against her breasts. Only a few days already, and he was falling into her snare after all, though it was not the snare she intended originally. He suddenly wanted her like he'd wanted no other woman before. Ever. For the first time in a long time, he was himself vulnerable. Why? He didn't know. Maybe it was the strain. Whatever, he kissed her passionately.

After a moment he withdrew. "Karola, I, uh, I can't. Not right now. I just can't."

"Why? Whatever you're involved in is no good, and we both know it. Oh, Jack. Opportunities like this come once in a lifetime. I love you, Jack."

He closed his eyes, willing himself not to say it, but he said it anyway. "I guess I feel the same way, Karola." *God help me!*

She crashed into him again. "Then let's do it, Jack. Let's get out of here forever."

He broke her grasp and stood apart, his head turning away. He didn't need this. Not now. Suddenly things were very, very complicated.

"Don't make me go back," she pleaded, tears threatening, a recalcitrant, pervasive fear returning to her eyes. "I don't want to face them anymore. Andrei. My father. Not anymore. Never again. Please?"

Calumet was screaming inside. He had set out to break her, but had surpassed even his own expectations. He had done more than break her, he had converted her beyond recovery. NASA couldn't bring her back now. In just a few minutes she had become a little girl again, with a little girl's simple wants. She was a young woman who simply desired to be loved. She craved bonding. She wanted to feel safe and secure. Those things had always been impossible for her before, but suddenly she discovered that it could all come true, and she was reaching for it with everything she had. She was begging him not to send her back into the lion's den.

But where Calumet was, there was no way out. In her original desire to entrap him, and in his determination to turn it around on her, they had both been ambushed by an unforeseen enemy. It was a cruel irony, of sorts. They had both been blindsided by something known as "true feelings," of all things. True feelings. Imagine that. Espionage and true feelings somehow seemed iconoclastic. The two just didn't mix. And to top it all off, Calumet was feeling pretty isolated himself. He felt as though his own people were deserting him, and he did not know why. So perhaps the hardest thing he ever did in his entire life was refuse her.

"Karola," he sighed, "you're going to have to trust me." She started shaking her head at that declaration, and her body trembled, as if monsters were about to overrun her position, but Jack took her by the shoulders to steady her. "Listen" he continued softly, "it will pan out. You can come with me when this mess is all over." Mercifully, pesky thoughts of how he was planning to work Diane into the equation didn't invade his mind just then. "It won't be long before we can be together permanently. We'll have nothing but time on our hands. I promise."

"Why?" she cried. "Why do you have to have further dealings with Andrei and my father? I hate them. Why?"

"Because." Calumet spoke distantly, as if the explanations were way beyond her powers of comprehension. "I just do. I have to finish what we've started."

She looked longingly into his eyes. "I don't want to go back," she whimpered. But she knew it was hopeless. She bowed her head in resignation and leaned against his chest, a squadron of tears once again dive-bombing her cheeks.

Calumet stroked her hair. "We'd better go," he said gently.

She jerked away and started fixing her face. "Fine!" she snapped angrily.

"Karola, I'll get you out. I promise."

"Forget it, Jack. If your little games are more important to you than I am, fine. I can deal with it."

He attempted to mollify her, but she would have none of him now. She had tunneled back inside her cocoon where it was safe, a tortoise on a four-lane. She huffed through the front door, Jack right behind her.

Once outside, they went their separate ways. Calumet was troubled. On the one hand, he felt as though he had overcome a major hurdle; on the other, he was emotionally drained and marginally depressed. From a professional standpoint, there was always the risk that she might betray him and give up this particular location, but deep down he didn't think so. He knew he had gotten to her, even though she had turned spiteful at the end. But what could he expect? For possibly the first time in her life she had made herself vulnerable, only to be spurned. At least in her own mind she had been spurned. And although Calumet didn't see it that way exactly, he remembered the old adage that hell hath no fury like a woman scorned. She was in a volatile state at the moment. There was no telling what she would do. Calumet admitted to himself that he had fallen for her, but he was not ready to admit it to her—not fully. Not yet. He had too many other irons in the fire, such as the debt of honor he owed to Conrad Thurman and family. He could not rest until that particular act of chivalry had been utterly dispatched—not when it was in his power to do the dispatching.

Calumet analyzed his confusion as he left the safe house. He began to wander the streets of Bern aimlessly, thinking it through, and in the final analysis, he concluded, he had performed admirably. He was pleased with the operational results of what had just transpired. In a way, he had won.

For all his acumen though, and completely unaware of a banal, hidden truth, he had, in reality, fallen just a tad short. While his interrogation of the woman had been classic, he had committed a single, fateful error: he did not press for the father's name. At this moment, he did not view the omission as significant.

CHAPTER 22

After a brief shopping tour where he picked up extra clothing, a suitcase, and toiletries, Calumet checked into the Hotel Ambassador at the southern tip of Bern, across the river Aare. He was able to wangle a room on the top floor of the nine-story establishment, registering under one of the aliases he had procured from De Boeck. He would not use the room for more than several hours, but in the meantime he felt he needed a base of operations. A safe base, isolated from the world of spooks, including Eitan and company.

In addition to his other purchases, he also counted among his recent acquisitions a pair of expensive Gleiss binoculars. His room faced the Aare and he could surveil a wide area across the river with them. It was more or less a long shot, but he decided to try and spot enemies—or even friendlies—making their way east toward the bear pits and his rendezvous with Vartanyan. The meet was still several hours away, so he would not begin his observances until the appropriate time. In the interim, he phoned his bank and instructed them to wire Gustav's money to the account number he had been given. After completing that task, he was satisfied that he had done all he could do. He tried to relax, restively awaiting his hour.

*

Vartanyan was also waiting, pacing back and forth impatiently. He was in the safe house when Karola arrived.

"How did you get inside?" she asked, startled.

"Are you alone?" Vartanyan countered.

"Yes."

He strode to the curtains and peered outside. "Are you all right?" he further inquired as he continued to watch the streets. He had barely glanced her way.

"Of course I'm all right," she answered flippantly. "Why wouldn't I be?"

He jerked his head slightly and gazed intently in her direction. *Something has changed,* he thought. For the merest instant he could have sworn her eyes reflected unrequited hatred.

Realizing how she must have come across, she sailed over and threw her arms around him. "I've missed you, Andrei." The admission sounded hollow.

He pushed her back and held her at arm's length. "Is everything okay?"

"Yes, everything is superb," she pirouetted. "Why? What's wrong?"

Vartanyan stared quizzically at her for a moment before responding. "Nothing," he said finally. "Where is the American?"

"He wouldn't come back with me. He told me to tell you that he'll meet you at the bear pits, as arranged."

Vartanyan nodded thoughtfully. "Did he stay here with you last night?"

"No," Karola responded forlornly. "He did not show up until early this morning." She sought a reaction in Vartanyan, but could not discern one. It obviously made no difference to him whether or not Calumet had slept with her. *Maybe Jack is right,* she pondered. She pulled away suddenly. "I need to sit down and relax. I've been on my feet all morning." She plopped into the nearest chair.

Vartanyan was perplexed; he perceived an ever so subtle change in her character. "Where were you that you were on your feet all morning?"

"Yes," her father's voice chimed in abruptly. The refined patrician stepped suddenly out of the hallway's shadows and entered the room. "Where were you, Karola?"

*

Calumet's original medical records arrived in Moscow in the wee hours of a balmy Russian morning. The inclement hour did not keep Nishka from marshaling his forces. His forensics team had been on standby ever since Nishka had been informed by George Menzel's cutout that the illegal had successfully fulfilled his obligation to the Party.

Nishka briefly perused the records, mainly just to make sure they were what they had been purported to be—namely, originals that matched his previous copy—then handed them to his aide. "Forensics!" he snapped. "I want a preliminary report by tomorrow evening."

"Yes, Comrade Nishka." The aide turned on his heels and began to march.

"And tell them I want them to concentrate on the inks first," the Russian spymaster called out after him. The inks were important; they could be the terminal exposé of the entire operation. *Besides, that's the same mistake Armbrister made in Istanbul,* he recalled.

*

Team Interceptor was beginning to feel like Regular Army—hurry up and wait. Minutes after Calumet's call the previous evening, they had been given the address of a CIA safe house near Bern and had been told to make their separate ways to that destination by the most expedient means commercially available. Two flew, two took trains, and Rossetti interpreted the order literally. Which is to say, he interpreted the order similarly to the way a seasoned burglar might interpret the placid setting of a house with an unlatched window.

The most expedient means commercially available, in his view, especially since it would not be considered good form to have three of them *flying* into the small Bern-Belp Airport, was what his old friends in the Bronx would have called a "ride." He rented, at the covert fund's expense, the fastest car he could lay his hands on. That turned out to be a black Ferrari Spider. And the black Ferrari Spider turned out to be fast. Very fast. Rossetti made a point of flushing the carburetors whenever the roadway appeared to be amenable to ballistic travel, and a few times even when it didn't. Amazingly, he had only five or six near misses over the course of the entire trip, and that wasn't bad considering the fact that he was in the peculiar habit of turning his lights off from time to time on the more isolated stretches of pavement. The primary cause of such an odd disorder could probably be attributed to a voracious thrill-demon lurking somewhere inside him, but there was also a smattering of something else. He seemed to challenge himself perpetually, in one way or another, and the challenge on this particular journey manifested itself when he got the crazy idea that he would make the most of a splendid opportunity by working on his night vision. After all, night vision was important in his line of work, and the extrasensory capability was more or less like a muscle–the more you exercised it, the stronger it became. At any rate, he got there safely. And now, once again, all five of them were caged up, sitting on their orders. Hurry up and wait.

Then Steve came bustling in. He carried a small bag in one hand and a map of the city in the other. "It's a long shot, but we want you to fan out and try to locate Calumet."

"Where is Robert?" Rossetti inquired.

"He said he had some other business to attend to," the DO replied. "Haven't seen him for a while." He set the bag down and spread the map out on a table. "We suspect Calumet will be meeting the Russians sometime today. Hopefully, the meet will take place out in the open where we have a chance of picking it up, instead of in a safe house. Bern Station is mounting a surveillance operation against the Russian Residency. With any luck, one of our two efforts will put us onto him."

"I don't understand," Rossetti said. None of them had been told anything. "Isn't Calumet on our side? Hasn't he checked in?"

Steve looked him in the eye. "Yes," he replied gravely, "he's checked in." After a slight pause he continued. "As to whether or not he's on our side, that's a question that is very much in a state of flux at the moment."

"What does that mean?" Rossetti asked.

"That's all you need to know," Steve remarked offhandedly.

Sure, Rossetti thought, *you hang him out to dry, and then when he initiates actions which are aimed purely at self-preservation, you immediately label him a potential traitor. I get it.* "So what do we do if we find him?" he asked.

Steve opened the bag and started handing out radios. "Report it immediately. The frequencies have already been set. Let's take a look at the geography." He pointed to a spot on the map. "Yardley, you take the west side and–"

"I'll handle the deployment of my men," Rossetti interrupted. His voice allowed no quarter for argument.

Steve surveyed the other members of the team and quickly concluded that he was not necessarily among friends. "Fine," he finally said to Rossetti. "Get started immediately then, as soon as you nail down the assignments." He nodded and walked out the door.

"Yardley," Rossetti commanded, grinning and overemphasizing

his words, "you take the west side." A chorus of laughter bounced around the room. Rossetti then doled out the remaining assignments and Team Interceptor went hunting.

*

"What do you care where I've been?" Karola asked her father.

Her father glared in response. She had never been easy. "Karola, my concern for your welfare is unfortunately not the problem here today. There are far more important issues at stake. Now, where were you?"

Vartanyan eyed her searchingly. His gaze retained a faraway look, as if he had somehow withdrawn his psychic presence in order to study the matter privately. *Something about her has definitely changed,* he postulated.

"I had breakfast with the American at the Bahnhof," Karola replied casually. "Then we walked along the Aare near the bear pits. He said he wanted to have a look before his meet with Andrei this afternoon."

Vartanyan returned from his netherworld. "Did he tell you why he did not spend the night here? Or did you even ask?"

"As a matter of fact, I *did* ask," she replied confidently. "He came up with some lame excuse about being under surveillance. He told me he checked into a cheap hotel and fell asleep."

The two men exchanged glances. "Why do you think you've been unsuccessful in compromising him?" Vartanyan accused.

If Karola had any doubts before about the efficacy of Calumet's words, they dissolved on this turn of the conversation. This moment became pivotal in her life. Vartanyan, her heretofore handler, lover, and confidant, had suddenly adopted the attitude of a royal inquisitor. He was toeing the party line obediently and operating by the stricture of the manual. If the slightest shred of humanity ever existed in his insatiate being, he had misplaced it long ago. He had now become so callous that he could readily ignore the subtle groans of his scheming, crusted heart, the fleeting enticement of power rendering him deaf to the *living* world—if he ever had a heart to begin with, that is. And for the first time in her life, Karola began to question her own beleaguered soul. She was digging down, sorting through years of travesty and deceit. In some small measure, she was confronting the pain of her own repressive past and discovering simultaneously, with great surprise, that her fear of such a confrontation after all this time had been much, much greater than the actual emprise of one day going through it. For the first time in her checkered, degraded life, she began to feel released.

She glared at Vartanyan. "You mean, why have I failed to compromise him *sexually?* Isn't that what you mean, Andrei?" She wanted to hear him say it.

"Precisely!" Vartanyan snapped.

"Probably because he knows I already belong to you. He's nobody's fool, Andrei." She glanced at her father. "Calumet is nobody's fool," she repeated.

"Does that include the CIA?" her father asked quickly. "He's not our fool; he's not your fool. Is he the CIA's fool, Karola?"

"Nobody's fool," she emphasized.

"You've been with him all this time," Vartanyan interjected. "You've talked with him, had a chance to analyze him, seen him at his weakest, perhaps. Are you absolutely positive that Jack Calumet is not a CIA provocateur, Karola?"

"He's a mercenary," she replied confidently. "Nothing more, nothing less. I'm positive!"

Vartanyan and her father locked eyes. The patrician nodded. Facing her once again, Vartanyan asked, "Are you willing to bet your life on that, Karola? Are you willing to bet your life that Jack Calumet is not working for the Americans?"

She glanced uncertainly at the two men, her head swiveling back and forth in a vain attempt to read them. *Are they merely questioning my loyalty?* she wondered. *Probably.* "Yes," she confessed. "I'd bet my life on that."

"That's a shame," her father responded evenly. "I've known Jack Calumet intimately for six years, and you just lost, daughter."

CHAPTER 23

Bern, although the capital of Switzerland, was more of a large provincial town than a city. At least it seemed that way. And yet, attempting to locate a single individual by fanning out and trolling the streets, well, that was certainly an ambitious undertaking no matter how you cut it.

The deployment of Rossetti's men was orchestrated not by the points of the compass, as Steve would have done if he had gotten his way, but by Rossetti's own peculiar formula. He knew Calumet was no traitor. Hell, Rossetti reckoned, any field man would be able to figure out what was really going on. Sure. Simple as pie. The racehorse was fighting the bit—that was all. A natural, completely predictable reaction. As such, Rossetti did not think too highly of Steve's plan for ferreting out a spy. In fact, Rossetti did not think too highly of Steve, period. Steve was a typical establishment man. Smart as a whip, no doubt, but a conformer, and the way Rossetti saw it, most conformers would usually conform to just about anything. Not that there was something wrong with playing for the team; he didn't mean that kind of conformer. Rossetti meant the kind of conformer who conformed out of blind regimen as opposed to conforming because he believed that the enterprise he was undertaking was truly the right thing to do. That kind of conformer.

Rossetti's stratagem for smoking out a spy, therefore, was fashioned primarily along analytical lines. He postulated that Calumet would refuse to meet the Russians on any ground where he could easily be killed or captured alive. This meant, the way Rossetti figured it, that the meet—if it occurred—would probably materialize someplace public, someplace with a slew of people around, someplace where an entire horde of pedestrians would be milling about and standing in as unwitting bodyguards for an American double agent. Even the Russians would much prefer to commit their sins in the darkness rather than in the presence of gaping onlookers. Unless it was in their own country and in front of their own people, that is—then it didn't bother them. In fact, their own people were so used to it by now, after seventy odd years of a police state mentality, that it usually didn't bother *them* either. At any rate, Rossetti strategically placed his team in and around public locations—tourist spots such as the Ogre Fountain, the Clock Tower, the Botanical Garden, the Art Museum, and so forth.

The reason Rossetti chose the easternmost end of Bern for himself was basically twofold. In the first place, he still had the Ferrari, and the road was scenic the way it looped around with the river on the eastern edge of the city. On the eastern edge of the city, the drive and the view were hard to beat. Plus, the way Rossetti envisioned it, the Ferrari itself would be pretty hard to beat if the Russians took a notion to do something crazy and then light out in getaway cars. Rossetti and his Ferrari would be ready for such an event, especially if he was ever fortunate enough to have something like that happen. Still, with his luck, he moaned, the Russians would probably step out of character and behave themselves for once, and all he would ever get to do is watch. *If* the meet took place on his shift, that is, and *if* it took place in his general locale.

Which is the second reason Rossetti chose the easternmost end of Bern for himself. He was beginning to get a sense of Calumet's mind-set. He thought he knew how the agent would be thinking at this stage of the game. Not only would Calumet choose a place that was public, crowded, but also, knowing Calumet, would probably select the location with an impertinent, calculated flair. Thus, Rossetti was betting on the bear pits. Calumet would have made arrangements to meet the Russian bear at the bear pits of Bern. In Calumet's mind, it would be a lovely symbolic irony. Just to spite them. At least that's the way the commando saw it. There were likely to be oodles of tourists around the bear pits, especially at this time of year.

Rossetti glanced at his watch. One-thirty. It was time again. He removed his radio and switched to a different frequency. Speaking into the built-in microphone, he said crisply, "Post one."

"Sitrep negative," came the immediate reply.

He similarly checked the remaining members of his team, then changed back to his original frequency. This routine was repeated every fifteen minutes. Rossetti had concluded that any sighting of Calumet by elements of Team Interceptor would be reported directly to him. He would then make the decision about when to pass it on—or *if* to pass it on—to Steve. In the meantime, he was wondering, *Where is Robert?* Of late, Robert's hallowed presence had been scarce.

*

Calumet gazed through his binoculars and took in the swarm of cars and pedestrians traversing the streets below. He observed a variety of people as they strolled capriciously along the walk of the Kirchenfeldbrücke, which gracefully spanned the river Aare. The bridge, not spectacular by itself, but coupled with the piercing blue water of the river, seemed to produce its own mysterious flavor of vintage nostalgia, hinting loudly at *Heidi*. Even the Bernese, he imagined, would admit to the analogy, so pastoral was the view. Watching, panning the overlook, he was able to measure the cultural variance in slices of human endeavor as the locals distinguished themselves by their headlong gaits, striding purposefully, while the tourists stopped and pointed and took a hundred pictures, and probably a hundred more again, from a hundred different angles, on the whole crafting a montage of mankind's desire to catalog his existence. Calumet was awed by the complacency of the bustle of life, and the ease of it when witnessed from afar. And, as always, he was mesmerized by the water. He deemed the water in this part of the world to be splendorous and overpowering in a serene way, but unassuming in its shining alpine purity, and he wondered how long it would remain capable of defending itself against the ineluctable onslaught of progress and pollution. Not long, he figured, because if ever there was a steamroller, it was progress. Or what sometimes passed for progress, anyway.

Calumet took note of the hour. It was 1:45. Time to go. So far he had spotted nothing significant. He flipped the binoculars to his eyes for one more look. The only object that piqued his interest was a black Ferrari Spider making its way east on Aarstrasse. *Another freaking playboy,* he thought, envious of the vehicle.

Before leaving, he picked up the phone and dialed the American embassy. "Steve Phillips, please," he said to the Swiss woman who answered. He could imagine her looking through her list as he waited. Robert or Steve would have alerted her by now to be on the lookout for a phone call to Steve Phillips.

"Hello," the familiar voice came on line. "This is Steve Phillips."

"This is Excalibur. Do you want me to come in?"

"Damn it, Calumet! This line is not secure."

"Do you guys want me to come in?"

"Of course not! Have you gone crazy or something? This is an *open* line. And you weren't supposed to call until four. What the hell—"

The phone went dead in Steve's hand.

Calumet walked briskly out of the room and headed for his rendezvous with Vartanyan. *I think I'm beginning to understand,* he told himself grimly.

*

Rossetti parked the Ferrari off Aarstrasse near the river and walked east toward the Nydeggbrücke. His manner was casual but his eyes were alert. This was his third trip to this particular vicinity today. He would keep roving until they all decided to call it quits. Or, until somebody spotted Calumet. Whichever came first, Rossetti guessed.

But it wasn't Calumet that Rossetti spotted; not initially. It was Vartanyan. As Rossetti was crossing the Nydeggbrücke, he saw the Russian ambling south on Grosser Muristalden. He was headed toward the bear pits. At first, the commando was not sure of the identification. He did not get a clear look at Vartanyan in Berlin due to the impending darkness. However, he saw enough to be reasonably sure of the assimilation now.

Rossetti leaned against the railing and peered into the water while Vartanyan passed by on a perpendicular path at the opposite end of the bridge. Although seemingly oblivious to his surroundings, his eyes were taking in *everything*, Rossetti noticed. That the Russian was a consummate professional was obvious. He had that certain air. *Careful, Rossetti.* Vartanyan was still a good thirty yards away, and there were plenty of people about, so Rossetti felt confident that he had not been made. He knew the Russian did not get a good look at *him* in Berlin, either.

The commando checked his watch as Vartanyan disappeared into the crowd. It would be another five minutes before the members of Team Interceptor changed over to their agreed-upon frequency. Rossetti walked casually after the Russian.

Rounding the corner of the bridge, he picked up Vartanyan once again. The Russian was standing near the bear pits, seemingly enjoying the scenery. The commando stepped back onto the Nydegg-brücke and waited. There was still no sign of Calumet.

*

Calumet approached from the south. A tremendous amount of soul-searching had led him this far. He was not sure when his un-derstanding of Armbrister's motives and the subsequent corollary events began to blossom in his apprehension of the truth. Perhaps his cognizance came to him in stages, from somewhere deep inside, undefined at first, then rose slowly and focused itself like a hunter dissolving a pesky blur with the adjustment of his rifle scope. At any rate, he thought he had the gist of it now. And Armbrister had been right—he had spoken the word *Odyssey* on purpose yesterday, sus-pecting that the usage would set off all kinds of alarms. The Rus-sians would be targeting the communications of the American embassy in Bern, and phone calls on open lines were sitting ducks. Calumet had taken a big gamble. If he had been wrong, they would have pulled him in and Odyssey would be over. At least for him. If he had guessed wrong, Jack Calumet would have been turned out to pasture by now and made to repent for his sin, probably for good. But he wasn't wrong. Steve had just assured him that they did not want him to come in.

Why? Because, he calculated, the crux of Odyssey had little to do with deep-penetration agents. Jack knew that now. He knew his mission was ultimately sacrificial. He could feel it. He could taste its bitter bile. *But why? To what purpose? Why are they running me into the ground?*

He could only speculate, but it seemed that the only logic which presented itself—the only dialectic that could somehow explain this strange turn of events—was a convoluted mesh that went way beyond the premise of secret moles and prolific penetration agents. If he was right, the crux of Odyssey was a very clever Gordian knot, woven intricately by Nishka and Lewis Armbrister. A knot which was so tightly wound that it entwined a cunning, diabolical campaign of deceit, lies, and disinformation. And disinformation, properly planted, might be more devastating to an intelligence ser-vice than any ten moles could ever dare to wish for.

As Calumet saw it, the bottom line was really very simple. For whatever reason, Armbrister had been laboring to drive him into the jaws of the Russians. The DDO's purpose was evident. He was attempting to sacrifice Jack Calumet, but he had to make sure that the Russians bought it; it had to be real. Jack was now certain of it, and it was like a knife piercing his heart. If it had just been Armbrister behind it, it would have been all right, but the pain was accentuated because, of all people, Robert had gone along with it. The only question in Calumet's mind was whether or not he was going to allow them to carry it through. On the one hand, he could not believe that Armbrister had acted out of malice. If Jack did not have a small measure of faith in Armbrister, he certainly held Robert in high esteem. Would Robert, his controller and friend for these past six years, allow him to be betrayed for no good reason? Or any number of trivial reasons? No! He could not bring himself to believe that. Not Robert. Robert had tried desperately to talk him out of this operation. Maybe Robert *had* known something after all.

So what are they after? Calumet deduced the answer to that question. He knew what they were after. No matter how many times he sorted through it, the fact that he was being set up as a sacrifice could mean only one thing: Armbrister wanted the Russians to discover that Calumet had been a loyal double all along, that he had been working strictly for the Americans from day one. The Russians had to believe that he was a legitimate American agent, an agent provocateur, and they had to believe that they had found him out as a result of their own cunning, without being led by the nose. In Calumet's mind, there was no longer any question about the goal. That was plain, but the real mystery—and the utter vexation of it—could still be defined in that one word: *Why?* He didn't have the slightest idea.

But he had made up his mind and he was determined to find out. He moved forward until he was standing next to Vartanyan. In all his ruminations, even before he had made the phone call fifteen minutes earlier, Jack Calumet had concocted a fish tale of epic proportions. He could only hope it worked.

*

Rossetti took out his radio. "Sitrep positive. Seven. Out." Seven was the numeric equivalent of the bear pits. Before embarking upon their quest, Team Interceptor had assigned numbers to various locations around the city. Instead of trying to memorize them, each commando had written them down on a piece of paper, but Rossetti did not need to refer to his. The number he had assigned to the bear pits was his own lucky number, and if he forgot it he figured he might as well go on home. The commando stuffed the radio in his windbreaker and leaned against the railing. He could just make out the heads of Calumet and the Russian down the way. The entire area was blanketed with tourists and onlookers, but, thus far, he had seen no sign of countersurveillance; Russian *or* American. Had he not been so intent upon observing Calumet and Vartanyan, however, he might have spotted the man whose eyes were riveted upon them all.

Across the street, slanting against a tree, clothed in rumpled garments and wearing a hat that nearly covered his sunglasses, the mysterious, elusive Robert stood watching.

*

"You have my money?" Calumet asked.

Both men were facing the river. Neither had so much as glanced at the other. Now Vartanyan turned his head slightly and scorched Calumet with a lethal stare. "Yes, Jack. I have your money." He removed an envelope from his pocket and passed it over.

Calumet accepted it very casually and slid it underneath his jacket. He said, "I suppose you want to know about my meet with Steve Phillips the other day."

"No, I think we can let that slide for now." Vartanyan did not elaborate, leaving the potential for miscalculation hanging precariously in the wind.

But Calumet would not climb into the ring with him. Instead he asked, "How's your lovely shrew?" If he had earned any success with Karola, he did not want to give her away. He chose to disdain her in Vartanyan's presence.

The remark had been potent. For an instant, Vartanyan seemed on the verge of exploding. It was in his eyes, ever so subtle, but it came and went quickly, like a flash. Then he laughed, not loudly, but robustly. "I believe she's still recovering from your adventures of the last two days."

Calumet was unable to get a read. He was looking for something that would tell him how she had played it, but Vartanyan gave absolutely nothing away. Jack smiled. "So where do we go from here, Andrei?"

Vartanyan turned to him, meeting his gaze. "Why don't you tell me about Odyssey, Jack?"

This was the moment Calumet had been preparing himself for. The moment of truth. "I'll be happy to sell it to you. It's one of the craziest stories you've ever heard."

CHAPTER 24

Artie Brandon and Chip Longstreet appeared first. Rossetti nodded them off, intimating that they should spread out and take up tactical positions in the surrounding area. Several minutes later, Kramer and then Yardley emerged from the throng. Translating the situation, they immediately dispersed and mingled with the crowd.

Screw it! Rossetti thought. *I'm not reporting this.*

A safe distance away, Robert had noted the arrivals. He edged farther back into the trees, his expression somber. *Don't get too cute, Rossetti,* he thought.

*

"How are you involved in Odyssey?" Vartanyan inquired.

"As I said, it's one of the craziest stories you've ever heard."

Vartanyan had no doubt of that. The bargaining had begun. "Okay, if I think what you have to say is important, we'll negotiate a price."

"Forget it!" Calumet barked.

"You have to give me something to go on," Vartanyan countered. "I can't buy something without knowing the specifications."

"Langley has been running a con on you for six years," Jack stated candidly. "Is that specific enough for you?"

Vartanyan put it together immediately. "That corresponds with your tenure as our agent, does it not?"

"You got it."

"And you've been involved in this con, as you call it?"

"Yes." Calumet threw his hands out, palms up. "But I didn't know it."

"When did you find out?" Vartanyan asked, his concentration suddenly immense.

"Within the last couple of days," Calumet announced.

"And what led to this sudden discovery?"

"That's all you get for now, Vartanyan. Besides, we can't discuss it here."

Vartanyan measured Calumet. This was not the same person he had met with only a few days earlier. The Russian concluded that he was seeing the real Jack Calumet for the first time. "I agree. We can't discuss it here. We have several safe houses in the area. We could go there right now."

"In the first place," Calumet explained, "we haven't arrived at a mutual understanding regarding payment. And secondly, I'll dictate the terms and the place of the debriefing."

"If you want to be paid," Vartanyan sniped, "you will be debriefed at our pleasure. After all, we can't stand on the street corner and hold a summit, can we?"

"I want one million dollars," Calumet informed him. "Cash on the barrelhead."

"Impossible!"

Calumet held his peace.

"Are you defecting?" Vartanyan asked suddenly.

"No," Jack replied. "But I'm betraying my country. I'll need the money to get away. Far away."

"I thought you had *been* betraying your country all along," Vartanyan said suspiciously.

"Not really," Jack answered. "Oh, sure. I've been selling you secrets. But we both know that nothing I ever gave you was earth-shattering. What I'm about to give you is."

Vartanyan looked at him, sizing him up. "Why don't you just defect to Russia? That would solve your fugitive problems."

"So will a million dollars," Calumet responded glibly. "And I wouldn't defect to that dump of a country of yours if my life depended on it. As far as I can tell, you don't seem to spend much time there yourself."

"What kind of con?" Vartanyan wanted to know, dismissing the insult.

"You got a million dollars in your shirt?"

Vartanyan mulled over the circumstances. "No," he finally replied. "But I can have a quarter of a million waiting for you this evening. If what you have for us is earth-shattering, I can have another quarter of a million the following day."

"That's very commendable, Andrei. Really. But when you have

a *full* million waiting for me, let me know. Until then, we have nothing to discuss."

He's for real, Vartanyan thought. *He really is planning to run.* If Calumet had been willing to negotiate, it would have been suspicious, and he knew it. If he had acceded to the Russian's offer, it would have raised a red flag.

"And if we decide not to take you up on your offer," Vartanyan speculated, "then you just keep pretending to play Moscow and Washington against the middle. Is that it?"

"I'm out of here either way. I'm on a short fuse, and we both know it. It would be nice if I could walk away from this a rich man, but either way, I'm gone."

"We can pay you one million American dollars," Vartanyan announced suddenly. "But we'll debrief you at the location of our choosing."

Sure! Calumet thought. *You could pay me a million dollars, but you have no intention of doing so no matter what I tell you. You were too obvious, Andrei.*

"The debriefing can take place in an isolated location if you want," Calumet agreed, "but here's how it's going to go down." He glanced around to make sure no one was eavesdropping. "I will obtain a location somewhere in the vicinity of Bern. A secure location. We will then set a time. You and I and whoever else you wish to be present will meet at some point in the city. No more than two people besides yourself, though. Bring all the recorders you want, but no radios. If I even smell a radio or other communication device, I'll vanish so fast it'll make your head spin. And no weapons. Once we've met and I'm satisfied that these conditions have been adhered to, at that point I will take you to the location I've selected. You will have four hours to debrief me. No more. And if you don't show me the money up front, I abort. For good. This is a one-shot deal. Understood?" Calumet was aware of the weakness in his strategy, and he was sure Vartanyan would see it too.

"I think I can agree to that." Vartanyan smiled. "What's your timetable?"

"Send Karola to the Bahnhof tomorrow morning at ten o'clock with twenty thousand dollars. Call it good-faith money. I'll give her the details then. And send her alone, Andrei. It would not do to make me nervous at this point." *The weasel hasn't pulled the cigarette case one time,* Jack thought.

Vartanyan extracted the silver case and snared a cigarette. Lighting it, he said, "Okay. Tomorrow morning at ten o'clock. Why Karola?"

Does he have mental telepathy or something? "Because I know her. I can handle her. Let's just say it's because that's the way I want it."

Vartanyan tossed his cigarette. "Ten o'clock tomorrow morning. Karola will be there alone." He walked briskly away.

Calumet turned and strode in the opposite direction.

*

Kramer was nearest Rossetti. Rossetti eased over and pointed out Vartanyan confidentially. "Stay with him. You and the rest of the boys, except Longstreet. Give him these." Rossetti handed him the keys to the Ferrari. "It's parked just down the street. Tell him to pick it up and head slowly in my direction." He pointed down Grosser Muristalden. "I'm going after Calumet."

Kramer nodded and set off to alert the other members of Team Interceptor. They had to move quickly but without attracting attention. Vartanyan was walking north on Grosser Muristalden, Calumet south. Team Interceptor moved out.

Robert held his position until everyone dispersed. At last he ambled slowly across the Nydeggbrücke and hailed a cab. He had no doubt that Andrei Vartanyan would slip the net. The three commandos would not be able to stay with him. He knew Vartanyan was one of the best, and it would take more than a team of three to beat him. The Russian would lose them. On the other hand, Robert was beginning to think that Rossetti was going to be a problem. The commando's calculated insolence could be tolerated only so far.

*

Calumet flagged down a passing cab on Grosser Muristalden and climbed in. Some sixty yards behind, Rossetti glanced up the road apprehensively. Longstreet was coming toward him in the Ferrari. Rossetti dove in and they went after the cab. While in pursuit, Rossetti set both his and Longstreet's radio to their prearranged frequency. There was no sense in adhering to fifteen-minute intervals anymore. They had acquired their target.

Sitting in the front seat, Calumet peered into the side mirror. He noted the Ferrari, but was unable to distinguish its passengers. He thought nothing about it; he simply filed it in his mind with the images of the other vehicles that happened to be on the road. If he saw the same vehicles twice, after he had changed direction, then he would begin to think something about it.

The cab deposited Calumet at Münsterplatz. The Ferrari cruised by, stopping about twenty yards beyond. Rossetti jumped out and ordered Longstreet to circle the block. Calumet purchased a tram ticket and climbed aboard. Rossetti did the same. By the time Longstreet returned, the two had vanished. He parked nearby and just sat, waiting for his radio to crackle with fresh instructions.

Calumet was immediately suspicious of Rossetti. He had seen the commando jump out of the Ferrari and then follow him without hesitation into the tram. For the next hour, Calumet baited and switched, and Rossetti stayed with him all the way. Calumet was no longer suspicious of the man; he was certain of him. The man was sticking to him like glue.

Who is he? Calumet wondered. He did not think his pursuer was Russian; they would have put a team on him. This guy was a solo act. Calumet made his way to Marktgasse and entered a small café. He sidled up to the bar and ordered a beer. He wondered how long it would take the man to enter. After a few minutes his curiosity was satiated. Rossetti sauntered in and, to Calumet's great surprise, approached him.

"It's time we talked," Rossetti said casually, his eyes sweeping the room.

Calumet appraised him, but said nothing.

"We've been covering you since Frankfurt, Jack," Rossetti continued. "We work for Robert."

Calumet raised his brows involuntarily. "You're the clown who put on that little show in Grunewald Park," he stated. "I recognize the voice."

"Yep."

"Where did you pick me up?" Calumet asked suspiciously.

"The bear pits. Robert has had teams out looking for you. I guess I got lucky."

Calumet eyed him warily. "I don't believe in luck, friend."

"I don't blame you," Rossetti sympathized. He signaled the bartender and ordered a beer. "Believe what you want, but that's the truth."

"How long before Robert gets here?" Jack asked, inferring disparagement and complicity.

"He doesn't even know *I'm* here," the commando confessed. "In fact, I'd be in trouble if he did."

Calumet took a swallow of beer and wiped the foam from his mouth. Something about the admission soothed him. He suddenly felt more at ease. "Why is that?"

"Because we were ordered to report it the minute you were sighted. I chose to disobey that order."

"What about your friend? The one who was driving the Ferrari. Does he feel the same way?" *This guy does not fit the mold. He's not an operations officer.*

"There are five of us in all. My boys follow me."

"Then you're military?"

"Delta Force," Rossetti answered in a hushed voice.

Calumet nodded, suddenly understanding. Robert had been first-rate for bringing them in, especially in Frankfurt where things could have easily turned nasty. If this hombre had meant him any harm, he could have readily drilled him in the park. But he didn't. He was definitely a friendly, Jack concluded. A new avenue of possibilities suddenly presented itself. "You got a name?"

Rossetti hesitated. Finally: "Rick Rossetti, but now that I've told you, you have to promise not to get captured."

Jack laughed. "I'll do my best. How did your man know to warn me about the woman?"

Rossetti quickly brought him up to date, explaining all he knew. Calumet listened intently. As Rossetti talked, Calumet found himself reliving his own story, but from another professional's point of view. In the end, Rossetti's version confirmed his interpretations. The operational campaign he had set forth for himself had been fortified in the commando's recital of events as he saw them. And he was inordinately pleased because the commando saw things in exactly the same way as he would have seen them had their roles been reversed.

After everything had been covered, Rossetti asked, "What are your plans from here?"

Calumet thought for a moment. He liked Rossetti. He sensed a kindred soul. The commando had been succinct and perceptive in his analysis of the situation as it had been presented to him. He possessed the ability to see the big picture and simultaneously retain his operational focus. He could read not only the letter of the law, as it were, but the intent of the writers of the law as well. In short, Rossetti knew what Langley was after. He was able to interpret the differences between Washington's maxims of applied psychology and compare them to the savagery of the real world. He understood their intransigent motives and subtle power plays, and, for the most part, he had no use for them. But he did have style. Calumet concluded anyone who had the moxie to rent a Ferrari with covert funds—without permission—and then disobey a direct order or two on top of it, well, anyone like that, Calumet figured, could most certainly be trusted.

"Do you have a curfew?" Calumet asked.

Rossetti smiled. "I suppose not."

"I think I may have turned Karola," Jack disclosed.

"The woman?"

"Yes."

"How?"

"That's not important right now," Jack answered, "but I've arranged for her to contact me if she feels so inclined. The location is a safe house near here. The problem is, I have a few other matters to attend to, and I won't know if she's tried to reach me or not—or even if it's a trap—because I can't watch the safe house. Plus, if it *is* a trap, the Russians will see me coming from a mile off. At any rate, I have to assume that the location is compromised."

"How long do you want us to watch it?"

"Several hours. Say until nine, nine-thirty."

"We can handle that. No sweat."

"Great! I wish I'd made a note of pay phones and numbers in that vicinity. That way, I could arrange to contact you."

"That's no problem," Rossetti grinned. "Steve was kind enough to give all of us radios this morning." He extracted his and handed it to Calumet. Jack quickly secreted it in his pocket. They quickly worked out a code. Neither was willing to take a chance on eavesdroppers.

Calumet related the address of the safe house. "When will you talk to Robert?" he asked.

"Couldn't tell you. I haven't seen him in a while."

"So who's been your liaison? Steve?"

"Correct."

"Well, don't deal with Steve," Calumet advised. "When you *do* see Robert, tell him we've met. Tell him I know what Armbrister wants from me. Tell him that I'm going inside to give it to them." Their eyes locked. Rossetti knew what Calumet was saying. He respected his courage. "But don't tell him about the girl or our overall conversation," Calumet added.

"When I tell him you're going inside, he'll want details."

"You don't know the details."

Rossetti remained stolid, impassive. He knew better than to try to dictate to Calumet.

Calumet appreciated the forbearance. "Don't worry. I'm not going in naked," he smiled. "I'll want you to cover me when the time comes."

"Good!" Rossetti remarked. "Because for a minute there, I was beginning to think you were a crazier indian than I already imagined you were."

Calumet smiled.

"Tell me something," Rossetti continued. "What are your chances of coming out of this thing in one piece?"

"Fifty-fifty," Calumet said nonchalantly. "I either will or I won't." Then he became serious. "I've got some personal business to settle with Vartanyan when this is over. And he thinks he's got some business to settle with me."

Rossetti nodded. That was one business he well understood.

Calumet related the operational contents of his meet with Vartanyan and told the commando where he was planning to meet Karola the following morning. Rossetti assured him that Team Interceptor would cover him and guard against Russian interference. Their business concluded, Rossetti departed first. He had a surveillance operation to mount.

Calumet gave him a ten-minute lead and then headed for another part of town and a telephone. He hoped Eitan could deliver on the new safe house because there was no way, he decided, that he was going to take a chance and return to his hotel. Events were transpiring rapidly now, and he could not afford to slip up. Not at this stage of the game. By now, he figured, the game was almost over.

In fact, it was really just beginning.

CHAPTER 25

Calumet placed his call to Eitan and discovered that the old spy had come through for him. They had arranged to meet at the north end of Kornhausbrücke, which is where Calumet was now standing, waiting for the man to show. Admiring the river Aare, he hoped the Israeli would not tarry long. He did not like being out in the open. On the other hand, he felt pleasantly lighthearted as a result of the overall turn of events. The revelation of Rossetti and his team had been a blessing. For the first time since Odyssey's inception, Calumet sensed he was not alone. He felt as though he had backup.

It was Jack's custom to retrace his steps mentally and think them through. Leaning on the bridge with his elbows, he did that now. He gazed wistfully into the water and considered his plight. He theorized about the recent events and how they had unfolded so rapidly, as if driven by a taskmaster. The more he thought about it, the more he appreciated Robert and his uncanny foresight. Of course, Robert evidently had no idea that Rossetti would turn rogue, thereby arbitrarily resolving to mount his own limited operation inside a larger one. Still, this particular commando had been selected for a particular reason. After all, they did not simply choose names out of a hat. No, Jack ruminated. Each individual in any operation was selected with extreme oversight. The entire biography would have been assimilated and sifted until a psychological makeup could be carefully constructed. After that, a searing analysis would have been performed and, if all seemed well, a decision would finally be taken.

So why had Rossetti been chosen? Jack pondered. Were the magicians at Langley that good? Was Robert that good? Or was Calumet just lucky? Perhaps. Perhaps it was nothing more than kismet after all, but whatever it was, Jack concluded, he was grateful. He now had at his disposal the resources to not only see this operation through, but also—as Rossetti had half-joked—to come out of it in one piece.

Eitan drove up and Calumet jumped in. Driving away, Eitan remarked casually, "In just a few hours you've become famous already."

Calumet suddenly became alert. "What do you mean?"

"Discreet inquiries have been made as to your whereabouts."

"By whom?"

Eitan presented him with a somber look. "By the Americans. Bern Station."

That would be Steve, more than likely, Calumet thought. He was gratified that he chose not to return to his hotel. They probably had that location by now. "Who were these inquiries directed at?"

"Friends of mine," Eitan answered cryptically.

Calumet was thinking. He wondered how it would come across if he asked for reassurance from the old spy that he would not give him away to his own people in the Mossad. But he did not have to think long.

"Don't worry," Eitan laughed. "The request was made at a rather low level. My people interpreted it as no-further-action-required. Apparently, it was not a high-priority request. More like a 'Please let us know if you see him' type thing."

"And—" Calumet began, but was quickly interrupted.

"And I haven't seen you." Eitan grinned.

Calumet joined in the levity, although he was annoyed at the Israeli's idea of a joke. Smiling, he said, "You *do* get around, don't you, old man?"

Eitan shrugged his shoulders. "I do all right, youngster. *You* should do so well if you ever reach my age." He dispensed a subtle sideways glance.

"Your mouth to God's ear," Calumet rejoined, suddenly caught up in the cultural vernacular. At the moment, he was more worried about reaching his next birthday than he was about reaching Eitan's age.

Their ride lasted only five minutes. The safe house was located on the northern sweep of Bern, situated in the midst of a row of small houses. Eitan handed Jack the key. Calumet thanked him and began to climb out, but Eitan rested his palm on Jack's shoulder, giving him pause.

"There has also been quite a lot of activity at the Russian embassy," the old man remarked. "Is there anything else I can do for you?"

"What type of activity?" Calumet was, not at all surprised.

"People coming and going. Communications. The regular buzz."

"Like you said." Calumet grinned, "when I blow into town, it doesn't take long for me to become famous. Thanks anyway, Eitan." He opened the door but was arrested once again by the old spy's unerring touch.

"That's not all," Eitan revealed. "A few line officers from the Russian embassy have also been making discreet inquiries as to your whereabouts."

That *did* surprise Calumet. *The Russians! What are the Russians seeking me for?* "As of when?" he asked intently. "When did you get this information?"

"About the Americans, this morning," Eitan responded. "The Russians, well, just recently. About a half hour ago."

The disclosure was a mystery to Calumet. Why would the Russians suddenly be looking for him since he had met with Vartanyan only a few hours ago?

"If you need some insurance," Eitan offered, revealing his paternal side, "I've got some boys who can be available on short notice."

Calumet was only half-listening. He was stymied by the odd disclosure.

"I would not charge you for this," Eitan continued. "I would simply want you to cover expenses."

Calumet surfaced from his thoughts and nodded. The last thing he needed at the moment was outside intervention, but he sought to mollify the Israeli, correctly perceiving that the old man was hungry for the action. "That's a good point, my friend. I may take you up on that. In the meantime"—he winked—"don't take any solitary action. It could compromise a very delicate operation. Do we have a bargain?"

Eitan smiled. "No problem. But you let me know. Okay?"

"Absolutely," Jack assured him. He finally extricated himself from the conversation and climbed out.

The safe house was another two-bedroom affair with a living room and a small kitchen. Jack picked up the telephone and listened. It worked. The phone amazed him more than anything. Whatever else he might think about Eitan and his overt enthusiasm, the old man certainly had something going for him to be able to furnish the house with a phone in such a short time.

He retrieved the radio and opened the refrigerator to browse. The revelation of the Russian inquiry was still consuming his thoughts. *What could that possibly be about?* He was disturbed. The Russian action seemed inconsistent somehow, prominently out of place. But he would have to analyze it later. At the moment, he was hungry. As he was scanning the refrigerator, he raised Rossetti, not really expecting to hear anything out of the ordinary.

"Bases are loaded," the radio crackled. *Emergency!* That was their signal for an emergency.

"Acknowledged!" Calumet snapped. He tore out of the safe house and found a cab as swiftly as possible.

Darkness spilled over Bern and was complete when he arrived. There was a crescent moon, but the sky was cloudy, making it difficult to see without the illumination of the city. He met Rossetti around the corner from the safe house.

"Four people went inside," Rossetti explained. "About twenty minutes ago. The girl and three men. One of the men was Vartanyan, another the blond who paid off the hoods in Berlin. The woman was being escorted. I couldn't tell if she was under constraint or not."

"What about the other one? The man, I mean."

"He was dressed in sunglasses, a hat, and an overcoat. Looked just like one of those old spy movies."

Calumet pondered the situation. Eitan had revealed just minutes ago that the Russians had put out the word—they were searching avidly for Jack Calumet. Vartanyan obviously wanted a fast meet. *But why?* Calumet concluded he must have said something earlier that created a panic in their ranks, something that Vartanyan hadn't picked up on. Whoever was running Vartanyan realized it after Vartanyan had been debriefed. *That must be it,* Jack speculated. *But what could I have possibly said that was considered so significant they couldn't wait until tomorrow for clarification?* After a moment, he asked, "Can you guys stick around for a while?"

"You're not going in there, are you?" Rossetti seemed amazed, as if that was the dumbest idea of the week.

"Yes," Calumet answered. "I've got to find out what this is all about. If it was a trap, they would have sent the woman in alone and then staked this place out." Suddenly he seemed troubled. "You've been on the lookout for countersurveillance?"

"Of course. There's been none—I can assure you."

Calumet nodded pensively.

Rossetti continued, "If you've made up your mind to go inside, you need to give me a time frame."

Calumet shook his head. "I want to play it by ear. I don't think this is a setup."

Rossetti shrugged, his eyes dancing. "If you're wrong, we probably won't be able to tell anything until it's too late. Until they come out of the door, for instance, and we go inside and find your body. You know that, don't you?"

"Anybody ever tell you that you have a way with words, Rossetti?" Calumet was sweeping the area with his vision. He felt uneasy about the countersurveillance.

"I'll give you fifteen minutes," the commando announced. "At the outside. Then we're coming in." The statement was not dogmatic; Rossetti was testing the waters.

Calumet held the commando's gaze. "This is my call. If things get out of hand, I'll be able to send out a signal." He pulled his Beretta and worked the slide, chambering a round. Returning the gun to his right pocket, his finger surrounding the trigger, he added, "Get my drift?"

"Yeah," Rossetti remarked, "I get your drift. But if you have to use that thing, you'd better send out *several* signals, if you get *my* drift."

"I just don't think it'll come to that." Calumet shook his head. "But then, that's what makes horse racing."

"Well, if it *does* come to that," Rossetti warned, "go down fast. When we come through that door, we'll be taking out everything standing."

"The girl may not be in on it," Calumet protested, allowing for the possibility that the commando just might be correct in his assessment of the situation. He did not want Karola to become an innocent casualty. Not now, not after what he knew about her. Regardless of whether or not she'd been turned, she was just another pawn. Jack did not want to see her die for that.

"Everything!" Rossetti asserted. This time it was dogmatic. "Everything higher than a dog's behind gets obliterated," he added, making sure Calumet apprehended the physics and was clear on the dimensions.

Calumet indicated he understood how the program worked. Then, switching to a less-controversial topic, he asked, "Have you been able to get in touch with Robert yet?"

"Hell no!" Rossetti answered, exasperated. "Nobody has seen him since Berlin."

What's his game? Calumet wondered. *Robert is supposed to be running this operation.* He handed his radio to Rossetti. "I don't guess it would be a good idea to get caught with this." The commando took the radio. Jack's eyes conducted a cursory survey of his surroundings. "Are you positive about the countersurveillance?"

"Of course," Rossetti emphasized. "I've got four men spread out around this place. We'd know it."

Calumet's internal radar disagreed, but he possessed no tangible proof. *Maybe I'm just jittery,* he rationalized. Though not completely satisifed, he said nevertheless, "Well, here's to swimmin' with beautiful women." He nodded at Rossetti and headed for the safe house.

Calumet knocked on the door. The first thing he noticed when Karola answered was the severe bruise on her cheekbone, under her left eye. She gave him no time to notice anything else.

Karola shouted, "Get out of here, Jack! They—" She was cut off rather abruptly.

The blond encircled her neck with his forearm, choking her, and simultaneously pointed a nine-millimeter Browning at Calumet's chest. "Won't you please come in?" he greeted.

Calumet was immediately incensed upon seeing her eye and then the forearm and finally the gun, but he hid his emotion. "So very nice of you to ask," Jack responded, smiling and stepping inside. He wondered if the blond had any idea that Jack's own finger was at this moment caressing the trigger of a Beretta cloistered in his right pocket—a nine-millimeter Beretta which contained a silver-tipped hollow-point load—and that he could disembowel the halfwit before he even knew what hit him. Calumet had never been one to hold men who beat women in high regard, and he was betting it was the blond man's fist that had awarded Karola the hideous bruise.

Vartanyan was standing in the living room, smoking a cigarette.

The blond GRU agent dumped Karola in a chair and took up a position by the front door, which was the only way in or out. He had returned his gun to its holster. There was no sign of the third man who, according to Rossetti, had also entered.

"Which son of a bitch did *that?*" Calumet asked Vartanyan, pointing to Karola's face. "You, or that slimy moron by the door?"

Vartanyan smiled. "The slimy moron did it, I'm afraid."

The blond GRU agent chuckled in the background. Calumet whirled and gave him a corrosive look, his gaze burning into the man.

Vartanyan dropped the smile and put on a menacing expression. "And Karola is part of the family. *Our* family, so she is none of your business, Calumet."

Ignoring Vartanyan and calculating the insult, Calumet turned to Karola. "Are you all right?"

Her eyes flickered and bounced furtively from one man to the next. She was scared. "Yes," she managed. Calumet smiled at her, hoping to instill a small measure of courage. She appeared to glean something from it.

"He won't do it again," Jack promised, nodding toward the blond. "If he does, I'll kill him." Again, his eyes bore ferociously into the GRU agent, sending a message.

"If you're through being a cowboy," Vartanyan quipped, "we can get down to business."

Calumet preserved the silence for several moments, letting both men know that he took the matter of Karola seriously. He suddenly felt responsible for her welfare. There was no longer any doubt about where she stood, about whose side she was on. And it was because of Jack that she was in this situation now. She asked him not to send her back, but he had. She seemed so innocent and vulnerable now. He was kicking himself for not having thought of something else, but it was all water under the bridge at this point. There was nothing he could do about it at the moment. "What business is that?" he finally snapped.

Vartanyan opened a briefcase. It was filled with American bills. "As you can see, I've brought your money. Well, some of it. I'm afraid a half million is all we could put our hands on with such short notice. We can arrange to pay you the balance tomorrow."

"No way, slick," Calumet rejoined. The Russians were suddenly attempting to dictate terms and he could not afford to let them succeed. He perceived it as a psychological ploy on their behalf and quickly concluded that he could not allow them to walk all over him. "We do it my way, or we do it the hard way."

Vartanyan grinned. "Before you try to become a hero, Jack, let me explain something to you. We mean you absolutely no harm. As you can see, Yevgenni"—pointing to the blond—"has holstered his weapon. It's just that we've suddenly become very interested in your offer. We've found it necessary to hear your story immediately. You see, we think you may be on the verge of making a big mistake. In our estimation, Jack, you can be of further service to us, and we are seriously concerned that you may do something to mitigate your usefulness in that respect." Vartanyan shifted his weight, the action apparently helping him find the words for his next sentence. "If you will play along, you will soon see what I mean. You have my word on that."

It was evident to Jack that the Russian was patronizing him, and he knew Vartanyan's word was about as good as Confederate money, but he was intrigued by the sudden change. What could he have said to set them off like this? Personal considerations aside, it was imperative he find out. "I get the half million before I leave, no matter what. Right?"

"Sure," Vartanyan agreed. "I don't think we have a problem with that."

Calumet exhaled deeply. "Okay. As I told you this afternoon, Langley has been running a con against you for six years."

Vartanyan looked quickly past Calumet into the hallway. It was an imperceptible motion, merely a slight flicker of the eyes, but Calumet caught it. He cocked his head and followed the Russian's gaze, but saw nothing other than an empty hallway. Returning his attention to the matter at hand, Vartanyan gestured for Calumet to continue.

Calumet thought, *Karola's father, the individual who, according to Karola, is running Vartanyan, must be back there manning the recorders. And whoever he is, he apparently sanctioned the violence committed against his own daughter. What a guy!*

"I originally began as a loyal double," Jack said. "The CIA was covering me from day one. They had the first meet cold. My first meet with Filatov, I mean."

"The CIA or the FBI?" Vartanyan inserted, his concentration intense.

"The CIA."

"That's odd, isn't it?" the Russian queried. "I would think the FBI might have been involved since it took place on American soil. Hmm." He appeared to ponder the admission, as if he was bereft of knowledge in these matters and had not the faintest clue about the methods of spooks and their secret world. "How did you get in touch with the CIA in the first place? Were you already working for them?"

He doesn't believe me, Jack thought. *I'm actually telling the truth on this part, and this genius doesn't believe me.* "No, I wasn't working for them. As it turns out, I mentioned Filatov's initial approach to a friend of mine and he passed it along to Langley. Then *they* got in touch with *me.*"

"I see," Vartanyan remarked, obviously skeptical. He nodded. "Go on."

"After a time," Calumet proceeded, "I began to become disillusioned. It was obvious that the CIA was just using me. They didn't give a flip about me personally. They were harsh in their debriefings, and half the time they withheld payment. They explained that I didn't do this one thing the way it should have been done, or I screwed something up—all the usual crap. At least, that was their excuse. Basically, they were bleeding me like a turnip and offering me nothing in return." His campaign had been carefully erected. He planned to lead them down the trail of the disaffected agent; the agent who, for one reason or another, can't cut it anymore and therefore crosses over. Except, in *his* fabrication, *he* would not have crossed over. Not yet.

"So you began to free-lance," Vartanyan jumped in, helping him along, even though Calumet hadn't asked for any assistance. "When you'd had enough—enough disillusionment, as you referred to it—you then sought alternate inroads with your *real* sources and ultimately started passing us *legitimate* intelligence, as opposed to the disinformation you were feeding us in the beginning. Correct?"

"As a matter of fact," Calumet responded, suddenly wary, "that's exactly what I did." *What is he up to?*

"Let me see if I've got this straight," Vartanyan chanted sardonically. "According to *your* story, the intelligence you were passing to Shevchenko in the beginning of your career was disinformation, and the intelligence you were passing along later, after Shevchenko had been compromised, was valid. Is that a correct interpretation of your words?"

Calumet did not like the Russian's abrupt effusion of confidence. He suddenly felt he was treading on dangerous ground, but it was impossible to back out now. "Yes, that's it in a nutshell. As far as it goes, that is."

"I'm afraid your story won't wash, Jack," Vartanyan accused out of thin air, as if he were holding an ace up his sleeve. "It's certainly not worth a million dollars."

"I haven't even finished," Jack insisted.

"It doesn't matter," Vartanyan countered. "I know where you're headed, and the fact is, your story stinks."

Calumet didn't think so, not the way he had planned to present it. He thought it was a whale of a story, and he could not for the life of him figure out why his nemesis wasn't buying into it. He had always assumed that the Russian would have dearly loved to hear him admit he was originally a loyal double. That sort of admission would make for high intrigue. Even broaching the subject and thereby casting a specter of doubt would normally set off all the alarms, but Vartanyan could care less. Something was wrong.

Just then, Jack sensed a presence standing diagonally to his rear, in the recess of the darkened hallway. He stoke a quick glance, to no avail. All he could discern was an outline in the shadows. The form seemed vaguely familiar and he longed to take another peek, but Vartanyan was fumbling around with the silver cigarette case again, and Calumet had developed a fixation for it. Ignoring the intrusion, he kept his eyes on Vartanyan and the silver cigarette case.

Vartanyan noted Calumet's obvious discomfort. He smiled devilishly. "I'll tell you why your story won't wash, Jack. Or rather, I'll show you." The Russian nodded, his attention directed to a point beyond Calumet. "Perhaps it's time you met Karola's father."

"Hello, Jack." The voice came from behind. A voice out of the past, a strangely familiar, eerie voice.

Calumet whirled around.

The figure stepped out of the darkness and into the light.

"*No!*" Calumet gasped. His mind was suddenly reeling.

In plain view now, not ten paces in front of him, and alive and well and as healthy as a horse stood a smiling, gloating Major-General Aleksandr Shevchenko!

PART FOUR

ROBERT'S GAME

CHAPTER 26

Calumet was speechless. An avalanche of possibilities rushed in, overwhelming him. The implications were too much to absorb all at once. Suddenly he remembered that enigmatic moment in his first meet with Vartanyan, and how Vartanyan had worn a mystical expression when Calumet had mentioned Shevchenko's treason, and he thought to himself, *That's when I should have known.* He knew the experts would have said he was berating himself for not being clairvoyant. *But still, I should have known,* his ego insisted.

"I, ah ... I thought you were dead, Aleksandr," Jack stuttered, as if the Russians required an explanation for his sudden shock. Especially since Vartanyan had himself admitted Shevchenko's execution only days ago.

"Certainly you're familiar with Mark Twain, Jack." Shevchenko smiled.

Calumet recovered quickly. "Yes, reports of your death have been greatly exaggerated."

Shevchenko nodded amiably. Stepping forward, he offered his hand. "Nice to see you again."

Jack shook his hand, warily. "What in the world is going on, Aleksandr?"

"Well, for one thing," Shevchenko stated blandly, "we've discovered that you certainly haven't changed, Jack." He laughed suddenly, amused at Calumet's predicament. "After all, you tried to pull a fast one on Andrei, here. You were about to try to sell us a phony story concerning your early involvement with the CIA and thereby fleece us for a million dollars." He and Vartanyan chuckled together. "Isn't that correct, old friend?"

Calumet shrugged, affecting a shy regret. He had no idea how to play it. The only thing he *did* know was that his own tale, the false legend he had been preparing, was shipwrecked. He thought he had correctly deduced the nature of Armbrister's intent and Langley's initial intelligence objectives for this operation, but now he realized he was wrong. Whatever the DDO's scheme, its purpose was far removed from Calumet's current interpretation of Odyssey and its overall import. As to the thrust of his own relegation in the affair, he was very much confused. He could only hope that the Russians would inadvertently leak a little insight.

"We understand this, Jack," Shevchenko said suavely. "After all, you are in hot water with the CIA at the moment. And the DEA."

Calumet feigned surprise at the remarks. In fact, he *was* surprised that they mysteriously *understood*. Unless, of course, the statement was simply a red herring, employed merely as a preface to sudden turnabout. The prelude to an ambush.

"Oh yes, Jack. We know that the CIA has had their screws in you for the past year or so. You've been searching for a way out. Isn't that so? You've been dabbling in the drug trade so as to garner enough cash to rupture the shackles of the CIA. That's how we read it, anyway. Would you care to dispute that, Jack?" Shevchenko and Vartanyan were both appraising him, seeking to gauge his reaction.

Calumet felt like a wild animal whose keepers were attempting to capture it for its own good. The Russians were posturing in his favor, but he was bewildered if he could see their angle. "No, Aleksandr. Minor details aside, I don't think I'd dispute that, exactly." He desperately needed to find out what they were driving at. "But I'm not sure you're one hundred percent accurate in your analysis of my biography. Why don't you tell me what you think you know?"

The two Russians exchanged glances. Shevchenko nodded, giving Vartanyan permission to take up the torch. "We know that you were compromised by the CIA about a year ago, Jack."

Although a tiny glimmer of insight pierced his thoughts suddenly, Calumet adopted a conversational virtuosity, saying nothing and expressing nothing.

"Yes," Shevchenko added. "You could have told me, Jack. We could have come up with something. I'm disappointed, actually, that you did not see fit to confide in me."

Calumet was pedaling furiously, trying to work it out. *For some reason, they think I was suborned by the CIA a year ago!* "I don't know what you boys are talking about," he retorted, as though he had been caught red-handed with his fingers in the cookie jar, but stubbornly chose to deny it anyway.

"I haven't come back from the dead to criticize you, Jack." Aleksandr smiled. "Just the opposite, actually. But you're going to have to be honest with us if we're to help you."

The revelation came slowly, but it came nevertheless. Calumet suddenly began to apprehend the brilliance of Armbrister's strategy. Shevchenko's own words had triggered the unveiling. The Russian had come back from the dead, and that—at least in part—was something Langley had been trying to resolve all along. They must have wondered. Had Shevchenko been legitimate? Or had he been a provocateur from the beginning? *How he was initially recruited is unimportant*, Robert had remarked.

Of course, Jack suddenly realized. Robert knew how Shevchenko's ostensible subornation began, but he could not afford to disclose it for many reasons, one of which was the fact that he considered it necessary for Calumet to march into Odyssey without any preconceived notions. Otherwise, Calumet—Robert well understood—would have been pushing too hard. He would have attempted to discover the truth concerning Shevchenko, and the Russians would have smelled it, thus compromising the entire operation before it ever really got its steam. One reason Calumet was here, he deduced, was to *learn* the truth concerning the major-general because the spymasters at Langley were not sure themselves. And there were other ramifications, chilling in their clandestine prospects. If Robert had been telling Jack the truth in Amsterdam, then Langley's own source inside Khodinka—if indeed the *source* had been the fountain of knowledge with regard to Shevchenko's execution in the first place—was also a provocateur, a clever plant from Nishka to dispense even more disinformation to America's intelligence elite. And still there was more, Calumet knew, but he did not have the luxury of time to sort it all out at the moment. It was enough that he began to see the serrated form of Armbrister's very clever knot, and Nishka's equally clever devices in rebuttal. *I've been on the wrong side of the applecart from the get-go*, Jack realized.

"What are you trying to help me with?" Jack inquired, purposely attempting to appear suspicious. His instincts were whispering to him about the direction in which the Russians were headed, but the details had not yet flowered in his mind. "And *how* are you planning to help me with whatever it is you want to help me with?"

"Why don't you stop dancing, Calumet?" Vartanyan exclaimed irascibly.

Shevchenko held up his hand. "Be patient, Andrei," he said soothingly, attempting to mitigate potential confrontation. "Jack is naturally suspicious of the situation. In fact, I'm sure he's suspicious of *everybody* at this point, considering what he's been through. Isn't that so, Jack?"

Jack learned long ago that people who were too nice on the surface could summon monsters on command. Shevchenko's daughter, sitting over there with a welt the size of a baseball, was proof enough of that. He simply nodded his agreement.

"Why don't we start with your subornation by the CIA?" Shevchenko suggested.

"You mean about a year ago?" Jack replied, picking up on the earlier conversation. He had no idea where they came up with this particular theory, but his only choice was to play along.

"Yes."

"There's not much to discuss," Jack began. "They caught me. I had no alternative."

"In fact," Shevchenko stated, his head bobbing up and down, indicating he had just heard the truth, "the *real* story is actually quite the opposite of what you were planning to sell for a million dollars. Correct?"

Calumet shrugged, reticent, an actor who forgot his lines.

"In other words," Shevchenko continued, "you provided quality intelligence for roughly five years. Then, a little over a year ago, we began to receive information from you that just didn't gel. When we took it back to Center and had it analyzed, it didn't hold up; it was rotten. Somehow the CIA got onto you, and to keep from going to jail, you allowed them to play you back. In case you're interested, we knew immediately, Jack."

That devious . . . Calumet was thinking of Armbrister. For some reason, Langley had changed the game in midstream. Up until a year ago, Washington had been providing him with intelligence that Moscow could readily digest. Then Langley threw a wrench into the program and began to shovel data that somehow got tagged as suspect. He couldn't wait to hash this one out with Robert.

"Yes," Vartanyan tacked on. "You admitted to me the other day that you were a double. You failed to mention, however, that you were really being run by Langley, that they had you dead to rights. In fact, Jack, you never *were* circumventing Langley and meeting with independent sources. Every crumb of information you've passed to us for the last year has come straight out of the bowels of the CIA, hasn't it?"

"No," Calumet sighed, exasperated. "That's not exactly true. I still managed to circumvent Langley and provide you with legitimate intelligence. Most of the time, anyway. Look, what do you want from me?"

Vartanyan and Shevchenko both appeared pleased, gratified with the answer. Shevchenko smiled. "Jack, loosen up. What we want is really very simple. We want to take you up on the offer you made to Andrei this afternoon. With modifications."

"You mean I get my million dollars?"

"Yes," Shevchenko said smoothly. "Once you've performed successfully. We *want* you to have your million dollars, Jack."

Sure! Just like you loved Karola's mother. Just like you love Karola. "That's reassuring, Aleksandr. What kind of modifications? What do I have to do?" Calumet suddenly wondered why they weren't pressing him for details as to how the CIA compromised him. Why weren't they concerned about how he got caught? Then it dawned on him. Calumet knew the answer, but he wanted to hear Robert admit it. Robert had been way ahead of the game all along.

"We want you to stick around and retrieve that package from Steve Phillips—the CIA's response to the bag of information Andrei gave you in Berlin. After that, we may wish you to run through two or three more cycles, but that's up in the air at the moment. For now, we are eagerly awaiting the package they send back."

"That's no problem," Jack said enthusiastically. *This isn't going to be so hard after all.* "None whatsoever."

"Good." Aleksandr exclaimed. "Uh . . . Jack."

"Yes?"

"Don't try to sell us to the CIA on this one. We'll know. And you'll need the million to get away."

"In the first place," Jack asserted, "I despise those turncoats. In the second, I don't like being in the position I'm in any more than *you* would. Don't worry. There's no way they'll know about this."

"Sensational," Shevchenko remarked. "Now, I believe you told

Andrei that you required good-faith money, no? About twenty thousand, if I remember correctly." He turned to Vartanyan and nodded. "Andrei."

Vartanyan plucked two stacks of bills from the briefcase and tossed them lightly to Calumet, who caught them. "There's your twenty thousand," Vartanyan informed him.

Shevchenko recited a phone number, ordering Calumet to memorize it. "Call us when you are in possession of the information."

"One more thing," Calumet said. Suddenly both men looked concerned, as if they were annoyed at his impertinence.

"What's that?" Vartanyan asked warily.

"Karola goes with me," Calumet asserted, his expression determined. He glanced at her and winked.

"I'm afraid that's not at all possible." Vartanyan spat. "That's just not going to happen!"

Shevchenko made no effort to intervene.

"Then get yourself another errand boy!" Calumet challenged.

Vartanyan came perilously close to violence. He took one step toward Calumet and quickly stopped, suddenly realizing what he was doing. There was murder in his eyes.

"I'm afraid Andrei is right, Jack," Shevchenko said pleasantly. "We simply cannot allow her to accompany you due to security considerations. I'm sure you must understand." He smiled deprecatingly. "However, perhaps we can work out a compromise."

Calumet heard him, but he and Vartanyan were momentarily locked in an apocalyptic struggle, blazing away at each other with lightning bolts in their eyes. Without severing his gaze, Calumet asked, "What kind of compromise?"

"We will send Karola to meet you when you call. She can lead you to us."

Calumet broke off his engagement with Vartanyan and looked at Shevchenko. He knew the major-general was right. There was no way they could let her walk out of here with him. She could blow the entire operation. "I'll agree to that," Jack stated. "But you hear me well, Aleksandr. If she doesn't look healthy when I see her, I'll back out of this operation so fast you'll think I was nothing but a blur in the sky. If there's one mark on her, I'm gone, and I'll let the CIA debrief me at their leisure. Before I'm through, they'll have every word that was spoken here tonight. I'll wager they'd be very interested in knowing that you're still alive."

Shevchenko laughed. "Don't get so hyper, Jack. Of course she'll be all right. I'll see to it. You have nothing to be concerned about."

Calumet turned to Karola. "You're going with me when this is all over. Try to be brave."

Vartanyan remained composed, although it was evident in his demeanor that Calumet had laid down the gauntlet.

Karola managed a weak smile. "Thank you, Jack. I'll be okay." An honest tear trickled down her cheek.

There's no telling what they put her through, Calumet thought. He knew that some of the most severe methods of interrogation left no visible signs of physical abuse, even though in reality the torture was excruciating. When coupled with the mental abuse, the combination was irresistible. Everybody broke. It was just a matter of time.

Calumet gave Vartanyan a screw-you glance, and then said to Shevchenko, "Am I dismissed?"

"Yes," Shevchenko replied. "We'll all leave together, though." He signaled to the blond with a nod that he and Vartanyan should assist Karola. The blond brushed Calumet's shoulder as he strolled by, and Calumet almost dropped him on the spot, but with some difficulty exercised restraint.

After Calumet watched them all walk down the sidewalk and climb into a waiting limo, he strode casually up the street toward Rossetti. He still felt uneasy about the surveillance. He suspected all along that his conference with the commando before entering the safe house had been watched. He could not afford to be discovered, not if Odyssey was to succeed, whatever Odyssey was. He was totally confused.

Rossetti appeared from behind a building and motioned him over.

Calumet was talking before he turned the corner. "I've got to get in touch with Robert. It's absolutely imperative that—" The words caught in his throat and he froze.

Robert was standing there, leaning against the wall, grinning like the old sorcerer that he was.

CHAPTER 27

"Nice of you to drop by, Robert," Calumet remarked, harnessing the ambush. He looked at Rossetti, his facial expression indicting the commando with conspiracy, but Rossetti shrugged his shoulders, as if to say, *I didn't have the slightest idea.*

Robert shook his head in contrite resignation. "What a pair you two are!" he sighed dramatically.

"Look who's talking," Calumet rejoined. Turning to Rossetti, he asked, "You didn't know about this?"

"No. In fact, I almost shot him. He snuck up on me."

"Rossetti told me about the girl," Robert commented. "Vartanyan, one of Vartanyan's thugs, and who else? Who was the third man?"

Calumet fixed him with a hollow stare. "Take a wild guess!"

Robert smiled. "The stride *did* look a bit familiar. A ghost, perhaps?"

"Very funny, Robert! You know who it was. And I want some answers!"

"Was it Shevchenko?" Robert asked intently.

"You guys could have had a little more faith in me," Calumet lectured, shaking his head. "I didn't just fall off the back of a turnip truck, you know. I've—"

"Was it Shevchenko?"

"Either that or a perfect clone."

Robert exhaled forcibly. "That's what must have gotten Filatov killed," he mused, more to himself than anyone else. His voice began to trail off as he continued, "Filatov must have seen Shevchenko in Berlin and wasn't supposed to."

"Oh, no!" Calumet exclaimed.

Robert looked at him, puzzled. "What's wrong with you? I didn't think you liked Filatov."

"I don't," Calumet replied tartly. "But you just said he's dead, right?"

"Yes," Robert remarked, still mystified. "Our information is that he was executed by direct order from Nishka."

"Great!" Jack remonstrated. "Just great! Considering the reliability of your sources lately"—his tone was brimming with accusation—"that means I can count on bumping into the bozo any day now, I guess."

Robert laughed, suddenly aware of Calumet's comedic inference. "No, Jack," he chuckled, "our information is solid on this one. I assure you." Then the spymaster withdrew abruptly into his own world, as though he was standing there completely alone. It was evident to Calumet and Rossetti that the wheels were spinning, his brain waves churning out whatever it was he manufactured in that cerebral computer of his. A slight smile crept up on his mouth, his eyes bright, lighting the darkness around them.

"How in the hell did you get here?" Jack asked the controller after a polite moment, rudely crashing in on his reverie. He began to scan the surrounding area, searching for Robert's team. Robert wouldn't be here without his team. But he saw no one.

"Not now, Jack," Robert advised. "Not here. Why don't we go to your safe house and discuss it? I want it all—the whole kit and caboodle."

Calumet's eyes narrowed. "What makes you think I have a safe house?" he asked, his inflection loaded with suspicion.

"Well," Robert remarked, "I guess I should have been more specific. Why don't we go to the third safe house you've rented since you've been in Bern? The one the old man acquired for you several hours ago."

Rossetti and Calumet traded blank stares.

"Let's move!" Robert ordered. "Now!" He began striding toward the street. Calumet and Rossetti remained in place, allowing him to gain some distance.

"Does he know about the Ferrari?" Calumet whispered to the commando when Robert was safely out of earshot.

"Not on your life, pal."

Calumet nodded blithely. "Good! Don't tell him."

Robert turned around. "*Now*, gentlemen, if you please. Rossetti, you go and collect your Ferrari and meet us there. Jack and I will take my car."

"That squirrelly little . . ." Calumet exclaimed sotto voce, eminently frustrated. He started to give Rossetti the address, but changed his mind. "I'll ride with Rossetti," he informed Robert. Before Robert could object, Calumet grabbed the commando by the arm and hustled him off.

"Here," Rossetti said, tossing Jack the keys when they reached the Ferrari.

As they settled in, Calumet gunned the engine, then turned to Rossetti and grinned. Rossetti thought briefly about strapping on his seat belt. Calumet's grin was devilish.

*

Nishka's mole was working late in the Pentagon. As the Assistant Secretary of Defense in Charge of Intelligence, James Richardson worked late quite often these days. He finally walked down the front steps at 9:00 under a quarter-moon and slid into the rear seat of a waiting taxi. Fifteen minutes later, the taxi deposited him at a quaint Chinese restaurant, where he took a booth in the corner, setting his thick black leather satchel on the seat next to the wall, clearly hidden from casual view. After a hurried meal, he paid his tab and added a 25 percent rider, then rose to leave. Instead of picking up the satchel he had brought with him, however, he took the duplicate beneath his chair.

Richardson had barely gotten five feet from his table when the busboy sailed in to tidy up. After making the table presentable, the busboy nonchalantly set the forgotten satchel on his cart and rolled it into the kitchen. There a slender man in a dark suit took charge, nimbly lifting the satchel off the cart. Without pause, the stranger skipped through the rear exit, leaving the doors swinging in the night. He managed to disappear before Richardson even made it out of the front entrance. Nobody works faster than a Chinese busboy.

Upon arriving at his home in Annandale, Virginia, James Richardson went directly to his study and placed a call on his scrambler.

"Yes?" Armbrister answered.

"Done deal," Richardson said softly.

The line went dead as both men simultaneously replaced their respective receivers in their respective cradles.

*

Robert was waiting in front of the safe house when Calumet and Rossetti came screeching up. "What took you so long?" he challenged, making a production out of glancing at his watch.

"Had to get some gas," Jack answered. Rossetti struggled ferociously to maintain a neutral expression, but he knew that Robert knew they had spent the last twenty or thirty minutes hot-rodding. Still, the commando thought, Calumet had his priorities straight when it came to fast cars. During their ride, Calumet had asked him if he'd managed to pick up any women with it. No, Rossetti had said, he hadn't had time yet, but he was working on it. Calumet nodded, indicating that he knew how frustrating it could be when the job interfered with the important things in life.

As they were walking to the front door, two of Robert's team magically appeared. Both were carrying large cases. Once inside, Robert motioned Calumet and Rossetti to silence while his two men swept the entire apartment for audio surveillance. Twenty minutes later, satisfied, the officers then planted small black boxes on each window. The boxes emitted noiseless electrical impulses which countered any attempts at laser penetration. Their business concluded, the two sound men nodded and quickly left. Robert unplugged the telephone as a final precaution.

"Rick," Robert began once they'd settled themselves in the front room, "you're in on this conversation because your operational judgment may be required to complete our mission."

He means I'll have to decide whether or not to pull the trigger, Rossetti thought. "What about Steve?" he asked. "Is he in on this?"

Robert smiled. "Don't judge Steve too harshly. He's a good detail man. He's done exactly what he was supposed to do, and that's a bit more than I can say about either of you." He gave them each a reproving look, but neither seemed to be moved by it, so he continued. "Steve is in on what I *want* him to be in on. Is that clear?" He tried the reproving look once more but got the same reaction. Except that Rossetti rolled his eyes slightly. "For now, Steve is not privy to what we're about to discuss. Okay?" Robert noticed that this last comment was well received when compared to the previous two. "By the way," he added as a blistering afterthought, "where do you get off leasing a Ferrari, Rossetti?" But he could see that the commando had been working assiduously on his explanation for a long time now, and his mannerism indicated he was revving up to let it fly. Just as he was about to speak, Robert held up his palm and sighed, "Never mind. I don't want to hear it. We'll go over that later."

"I think it was a good move, myself," Calumet interjected. "Nobody would expect one of us to be driving a shiny black Ferrari. It's too conspicuous. See the beauty of it, Robert?" Rossetti smiled inwardly, pleased that he had let Calumet drive.

Robert just shook his head. "Uh-huh. Sure, Jack. Gentleman, let's stop clowning around and get down to business." He turned to Calumet. "What was Shevchenko's agenda?"

"First of all, Shevchenko gave me a phone number to memorize." Calumet told him the number. "Why don't you get your people working on that?"

Robert nodded and stepped outside a moment. Returning, he took his place and repeated, "Now, what was Shevchenko's agenda?"

Calumet related in precise detail the content of his discussion with the major-general, and also expressed his desire to get Karola out one way or the other, briefly explaining her harrowing ordeal.

"It's too bad about the girl," Robert replied. "We'll certainly bring her out if we can. I'm afraid, however, she is not our primary concern in this operation."

Calumet had been pushed as far as we was willing to be pushed. "Well, it may not be *your* primary concern, or Armbrister's either, but the fact is, Robert, neither of your concerns mean much to me right about now. Neither of you have shot straight with me regarding Odyssey or my involvement as it relates to Odyssey, so unless you're prepared to bring me all the way into the fold, and I mean *all the way* into the fold, then the woman is *my* primary concern in this operation, and that's *exactly* the way Odyssey is going to be played from here on out. You can take it or leave it, because there *is* no operation without me. Not at this point."

"Is there an emotional relationship between you and the girl, Jack?" Robert's concentration was intense. If Calumet had gotten involved with Karola emotionally, he could ruin the entire mission, and Robert knew it. In fact, he had seen it happen before.

"No," Calumet lied. "Not at all. But I promised her I'd get her out."

Robert showed no signs of contention. He apparently bought it. In fact, he smiled lightly, remembering back to his own days when Langley had been recalcitrant as he requested permission again and again to salvage a defector whom *he* had turned. Langley wanted the defector to remain in place a while longer, but Robert was convinced that the man was about to be blown. The standoff ultimately came to a head when Robert and some twenty operations officers threatened to resign on the spot and then bring the defector out themselves if Langley would not concede the point. In the end, Langley conceded the point. A defector whom an agent or an officer turned became special to that agent or officer, and often the agent or officer sensed the pulse of danger more readily than the analysts in Washington, so Robert understood Calumet's fervor. Still, Robert had an operation to run.

"What you say certainly has a measure of validity, Jack. I'm going to take you back and walk you through Odyssey, only this time, I'm going to shoot straight with you, as you put it."

"Why didn't you shoot straight with me in the first place?" Calumet demanded.

"Perhaps the answer to that question will become evident as I explain the dynamics of Odyssey, Jack." At that point, Robert determined he was not going to be pushed any further himself. "If that's not satisfactory, you can pull out right now. You can be on the next flight home. Just say the word."

"If I pull out, I won't be on the next plane home. I'll get Karola out myself."

Again, Robert saw himself in Jack's own insurrection and smiled momentarily. Then he became very serious. "Jack, don't test me on this one. If you pull out, I'll make *sure* that you're on the next flight home." Changing back to the smile again, he continued, "But I don't think that will be necessary. I believe you'll soon see that this avenue of discussion is academic. Shall we continue?"

"I'm listening," Calumet said evenly. And then he suddenly realized that Robert was the one who had precipitated this particular avenue of discussion in the first place. *The crafty old fox could probably make a circle believe it was pointing in the wrong direction,* Jack surmised. At any rate, in case he did not like what he was about to hear, he began to formulate his own campaign for evading Robert and his secret hordes. His first concern was Rossetti. He could not be certain how the commando would play it if he decided to rebel, but he nevertheless worked out quickly in his own mind how to go about incapacitating Rossetti should it become necessary. *A blazing right-cross to the jaw ought to do it,* he concluded. Suddenly he wished he had held onto the keys to the Ferrari, but he had given them back to the commando when they arrived.

"It was necessary," Robert began, "for me to be less than candid with you, Jack, for several reasons. But let me begin at the beginning." He sighed, as though he had a large task ahead of him. "I initially told you that we bought Shevchenko in the early days of Yeltsin's administration. That much is true." Robert held Calumet's gaze, intimating that his next comment should be considered significant. "He was a walk-in."

"So you were immediately suspicious," Jack stated.

"Yes. Immediately."

"Did you know that he worked for Nishka?"

"Don't get ahead of me Jack, please," Robert admonished. "Shevchenko told us that he knew Nishka when Nishka was First Deputy Chief of the GRU, but claimed that he never saw Nishka again after Nishka dropped out of sight and went underground. Of course, we had no way to verify this, although we were skeptical."

Rossetti wondered, *Who is Nishka?* But he knew better than to interrupt.

Robert continued, "You see, Jack, Shevchenko trod very carefully with us at first. He was positioned to do tremendous damage to the Aquarium by virtue of the fact that he actually had oversight of the GRU Resident in Washington. This obviously meant that you weren't his only source; he had access to several others as well, even though he did not actually run most of those other sources. Initially, we couldn't get a handle on his motives. We speculated— was he a provocateur? Or was he merely feeding us his intelligence piecemeal in order to drag it out and thus garner longevity for himself? In other words, was he attempting to get the most bang for our buck by doling out his sources on a staggered schedule?" Robert shrugged. "Well, we could never really be sure. You see, some of his intelligence was golden. He exposed several people about whom we hadn't the slightest suspicion. Several illegals and a couple of NATO officers, as it turned out."

"What about Murdock?" Calumet asked.

"I was coming to that," Robert replied. "But no, he never mentioned Murdock. We were planning to confront him about Murdock after Murdock's arrest, but we never got the chance. By then, we had received information that Shevchenko had been executed."

"Well, blast it!" Calumet exclaimed angrily. "You *must* have been suspicious of the whole setup at that point. You could have warned me!"

Robert smiled. "Yes, we were suspicious. We'd been suspicious all along, if you want to know the truth. Of course, it *is* conceivable that Shevchenko did not know about Murdock. Or maybe he was holding back, planning to sell Murdock to us later on. There were several possibilities, Jack. We were keeping our options open."

Calumet started to speak, but Robert waved him off. "You must understand, Jack, there were other prongs to Operation Odyssey, which really began when Shevchenko ostensibly turned. You and Shevchenko were just one front in this little war. There are additional fronts about which you know nothing. And never *will* know, actually."

But Calumet thought he *did* know. Suddenly it was obvious. Initially he had the whole scheme figured backward. Now he began to see it in linear terms. The Shevchenko ruse gave it body. He ventured his speculation. "Oh? You mean I'll never know about Nishka's American mole who is really a high-level plant by Armbrister. Is that what I'll never know about?"

There was a perceptible change in atmosphere, as if the room suddenly acquired an eerie silence typified in the aftermath of a bomb detonation. Robert almost leapt at Calumet. "Where did you get that?" he asked rapidly.

Calumet had never seen his controller more concerned. "I deduced it. It's only logical."

Robert eyed him suspiciously. "Jack, don't screw around with me. Did you deduce it? Or did Vartanyan or Shevchenko precipitate it? I *must* know."

"I just deduced it," Jack said sincerely. "Just this very moment, in fact. You have my word."

Robert turned to Rossetti. "You'll forget you've heard any of this, Rossetti. Understood?"

Rossetti nodded.

"And you'll forget it too, Jack," Robert admonished sternly. "I mean it. That information is grounds for pulling you out of this operation right now."

"I still don't see why you couldn't have been more forthcoming with me," Calumet remarked.

Robert frowned. "Let me put this in perspective for you, Jack. *You* work for *us,* not the other way around. It's that simple." Robert shook his head. "Jack, you are undoubtedly the most intelligent and instinctive agent I have ever known, bar none. But you are not the final authority on American policy and intelligence tasking. There are a great many equally intelligent individuals who have been masterminding Odyssey since its inception, and they have additional sources of input to which you are not privy. Don't try to second-guess me, Jack. The fact that I withheld information from you very likely saved your life."

"How is that?" Calumet asked skeptically.

"For one," Robert explained, "your first interview with Vartanyan. What if Vartanyan had decided to conduct a hostile interrogation?"

"He didn't," Calumet said plainly, although his tone indicated he realized his ground was weak.

"That's right," Robert stated. "Do you know why? Because certain measures were taken to make it unfeasible for the Russians to put you under drug inducement or physical duress."

Calumet was about to question that, but Robert held up his palm. "Never mind. On the other hand, it was not a given that the Russians would heed our little ploy. The possibility existed that they would go ahead and submit you to hostile interrogation anyway. In that case, you would have spilled the beans and given them everything. If we had told you the whole story up front, everything would have been blown, and they would have killed you on the spot. In contrast, by knowing nothing, even if they had forced you into a hostile interrogation, in the end they probably would have let you live and proceeded to play you back, just as they have done."

Calumet saw the logic in that, and nodded, acquiescing.

"Don't forget, Jack," Robert smiled, "I was running agents when you were still a gleam in your daddy's eye."

"A gleam, my foot!" Rossetti interjected. "Calumet was a mistake, and everybody knows it."

The atmosphere had been somewhat tense up until then, but

Rossetti's witticism defused the pressure. Everybody had a good laugh.

"Jack," Robert said after they had settled back down, "one reason we ran you the way we did was to discover Shevchenko's status. He is a crucial piece to this entire puzzle. By sending you in blind, by forcing you into a conflict with the BND, we were attempting to ingratiate you to the Russians while simultaneously striving to preserve your cover and your very life. After all, we couldn't very well cable Nishka and ask him to please buy into our little scheme, could we?"

"And the proof is in the pudding," Calumet remarked, conceding the point. "I mean, they fell for it and Shevchenko revealed himself, didn't he? Which is just what you wanted."

"Yes," Robert smiled, "because you forced them into it with your last little act. They were afraid you were on the verge of flying the coop. Of course, we couldn't predict the details of how it might all play out, but the end result was exactly what we were after—as far as it goes, that is."

"As far as it goes?" Calumet wondered out loud. "What does that mean?"

"Aren't you the least bit curious why Shevchenko is convinced that you were initially a legitimate double and then had been compromised by Langley only a year ago?"

"Absolutely," Jack agreed. "I was getting ready to ask you about that. Why do they think that?"

"Very simple," Robert answered. "Shevchenko did not sell you to us until about a year ago."

An exclamation of surprise flew onto Calumet's face, but Robert held him off again. "You see, Jack, Shevchenko kept your identity hidden from us for two years. Then suddenly one day he sprang it on us."

"Well, now that we know he's been working for Nishka all along, why would he do that? What are they up to, Robert?"

"Ah!" Robert grinned. "Here's where the plot thickens. Jack, listen very carefully, because everything I told you before was simply a smoke screen. But no more. I'm about to reveal the pivotal meaning of Odyssey."

CHAPTER 28

Calumet was in no mood to exercise patience. "I'm listening," he said enthusiastically.

"From the beginning, Odyssey has been an immense conflagration of disinformation," Robert disclosed. "On *both* sides. You see, Jack, we have been throwing reams of disinformation at Khodinka for several years, and they've been throwing it back. You were just one of our sources in this scheme. To make it more palatable, let me tell you how it worked."

"Be my guest," Calumet remarked.

"Although I told you in Amsterdam that we were giving you genuine intelligence and then exchanging it with Shevchenko before he passed it along to Moscow, that's not exactly true. Again, the reason for the subterfuge was in case you were forced to submit to hostile interrogation. In reality, we were investing you with carefully construed disinformation. There were two reasons for this. The first, as I mentioned before, was to validate your legend as a traitor in Shevchenko's eyes. The second reason is because we were suspicious of Shevchenko all along."

"That's all well and good," Calumet interjected, "but it doesn't add up exactly. If you had other sources, then any disinformation I was passing to Shevchenko could have been corroborated or disavowed by all the other sources you mentioned."

"Very perceptive, Jack." Robert smiled. "That's exactly the point."

"I don't understand."

"Let's look at it this way," the wily operations officer explained. "If you take a jigsaw puzzle and attempt to put it together, you must first be confident that you possess all the necessary pieces. Right?"

Calumet nodded.

"Good. But what if you don't have all the pieces? What then?" Robert didn't wait for an answer. "You see, Jack, we were investing you with only certain pieces of the puzzle. Your information, on the whole, would be useless unless it was combined with information

from additional sources. In other words, Nishka not only required
your information, but he also required the information from at least
one other source in order to make it work. Your intelligence by
itself, and our other source's intelligence by *itself,* was an incomplete
jigsaw puzzle. Do you see?"

"Yes," Calumet stated blandly. "That's not too difficult to comprehend, Robert. Even somebody like Rossetti could understand
that." Everybody chuckled. "But you said that the information you
were providing to me and this other source was all disinformation,
right?"

Robert nodded. "Not all of it, but most of it. Yes."

"Well, then something doesn't jibe, Robert."

"What's that?"

"Eventually the Russians would discover it was disinformation.
Eventually they'd find out that something didn't work, and they'd
know. You wouldn't be able to pull it off forever."

"That is correct," Robert smiled. "And we knew that from the
beginning. That's why we began to muddy the waters."

"What do you mean?"

"I'm not going to hit this one too hard, but I'll give you the basics. You see, we had *several* sources, not just two. After a certain
point in the operation, we were able to infiltrate additional sources
into the ball game. The whole scenario was carefully constructed.
In essence, we began shoveling conflicting disinformation down the
Aquarium's throat. They would be forced to try and sort out what
fit and what didn't, thus keeping their minds off the fact that it was
all disinformation in the first place. In other words, we were disguis-
ing what was purported to be genuine intelligence by feeding them
conflicting disinformation. Our hope was that one set of disinformation would act as a smoke screen. We were hoping that they
would ultimately discount one set of disinformation and then say,
'Aha! Now we've uncovered what was false, so the other must be
real.' Are you with me?"

"Sure," Calumet answered. "But again, you could only pull it off
for so long. As I said, eventually, they'd make heads and tails out of
it and the operation would be over. I'm sure that you could set them
back a number of years, assuming they bought it all, but it certainly
doesn't seem to be worth all the effort."

"Well, I disagree," Robert said. "It would definitely be worth the effort, especially if they bought it all. However"—Robert's eyes suddenly acquired a brightness—"this particular prong was never the real crux of Odyssey anyway. The disinformation, the shuffling of provocateurs, the mixture of truth and lies—none of these things were ever intended to be the visceral motivation behind Odyssey. None of these things were what drove us into this affair in the first place."

Robert preserved the silence at this point and began to appraise Calumet and Rossetti. Finally unable to contain himself any longer, Calumet spoke. "Well, do I get to know or not? Or are you going to try to make me divine the riddle all by myself?"

Robert sighed. "Jack, in order for this operation to continue, you're going to have to go back inside."

"I know that. Tell me something I *don't* know, Robert."

Robert stood and paced the room for a minute. Finally, sitting back down, he looked Calumet in the eye. "I want you to know, Jack, that you can back out of this operation at any time. I just want you to know that. And I mean it."

Calumet glanced at Rossetti, who shrugged. "Robert," Calumet remonstrated, "what in the world has gotten in to you? Are you going soft on me all of a sudden? What's the big deal?"

Robert extracted a glossy coin purse from his pocket. Opening it, he plucked a small capsule from its interior and laid it on the table in front of Calumet. "Cyanide," Robert stated plainly. "If you go back inside, you'll need to carry that with you. And, if things don't go the way they should, you'll have to eat it. There can be no screwups from here on out, Jack." Robert grimaced slightly and gazed intently at Calumet. "If I were you, I'd leave that capsule right there on the table and go on home."

Calumet's eyes darted back and forth between the capsule, Robert, and Rossetti. After a moment, he said with levity, "Doesn't Rick get one?"

"He won't need one," Robert answered seriously. "Rossetti will have several targets to concentrate on. And Jack"—the operations officer leaned forward—"if Rossetti sees you being led away by the Russians, *you'll* be one of those targets."

"I can't do that!" Rossetti protested.

"You'll do what you're told, soldier!" Robert snapped.

Rossetti started shaking his head, but Calumet quickly intervened. "It won't come to that." Jack scooped up the capsule and put it in his pocket. "Don't worry about it."

"The capsule's lining is insoluble," Robert said. "You'll have to bite it." The statement sounded insensitive, but there was really no other way to put it.

Calumet nodded. "So what's this all about, Robert." Secretly, the capsule freaked him. He would rather charge single-handedly into a hostile army than think about eating cyanide, but he evidenced no outward display of emotion.

Robert sighed heavily. "In a sense, you could say that Odyssey's momentum revolves around a very grave secret, Jack. Perhaps the biggest secret since Operation Overlord in World War Two."

"Hold on," Calumet interrupted. "Before we go any further, Robert, I want to know something. I just put the cyanide in my pocket. That means I'm committed. But I have to know if what you are about to tell me is the absolute truth, or just another subterfuge. You owe me that much."

"Yes," Robert agreed, "I *do* owe you that much. And you have my word that everything I've told you tonight and everything I'm *about* to tell you is gospel. My absolute word. In fact, I'm about to tell you *some* things I'm not really authorized to tell you, and that's the truth as well."

"Fair enough." Jack nodded. He could read the sincerity in Robert's eyes. "Go ahead."

"You might say that Odyssey has been winding down ever since it began. Odyssey was conceived in large part for the purpose of obscuring another operation that was already in sanction. Let me digress a bit, Jack." Robert leaned back in his chair. "You see, although you never knew the exact contents of your products, the intelligence contained therein served a special purpose. Along with other bits of information, we were also placing within each package a smattering of technology concerning our KH-12s."

That shocked Calumet. "You mean our satellite technology?"

"Yes," Robert responded. "With particular emphasis on SIGINT." He glanced at Rossetti and explained, "Signals intelligence."

"Yeah," Rossetti acknowledged. "I know." Of all the hardware sent aloft, the SIGINT platforms, sometimes referred to as ferret satellites, were the most secret, and served as the very heartbeat of DEFSMAC.

Calumet knew that every shopping list given him by the GRU had contained specifications regarding American satellite capability, but he always told them that he would see what he could do, doubtful that Langley would disclose any information along those lines. Now he saw that he had been wrong. Before he could question it, Robert took up again.

"You see, Jack, we were providing minute details—not all of it legitimate, of course—about the hardware specifications of the satellites themselves. We figured that was as far as we could push it on your end. After all, the hardware technology, although top secret, is not so dark that information about it could not be gleaned from certain sources. What *was* too dark to give to the Russians through you, on the other hand, was the sensor packages. In other words, the ins and outs of the sensor capabilities of our KH-12s."

"So for that," Calumet deduced, "you had another source. One who is much more highly placed than myself or any of the contacts I might have laid claim to."

"Precisely," Robert agreed. "We fed them the hardware through you, and the sensor packaging through another conduit."

Calumet whistled. *This is heavy!* he thought.

"Eventually," Robert continued, "we knew that the operation would have to come to an end. Eventually we knew that they would discover our ploy. As a result, we began to attempt to steer Odyssey into a subtle meltdown. All the while, Nishka has been manipulating his sources back and forth in an effort to get a handle on what's real and what's not. It's been a game of pin-the-tail-on-the-donkey for both of us. That's why Shevchenko waited two years before revealing you to us as his asset. At that point, Nishka had apparently decided to attempt to penetrate the puzzle from another angle. After about a year, however, he evidently concluded that he hadn't gone far enough, so he turned up the heat. By recently leaking the information about Shevchenko's execution, Nishka was attempting to force our hand. Do you see?"

"I see the reasoning behind it," Calumet remarked, "but the logic escapes me on one point."

"And what point is that?" Robert queried.

"Well, I'm not a rocket scientist, but it would seem to me that this game has gone on too long. I would think their scientists would have been able to take your disinformation and piece it together by now and see that it doesn't work." Calumet suddenly had a thought. "Or *does* it work?"

Robert smiled. "No, Jack, it doesn't work. Not exactly. And you are right, as far as it goes. Normally, their scientists *would* have been able to piece it together by now. Normally."

"Normally?" Calumet appeared puzzled.

"Yes," Robert grinned. "You hinted at it yourself. Rocket scientist," he added cryptically.

You're kidding! Calumet thought. He believed he knew what was coming.

"That's right," Robert beamed. "Our big secret." He reached into his jacket and extracted a dossier. Flipping it open, he pulled out an eight-by-ten photograph and laid it on the table. He turned the picture so both Calumet and Rossetti could see it.

"Who is he?" Rossetti asked.

But Calumet knew who he was, although he'd never seen the man before in his life, and he didn't know the name, yet he nevertheless knew who he was. He ventured his supposition: "Let me guess, Robert. One of Russia's top rocket scientists. Correct?"

"No, not *one* of Russia's top rocket scientists. *The* top rocket scientist. Sergei Ivanovich Kulagin. Director of the Aquarium's SIGINT program." Robert exhaled forcefully. "And he's been working for us for the past five years."

"Unbelievable!" Calumet exclaimed. "So he's been keeping their program at bay and turning our disinformation into something that could ostensibly be viewed as legitimate. Something that would *appear* viable, but wouldn't really work. Amazing!"

"Exactly," Robert rejoined gleefully.

Calumet thought momentarily. "Then where do I fit in?" he asked. "Other than the fact that Kulagin has been using the intelligence procured through me and other sources to prevent the Russians from obtaining our capabilities, how does that fit in with Odyssey and my involvement with Vartanyan and Shevchenko?"

"It's really very simple," Robert answered. "Kulagin's time is running out. He's about to be blown. It won't be long before his associates discover his treachery. That's why Nishka has forced our hand where you are concerned. He wants to see how Kulagin will explain the intelligence you give them in your next package. You see, Nishka *knows* that the information you will be handing over this time is disinformation. There won't be any doubt about that. Right?"

"Right," Calumet agreed.

"So," Robert expounded, "he won't tell Kulagin that. As far as Kulagin is concerned, in Kulagin's own mind, Nishka will think the information is legitimate, just like in the past. In reality, however, Nishka knows that the information is bogus."

"Ah," Calumet deduced. "So Nishka is laying a trap for Kulagin."

"Yes," Robert said seriously. "Precisely."

"Why doesn't Nishka just arrest Kulagin and submit him to hostile interrogation?"

"There are several problems with that, Jack. First, Nishka doesn't know that Kulagin is the bad apple. He knows only that their program is virtually defunct: they have made no real progress for the past five years. At this point, Nishka has only a list of suspects. By beginning with Kulagin, he's starting at the top. If it's not Kulagin, then he'll move on down to the next scientist in the link. Of course, we both know that it *is* Kulagin, and if Nishka is allowed to carry out his little machinations, then Kulagin is finished. As far as submitting Kulagin to hostile interrogation, Nishka can't afford to take the chance. The interrogation would more than likely fry Kulagin's brain, and Nishka knows that if he is wrong, he's just wasted their top scientist."

"That makes sense," Calumet ventured. "But since they think Langley compromised me about a year ago, they know that my information for the past year is suspect. Wouldn't that be enough to expose Kulagin?"

"No," Robert remarked. "Because we forced an exchange with Shevchenko before he passed the documents back to Moscow. For all they knew, you were still circumventing us on the sly. Remember?"

"Oh yeah," Calumet nodded vigorously. "So they think that the information I'd been passing to Shevchenko was real, and that Langley was just playing me along. They didn't know what to make of it at that point because you had managed to muddy the waters, as you said."

"Yes," Robert agreed. "But Nishka has been tightening the noose for the past several years, closing in slowly. And now, with the deception of Shevchenko's execution, he has revealed his hand. We know that he's close, and that Kulagin is on borrowed time."

"So what are we going to do?" Calumet inquired.

Robert stood and began pacing again. "This is where it gets tricky, Jack, so listen carefully. And you too, Rossetti. Pay attention."

Calumet and Rossetti looked at each other questioningly.

"Gentlemen," Robert explained, "we have indisputable information that Kulagin is here in Bern."

"Right on!" Calumet exclaimed.

"Nishka wants a quick answer," Robert continued. "Sergei Ivanovich Kulagin was flown into Berlin the day before yesterday and driven here this morning under heavy guard. He's traveling under the aegis of Russian diplomatic immunity and at this moment is sequestered inside the Russian embassy. They're keeping an extremely tight watch on him. Why was he brought here in the first place? Because Nishka will order Kulagin to analyze your information on the spot, Jack, and by that I mean that they will attempt to hold you until your package is taken back to the Russian embassy for Kulagin's perusal. That's one reason for the cyanide. Under no circumstances are you to be taken alive, Jack—not knowing what you now know. But you'll have some time. We don't think they plan to let Kulagin out of the embassy at all. It's far too risky on their part. Of course, if Kulagin slips up on his analysis, he's dead. And probably so are you." Robert paused, then added, "For what it's worth, you performed brilliantly, Jack. They would not have flown in Kulagin if they hadn't bought your legend. You managed not only to succeed beyond our expectations, by virtue of the fact that they flew Kulagin out of Russia and brought him here, but you also managed to bring about the results much faster than we originally thought possible."

Robert frowned, as though eminently concerned. "However, here's the bottom line. Kulagin is on the verge of being discovered. If that happens, his life isn't worth a plugged nickel." Exhaling forcefully, the controller continued. "Therefore, we have a very grave problem here, gentlemen. If Nishka is allowed to pick Kulagin's brain, he will not only be able to force the scientist to retrace his deceptions backward, thus quickly repairing their own satellite program, but he will also be able in large part to dissect *our* SIGINT structure. After all, since Kulagin knows what *doesn't* work, he is very capable of easily deducing what does. How? It's simple, really. You see, in order to submit our carefully conceived disinformation, it's been necessary to mix in a little sprinkling of truth along the way. So if Kulagin is blown, we will have lost possibly one of the biggest gambles we've ever taken. And make no mistake, gentlemen, Odyssey has been a gargantuan gamble on both sides. Instead of characterizing Odyssey as a huge success, it will be nothing less than a catastrophic failure if we don't succeed with this final phase of the operation. In essence, Kulagin is at this point the little boy with his finger in the dike. In other words, we are now between a rock and a hard place."

Calumet appeared to appreciate the gravity of the situation. "Like I said, Robert, what are we going to do?"

Robert stopped pacing and stood directly in front of Calumet and Rossetti. Leveling his gaze at them, he said simply, "We're going to attempt to bring Odyssey to a close, gentlemen. We're going to try to get Kulagin out."

CHAPTER 29

Calumet picked up the package two days later, just before noon. It was a drab, chill Friday. The sky was overcast and sultry clouds covered the horizon in an ominous sheath of black and gray. They were draped so low that they seemed to smother the land like a field of wild mushrooms after a saturating spring rain. The next two days were days that Jack Calumet would remember for the rest of his life.

The meet with Steve to pick up the package had been brief and took place in the open. The Russians had been watching and listening, shadowing Steve out of the embassy and staying with him all the way. Robert's ghosts had been tailing the Russians and followed them back to the Russian embassy after the meet was concluded. In contrast, several members of the Russian countersurveillance squad made an attempt to box Calumet and trail him back to his lair, but Calumet dry-cleaned himself successfully and lost them after thirty minutes. In all, everything had gone smoothly.

Calumet's safe houses had been abandoned. Calumet, Robert, Rossetti, Team Interceptor, and other members of Robert's cadre were now situated inside another safe house on the outskirts of Bern. The phone number given Calumet by Shevchenko, and later given to Robert by Calumet, had turned up dry. Robert's technicians were able to trace the number to the Russian embassy, but no further. They were quite positive it was being rerouted to a separate safe house where Shevchenko and his gang were holed up, along with Karola.

Karola. What a tragedy, Jack thought. Her whole life had been one of disruption, heartache, and deception. It would take years to straighten her out, if she ever *could* be straightened out. And yet, Calumet sensed, somewhere in her inner recesses, she secretly nurtured a deep-rooted desire to turn over a new leaf. The hidden appetite had probably been there all along, like a volcano waiting to erupt, but mysteriously had never really latched onto the opportunity to flourish.

Well, that was about to change. Robert and Odyssey aside, Calumet decided he would make it his business to get her out. He would make it his business to give her, finally, a real shot at a slice of the good life. A wholesome life. He owed her that much. Not simply because he had turned her, though. He knew, ultimately, that no one could be turned unless they truly coveted the transformation in the first place, and Karola, he surmised, had simply been looking for a way out of her twisted world all along. She had been coerced into becoming something she had never really wanted to be, and now she saw a tiny glimmer of hope, a dimly lit, elusive pathway which might possibly allow her to shed her abomination and become what her mother had sought for her to become before she was viciously murdered on a cold street in West Berlin.

Jack was sure that Karola's single hope lay in him and him alone, in the strong hand of a man whom she had been unable to conquer sexually. But it also went further than that, he knew. The truth about her father had lingered just beneath the surface of her recognition for all these years, and although not crystallized in her thoughts, its subtle intuition had tenaciously stalked her soul and whispered continuously the horrifying reality that she had heretofore been unwilling or afraid to face. It took Calumet's own intuitive interpretation of her Shakespearean tragedy to bring it home. For her to let go of the placid lies and grasp at the merciless truth, to abandon the safety and simplicity of all she had known throughout her mature and wanton life, was a monumental leap of faith, an act of triumph and courage, and an effort of will that should not go unrequited. Thus, in the final analysis, Jack decided, whatever her motives, Karola had stood up against her father and Vartanyan for *his* sake and for her mother's. Now Jack Calumet would stand up for her. In Jack's mind, it was that simple. For him, it was not only a matter of honor, of his own cussed belief that you stood by your friends through thick and thin, come Heaven, come Hell, but also a matter of principle, and although to the untrained eye Jack Calumet might appear wild and reckless and prone to impetuous flings of heated passion, in reality he lived and breathed by his principles. To that end, he made a solemn vow. *Yes,* he determined within himself, one way or the other, he would quell Karola's masters and somehow get her out. Or die trying. In Jack's mind, it was that simple, and there were no in-betweens.

But Robert had another agenda. Fortunately, however, his game plan included Karola. From an operational standpoint, the spymaster devised a scheme which encompassed using Karola in an overall effort at bringing both Calumet and Kulagin in from the cold. If it worked, Karola would get out safely as well. And, as usual, Robert's plan required a rogue to pull it off. Calumet was the key.

Calumet waited until 3:00 to call the number Shevchenko had provided and inform the Russian that he was now in possession of the package. Shevchenko wanted a meet that evening, but Calumet put him off. "Not tonight," he told him, buying time, as Robert had instructed. "Tomorrow morning at ten." The Russian reluctantly agreed. They arranged a public location. From there, Calumet would be led to Shevchenko's lair. "No problem," Calumet had said, "but I want to see Karola healthy and whole."

The biggest break in the operation came at about 4:00 that afternoon. The Mossad asked for and received an immediate appointment with Bern's COS. At 4:30, Elihu Ben Geddi met with Edward Vermillion, the CIA's Chief of Station in Switzerland, and remarked offhandedly that the Russians had rented a large warehouse several years ago just north of Bern. According to Ben Geddi's sources, the warehouse had become operational only in the past few days. In further explanation, the Mossad man revealed that the Russians had used an illegal whom the Mossad had known about for some time to acquire the lease. The reason the Israelis were interested in the first place, Ben Geddi then propounded, was because of the Israeli government's ever-vigilant concern that the warehouse might be used as a staging area for the infiltration and dissemination of weapons to various terrorist cells throughout Europe. "Just thought you might want to know," Ben Geddi told Vermillion with a twinkle in his eye. Certain relevant findings in Odyssey's postmortem, which would not be conducted until much later, would ultimately attribute Calumet's utilization of Eitan as having been most fortuitous. Calumet should have been tipped off to Eitan's true allegiance by the phones in the safe house. Nobody could have orchestrated such things so quickly unless they had some very special help.

Robert got the news at 4:50. At that point, there was a considerable buzz in the safe house. Robert et al. became excited at the prospects of having found Shevchenko's lair. The spymaster dispatched a surveillance team immediately. At 9:45 that evening, the surveillance efforts paid off. Andrei Vartanyan was observed riding in a vehicle entering the dirt road leading to the warehouse with three accomplices, one of whom was in heavy disguise. Operation Odyssey was now primed.

All they had to do from here was figure out how to lure the Russians into bringing Kulagin to the warehouse to analyze Calumet's intelligence, as opposed to delivering the intelligence to the Russian embassy and having Kulagin analyze it there. In the end, Robert concluded that only Calumet could make that happen. Calumet would have to walk a delicate tightrope in order to pull it off. Still, Robert was confident. He knew that if anybody could walk that tightrope and preserve the balance, it was Jack Calumet.

*

Calumet showed at the Clock Tower at precisely 9:55 the next morning. The sky was still overcast, and the clouds still drizzling.

The Clock Tower was originally built in the twelfth century and restored in the sixteenth. Four minutes before every hour, crowds gather in front of the clock to witness the oldest horological puppet show in the world. Replete with mechanical bears, jesters, and emperors, the show is always quite fascinating to watch. Which is exactly what Calumet was pretending to do when Yevgenni, the blond GRU agent, approached him.

"Comrade Shevchenko is waiting for you," Yevgenni remarked arrogantly. "Do you have the package?"

At first Calumet ignored him, ostensibly caught up in the splendor of the show. Then, slowly, he turned, faced the Russian, and responded contemptuously, "Where is Karola?"

Yevgenni smiled cruelly. "She is with comrades Shevchenko and Vartanyan."

"That wasn't the deal." Calumet leashed his temper.

"That's the deal you will accept," Yevgenni stated dauntingly.

Calumet mentally counted to ten. "Which way?"

"Follow me."

They began to distance themselves from the crowd. As they came to the intersection of a side street, Calumet said, "Hold on a minute." He inclined his head in the direction of an alley and strolled into it casually. Yevgenni, suspicious, followed warily. After several steps, Calumet stopped abruptly. Without turning around, he suddenly launched into a lightning roundhouse kick, planting his foot squarely into the epicenter of Yevgenni's chest, who was correspondingly planted squarely into the brick wall of a nearby building. Calumet followed up rapidly with a hammer strike to the solar plexus, and then an elbow to the bridge of Yevgenni's nose. Blood spurted like a geyser as Yevgenni dropped heavily to the ground.

Calumet inspected his sleeve. Good! After delivering the point of his elbow to the bridge of Yevgenni's nose, he had withdrawn his arm in time—there was no blood on his jacket. "The deal I will accept," Calumet then lectured, satisfied that he had avoided the splattering blood, "is the deal I have made. You go back and deliver that very message to Shevchenko. In fact, since he's seen fit to abrogate the initial terms of our arrangement, you tell Shevchenko that my intelligence will now be provided in stages. A little bit at a time. The first installment will cost you fifty thousand dollars. If there is any more betrayal, or if anything happens to me, the remainder of my intelligence will be lost."

"What do you mean?" Yevgenni grunted, still terribly confused. "What are you talking about? Stages?"

"Never mind," Calumet answered. "You're too stupid to understand anyway. Just tell Shevchenko. I'll be back at the Clock Tower in one hour. Karola had better be there this time, or I'll vanish." For good measure, because of what he'd done to Karola, Calumet kicked Yevgenni resoundingly in the ribs. "Got it?"

The Russian nodded weakly, gasping for air. Calumet stormed off.

Fifteen minutes later, Robert was about to go ballistic. "What the *hell* do you think you're doing?" He had witnessed it all from a distance, and now he, Calumet and Rossetti stood in a secluded area going over the details.

"I was controlling the meet," Calumet answered defensively.

"Balls!" Robert almost shouted. "You were indulging in a personal vendetta."

"I know what I'm doing," Calumet snapped back. "You wanted me to set it up so as to deliver the intelligence in stages. I've just done that. The fact that I roughed up that idiot only adds to my credibility. They'll think I'm temperamental and that the only reason I insisted on the stages is because of what just happened. They won't think the whole thing has been calculated, they'll think I came up with it on the spur of the moment."

Robert shook his head. "Maybe so," he agreed reluctantly. "But your motives are what concern me, Jack. And you *are* temperamental. I told you, we will do our dead level best to rescue the woman, but she is *not* our primary objective. Kulagin is."

"I understand the program, Robert."

Robert was on the verge of really lighting into Calumet, but suddenly thought better of it. Secretly, he felt confident that Calumet would not screw it up. If push came to shove, Calumet would do the right thing. He would place a premium on Kulagin's life if it came down to a contest between the Russian scientist and Karola. Robert decided to express reliance in his agent. "I just hope you know what you're doing."

Five minutes later they dispersed. Everyone knew their assignments. Calumet cooled his heels in a café with coffee, pastries, and a newspaper. Forty minutes later, at 11:00, he was back at the Clock Tower.

This time there were four of them. Vartanyan, his two Spetsnaz assets, and Karola. The two assets were either side of Karola, helping her walk, whether she needed the help or not. Vartanyan was slightly out front, his eyes spitting fire. Jack joined them and all five moved away from the crowds.

"You're on the verge of being sucked into a whirlwind, Calumet," Vartanyan threatened. "This is the second time you have assaulted one of my countrymen without provocation. Don't ever let there be a third."

Calumet greeted Vartanyan's gaze with his own flame. "Save your threats, slick. You can't back them up." Calumet purposely let that hang while both men engaged each other in eye combat.

Finally Vartanyan said, "Let's get down to business. As you can see"—he nodded toward Karola, who was standing a few feet away, wedged between the goons—"Karola is safe and sound. On the other hand, your terms are not acceptable."

"What terms are those?"

"The stages. If you want to do business, you'll provide the entire package simultaneously. Otherwise you can forget your million dollars." Once again, Vartanyan inclined his head toward Karola. "And you can say good-bye to your new girlfriend."

"Fine," Calumet responded, his face set to stone. "The deal's off, then." Jack paused, letting his words sink in. "If you think I'm bluffing, just try me."

Vartanyan ignored the challenge. "Am I to assume that you don't have the entire package on your person?"

"You're welcome to assume any anything you like, Vartanyan. As I told that Mongoloid, Yevgenni, we're going to do this in stages if it's to be done at all. In this case, though, you happen to be correct in your assumption. I have only a partial package on my person at the moment. You show me fifty thousand dollars and it's yours."

It was evident that Vartanyan had carefully planned his channels of negotiation beforehand. He said, "I don't like to repeat myself, but I will. Your terms are unacceptable. You're not dealing with Filatov this time, Calumet. Perhaps, however, we may be able to reach a compromise."

Calumet breathed easier. He knew this deal had to go down. He and Robert had worked out the mechanics the previous evening. Their goal all along had been to force the Russians into some sort of conciliation, which is what Vartanyan was now offering. The only question that now remained was what kind of compromise Vartanyan had in mind. So Jack asked, "What kind of compromise?"

"We're not going to pay you for information sight unseen. Not this time. If you want to be paid at all, your intelligence must first be analyzed by our people."

Perfect! Calumet thought. That's just the way he and Robert had constructed the scenario in their safe house the night before. He pretended to mull it over. Finally, he said, "You mean your people in *Russia?*"

Vartanyan smiled lightly, sensing he had scored a minor victory. "No. Our people here in Bern."

"I'm not sure I understand. Since you know that this package is going to be nothing but disinformation, why would you want to analyze it?"

"We might desire clarification on certain points. And you will not be paid prior to our complete satisfaction, even if we have to ask you to go back to the CIA and retrieve such clarification. If you think *I'm* bluffing, *you* try *me.*"

Calumet nodded quickly. "Okay, I guess I can do that. You're welcome to take this package now, but at our next meet, before I hand over the second installment, you pay me the fifty thousand."

Vartanyan's demeanor reflected blatant disgust. "And how many installments do you envision?"

"Five altogether," Calumet responded. "The payment for each installment will increase until we've reached a million dollars. And Karola goes with me after you receive the final package."

A tiny flicker of anger registered in Vartanyan's eyes at that remark, but he brought it under control quickly. "That could take us several days. Especially when you consider all the time that would be required to analyze your information. We'll do it in two installments. This one, and a final one to follow."

"Three is as low as I'll go," Calumet countered. "And I'll accompany you on the final installment. Payment will be made before you analyze the package. I'll wait until you're satisfied that the information is legitimate, however, I won't wait longer than thirty minutes. You make sure your people are on station. They can analyze the intelligence on the spot. Then I take Karola and we leave. At that point, our business will be concluded for good."

Vartanyan knew Calumet was too smart to place himself in such a tenuous position. He said as much. "Something just doesn't ring true, Jack."

"What's that?"

"You and I both realize that we have no reason or incentive to pay you after you deliver the final installment. What's to prevent us from absconding with your package and leaving you hanging? And since neither of us is a neophyte, I won't beat around the bush. What's to keep us from tossing you in the river?"

Calumet smiled. "Ah! I wondered if you'd pick up on that, Andrei. It's really very simple. I'm holding out on the last piece of information. It's a very critical piece of information, as I see it. Although I'm no rocket scientist, I can read. The particular piece of information I'm referring to has to do with the sensor capabilities of America's KH-12s." Robert hoped this last slice of bait would be irresistible. In the Russian's view, the sensor capabilities could be the straw that broke the camel's back where Kulagin was concerned. If Kulagin pronounced the intelligence as workable, it would expose him, and his complicity would be undeniable. If not, it would confirm to the Russians that Kulagin was not their mole, and they would then be forced to move on down the line in the Aquarium's schematic search for a traitor.

Vartanyan pondered Calumet's disclosure for a moment. "How will we come into possession of this critical information after you leave?"

"Simple. I'll give you its location. All you'll have to do is go and pick it up." And therein, Calumet knew, lay the transparent weakness in his strategy. If he carried the location in his head, the Russians were positive they would be able to get it out of him. They were merely toying with him at this point, appeasing him, playing a game. They never planned to let him keep the bulk of the money in the first place. When they finally had Jack Calumet where they wanted him—in the warehouse—the niceties would be terminated. And so would Calumet, once they bled him dry. At least that was the way Calumet and Robert hoped they'd see it. The whole operation hinged on it.

"I think I can live with that," Vartanyan smiled.

At this juncture, Calumet demanded to speak privately with Karola. Vartanyan and his two assets kept a tight rein on them while they talked. The conversation itself was very brief. Calumet revealed nothing operational to her; he merely reassured, though his heart ached for her as he stood there. She seemed so helpless suddenly, so frightened. And he felt responsible. He had made her go back. He desperately wanted to take her in his arms, but he dare not exhibit affection for her in front of Vartanyan. That would only endanger her more.

Afterward, Calumet and Vartanyan set up the location of the second meet, and Calumet handed over the initial package. Vartanyan acutely desired that the second rendezvous take place within the next hour, but Calumet strung it out, insisting upon 2:00, three hours away. Another small argument ensued, but Calumet was adamant. Stringing out the meets was paramount if they were to have any chance of rescuing Kulagin. The Russian finally assented. The first meet was over. All participants departed.

The second meet comprised the same players, but went much more smoothly. Calumet spoke with Karola again and then delivered the second installment package to Vartanyan. In return, Vartanyan relinquished a small suitcase containing $50,000. They scheduled the hour for the next meet at 4:30 and once again went their separate ways.

Calumet dry-cleaned himself and returned to the safe house. There, everyone present milled about in a state of anxiety. They were praying their strategy would pay off. By stringing out the meets, the CIA was attempting to force the Russians to take Kulagin out of the embassy and deliver him to the warehouse. Robert surmised that by handing over the intelligence in stages, Nishka or Shevchenko—whoever happened to be calling the shots in the field—would become impatient and possibly consider himself to be stretched too thin. The spymaster fervently hoped that the Aquarium would find the nuisance of accepting Calumet's intelligence piecemeal—thus ensuring a constant flow of traffic in and out of the embassy—to be too much of a burden. Khodinka would have to believe, the way Robert saw it, that it would facilitate matters immensely if Kulagin was on location in the warehouse to conduct his analysis because Robert knew something that the others didn't. He knew that Nishka was racing a clock. Even Nishka had a master, and his master was demanding results. It was now painfully evident to the Russians that the Aquarium's SIGINT program had been stymied for five years, and that was long enough. In Nishka's mind, every single day and every single hour counted at this stage of the game.

In any case, failing the success of the first phase of their strategy, Robert had devised a fallback. Perhaps Calumet's insistence that the Russians be allowed only thirty minutes to analyze his last delivery would do the trick. However, if worse came to worst and Kulagin remained confined to the embassy, then all Robert could hope for was that Kulagin would be perceptive enough to discern the motivation behind his own recent turn of events. The fact that the GRU had spirited him out of Russia and had delivered him to Bern to analyze pilfered intelligence would be a very strange occurrence to say the least. Hopefully, Kulagin would pick up on it and act accordingly. But, to the CIA's immense relief, the worst did not occur.

At 3:45, Robert's strategy was handsomely rewarded. A surveillance team picked up the Russians secreting Kulagin out of the embassy in a van. At 4:10, the van was spotted entering the dirt road leading to the warehouse.

"So far, so good," Robert said. But his expression was one of grave concern.

CHAPTER 30

Team Interceptor had been reinforced by eight commandos from Delta Force. Like Rossetti and his band, all had seen action in Panama, the Gulf, or both. They had flown into Bern the day before and spent most of the night in briefings and strategy sessions. Earlier this morning, after carefully studying maps of the immediate area surrounding the warehouse and a diagram of the warehouse itself, they were once again briefed on their mission and ordered to begin making preparations to deploy. Finally, at just after 2:30 in the afternoon, it was time. Each member of the assault force, which consisted of everyone but Rossetti, Yardley, and Kramer, was attired in body armor and each sported all the other accoutrements specific to his peculiar profession. Rossetti led the assault force to the staging area, which was some four miles distant from the warehouse, and supervised their deployment. They were told to be in position by 4:30, and that was no little feat considering the fact that they would have to hump it through the forest to get there. Russian countersurveillance would be heavy in and around the warehouse, especially with Kulagin on location, so they could not afford to take any chances by motoring in close and then dispersing. Nor could they afford to take chances by being in place any longer than necessary and thus risk discovery. As a result, their deployment took place just after 3:00, giving them less than an hour and a half to cover four miles across hostile terrain and then get set. Of course, they knew that the army would not have referred to the landscape as hostile terrain. The army would tell them that the terrain was a neutral adversary. Right. In any event, it was a given that the Russians would be scanning, so their radios would not be turned on until after they had witnessed Calumet's arrival.

Calumet rendezvoused with Vartanyan, the two GRU agents, and Karola at the Samson Fountain on Kramgasse. Before handing over the package or collecting the money, he insisted on speaking with Karola once again. This time, however, he gave the two assets a withering look when they stood too close. He moved her a short distance away and whispered in her ear, "If it looks like there's going to be trouble, try to stand near one of the windows in the warehouse and run your fingers through your hair." She indicated silently that she understood.

"Karola," Jack whispered. "I, uh, I'm sorry. About making you go back, I mean. I had no idea."

She smiled. "It's okay, Jack. I understand."

Somehow it wasn't enough, though. His words seemed so hollow. "I'll get you out," he promised.

Karola brushed his face with the back of her hand. "I know what's going on here, Jack. You felt you needed to use me, and now you're regretting it. Don't. It's okay."

"No," Jack winced, "it's not. I can't explain it to you right now, though."

"You don't have to explain anything, Jack." She inclined her head toward Vartanyan. "He's been using me all along, as you said.

And he could care less. He has no conscience, Jack. But you"—she smiled warmly—"you have a conscience. You care. And that's the difference between you and Andrei. Andrei doesn't think twice about using people. You, on the other hand, Jack, you despise it." She was staring straight into him, into his soul. "You would much rather be used than to use someone yourself, and I love you for it. In fact, as difficult as this may be to understand, you're the only man I've ever loved, Jack." But Jack thought he did understand that part. She was seeing the world in a different light now. She was no longer caged by her fears. "And please don't think that I am unaware of what's really going on here, my love, because I can see all the undercurrents." Her eyes sparkled with a woman's secret knowledge. "You've given me the courage to face life once again, and I'll always be grateful for that, Jack. Always. No matter what happens." Casting a contemptible glance at Vartanyan, she added, "He can't hurt me anymore. You've helped me face the truth, Jack. I could never have done it without you."

Calumet wanted to scream. He wanted the two of them to be anyplace but where they were at the moment, somewhere free to talk and to touch. His heart yearned for her. She was a completely different Karola than the one he had first met. She was no longer the wanton, vituperative voyeur, ever seeking to ensnare. Rather, she was so serene and accommodating now. He wanted to take her right this minute and just fly away. And he wanted to tell her that he loved her in return, because he truly did. Here, now, he loved her, and he knew it. Instead of telling her though, he became hardhearted suddenly, determined. He required all of his faculties to see this operation through, and he could not allow himself to become clouded with distractions, not if he was going to get Karola and Kulagin out, and then walk away in one piece himself. He would explain it to her afterward, he decided, when it was all over. He gave her a reassuring nod and they both returned to Vartanyan.

Calumet said, "The money." Vartanyan handed him another suitcase, presumably containing $150,000 this time. At that point, Calumet raised his left hand and snapped his fingers in the air. Presently a car pulled away from the curb several meters down the street and rolled alongside. Calumet handed the money through the open window to Yardley. Then the car raced away.

Vartanyan evidenced sudden concern, but Calumet precluded

him. "Local talent," he explained. "Someone I've done business with in the past. I'm sure Karola must have told you about my acquisition of the passports and safe houses."

"And does this local talent have possession of the last little bit of information you're going to provide to us after you disappear?" Vartanyan inquired intently.

"No way!" Calumet responded. "I wouldn't put that kind of information on the street." In fact, he knew the Russian wasn't really worried about the information being on the street. Vartanyan was heavily concerned about his ability to acquire the information after they had subjugated Calumet physically. He and Shevchenko had no intention of letting Calumet or Karola walk out of that warehouse alive, and if Calumet had taken the extra step of safeguarding the information by letting a live body hold onto it until the live body was sure Calumet had effected his getaway, it would make the Russians' job that much more difficult. The Russians' ability to obtain the final packet of information would be in peril. So Calumet reassured his nemesis, "The last packet of intelligence is in a safe place, in a fixed location. I'll tell you where it is when your people have analyzed this." He handed Vartanyan the third installment package.

Vartanyan accepted the package, but still appeared troubled.

Sensing Vartanyan's discomfort, Calumet remarked extemporaneously, "Well, you didn't expect me to carry the money on my person, did you? Not when we're about to travel to your turf."

Vartanyan shrugged, then sprang his own surprise. A black van pulled alongside and the sliding door belted open. "Get in," Vartanyan said, motioning to Calumet and Karola. His voice was casual, eliciting nothing sinister or threatening, but Calumet knew this was it. It was either cut and run right now—at Odyssey's expense, and Kulagin's and Karola's detriment—or it was walk into the lions' den willingly, and these thoughts actually grazed briefly upon infertile ground in his mind. After only a second's hesitation, he helped Karola step up, then, feeling the cyanide capsule between his fingers in his left pocket, and the Beretta in his right, he entered himself. One of the three GRU agents within the van slammed the door shut as the vehicle screeched away from the curb. Vartanyan and his two assets followed closely in a black Mercedes sedan.

*

Several time zones to the east, the lights burned brightly inside the Aquarium as Nishka sat hunched over his desk, engrossed in the forensics report on Calumet's medical records. While perusing the annotations made by his forensics team, the devilish figure began to smile. Fifteen years ago in Istanbul, Armbrister had attempted to levy a playback against one of Nishka's successful penetrations. The playback failed due to Nishka's diligence. The Russian spymaster had been able, in the end, to uncover the mask behind the DDO's Byzantine strategy, although he never let on that he knew. For several years, the Russians behaved as though they had bought Armbrister's story lock, stock, and barrel. They acted as though the disinformation being fed them by Langley was genuine. It took several years and countless operations before Langley discovered they had been duped. Finally, as Robert had explained to Calumet in Amsterdam, both sides eventually rolled up their nets and moved on to other ploys. However, Nishka never forgot. He remembered the methods. Armbrister had attempted to doctor original documents which would ultimately have led the Russians down a primrose path, but Nishka had found him out. The giveaway was in the inks.

There is a national data base, currently maintained by the Bureau of Alcohol, Tobacco and Firearms, which contains a precise breakdown of the rare-earth elements found in manufactured inks. With the cooperation of the principal ink manufacturers, trace amounts of these rare-earth elements are varied on each successive year, thus making it possible to identify the dates and chronology of the purchase of a specific ink. It was in this area that Nishka was able to establish the discrepancy.

Nishka noted the entries in Calumet's medical records, concentrating specifically on the dates and the corresponding entries depicting Calumet's nasal and cardiac abnormalities. He cross-checked each entry with the annotations in the forensics report and found what he was looking for. Several entries predate the inks. Thus the logic was incontrovertible: Jack Calumet's medical report was a fabrication. Nishka sat back in his chair, frowning.

It all made sense now. Calumet's longevity, his ability to elude the CIA after Shevchenko pronounced to them that he was a traitor, his apparent invulnerability to confrontation and arrest, all these things explained the methodology behind Armbrister's clever campaign of disinformation and the cunning proclamation of deceit that Langley had been waging against the Aquarium for the past six years. The reason for the stagnation of the Aquarium's SIGINT program was now clear. There was definitely a mole inside Khodinka. There could no longer be any doubt. Armbrister had finally gotten even for Istanbul. Nishka would have to answer for the duplicity, but in the meantime he would extract his own measure of vengeance. And the object of that vengeance was certain. As Nishka reached for the telephone, he knew there was no question now.

Finally, after six years, Jack Calumet–the Teflon double–was blown.

*

The dirt road leading to the warehouse was approximately one mile long. Unknown to Calumet, two Russian sentries were concealed in the bushes at the turnoff. The road itself was rough, with ruts and bumps, and the van and its passengers bounced incessantly as they rattled slowly along. Four men from Rossetti's assault force, stationed in the trees in the immediate vicinity of the warehouse, observed the van and the trailing Mercedes as the two vehicles arrived and disgorged their occupants. Both vehicles were splattered with mud due to a light drizzle.

The two-story corrugated aluminum warehouse was very large. There were two doors, front and back, with the front door on the far right corner of the building. A huge sliding panel, now closed, was situated next to the door. It could be opened electrically and was used for large cargo. Calumet knew from the schematics they had studied in the safe house that the building had twelve windows: two on each wall on the first floor, and one on each wall on the second.

As Calumet, Karola, and the Russians exited the vehicles, Jack noticed other sentries posted around the warehouse. He hoped the members of the assault force were as good as they were rumored to be. The Russian sentries were cradling Uzi machine pistols, held at the ready, and they looked like they knew how to use them. No doubt they were all Spetsnaz officers and were there specifically to safeguard Kulagin and the meet. *Where is Rambo when you need him?* Calumet wondered privately.

Calumet and Karola were led inside.

*

The two Russian sentries who were posted either side of the road and concealed in the brush near the turnoff had alerted Shevchenko when the van and the Mercedes passed by. Rossetti hoped they were not expected to check in again unless there was trouble. Although he originally had no confirmation that those particular sentries would be in that specific location, it only made sense. As a result, he, Yardley, and Kramer had humped in through the woods, expecting the sentries to be there. And they were. Having discovered them, Rossetti sent Kramer and Yardley back to the Ferrari while he concealed himself in the bushes on the near side, well behind the first sentry. Several minutes later, he watched the first sentry watch the Ferrari as it cruised by on the main artery, bypassing the turnoff. Three minutes later, Rossetti observed as Yardley, dressed like a Swiss farmer, strolled into view. Rossetti inched toward the first sentry. Kramer, he knew, would be on the other side, sneaking up behind the second.

Yardley was kneeling in the middle of the dirt road now, pretending to fiddle with his shoes. Just as the first sentry was standing, apparently having decided to confront the farmer, Rossetti pounced. In the midst of his leap, he heard a commotion across the way. Good! He and Kramer were in sync.

Rossetti delivered a penetrating blow with the knuckles of his right hand to the left temple of the sentry. It was all that was required. The sentry went down, completely unconscious by the time he hit the ground. Kramer had been equally effective. In the event that either of the two commandos hadn't been so effective, however, Yardley—magically transformed from the simple farmer into the deadly soldier—could now be seen crouched in a combat stance, his weapon drawn and ready to fire. The gun looked menacing with the silencer attached. Although Rossetti was not fond of taking human life, he had suggested to Robert earlier that in order to maintain operational integrity, it would be much cleaner to shoot the sentries rather than risk allowing them to get off an alert via their radios, but Robert nixed the idea. In any case, the outpost had now been neutralized.

*

Calumet stepped inside the warehouse, followed closely by Karola. Vartanyan and his team brought up the rear. The first thing Calumet noticed was Kulagin. He was standing next to Shevchenko on the far side of the warehouse, just outside an inner office. Next to them stood Yevgenni and his bandaged face. Calumet glanced up quickly. At least the rafters directly above him were clear. But not the loft. As he had learned from the schematic, the second floor was more of a loft than anything else, encompassing only about half of the space overhead. It was set farther back in the warehouse where a set of metal steps rose up to meet it. A forklift was parked underneath, shunted off to one side. The loft contained what were apparently crates of some sort, but it was hard to tell exactly because they were covered by olive-drab tarpaulins. In front of the tarps, three sentries with machine pistols leaned against a railing, spread out along the loft's width. Below was more of the same—crates and tarpaulins set about in rows. All of this caused Calumet to discreetly examine the forklift more closely in an effort to figure out if it would provide sufficient cover. In any event, the entire panorama was sobering. Jack did not like what he saw. Although he knew the Russians would be taking pains to make themselves secure, he wasn't prepared for their numbers. The place was crawling with Spetsnaz commandos, and Calumet knew that they were as well trained as any force in the world. *Robert was right,* he suddenly decided. *I should have canceled the meet with Filatov and come in from the cold.*

While Vartanyan—package in hand—made a beeline for Shevchenko and Kulagin, Calumet stole a quick glance to his rear. In addition to two GRU agents positioned on either side of the door inside, he could just make out one of the sentries through the window, obviously defending the portal against all comers on the outside. He had counted six sentries before entering, but those were only the ones posted along the front and right face of the building. Vartanyan had not offered him the opportunity to stroll around the perimeter to check for more, and Calumet thought it best not to ask.

*

To those Bernese citizens who were perceptive and who happened to be listening to an extremely popular radio program that day, they might possibly have found reason to complain later about the slight glitches of interference that occurred between 4:30 and 5:00 in the afternoon. Fortunately for Robert, they would never know that it was mostly his fault. Since the Russians would no doubt be actively scanning, Robert decided to snuggle up to that particular radio station's frequency in an effort to mask his own team's communications. It wasn't a foolproof scheme, but since his people would be speaking in code and all conversation would be kept to an absolute minimum, it just might work.

The assault force turned on their radios and reported that they were in position. Robert knew the announcement wouldn't have been made had Calumet not already gone inside. However, now that he had received confirmation, the spymaster sealed off the dirt road. Nobody was getting away without his blessing.

"I've got to be up close," Rossetti told Robert.

Robert gave him an appraising look, letting the silence grow. Rossetti's eyes didn't so much as flicker. Finally Robert said, "Go for it!"

Rossetti nodded, gave Kramer and Yardley a thumbs-up, then took off through the woods toward the warehouse.

*

Calumet and Karola were standing in the middle of the warehouse by themselves. They watched as Shevchenko and Vartanyan spoke to each other. Vartanyan had given the package to Kulagin, who was now going through the motions of analyzing it. Although about twenty-five paces separated them, Calumet could see Kulagin's perspiration from where he was standing.

Suddenly the conversation between Shevchenko and Vartanyan became animated, with Shevchenko pointing at Calumet, and Vartanyan shooting sinister glances in his direction, a cruel smile lighting his face.

"Something is wrong," Calumet whispered to Karola.

"I know," she whispered back. And then she looked him in the eye. "Jack," continuing to whisper, "I have to know something."

He met her gaze. "Yes?"

"Are you a free lance? Or are you CIA?"

If he went by the book, he would stick to his legend. He would reveal nothing about the true nature of his assignment. But Calumet went by the book only when it suited him. It did not suit him now. "I've been a loyal double all along, Karola."

Neither spoke for a full thirty seconds. She just stared at him, her eyes laughing. "Look," Jack explained, "I lied to you about that, okay? But I didn't lie to you about the other. I care about you and I've made arrangements to get you out."

She was unfazed, as if she had already known.

"If you don't want what I have to offer," Jack said lamely, "then I suggest you walk over there to your father and tell him what I've just told you. Then he can have me killed just like he had your mother killed."

"I love you, Jack," she said simply. "And I knew you were a loyal double ever since our little talk in the safe house that day."

He was at a loss momentarily. He wasn't sure how to respond. He was trying to remain aloof and in control. He didn't need distractions at this point.

Karola let him off the hook. "I know you're probably not in love with me, Jack, and that's okay. I don't have to have your love, but I need your trust. Do you trust me, Jack?"

Calumet looked deeply into her eyes, wondering what she was up to. "Yes," he said finally. "I trust you, Karola."

She put her hand on his face and kissed him quickly. "You must trust me," she ordered.

She began to pull away from him but he stopped her. "And I love you, too, Karola." There. He'd admitted it, and not just in the heat of the moment. "When this is over . . ." He let it hang, knowing she understood.

Her eyes lit up like bonfires. She knew he was completely sincere. In spite of their predicament, Calumet could see that she'd never been happier in her life. She winked discreetly, then broke away and ran toward her father, shouting, "Oh, Daddy, Daddy!" Tears began to cascade down her cheeks. "Forgive me, Daddy," she cried.

*

Rossetti circled around to the back of the warehouse, checking the position of each member of the assault team as he went. He noticed two Spetsnaz sentries covering the back. Through the second-story window, Rossetti could also make out one of the Russian soldiers in the loft. He glanced at his counterpart, concealed in the brush nearby. The commando maintained an unerring bead on the first sentry. Fifteen paces away, a second commando was aiming a grenade launcher at one of the windows. It was loaded with percussion rounds, also known as stun grenades. Rossetti smiled, then silently worked the slide on his Heckler and Koch MP-5. HK MP-5s were good for close-in fighting, he had always said.

*

Shevchenko was momentarily taken aback as Vartanyan stepped in front of him, apparently to shield him from his daughter's assault on the major-general's pity. Vartanyan grabbed Karola by the wrists, subduing her motion. "Please," Karola continued, crying, "I'm sorry. Daddy. Andrei. Please forgive me," she implored. "Give me another chance. I'll make it up to you, I promise."

Vartanyan and Shevchenko exchanged looks. Then Vartanyan, continuing to maintain a tight hold on Karola's wrists, shrugged.

Shevchenko nodded, signaling to let her go. Karola rushed up and threw her arms around her father, crying profusely. In fact, her tears were real, a reflection of all her sorrows, but her motives were completely disingenuous. She hated and despised the monster she was now embracing. Sometimes, though, even monsters have a soft spot, and Karola's performance was a wrap. Shevchenko enveloped her in his arms, stroking her hair. "There, there," he soothed.

Calumet smiled. *That is one sharp lady,* he thought. He was proud of her, but still nervous. In her confused state, too much kindness from her father might set her upside down again. But Calumet need not have worried.

True to form, Shevchenko brushed her aside suddenly. "We'll discuss this later," he admonished.

All attention reverted to Calumet as Karola moved next to a window.

*

The message crackled in Robert's radio. "Sparrow sighted near east window." Sparrow was the designation assigned to Karola. The operation did not hinge upon her; Robert wasn't convinced that she could be trusted, or that she would even be able to maneuver into position to signal, but she was nonetheless factored in as a fallback. The other commandos, he knew, were gazing into the warehouse with high-powered binoculars and thermal imaging scopes, which could literally "see" through buildings. In fact, during the Gulf War, one commando was purported to have "made the touch" on an Iraqi general at twenty-five hundred yards through a cement wall with a 50 caliber-bolt action rifle. So, while Rossetti's commandos would not be able to give an exact accounting of what was happening inside the warehouse, they would nevertheless be able to discern any amount of untoward activity. Calumet would not go down easily.

"Get ready," Robert instructed Kramer and Yardley.

They climbed into the Ferrari. It was parked on the dirt road, pointed at the warehouse approximately a mile away.

*

Rossetti nodded to the two commandos nearby. They took careful aim and shot both Russian sentries covering the back of the warehouse. The falling bodies made more noise than the weapons that had sealed their doom. The silencers these days were very, very good. The weapons, discharging subsonic projectiles, made almost no noise whatsoever. The two commandos crept down and pulled the bodies back into the brush. Then they and Rossetti crouched beneath the rear entrance of the warehouse, waiting, anticipating. Rossetti faced the door, surreptitiously peering through the window, while each commando faced an opposite corner of the building in case one of the other sentries came around the corner.

As far as the official record was concerned, Rick Rossetti had just made one of those operational judgments Robert had referred to in their conversation a few nights ago.

*

Shevchenko motioned Calumet forward. The atmosphere was noticeably tense. Kulagin glanced up as Calumet approached, the scientist's facial expression reflecting immense stress, almost pleading. Calumet did not look at him, did not meet his gaze, did not acknowledge him in any way. Kulagin had no idea who Calumet was, but he naturally assumed Jack was somehow connected to the CIA. To Calumet, it was blatantly obvious that Sergei Kulagin was a worried man. The scientist was on the verge of losing it. *Just hold on, buddy,* Jack thought.

Although Calumet perceived that something was amiss, that something was very wrong, he sustained the charade. "You got my money?" he asked Shevchenko.

"It wouldn't do you any good," Vartanyan interceded quickly, a malevolent grin masking his expression.

Calumet eyed him with suspicion. "Why is that?"

"Because," Shevchenko joined in, "your game is up, Jack."

There was a certain finality in Shevchenko's voice, one which communicated to Calumet that the Russians knew. Still, he held his ground. "What are you talking about? Are you upset because I insisted on doing this in stages or something?"

"We should have let you talk the other night when you began to tell us about Odyssey," Shevchenko remarked, as though he hadn't heard Calumet speak. "You see, Jack, we now know that you have been a loyal double all along."

Calumet darted in quickly. "I'm not sure what you mean by loyal double, but if you're saying what I think you're saying, you're right. I've been loyal to you guys all the way."

Even Shevchenko appeared to admire Calumet's footwork, evidenced by the slight curl of the major-general's upper lip.

"I'll say this for you," Vartanyan quipped, smiling menacingly. "You may very well be the shrewdest operative I've ever laid eyes on." After a slight pause, he added, "It's a shame you have to die for it."

"We know about the medical records, Jack," Shevchenko said.

Calumet's surprise was legitimate. He didn't know what to make of the major-general's statement. He thought the remark came out of left field, and he said as much. "Medical records? I'm afraid we're dancing to different tunes, Aleksandr. What are you talking about?" He wondered if the Russians were up to snuff on double entendres.

"Ah," Shevchenko intoned. "Possibly they would not have made you aware of that. You see, Jack, Lewis Armbrister fabricated your medical records. He made it appear as though you had a cocaine habit and a corresponding heart problem. Our guess is that he did not want us to induce you to chemical interrogation."

Calumet thought furiously. *Okay. Try this one, boys.* "Well, that means that old magician is trying to set me up, then. Don't you see?"

"Yes," Shevchenko frowned, "I *do* see. We've been snookered, to use an American term. All we can do now is limit damage. Your efforts have been commendable, Jack Calumet. You were really very good. But I'm afraid it's over."

Calumet knew it was useless. Even if he *wasn't* a loyal double, the Russians were convinced beyond the efforts of any argument he might be able to present. He exhaled heavily. Removing his left hand slowly from his pocket, he performed a cursory inspection of his fingernails. The cyanide capsule was concealed in his palm.

Then, glancing around the warehouse and noting all the firepower, he remarked casually, "After very careful consideration, I've come to the conclusion that I'm up to my rear end in alligators here, fellas."

Standing next to window and taking in the conversation, Karola ran her hands through her hair.

*

"Sparrow feeding!" the radio crackled.

"Go!" Robert told Kramer, who was sitting behind the wheel of the Ferrari.

Kramer stomped on the accelerator, the fishtailing Ferrari creating an avalanche of flying mud.

Then Robert alerted the assault force. "Echo Zulu!" Their prearranged code for "Green Light." "Repeat! Echo Zulu! Go on blackbird!" After releasing the button, he added an afterthought. "And God help us."

*

"You can relax, Jack," Vartanyan said easily, at the same time extracting the silver cigarette case. "Nothing is going to happen to you immediately."

Calumet noticed the almost imperceptible flick of the finger as Vartanyan brought the case forward. He didn't know what the Russian had done exactly, but he had done *something*.

"We're not barbarians, you know," Vartanyan continued smoothly. "Are you sure you wouldn't care for a cigarette?"

But Calumet was already diving to his left when the hidden canister exploded, discharging its noxious gas, and his right hand was coming out of his pocket with the Beretta. At that point, everything suddenly seemed to be happening in slow motion. Bedlam broke over the warehouse in a tidal wave, invoking panic and confusion all around. Jack noticed Vartanyan and Shevchenko scrambling furiously as the percussion grenades slammed through the windows.

CHAPTER 31

Rossetti came through the door like a runaway freight train. A murky haze redolent of cordite permeated the air. Rossetti rushed straight ahead through the smoke while the two commandos charged up the back steps to the loft. Staccato bursts of gunfire sounded within and without.

The concussion grenades gave the assault team an initial slight advantage. Everyone within the warehouse was momentarily disoriented. The loud bang and the force of the explosive concussion had achieved the desired effect. However, the Spetsnaz officers were rugged professionals, and they recovered almost immediately. Hard men. They engaged the commandos the second the commandos began infiltrating through the doors and windows.

The action outside had been much different. The Russian sentries never had a chance. After Rossetti and his cohorts took care of the two behind the building, eight remained. Yardley shot three through the window of the Ferrari as they raced up and went into a violent sideways skid, that due to Kramer's masterful driving skills. The remaining Spetsnaz sentries were taken out instantly by other members of the assault force while two commandos simultaneously blasted percussion rounds into the warehouse. Then everybody poured in.

Vartanyan and Shevchenko must have heard the Ferrari and the commotion outside because they were going to ground at the same time Calumet hit the floor, his Beretta extended. Calumet actually fired once, but the bullet sailed just over Vartanyan's head. At that instant the first explosion erupted in the warehouse, stunning them all. The first percussion was followed quickly by a second, and then a third. And finally a fourth. Maybe five seconds elapsed—an eternity in a firefight—before they were all moving again.

Vartanyan had magically produced his own automatic. He might have even shot back, but there was so much confusion Calumet didn't notice. Then the picture began to focus. While Shevchenko

was scrambling toward the inner office, Vartanyan attempted un-
successfully to pull Kulagin off the floor. Fortunately for the Americans, he was rudely interrupted. Calumet fired once again at the
Russian, but was forced to shoot wildly. He sensed movement behind him just as he was squeezing the trigger and reflexively jerked
his body into a roll. Vartanyan released Kulagin and leapt backward. He was on the verge of returning Calumet's fire when he was
briefly distracted by the sudden onslaught of intruders. Kramer
suddenly burst through the front door and took aim at a GRU
agent. Before he could complete his mission, however, his world
caved in. Vartanyan dropped into a combat crouch and shot
Kramer four times in the torso. The second bullet severed the commando's aorta, killing him instantly. Yardley, who suddenly
materialized in the doorway and saw what had happened, drew a
bead on Vartanyan but never got the opportunity to fire. He was
instantly engaged by the GRU agent Kramer had originally tar-
geted.

Calumet turned and saw Rossetti charging forward through an
aisle of crates. Jack was about to turn his concentration back to
Vartanyan when two Spetsnaz commandos, previously undetected,
popped into an adjacent aisle. They were in a perfect position to
ambush Rossetti. Just then, Calumet saw other Spetsnaz commandos flush from the heap of crates as well. It was obvious that an
entire contingent of eight or ten Spetsnaz commandos had been in
hiding. Calumet dropped the two Russians waiting in ambush, then
signaled Rossetti that there were more and that they were scattered
all over the place. Rossetti nodded and disappeared behind a sheet
of tarpaulins.

By this time, the firefight was raging inside the warehouse. A
Russian sentry got blown off the loft and landed inches from Calumet. Yevgenni, whom Calumet had forgotten about, suddenly
drew attention to himself by going for Kulagin. Calumet could not
get a clear shot because Yevgenni had managed to get the scientist
on his feet now, and he was using Kulagin to shield his own body as
he attempted to drag the scientist into the office. Calumet covered
the ground between them like a charging lion. He threw a body
block into Yevgenni's legs, forcing both Yevgenni and Kulagin to
go crashing down, Calumet rolling on top of them. Calumet de-

cided this was no time for protocol. He shot Yevgenni point-blank in the face. It was one kill for which he would never feel the slightest remorse. It was also a kill which almost cost him his life.

Vartanyan was crouched just outside the office. Calumet sensed his presence, causing him to whirl around suddenly. That's when he knew he'd never make it. As though a distant participant in his own dream, somehow removed, watching himself in slow motion, a kaleidoscope of tracers and bright muzzle flashes posing for a backdrop, he could see Vartanyan's weapon pointing at his heart, and his mind's eye envisioned the Russian's finger squeezing the trigger. Even though Calumet launched, it was not in time. The only thing that saved him was Karola. She hurled her body between Calumet and Vartanyan just as Vartanyan yanked on the trigger. The impact of the bullets flung her backward onto Calumet's legs.

Vartanyan dove toward the office cubicle as Calumet got off two hasty rounds. This time the Russian wasn't quick enough, and Jack didn't miss. Both rounds caught Vartanyan smack in the chest, dead center. His body jerked sideways, slamming him into the door frame. *That's for Karola. And for Ankara.* Calumet was about to turn his attention to other matters when it happened.

Amazingly, Vartanyan leapt up. Before disappearing swiftly through the office door, he squeezed off two rounds of his own. The second bullet missed, but the first grazed his side and perforated his bomber jacket and his favorite shirt. *Vartanyan was wearing a vest this time.* Calumet was carrying a hollow-point load. It was useless against armor.

Jack did not dwell on his misfortune. Karola was still breathing. He consoled her with a few quick words, then dragged her to the wall, out of the line of fire. Next, he crawled over to Kulagin and assisted him to the abutment as well. "Lie there and don't move," he ordered. Then he began to search for targets. No joy.

With the exception of the office, the assault team had finally taken the entire warehouse and was now in total control. Calumet observed Rossetti and several commandos pelting the cubicle with a savage volley. What confused him, however, was the exchange fire. It was withering. And it was coming from the office. Calumet thought only Shevchenko and Vartanyan had escaped into the office. In fact, he was sure of it. *What's the deal?*

Suddenly Calumet saw one of Rossetti's commandos launch another percussion grenade. A second later it exploded within the cubicle. Rossetti and his commandos rushed in, spraying the entire enclosure with a rapacious, devastating fusillade. *Nothing could survive that,* Jack thought. He was sure that everything inside was now dead. Shevchenko. Vartanyan. Dead. Finally. A gossamer silence took command of the situation as an eerie calm drifted in and settled upon the scene. It was all over.

Calumet rushed to Karola's side. She was gasping for air, her lungs gurgling with every strained breath. Calumet kneeled, then lifted her gently and cradled her in his arms. "You saved my life, Karola." He thought it was a dumb thing to say, but nothing else presented itself to him. He smiled wanly.

"I love you, Jack," she whispered hoarsely.

Calumet checked her wound. The Russian had shot her twice, not once. Both penetrations were just above the solar plexus. "I love you too, Karola," Jack said softly. He could tell she wasn't going to make it. "Just hang on. Help will be arriving soon."

"My father?" she groaned. "And Andrei?"

Calumet shook his head. "No." He stroked her hair.

Karola nodded weakly. "You're the only one—" she began, then grimaced suddenly.

"Don't try to talk, honey,"

"Yes," she persisted. "You . . . you called me honey?" Her face lit up a bit. "You're . . . the only . . . one who ever . . . cared for me, Jack." Every word was an agonizing struggle.

Tears welled in Calumet's eyes. "Just hang on, Karola. I love you more than you know. I—" His adrenaline was pumping so fast that his mouth could not keep pace with his thoughts. He wanted to tell her more than that. He wanted to tell her how much he respected her suddenly, and how he would have made her happy for the rest of her life, and a thousand other things, but the words were blitzing through his mind too quickly. He couldn't snag even one, let alone a complete sentence. He wanted to make up for all the things he hadn't told her when he had the opportunity. He wanted to speak volumes, but the race to catch up to his thoughts was overloading his circuits. Suddenly his soul was feverish, on fire, blazing out of control. His head was spinning. The rumblings in his mind were incessant. Could I take your place, Karola? Right now. Could we do that? Is that possible? Can you ever forgive me for making you go back? Can we get those bullets out of your body and into mine somehow? Sure. That's what we'll do. Got to be possible. How can we work this out? There's got to be a way. Calumet was having a great deal of trouble with reality. Her words began to mix with his own. *Don't make me go back, Jack,* she had said. No! Maybe we could . . .

"Jack," she smiled. He jerked abruptly, snapping out of it, and mysteriously, for the first time, he saw a purity and a sweetness sail into her eyes like never before. As if suddenly she was a little girl again, and her life was just beginning. *Oh, God! Don't let her die! It's my fault! It's all my fault!*

"You're the only . . . one . . . who ever showed . . . me respect." His tears were dropping on her face now, wetting her cheeks, her lips, her hair. He brushed them away. "You're . . . the only one . . . who told me . . . the truth, Jack. You were . . . you were real. Nobody was ever . . . real to me . . . before."

"I loved you almost from the first day, Karola. And I believed in you." His voice quivered, and he could do nothing to abate it. "Just like I believe in you now. You're going to be okay. Just hang on. We'll go for long walks in the moonlight. We'll . . ." He couldn't continue. His Adam's apple rose up into his throat.

She reached her hand up, gingerly touching his face. Her forgiving smile devastated him. "I . . . Maybe . . . maybe in . . . another . . . life, Jack. I . . ." Suddenly she collapsed, and the breath went out of her.

Reflexively, Calumet checked his watch: 5:12. Time of death. He held her for a full minute or longer, oblivious to everything around him. Though partially in shock, he had never felt as worthless in his life. This woman had staked her future on him. She had turned against her own people for him. She had bet it all on him, and she'd just lost. *How could it be?*

Suddenly his life was a blur. A woman whom he had known only a few days had purposely sacrificed herself for him, and she knew what she was doing. For Jack, even in his vapid state of confusion, that was the ultimate guilt trip. She knew before she ever hurled her body that shielding him would cost her her own life. *Where is the justice?* He eased her gently out of his arms and rested her limp, lifeless form on the concrete floor. Soon her body would be as cold as the floor.

He felt a hand on his shoulder. The hand pulled on him, helping him stand. Calumet looked around, though his eyes wore a blank stare. He sort of noticed Robert, but recognition was difficult at the moment. Everything seemed out of kilter. In his disorientation he felt he had to speak. "She took my bullets, Robert."

Robert might have said something soothing at that point, though comforts at times like this were never welcome. Besides, there was a surge of activity all about. Jack noticed that the spymaster's team was also inside the building now. Some ten or twenty or maybe even a hundred DOs. But who cared?

And there was Rossetti. The commando was storming around, walking back from the front of the warehouse, his eyes glowing red, propelling razor shafts of white-hot fire. He was already talking as he marched up and got in Robert's face. "We can't let them get away!"

And Calumet suddenly came alive again. "Let *who* get away?"

Rossetti looked at him, as if he just realized that Calumet was there. "Vartanyan and Shevchenko," he explained. His tone of voice would have been very difficult to describe.

Calumet registered momentary trauma. He glanced at the office, then back at Rossetti. "Weren't they in *there?*" he asked, pointing to the office.

"Take a bloody look" was the way Rossetti chose to clarify it.

So Calumet did. He ran over to the cubicle and peered inside. Besides five or six bodies, none of whom belonged to Vartanyan or Shevchenko, there was a trapdoor. It was open, revealing a tunnel leading down into the ground. Calumet rushed out of the office, his eyes now competing with Rossetti's for ferocity. He looked around until he saw an Uzi. He picked it up, along with a couple of loaded magazines.

"No!" Robert ordered. "Sorry, Jack, but no!"

Several of Robert's DOs began to close in on Calumet, restraint heavy upon their minds. One made the mistake of coming within striking distance, so Calumet struck. He threw a circle kick and swept the legs out from under the man. Nothing serious at this point.

It wasn't that Jack snapped, exactly. It was just that he had run out of decency. His ideological motivations and his moral justifications no longer exerted any influence upon him. To him, everything could now be measured in absolutes. In a way, it was an oversimplification of an eye for an eye, or the golden rule. Or something. Or maybe it was just pure, unadulterated vengeance. Whatever it was, though, he wasn't going to be denied. "Don't mess with me, Robert!" Like Rossetti, his tone of voice would have been very difficult to describe.

At this point, several other DOs gathered round, and several took it upon themselves to pull their own weapons, probably just as a show of force. On the other hand, maybe they thought Calumet might get frisky with the Uzi. After all, he *did* appear to have run out of decency at this point.

Rossetti popped the action lever on his own weapon and drew down on the DOs. The remaining commandos—three had been killed, including Kramer, and several others wounded—joined in with Rossetti. Nobody was in a very good mood, it seemed.

Robert attempted to mediate. "Jack, it's over. We've won. Odyssey is finished, and it's been a sensational victory for us. In fact, Vartanyan and Shevchenko may not survive it. Nishka will have to have scapegoats. Let it go, Jack."

"Robert," Jack countered, "don't take this as a lack of respect, because I respect you more than any man alive. I think you know that. But I'm going after Vartanyan, and I pity the person who tries to stop me. Period."

They locked eyes. Perhaps, more than anybody, Robert knew the stress that Calumet was experiencing. And honestly, he couldn't convince himself that he would not be guilty of the same violation if the positions were reversed. At any rate, he figured you just had to let some mutinies run their course. "Okay, Jack. Do what you have to do." He looked at Rossetti. "You, too."

Calumet and Rossetti disappeared into the tunnel.

"How many bodies in the back?" Robert asked one of his DOs.

"Nine Russians," the DO responded.

"And you're positive that Rossetti was the only one back there?"

"That's what the other commandos tell me."

Robert shook his head in wonderment. He knew Rossetti was

good, but had he actually dispatched nine Spetsnaz commandos single-handedly? Amazing!

Actually, Robert had been misled slightly. Rossetti wasn't really that good. Calumet had gotten two of them.

CHAPTER 32

The tunnel was a maze, twisting first one way then the next. It was replete with electric light bulbs, cement walls, a fortified cement ceiling, and a cement floor. And it was a complete surprise to everyone. Everyone on the American side, that is. The schematic that Team Interceptor had studied in the safe house in preparation for their assault never depicted a tunnel. But that wasn't so surprising.

Although the warehouse had been under lease for several years, the locals evidently assumed it was in disuse because no one had ever witnessed any cargo being driven in the building's direction. In fact, the entranceway to the dirt road leading to the building had been barricaded by a chain-link fence, and the fence, up until several days ago, was rusted and overgrown with brush. To any passersby who might have been interested in the location, such as the Israelis, for instance, the entire area appeared to have suffered from a bad case of neglect. In reality, however, neglect was not the case at all. The real problem was that nobody, *including* the Israelis, had ever been able to make the correlation.

Three and a half kilometers up the road, a similar warehouse had been a cornucopia of activity. Heavy machinery, heavy cargo, and heavy traffic in abundance. Seven days a week sometimes. And the Russians had been much smarter in its procurement this time.

In fact, the Russians had actually built the second warehouse from the ground up, though no one was ever wise to the fact that the Russians were the money behind the building's construction in the first place. The company that now owned the building—*V. Schilling* it was called, named after its founder—was legitimately Swiss and had been legitimately incorporated some fifteen years earlier under proper Swiss law. And, as with its founder, most of the company's employees were native Bernese. But that didn't tell the whole story. A select few of those fortunate enough to have risen to top management within the esteemed company of V. Schilling, if pressed, could successfully trace their genealogy all the way back to Russia. As could V. Schilling himself, if pressed. What a surprise.

In essence, the Russians had managed to penetrate Swiss industry in a major way and, in the process, provide their operatives with a lucrative base of operations from which to craft battalions of intrigues, ultimately zinging them like boomerangs into the Western hemisphere and then waiting patiently to see what they would bring back. And V. Schilling was just one enterprise. Certainly there were others, though they never knew for sure how many of those might have been compromised by Western intelligence along the way. Of course, Moscow Center didn't expect to receive a memo from Langley advising them of such, but they nevertheless felt confident that they knew about those that had been exposed, and about those that hadn't, and they were certain that V. Schilling was one of those that hadn't. Until now. What they couldn't know at this point, but would soon determine, was that Odyssey was about to burn V. Schilling to the ground. The discovery of the connecting tunnel would not only explain all the activity, but it would unequivocally sound the company's death knell as well. In a nutshell, V. Schilling's game was about up.

Calumet and Rossetti charged forward, Jack in the lead, the commando close behind, both disregarding caution completely. They were simply in one of those moods. The thought of catching Vartanyan took precedence over their own safety, although Rossetti's extensive training by now had a kinesis all its own. His training hadn't taken a complete hiatus. He had been a warrior for so long that his discipline was automatic. Consequently, though sprinting to keep up, he managed to smash every light bulb he and Calumet passed. He concluded it would be a good idea if they didn't make it *too* easy for the Russians. After all, appearing in silhouette was a very good way to get shot. Besides, he had practiced his night vision all the way from Berlin, and it would be a shame to let that go to waste.

But nobody is perfect. In his rush to extinguish the lights, Rossetti never noticed the odd-shaped contraptions randomly affixed to the tunnel wall with some kind of epoxy. But Calumet did, and he thought he knew what they were for. Nevertheless, he didn't care. Jack wanted Vartanyan at all costs.

*

Sergei Ivanovich Kulagin was in a daze. He was not a man of war, though he'd spent the majority of his life devising and building devices strictly for that purpose. And he was proud of his achievements. Very proud. He was especially proud, in fact, of his calculated duplicity and his aggressive participation in an operation known as Odyssey. To tell the truth, his treachery was the one thing in his life that made him whole. Every man, they say, has a reason for betraying his country. Exceptional in his profession, Sergei Ivanovich Kulagin was nevertheless no exception to the rule. Like those before him, he also had a reason.

"I am not betraying my country," he had repeated to his handler on those few occasions when they had met. "I am betraying this monster of a government." And his handler wrote in his notes how the scientist's demeanor would change when he talked about his betrayal, and how he would tremble with rage. "The government of Russia has been ravaging my people for centuries," the scientist would say, "and they have offended humanity with their policies of murder and deceit for far too long. The truth of the matter," Sergei Ivanovich Kulagin would almost shout, "is that my government has betrayed *me!*" And then more softly, sometimes with tears, "And all of my people as well."

He did not want money, he insisted. Avarice had nothing to do with it. He wasn't demanding a condo on the beach and a shiny red Porsche in the driveway. Those things were completely out of the picture. No, it was simply a matter of principle and decency as far as Sergei Ivanovich Kulagin was concerned. It was a matter of honor. What he was doing, he was doing for purer motives, and he wanted his handler to know that especially. If his handler knew nothing else, the scientist said, he wanted him to know beyond the shadow of a doubt that he was doing what he was doing for noble reasons. Virtuous motives, he asserted. For the good of humanity, he expounded, and the stern look in his eye convinced his handler that he meant it.

The first approach took place at an astronomical symposium in Vienna five-and-a-half years earlier. The CIA simply walked up to Sergei Ivanovich Kulagin and introduced themselves. "Comrade

Kulagin? John Doe, CIA." Well, sort of. At any rate, times were gentler then, at least from a political standpoint, and the phrase "nuclear umbrella" seemed to have become a distant watchword. The wall had already come down, the Soviet Union had been broken up, and the nations were more or less talking to each other. There was hope after all.

Yet the nationalists inside Russia and the Baltics inculcated almost no one with farfetched illusions concerning global peace and worldwide prosperity. No one who understood a politician's mindset, that is, and the perpetual ambitions of those whose black hearts refused to be quelled under any circumstance, regardless of the platform. Sergei Ivanovich Kulagin certainly did not suffer from such delusions. He might have lead a sheltered life, as most scientists of his caliber do, but his thoughts were ever voyaging. He knew the difference between good and evil, right and wrong, justice and injustice. And he knew about ambition. He knew about the men who had it, and about how it drove them. Some of them, anyway. And he knew what it could lead to if they succeeded. Yes, he knew.

So the first approach by the CIA—and his reaction to it—was not so astounding. Not really. The first approach resulted in what was sometimes known in the trade as a *cold hit,* which is to say, Sergei Ivanovich Kulagin made a snap decision and bought in to the game without reservation right there on the spot. Bingo! Mark that lucky card.

Thus Odyssey was born.

*

Calumet and Rossetti were beginning to wonder what they had gotten themselves into. The passageway crooked back and forth in a strange fashion, its walls smooth and cool to the touch, yet the atmosphere was dank. Tire markings were evident on the cement floor, which obviously meant that some sort of transit system was supported by the tunnel, though the two pursuers had come across no vehicles thus far. They had been clipping forward at a rapid pace for about five minutes, meandering back and forth around the curves, when the passageway suddenly began to narrow. It was only about six feet wide now, whereas before it had been much wider. Completely unaware of the other warehouse, Rossetti figured that the change in contour meant they were approaching the end, though the end did not yet appear to be anywhere in sight. "Hold it!" he half-whispered.

Calumet skidded to a stop. "What?"

Rossetti moved close so they could keep their voices low. Both were breathing heavily, but as quietly as possible. They hugged the wall as they conversed. "I think we've been lucky so far," the commando remarked. "They could have this placed rigged with explosives and monofilament."

"We've passed three explosive charges already," Calumet informed him. "You didn't see them because you were taking out the lights." Rossetti's expression remained implacable. He wasn't the least bit surprised. Calumet continued, "As far as monofilament trips, I don't think so. Did you get a good look at those Spetsnaz bodies up in the office?"

Rossetti nodded, indicating he had.

"Well, two of them were carrying satchels," Calumet explained anyway. "I think they were supposed to fight a retreating action and then set the trip wires as they backed off. Thanks to you and your team, they never got the chance."

"Still," the commando insisted, "they'd have a backup. Probably a remote capability. And those satchels could contain just about anything: explosives, ammo pouches, or their lunch for that matter. To tell you the truth, we should have checked."

"Well, we didn't," Calumet barked, suddenly annoyed. "What do you want to do? Turn back?"

"No," Rossetti answered grimly. He gave Calumet an incisive look, as if to convey a message. *This is my kind of game, Jack. This is what I do.* "I'm taking the point," he stated. He lurched forward. "You take out the remaining lights," he called over his shoulder.

"Vartanyan's mine," Calumet warned, jogging rapidly to catch up. *Rambo or not, the sucker better not do Vartanyan. Vartanyan's mine.*

*

"They're not coming," Vartanyan said. "There's no sound of gunfire, and they'd be here by now if they had been able to get away."

"I'm afraid you're right, Andrei," Shevchenko responded. He nodded toward the bustle of activity in V. Schilling's warehouse. Spetsnaz commandos were scurrying around like ants. "Are they about finished?"

The two Russians were standing just inside the building in proximity to the south wall. The south wall buttressed a hill, and it was here that the tunnel entrance had been constructed. The entrance itself was approximately eight feet high and nine feet wide. Three golf carts, converted so they could haul equipment, were parked in a semicircle nearby. Though daylight was spilling into the warehouse from open windows to the north, a faint light trickled in from the tunnel's aperture, its glow giving the entranceway an eerie appearance overall. In the background, the whir of a helicopter droned, adding to the unabashed furor surrounding them.

"Almost," Vartanyan replied. "They're shredding documents and immersing them in acid. It shouldn't be much longer."

"What about our illegals?"

"Schilling has already left. So have most of the others. They'll be trying to make their way out of the country as quickly as possible. Separate routes."

"And the armaments?" Shevchenko persisted. "What has been done about those?"

Vartanyan held up a transmitter. "The armaments will be safely sealed off and the tunnel will cease to exist when we leave." He returned the transmitter to his pocket.

"Good," Shevchenko ruminated. "Very good." He pivoted and began to observe the ongoing frenzy of activity. "It's a shame that V. Schilling is blown," he said reflectively, "but we'll still be able to salvage some of our assets, so it is not a total loss, I guess."

"No," Vartanyan remarked evenly, his eyes boring into the major-general's back. "Not a total loss, but a loss nevertheless. And someone will have to answer for it."

Something about Vartanyan's tone of voice startled Shevchenko suddenly. He whirled around and faced him. And then he froze.

Andrei Vartanyan was pointing a Makarov at the major-general's heart.

"What are you doing, Andrei?" Shevchenko gasped. "What is this about."

"Your operation, your responsibility," Vartanyan explained coolly. "You should have handled Calumet. Unfortunately, it happened the other way around. Calumet handled you. I'm afraid your ineptitude cannot be tolerated, comrade."

"Have you gone crazy? Nishka will have your head if you go

through with this, Andrei. For goodness's sake, put the gun down and let's talk this out."

Vartanyan smiled, his expression menacing. "You are quite wrong," he began, cocking the hammer with the thumb of his right hand. "You see, Comrade Shevchenko, Nishka is the one who ordered this execution in the first place. Moscow rules." He extracted a cigarette with his free hand and lit it, then held it to the major-general's lips. "But we have a few minutes. Smoke?"

Shevchenko shook his head, fear lighting his eyes. He knew Andrei Vartanyan too well. And he knew Nishka.

"No? Hmm. Pity, actually. Here I am trying to offer you my hospitality, and you turn me down flat. Is that any way to treat a junior officer, comrade?" Vartanyan might have been discussing inclement weather for all anyone could tell. He flicked the cigarette away, his dyspeptic gaze never leaving Shevchenko. "Well, no matter. I'm sure you're upset. If it's any consolation, though, you were right about one thing, Aleksandr."

"What's that?" the major-general asked, now quivering.

"The anatomy," Vartanyan remarked mysteriously. "The head. You were right about Nishka having somebody's head." In one swift motion he brought the Makarov level with Aleksandr Shevchenko's eyes and pulled the trigger twice in rapid succession. All activity within the warehouse came to an abrupt halt as the sound of the two gunshots clamored off the walls. Startled faces popped up in alarm, suddenly confused. Everyone became still. Completely still, like statues, abruptly frozen in the midst of whatever exercise each had been pursuing. And they knew. All were fully aware of the judgment that had just been rendered. In one of life's cruel paradoxes, the initial ruse of Major-General Aleksandr Shevchenko's execution had suddenly become a self-fulfilling prophecy. The provocateur had been taken in his own trap.

Nishka's protégé sighed while Shevchenko's body collapsed. He seemed bored with the entire affair. Placing the gun in its holster, he stood silently for a moment, his eyes inspecting Aleksandr's brains as they spilled onto the floor. "Then again," he finally whispered, frowning, "Jack Calumet is *also* right about one thing, comrade." He spoke matter-of-factly to Shevchenko, as if the major-general could still hear him. "Operation Odyssey, as it turns out, *is* one of the craziest stories I've ever heard."

*

Rossetti was moving very cautiously now, and it was infuriating Calumet. The slope of the tunnel had begun to rise conspicuously, becoming steeper with each step, and the passageway was no longer twisting and turning. The commando noted it had been as straight as an arrow for the past quarter kilometer, and the transformation made him wonder once again if they were about to reach the end. All of which contributed to his sudden vigilance.

"This ain't a Sunday stroll, Rossetti," Calumet whispered harshly. "Move it!"

Rossetti glared back at him. "You won't get a shot at Vartanyan if you're dead, Jack."

"The only way I'm going to die is if you bore me to death with caution before we reach the other side. I'm telling you, Rick, they haven't employed any trip wires, and they haven't orchestrated any surprises. Vartanyan and Shevchenko were both running for their lives. And they're both going to get away if we don't get on the stick."

Rossetti paused and glanced around, thoroughly unconvinced. "Then what do you make of the abrupt increase in elevation? And what about the tunnel? This tunnel has been weaving back and forth all the way. Now it's suddenly straight?" He shook his head incredulously. "Why would they do that? What could it mean?"

"It means we're a little bit higher than we were a few minutes ago," Calumet retorted. "And it means we won't get vertigo. How would I know? Maybe they had to burrow around hard rock or something. Or maybe they needed a downhill slope for skateboard practice. What difference does it make?"

"It obviously made a difference to the Russians," Rossetti reflected. "In fact, why did they build this tunnel in the first place? Ever think of that?"

Calumet moved in front of Rossetti and retook the point. Striding into a trot, he called back, "I'll ask Andrei Vartanyan for you when I catch up to him. In the meantime, don't worry about the way the blasted tunnel is laid out. They probably just built it this way because some vodka-swilling engineer thought he was an artist."

But Rossetti wasn't so sure. He was just about to take off after Calumet when he saw Calumet suddenly hit the floor. *What the . . . ?* It didn't make sense. Jack was no more than ten paces in front of him, yet Rossetti was unable to discern the reason for Calumet's going to ground. Whatever it was that caused it though, the commando instinctively did the same. He watched Calumet as Calumet craned his neck, apparently striving to peep around a corner, but Rossetti could not for the life of him make out any corner. All he could see from his own vantage point was the tunnel furling into the distance.

Calumet gave the signal to advance. The commando double-checked his weapon and slithered up noiselessly. And then he understood.

*

"Bring it forward," Vartanyan directed.

Eight Spetsnaz commandos guided the granite slab while a fork-lift propelled it from behind. The slab was four feet thick, almost nine feet wide, and almost eight feet tall. About the same size as the entrance to the tunnel, in other words. Sixteen heavy-duty ball-bearing rollers had been bolted to the bottom, as well as one on each side.

"What about the strategic material?" a Spetsnaz officer asked Vartanyan.

"We'll leave it for now. There is only one other way to access the tunnel, and I am confident it will not be discovered. There haven't been any spelunkers in this area for years, I'm told. In any case, we'll retrieve the strategic material at a later date. For now, our granite slab will fulfill its purpose and safeguard our cache."

The Spetsnaz officer nodded. "Your helicopter is waiting, Colonel Vartanyan. If you prefer, we can handle the rest."

Vartanyan looked around. *What a waste,* he thought. Though prepared, the last thing they had expected was that shootout in the warehouse, along with the ultimate discovery of the tunnel by the other side. They had planned for it, for the possibility, but they had never expected it. Yet suddenly it had happened. Oh, well. *C'est la vie.* It was all water under the bridge at this point. They would simply have to follow through with their emergency contingencies and do whatever it took to ensure that the strategic material remained a secret.

"I'll wait until the slab is in place," Vartanyan decided. He removed the transmitter from his pocket and handed it to a technician standing nearby. "Then I'll leave," he added.

*

"It's a storeroom of some sort," Calumet whispered. A seven-by-three-foot doorway was carved into the cement on his right, opening into a cavernous area. Jack counted five steps advancing downward, and what he saw only intensified his curiosity. The fifth step came to rest not on concrete, as he expected, but on solid earth, which led him to believe that the cavernous area was not man-made. Illumination poured in from a light bulb farther up the corridor, making it possible for them to distinguish crates and equipment of one kind or another in the forefront of the cave, but the remainder of the room was completely obscured by a yawning darkness.

"A storeroom, huh?" Rossetti's tone was sarcastic. It was rather obvious that the cave was being used as a repository of some sort. Otherwise, why would there be a door? The commando was unable to resist further innuendo. "You figured that out all by yourself, did you?" But he spoke again before Calumet could respond. "Stay sharp. I'm going to have a look." He dashed inside, his weapon ready.

Calumet ignored the verbal jab and examined the tunnel. He hated to admit it, but he was beginning to think that maybe Rossetti had a point about its construction. The passage was only about six feet wide where he was lying. Just before him, however, the corridor became comparatively expansive, its width approximately nine feet. And the additional footage seemed to be evenly spaced. One and a half feet on the left, one and a half feet on the right. Apparently anything coming from the other direction and broader than six feet would be unable to move past this point. Anything broader than six feet, in other words, would only be able to travel as far as the entrance to the cave. Then it would run into cement bookends. Jack furrowed his brow, a reflection of his desire to snag a tiny modicum of insight. Strange. Very strange. Rossetti's words suddenly came back to him: *Why would they do that? Why indeed?* he thought. The answer was forthcoming.

"I know why they built this tunnel," the commando stated excitedly, returning. He handed Calumet three fragmentation grenades and a satchel containing spare magazines for his Uzi. He also kept three for frags for himself, in addition to his own satchel of extra mags. "Just in case," he rationalized.

Calumet stuffed a frag in each pocket and hung the third from his belt. He knew Rossetti had just pilfered them from the cave. He also knew the frags and the additional ammunition were not what the commando was alluding to. "Why did they build the tunnel?"

"Are you familiar with any of the various contingency measures special forces teams are prepared to employ in the event of war?"

"You mean things like sabotage and so forth?"

"Exactly. We are prepared to go in on the ground to commit acts of sabotage and foment disruptions within Russia in the event of global confrontation. The Spetsnaz boys are prepared to do the same thing to the United States and Europe."

"What's that got to do with this tunnel?" Calumet's suspicion was growing suddenly, but of Vartanyan and his sinister schemes, not of Rossetti. He knew Rossetti wasn't in the habit of making small talk. The commando looked as though he was about to drop a bombshell.

In a way, that's *exactly* what he was about to do.

CHAPTER 33

"How much longer?" Vartanyan demanded impatiently.

"I should have the transmitter hooked up in a minute or two," the technician responded. He was referring to the same transmitter Vartanyan had given him moments earlier. "I presume you possess the code?"

"Yes," Vartanyan replied. "With the major-general dead and Schilling gone, I'm the only person in this warehouse who knows the proper sequence now. Advise me the minute you get the box attached."

"Certainly, Colonel Vartanyan." The technician went back to work. He was integrating the wiring of the transmitter with that of the building's main power supply, which was adjacent to the tunnel entrance. The transmitter itself was rectangular and bore a keypad enumerating the digits 0 through 9. Four wires protruded from its plastic casing, each a different color, but that presented no problem for the technician. He knew where they all went.

Under different circumstances, Rossetti might have been gratified to learn that he was ultimately correct in his assessment of the
tunnel's configuration, albeit, given his current predicament, it is
doubtful he would revel in such knowledge at the moment. In fact,
the tunnel had been conceived with maximum precision and then
assembled with painstaking care. And the entire production had
been implemented with security in mind. For example, had the explosives seen by Calumet been wired to receive signals from a radio
transmitter, Vartanyan and Shevchenko might never have made
good their escape. The tunnel very likely would have been blown
long before now. If static electricity didn't do it, radio transmissions
might have triggered a premature detonation somewhere along the
line, tripped accidentally by police communications, citizen-band
communications, hobbyists with walkie-talkies, or a host of other
nightmarish reasons. And that would have been totally unacceptable. The tunnel was of paramount importance to the Russians, and
they could not afford an accident.

Initially, the tunnel was to be utilized as a secret cache for small
arms and tactical weaponry, most of it for sale or contribution—
depending upon the client—and for protecting the integrity of V.
Schilling. Transactions were slated to take place only at the second
warehouse, and separate charges could be put in place swiftly to
seal off that end of the tunnel if the need ever arose. All of which, of
course, would have answered Rossetti's question concerning the
twists and turns in the beginning. The twists and turns had been
built in for a reason. Namely, the charges would be able to achieve
maximum breaching efficiency on that end of the tunnel, thoroughly sealing off each section. The Russians were gambling that
the authorities would more than likely conclude that a small cave
had been demolished, not a tunnel. In fact, they would have no
reason to think otherwise. Consequently, the cavern containing the
armaments would still be accessible from the V. Schilling warehouse, but the other end would be almost impossible to excavate
afterward, thus preventing detection of the Russians' true base of
operations. By the time the tunnel was completed and the lease on
the other warehouse had been acquired, the scheme seemed foolproof. And it was.

But then Moscow decided to up the ante. Dangerously high.
That's when the introduction of additional fixed explosives and the

sculpting of the slab became necessary. And that's when the fail-safe was devised, to be activated only in the event of a dire emergency. Which is exactly what the Russians were now facing. Switzerland might be a neutral country, but nobody breaks Swiss law on Swiss turf and then walks away scot-free. Least of all renegade Russians with nasty toys. When all was said and done, after this day's activities finally came to the attention of the local authorities—which was about to happen quickly—Russian diplomats posted to Bern would be in for a big surprise. Those who were allowed to stay would find themselves under an extremely tight rein for months to come. Then again, so would the Americans. All gratis Odyssey. "Next time, let the big boys play in somebody else's backyard," the Swiss intelligentsia would soon be saying. At least the Swiss were fair.

For now, though, the Russians had to move fast. Once the transmitter was connected, the explosive charges within the tunnel could be detonated by sequentially entering the correct numbers on the keypad. At that point, the electric cables running from the warehouse into the tunnel and thence through the cement walls would send a signal to a switching apparatus which had been positioned between the main power supply and the explosives. The switching apparatus, accessible through a locked compartment inside the tunnel wall, would verify the electronic code and then take appropriate action. If the code was incorrect, for example, there would be no action. In that case, the receiver would not close the circuit, which in turn would prevent any flow of current from ever reaching the detonators. In the interest of security the code had been entrusted only to a select few. The Russians did not want a disgruntled agent or envious worker bringing down the tunnel on an angry whim, especially since the tunnel and its current contents had been approved at the highest levels within the Russian government. The way the Russians saw it, this particular tunnel was ultrastrategic.

Vartanyan motioned to several Spetsnaz commandos nearby. "Take the major-general's body and place it in the tunnel," he ordered. "Past the cavern."

The commandos began to move.

*

Rossetti repeated Calumet's question for effect. "What has that got to do with this tunnel? I'll tell you what it's got to do with this tunnel." His expression was grave. "They've got nuclear backpacks in that room, Cochise." The commando clicked his tongue and winked.

Calumet dropped his jaw. Nuclear backpacks were state-of-the-art demolition packages carried by special forces commandos. They were small, portable units which could take out any bridge or similar target with no trouble whatsoever. The implications settled upon Jack like a ton of bricks. The Russians were in violation of more treaties and agreements than anyone could possibly imagine. They were virtually guaranteeing that the West would scramble a global alert if the material was ever discovered. Which is exactly what had just happened. Calumet wanted to whistle, but he knew better. Instead, he whispered, "Are they actually assembled? Are they live?"

"No," Rossetti answered. "But they've got all the material. The special clothing, the backpacks, everything. I know, I've strapped one on in training before. The fissionable material is encased in lead cylinders, and the cylinders are buried in holes. They're all marked. At least, I assume it's fissionable material. I wasn't about to open them."

Calumet appeared reflective. Odyssey, Karola, and Vartanyan were momentarily forgotten. "It's perfect when you think about it. Constructing this tunnel and then burying the material deep underground where gamma rays and neutrons can't be detected?" He let out a low whistle in spite of himself. "You know what this means, don't you?"

Rossetti shook his head. "No. What?"

Calumet locked eyes with the commando. "It means one of us has to go back right this minute. We can't take a chance at this point. This is even bigger than Odyssey or any personal considerations we might have. Robert must be told immediately."

Rossetti nodded in agreement. Calumet was suggesting the smart play, and he knew it. His discipline and instinct surfaced without warning. "Get moving," he stated, flicking his head sideways, indicating the direction from which they had just come. He was telling Calumet to retreat.

"Nice try," Calumet responded, "but you're second in command here." His tone was ominous and his eyes were as hard as the granite that surrounded them. "I appreciate your assistance thus far,

Rossetti, but I'll handle Odyssey from here on out. Go back and warn Robert. I'll catch up to you when I'm finished with Vartanyan."

"Fat chance!" the commando rejoined, his demeanor menacing. "Look, Jack, this is what I'm trained for. I'll get Vartanyan for you. This is my kind of game."

"Maybe so," Calumet retorted, "but in this particular game I happen to be the freaking quarterback, and I'm not going to debate the issue. Now move it!" His posture was threatening, intimidating. He appeared to be on the verge of attacking Rossetti.

But Rossetti did not budge. Instead he decided to be blunt, knowing that the only way out of this particular standoff was compromise. "Okay, listen. It's obvious that neither of us is going to give in, so why don't we quit dickering, Calumet. After all, we're wasting precious minutes. Let's both get Vartanyan right now. Then we can go back and tell Robert together."

Calumet sighed. "Stubborn son of a gun." In reality, he never expected the commando to comply. Neither would he, if the positions were reversed. Jack's eyes suddenly took on a mischievous quality. "You're right, I haven't got time to argue with you. But just so you understand, the responsibility for the free world is on your shoulders. If for some reason we don't make it back and nobody ever finds out about the strategic material in that room, it's all your fault. I just want you to know that."

Rossetti grinned. "Understood, pantywaist."

"C'mon," Calumet smiled, moving forward. He glanced back and whispered, "By the way, Rossetti, you're beginning to glow."

*

The first portion of the tunnel from the V. Schilling side sloped uphill. After about a hundred feet, however, it crested and then began to roll into a downward slant. The four Spetsnaz commandos were approaching the crest. Two were dragging Shevchenko's body; the other two were walking point. They weren't taking any chances.

"How much longer?" Vartanyan asked impatiently.

"Just one more wire," the technician replied calmly. "Then you—"

A massive burst of gunfire erupted in the tunnel.

*

Calumet and Rossetti heard them coming. They dropped the point men simultaneously with short bursts from their automatics, then jumped to their feet and sprinted forward. The second pair of Spetsnaz officers released Shevchenko's body immediately upon hearing the shots and began to raise their own weapons, but both were dead before they ever really understood what was happening. One, however, managed to clamp his finger on the trigger as he was collapsing. His muzzle flailing wildly, bullets began to pepper the tunnel walls. Calumet and Rossetti were forced to hug the ground to keep from being hit by ricochets. Two or three seconds elapsed before the fusillade ceased. Then, without glancing at one another, both were up instantly and racing toward the entrance.

Although Calumet and Rossetti had never worked together before, not in combat anyway, they were nevertheless in sync. Each knew that the other hadn't been hit. They did not have to look at one another or inquire about it to tell; they just knew. For some men, combat became a battle against sheer panic, a maximum effort to simply execute and hold out, and those who were able to master the panic could truly be considered brave. For others, however, a good firefight became a cinema in slow motion, almost surreal. While both classes are initially induced with a surcharge of adrenaline, in the latter group unusually massive doses of epinephrine are squirted from the adrenal gland into the central nervous system, thereby triggering uncommon physical reactions. In this case, glycogen in the body is rapidly converted to glucose, resulting in exponentially heightened senses of awareness and overflowing stocks of energy. In fact, heroic achievements in athletics and other human endeavors have been accomplished in precisely this manner.

The process was a naturally occurring phenomenon: you either had it or you didn't. Calumet and Rossetti had it. Their minds worked hundreds of times faster than the fastest computer. Their reactions could be measured in mere milliseconds. Their instincts were governed by an unsearchable force rather than by logic. Choosing to obey logic instead of instinct would more than likely get them killed anyway. And they knew that. At this point, even their knowledge was instinctive. Consequently, they had moved in unison without benefit of consultation. They were completely in tune. They were wired.

Vartanyan immediately ordered the forklift to resume. It began propelling the slab slowly toward the entrance. Eight commandos were standing by to guide it, their weapons primed. They couldn't decide exactly what to make of the activity inside the tunnel, but they were prepared for any eventuality. If they had known that their comrades were already dead, they would have saturated the tunnel with firepower, but they didn't know. Not yet. Vartanyan moved behind the forklift while the technician struggled to attach the final wire.

Calumet and Rossetti were fifty feet from the entrance when Rossetti threw the first frag. He thought he yelled "Fire in the hole!" or something like that, but he would never remember one way or the other. Neither would Calumet. In any event, both dove to the ground as Rossetti's hand released the grenade. Both were concerned about the burst radius. Rossetti was cutting it close.

The grenade caromed off the approaching slab, still fifteen feet outside the tunnel, and exploded. A second grenade followed immediately thereafter, also careening off the slab before detonating. Calumet had thrown that one right behind Rossetti's, though he couldn't recall ever having had one in his hand in the first place, much less pulling the pin and then tossing it. It must have been automatic.

The technician was basically shredded. Three of the eight Spetsnaz commandos accompanying the slab were also taken out. Two others elsewhere in the building received debilitating wounds as well. But the slab was unharmed. It kept rolling toward the entrance.

That's when Calumet and Rossetti knew they'd never make it. They had not been prepared for an additional phalanx of Spetsnaz commandos. They figured Vartanyan's coterie would be composed of two, maybe three henchman at the most. Calumet was aware of Shevchenko's body lying on the floor, but he did not dwell on the realization.

The Spetsnaz commandos moved in and took up positions either side of the tunnel entrance. Calumet sprayed the passageway while Rossetti simultaneously reloaded and retreated. Then Rossetti went to ground and painted the killing zone while Calumet reloaded and retreated. They were leapfrogging each other. Both had been hit, Calumet in the left side, Rossetti in the right. Fortunately, however, their injuries were just flesh wounds. The pair made it over the crest when Rossetti threw his two remaining frags, but the Spetsnaz crowd had not followed them in and the frags never made it through the entrance, so all he'd done, in effect, was make noise.

Andrei Vartanyan could have ended it right there by ordering the slab into the tunnel, but he didn't. He wanted Calumet as badly as Calumet wanted him. Therefore, he implemented an impromptu plan which was designed to forestall Calumet's escape. Vartanyan and six commandos moved into the tunnel, pasting the air with automatic bursts.

Calumet and Rossetti made it to the cavern under a hail of bullets. Their ears were ringing incessantly now. Vartanyan and his Spetsnaz officers positioned themselves just the other side of the crest. They were continuing to scorch the tunnel with gunfire. If Calumet and Rossetti tried to make a run for it now, the Russians had clear a killing zone from the top of the stone ridge.

"They won't throw frags," Rossetti stated confidently, heavy of breath. "There's too much explosive stuff in this cave. What do you think?"

Calumet shrugged, also winded. "You're the commando. You tell me." The gunfire ceased abruptly. Calumet and Rossetti glanced at each other, then Calumet poked his head out for a quick look. "They're staying put for the moment," he advised.

"The way I see it is this," Rossetti conjectured. "As long as they're in the tunnel, we can wait them out. Vartanyan can't afford to hang around. The Swiss authorities will be swarming over this entire complex shortly."

They heard the grenade hit the tunnel floor an instant before it exploded. Both dove to the foot of the steps for cover. The heat from the blast washed over them, but neither was harmed.

"You got any more brilliant predictions?" Calumet whispered.

Rossetti simply rolled his shoulders, though he seemed ready to explode himself. He despised being proven wrong.

"Calumet!" The voice came from Vartanyan.

Calumet remained silent.

"Calumet! Can you hear me?"

"Aren't you going to answer him?" Rossetti asked. He peered warily into the tunnel. "Well I'll be goosed!"

Calumet immediately took a look himself. "So much for waiting them out, I guess." The Russians had moved one of the converted golf carts to the top of the crest. It would provide good cover if they decided to advance.

"You fellas have some pretty nasty toys stashed in this cave, Andrei!" Calumet yelled.

"Jack," Vartanyan chuckled, "you shouldn't concern yourself with such trivial matters. Rather, you should be concerned about seeing the sun rise tomorrow. You've got five minutes to come out, otherwise we're coming in. You can live or die. It's up to you, Jack."

"I wouldn't make any hasty moves, Vartanyan. My friend here is Delta Force. He knows all about nuclear backpacks. In fact, he's assembling one as we speak. You move in and we'll all be reclassified as radioactive waste."

"I think you're bluffing, Calumet. You've got five minutes."

"I think Vartanyan is the one who's bluffing," Rossetti whispered. "An advance would be suicidal on their part, and they know it."

"How far do you figure it is back to the winding part of the tunnel?" Calumet asked.

"Half a click."

Both had reloaded and picked up more grenades. "The only way we'll have a prayer is if I'm the decoy," Calumet stated matter-of-factly. Jack knew Rossetti was a crack shot. At Range 19, Delta Force headquarters, the commandos fired hundreds upon hundreds of rounds on a daily basis. It was simply a way of life. Everyone participated, and at Range 19 there were virtually only two excuses for missing shooting practice: you either had to be dead, or not alive. Other than that, you shot. Period. Calumet was certain Rossetti could take a twig off a tree at a hundred feet in his sleep.

Rossetti nodded, indicating that he concurred with Jack's tactical appraisal. Calumet would have to expose himself in order to draw their fire.

"You could at least try to talk me out of it," Calumet remonstrated, shaking his head.

Rossetti smiled and slammed a fresh magazine into the breach. "Ready when you are." He knew what he had to do.

Calumet pulled the pin on a frag. Hefting his weapon, he rolled into the tunnel, threw the frag over the rise, then brought his Uzi to bear. Rossetti was propped on the top step of the cave entrance, waiting for the Spetsnaz commandos to show themselves.

But the explosion never came. "Ruskie munitions," Calumet exclaimed sotto voce. The grenade was a dud. Both he and Rossetti mentally prepared themselves for the advance. Nothing, at first. Then the golf cart began to move. Only backward, out of the tunnel. The Spetsnaz commandos remained hidden; they did not slither over the rise.

Calumet dove back into the cavern. "What are they doing?" he asked, as if Rossetti were privy to the Russian's strategy.

Rossetti thought for a moment. "Did you notice those other explosive charges? They're scattered throughout the tunnel."

"Yeah," Calumet acknowledged. "I saw them."

"They're trying to keep us pinned down," Rossetti speculated. "Vartanyan had no intention of risking his people by attempting a frontal assault. It was just a ruse. The tunnel explosives probably have to be detonated electronically. If I had to guess, I'd say they had a fail-safe in place. In other words, those charges weren't wired yet. Too easy to have an accident that way."

"So they're stalling until they can hook up whatever it is they have to hook up in order to trigger the charges," Calumet added.

"Right," Rossetti agreed. "They want to keep us here until they can trip the explosives and seal us inside. Permanently."

Calumet nodded. "Makes sense. Did you notice that slab of granite?" He didn't wait for an answer. "I know what it's for."

"So do I," Rossetti intimated. "It will roll only as far as the entrance to this cave." He pointed to the rear of the cavern. "I saw a thin shaft of light back there on my first visit."

"Can we get out that way?"

"No. The aperture is about forty feet up, and there's no way to scale the walls. But that's why they're willing to seal off the tunnel. They can come back at a later date and rappel down here. The slab will keep the rest of the tunnel from spilling into the cavern when they blow it. And if anyone tries to excavate afterward, the slab will be all but immovable."

Calumet agreed. "I think your analysis is on the money. Five will get you ten that they've already deserted their position on the ridge."

Just then a giant rumbling sound reached their ears. Both sprang into the tunnel, hugging the walls. They ran the eighty feet back to the top of the crest. Calumet was right. The Russians and the golf cart were nowhere in sight. But the slab was. It was being propelled up the incline by the forklift. When it reached the crest, it would begin its descent and would not stop until it had completely blocked the entrance to the cavern. Then the Russians would blow the tunnel.

Calumet and Rossetti turned and ran for their lives.

*

Robert and his people were tidying up, collecting the bodies of their own compatriots. And Karola's. The spymaster insisted upon doing that for Calumet. Kulagin had already been ushered out under heavy guard and was now on his way to the American embassy and a new life.

The explosion shook the foundations. The blast propelled debris and soot and smoke out of the tunnel's entrance. After an involuntary flinch, Robert strode slowly toward the office, his head hanging. *I should have stopped them.* Self-incrimination immediately began to haunt him.

And then Calumet surfaced, covered in a sickly white powder, cussing like a sailor. Rossetti followed right behind, cussing like Calumet. They angrily explained everything to Robert, who suddenly became animated when told about the nuclear backpacks.

Calumet looked around for Karola's body, but was unable to locate it. Robert told him gently that she'd been taken care of. Calumet nodded forlornly. Rossetti did not have to ask about Kramer. His teammates would have certainly seen to Kramer's corpse by now.

Calumet and Rossetti were quickly treated by two paramedics for their flesh wounds. Both refused to go to a doctor or have the holes stitched. They weren't that big anyway.

As they all strolled outside, leaving the warehouse in their wake, the rain washing the mud off the Ferrari, Calumet and Rossetti and Robert glanced up, attempting to define the sound. They saw the helicopter bank sharply, dip slightly in their direction, as if waving, and then watched it speed off and disappear beyond the horizon. Vartanyan had made good his escape.

"They also had a few Stingers in that cavern, didn't they?" Calumet asked Rossetti, referring to shoulder-mounted rockets used for shooting down helicopters and low-flying aircraft.

"Yep."

Neither could have foreseen the necessity.

Odyssey was over.

*

Calumet caught the next flight out. Even though Robert strongly encouraged him to travel to Langley and undergo a marathon debriefing, Calumet refused. He made it known in sparkling terms that he was headed straight to Atlanta, and furthermore, if anybody showed up at his house to try to debrief him there, they would be doing so at their own risk. Robert said something about psychologists at that point, and Calumet dealt handily with that issue as well. He assured Robert that Langley's psychologists would wind up plying their trade from a hospital bed if they got anywhere near him. Basically, Calumet was contrary to everything.

As for Rossetti, he finally found a girl. Some model who had been in Bern on a shoot. She and Rossetti were sitting in the Ferrari, the commando's eyes bloodshot, his face sporting a stubble.

"Have you ever been to California?" Rossetti asked her.

"You mean in Amerika?" she said, pronouncing the word with a hard "k," her voice denoting wonderment, as though such places were only found in fairy tales.

Rossetti turned his head slowly, his bloodshot eyes attempting to focus after rolling them slightly. He actually glanced around, apparently to make sure nobody else could have said such a thing. Then back at the girl. *Not only pretty, but smart, too,* he thought wryly. "Yeah, in Amerika," he said, also with the hard "k." When in Rome.

"No! I've never even been to Amerika, much less California," she said liltingly, an enormous smile stretched across her face.

"Good!" the commando exclaimed. "Let's see how long it takes us to get there!" Rossetti slammed the gearshift into first and stood on the pedal.

CHAPTER 34

It took a week and some high-level diplomacy to straighten things out with the Swiss. It took three weeks before the press turned loose of the story. In Washington, a presidential finding was issued ex post facto, primarily because that appeared to be the only politically correct way to save face, and the current president grew up under the tutelage of the old school and felt that neutrality should carry a price tag anyway. Robert would later characterize the president's support by remarking that the ex post fact occurred only because of the ipso facto, thus justifying Operation Odyssey's illicit beginning. Robert had always been fond of his Latin. The State Department refused to be mollified and would remain enraged for a year or more. As far as they were concerned, Langley's yahoos had once again managed to catapult diplomacy back into the Dark Ages. The DEA preserved a virtuous silence throughout.

The Russians spontaneously came to the conclusion that good-will had its place, and therefore pronounced themselves amenable to reopening discussions on nuclear weaponry and strategic arms limitation and whatnot. The State Department took the credit, of course, in spite of Langley's yahoos. On this point, Robert's Latin suffered a slight setback. When he got wind of it, he merely said something about bovine scatology. Those who heard him weren't sure if he was referring to the Russians or the State Department. Or maybe both.

In reality, the Russians were being blackmailed by Langley. Langley made it known that Washington had no plans to embarrass Moscow over the little matter of Russian nuclear material on Swiss soil as long as the Russians didn't get too cocky about certain things. Langley also politely informed Moscow Center that there would be no need for them to try to recover their lost merchandise from the cave. Langley would be more than happy to handle that for them, they said. Moscow Center impolitely agreed.

Lewis Armbrister received an official reprimand and two or three dressing-downs, but privately he was toasted throughout the intelligence communities on both sides of the Atlantic, and from the White House to Whitehall. The DDO had taken pains to make sure that Robert's career remained unscathed. Robert's role in Odyssey was also celebrated by those in the secret world. The Master Handler, they all said, for no agent could have ever been more difficult to run than Excalibur.

It was two weeks after that somber day in Bern when Robert and Armbrister finally met face to face. They were seated in Armbrister's office on the seventh floor at Langley.

Armbrister smiled, almost forlornly. "Odyssey was my last hurrah, old friend."

Robert evidenced surprise at the remark. "What do you mean?"

"I'm afraid I'm stepping down."

"What on earth for? Does it have anything to do with Odyssey?"

Armbrister sat in contemplation before responding. "In a way, yes. Don't worry," he smiled. "No one has asked me for my resignation. It's just that I have nothing left to achieve in this business, Robert. I've reached the pinnacle regarding covert operations."

"I can't believe that this has merely been a contest for you, Lewis. I've known you too long. Patriotism has always played a transcendent role in your affections, and you'll never be able to convince me otherwise."

"Of course," Armbrister agreed. "Patriotism has been my supreme motivation from the beginning. It's just that my methods are known now. And, to tell you the truth, Robert, I'm just plain tired. It's been a long haul. A satisfying haul, but a long one, too."

Robert projected understanding. You couldn't do much with an old horse whose only desire was to graze in peace. "Tell me," he said. "You meant for Nishka to discover the truth about Calumet all along, didn't you?"

Armbrister smiled. "He'll never forgive me for that, you know. Calumet, I mean." Leaning back in his chair, he continued, "I was playing it safe there, Robert. I could never be sure how the timing was going to converge in this operation, but sooner or later I figured Nishka would go after Calumet's medical records."

"And you knew that he'd run them through forensics and discover they were a fabrication."

"Yes. And you're right. I was prepared to sacrifice him. Not willing, but prepared."

Robert nodded, indicating he knew. "Because in the long run, if worse came to worst, you still had Jim Richardson over at the Pentagon. And it was imperative to keep him in play if everything else failed."

"Yes," Armbrister stated simply. "You know," he then added, his tone and demeanor reflective, "I remember what Le Carré once said through Smiley. He said, 'When our enemies lied, they lied to conceal the wretchedness of their system. Whereas when *we* lied, we concealed our virtues. Even from ourselves. We concealed the very things that made us right.' There's a mountain of truth in those words, Robert. After so many, many years, there comes a time when we have to set ourselves right. There comes a time when we have to drop the cover. My time has come."

With those words, Robert could tell that his old friend was having problems with the justification. He had fought for more than thirty years, and through it all performed magnificiently, but the machinations no longer fired his soul. The trade that had made him, he couldn't countenance any more. And Robert understood that. There *does* come a time when a man has to settle on his reckoning and answer for his past. For some, it comes earlier than for others, but it always comes. For most men, anyway.

But Armbrister still had a few bombs in the bay. "I've recommended you to succeed me, Robert."

Robert was so stunned he was calm. "Then you *have* gone bonkers, Lewis. I'm no good on a desk. You know that."

They bantered back and forth for another thirty minutes. It was a memorable time for both of them. They had shared the early days of the OSS and ridden a thousand storms together since then. And they had survived. Watching them told you something about the men and women who brought America into the twentieth century, and about those who kept us there. Sitting there, the world revolving around them, they represented the finest portion of the next generation's heritage. But would those who followed them remember? Hopefully, because without them, the present generation was meaningless.

Finally Robert stood and they shook hands. Robert walked to the door, and Armbrister called out to him. Robert turned.

"He was brilliant, wasn't he?" Armbrister asked.

"Calumet?"

"Yes."

"So were you, Lewis," Robert answered. "So were you."

After Robert departed, Armbrister went downstairs to the main lobby. His career was coming to an end, and he felt melancholy. And slightly troubled. His willingness to sacrifice Calumet, just like others he had never known personally, gnawed at him. He always wondered if it was worth it. He walked over to the memorial of fallen CIA officers—a protruding slab mounted on the wall—and began to read the names. After spending several moments there, reading the names and thinking about what they had done, his troubles began to dissipate, and his resolve became fortified. Because of those who had gone before, he decided, it was worth it. As long as America had enemies, it always would be.

*

Calumet was in a bad way. In just two weeks he'd lost fifteen pounds. And he had picked up the cigarettes again. He shaved only sporadically, and slept less. He spent his days playing solitaire on the computer, or sometimes on the rug. Over and over and over. Diane Shylock had moved in with him, determining he needed somebody to look after him. When she brought him food and tried to get him to eat, he growled at her. Other than that, he completely ignored her. And everybody and everything else as well. His mail sat unopened, scattered about his study. He would not take phone calls. He would not talk. He virtually redefined lethargy.

Diane was worried and at her wit's end. She did not know all the reasons for Calumet's despair, of course, though she might have suspected. She might have guessed. Still, she didn't push. She was there to help, not to hinder. And he definitely needed the help; that much was plain. She had never seen him like this before, and it scared her. It would have scared anyone who knew him. No matter how hard she tried, concocting this and crafting that, she could not draw him out. Robert had called a couple of times. When Calumet wouldn't come to the phone, Robert talked to Diane. She felt better for a while, but it never lasted because of Jack. He was indomitable in his shell. His only activity would be long drives in the middle of the night, and she always wondered if he was coming back. In his mental state, anything could happen.

Sitting there playing solitaire, Calumet recorded Odyssey over and over and over again in his mind. Each card dealt was a different phase of the operation, a sinister reminder of an affair gone sour. He relived Odyssey every moment of every day, and every time he got to Bern, he died in the warehouse along with Karola. Or *instead* of her maybe. She was dead because of him, because of his practiced manipulation, and the guilt was stifling. It wouldn't have been so bad had he been honest with her, had he expressed his feelings for her more forcefully and told her who he really was back there at the safe house when he first exposed her, but he didn't. He sent her back into harm's way, even though she had begged him, pleaded with him, not to. And when he remembered her leaning against his chest and whimpering, crying out, "Don't make me go back, Jack," arrows pierced his heart. *What have I done?*

Actually, he had only used her. That's what he had done, and he knew it. And the pain was unbearable. In the beginning she was nothing but a formula in a larger equation, an asset to be pushed across the board, but then his emotions cracked, and he ended up breaking all the rules. In spite of himself, he started to care. And in a way, he cared for her as he had cared for no one else ever before. A paternal care, in his assessment, mixed with romantic affection. Ultimately he saw her as a harlot-turned-maiden with a new lease on life and himself as her protector, her guardian, yet he simultaneously desired her as a woman. Perhaps the real tragedy was the fact that he never really got a chance to tell her.

Could Odyssey have gone ahead without her? Was Odyssey really all that important in the first place? Could he have spirited her away from the safe house that day and still managed to pull off the operation? After all, she had never been crucial to the Russian's strategy, or to his. Neither side really needed her. The Russians were merely using her as an extra ace up the sleeve. Her role was never meant to be one of paramount importance. So could he have gotten her out somehow? Before he made her go back in, that is?

Thoughts such as these perpetually haunted him, like a yo-yo on an endless string. His heart ached for her, and for his own feelings for her, and for the tragedy that blanketed her entire life. His mind whirled with self-incrimination for what he had done. Or had not done, actually. He thought of himself as the white knight who promised to come to the rescue and then failed to show. But even that analogy wasn't punishing enough in his own mind. In his own mind, he had done more than just fail to show, more than just fail to deliver. The pivotal matter of the whole sordid affair, the way he saw it, was a voracious reality that simply could not be ignored. It was the only conclusion that he could draw, inescapable in its indictment. Namely, he had killed Karola as surely as if he had fired the gun himself. He had forced her back into the jaws of vengeance. That's what he had done. After all, who else could she have run to, if not to him? Her mother was dead and her father was a devil. So it was all Jack's fault, the way he saw it. His recalcitrance at the safe house and her violent death at the end—these two things together were the proof. And the judgment.

To compound matters in his present state, he thought of Diane once in a while, and cringed when he realized what he was putting her through. What he had *already* put her through. But there was no turning back. Not from where Calumet was.

Calumet, a vacant look masking his eyes, was on the patio in the backyard when Robert showed up. It was a bright, sunny Saturday, the clock just passing noon.

"Hello, Jack," Robert said, stepping through the sliding door.

Calumet sat cross-legged on the wooden deck, facing away. He didn't budge. Behind Robert, still inside and half-hidden by the shadows, Diane stood, biting her lip. Tears began to make their way down her cheeks.

Robert sauntered around and pulled up a lawn chair. Placing it near Calumet, he took a seat and said, "Nice view you have here, Jack. Lots of trees, I see. I've always liked lots of trees myself."

But Robert could have been speaking to a statue for all anyone knew.

"Well," Robert continued, "I won't stay long. Just dropped by to bring you up to date." Turning to Diane, he said, "Could I trouble you for a glass of iced tea? Somehow," he grinned, "I've always thought the tea tastes better here in the South. No explanation for it, really. Must be the atmosphere or something."

Diane forced an accommodating smile and went to fetch the tea.

Robert took up again, his tone as pleasant as you please. "We returned . . . er . . . what was her name? Oh well, we returned the girl to Potsdam for burial. We—"

"Karola," Calumet snapped. His lips were all that moved.

"Ah! Yes," Robert smiled, but not too obviously. "Thank you. Karola. As I said, we returned her to Potsdam for burial. We gave her a nice headstone and funeral. Placed her right next to her mother. Just thought you might like to know."

Diane returned with the tea and handed it to Robert. "Thank you," Robert said pleasantly. Then he indicated to Diane that she should go back inside. After she was gone, he continued, "Normally, I would consider what happened to her to be tragic, especially when one considers all the heartache that pervaded her life. In the end, however, I believe she was very fortunate."

At this, Calumet's head turned slowly, his eyes seeming to come into some semblance of focus. Still, he uttered not a word.

"Yes," Robert persisted, "very fortunate, I would say. For a person who knew nothing but sorrow all her life, she was ultimately afforded the opportunity to die an immensely happy woman."

Suddenly; "How the hell do you figure that?" The outburst was accompanied by just the slightest flare in Calumet's pupils.

"Hmm. I thought that was obvious." Robert chose to be coy and let it hang.

But Calumet wasn't brain dead. "Just finish your tea and get out of here."

"The way I see it," Robert said agreeably, completely oblivious to Calumet's antisocial solicitation, "is that Karola felt an element of self-worth for the first time in her life. She felt fulfilled, wholesome. And you gave that to her, Jack."

Calumet glared at him, but said nothing.

"You see, Jack, you made this woman confront her demons. By doing so, you forced her to see herself, and once having seen herself, once having seen the *truth,* she was able to overcome all the lies and deceit that had characterized her entire existence. She had lived in fear for all those years, chained to the lies and the deceit, and you freed her from all of that. To be honest with you, I don't even think she was really in love with you at that point, after she was released from her chains, that is. I think she was just eminently grateful."

"Oh, ab-so-*lutely!*" Calumet chanted, his sarcasm ominous. "I'm sure she considered it a blasted *privilege* to get killed for me. Who *wouldn't* be grateful for an opportunity like that? Idiot! And yet, there appeared to be a glimmer of hope in his eyes, as if he was praying that Robert could somehow come up with a solution that would make everything all right.

"Actually, you're not far off base with that comment, Jack. In fact, I believe she *did* consider it a privilege to sacrifice herself for you. I think life itself was so horrendous for her that she wanted out. The problem, before you came along, was that she was more afraid of death than she was of life. However, once you set her free, once she saw that there was somebody in this world who respected her as a person, it made the prospect of death palatable. In the end, she wanted to be with her mother, and I honestly believe she thought death would bring about that union. The fact that she sacrificed herself for you was a act of supreme courage. She could not have done that without feeling mighty good about herself."

Something about Robert's words rang true. As is often the case, a deeper understanding takes place in the spirit than words can sometimes convey. It was so with Calumet. The bands of guilt that had shackled his soul began to disintegrate ever so slightly, just as the morning dew begins to evaporate with the sun. Still, a person does not march in and out of Hell and come away undamaged. And Hell is where he'd been, he figured. When all was said and done, she was still dead, and he was still to blame. It would still take some time to heal. Calumet gazed out at the trees, yet forlorn, once again drawing back into the safety of his shell. "I should have gotten Vartanyan," he whispered, more to the pristine sky than to Robert.

Robert heard him, however. "Don't worry, Jack. He'll be back. Wherever the Russians are causing trouble, Andrei Vartanyan won't be far away."

But Calumet was gone again, swimming in the depths of his own scorched soul.

Robert paused just then, diagnosing his patient, searching for a prizewinning cure. In the background leaves rustled gently on a tender breeze, but Robert's silence was thunderous. "Besides, Jack," he finally took up again, "you are not responsible for Karola's death. I know you feel that way, but you overestimate yourself by a wide margin if you think you could have foreseen all the contingencies. What you're experiencing is similar to commanders who have lost men in combat. 'What could I have done differently?' they ask themselves. There are never any easy answers, Jack. Not then, not now. We simply have to move on. Eventually, there is only one issue you must confront, only one issue you must come to terms with, and that is the disturbing mystery of why Karola ultimately chose to sacrifice herself for you."

He hesitated, allowing his words sink in. Although Calumet appeared to be locked in a furious trance, dead to the universe, Robert knew he was secretly paying attention. "So," the spymaster continued, "why did she sacrifice herself for you? Especially since she had pleaded with you not to force her to return? It's really very simple. She concluded that your life was more important than hers. She was giving back to you what you had already given to her. Before you came along she had no life, and she knew it, but in the last days of her existence she became the woman she had always longed to be, and she had you to thank for that, Jack. She received from you something that was priceless, something that meant more to her than all the treasures in the sea. You gave her a foundation for the first time in many, many years, and that's the one thing she had been searching for all of her adult life, or even before she was an adult actually, ever since that ugly, murderous day in West Berlin long, long ago, when her foundation was ripped from her soul."

Again, Robert momentarily held his peace. Jack had told him how her face lit up in the warehouse that day when he finally admitted he loved her. The spymaster wanted him to visualize in his mind's eye the comparison between the two; between the abomination of her mother's death and the ectasy of finally discovering that she was worthy on her own, without the lies and the seductions and the deceit, and all the wasted years in the middle. He wanted Calumet to measure the difference between the high and the low, between the nightmare of her youth and the wake-up call she received in the safe house that day at the hands of his blistering interrogation, because in his own wisdom Robert knew that relativity could sometimes be a great persuader. "You see, Jack, you once again managed to give purpose to her life by forcing her to open her eyes to the truth, and that in turn set her free to love, just as she loved when she was a little girl, before her mother died. To Karola, it was like a breath of fresh air, and one that she had completely forgotten existed until you came along."

Robert's voice exuded praise as he administered his last herb. "Don't you see, son? You managed to complete the circle for her, Jack. You returned to her all of her virtues. You managed to make her whole, and that's how she died. Proud and whole."

Calumet fought the tears, determined to keep them at bay. He suddenly understood what Robert was doing, and in spite of the psychology, the spymaster's clarity was compelling. Jack realized he was being forgiven suddenly, not by Robert, but somehow by Karola, through Robert's words somehow, as though Robert was holding court with the spirits, summarily conjuring a traveling séance and taking his act on the road, redemption his theme. Karola was smiling down upon him at this moment, it seemed, telling him that it was all okay, that the world was finally back in harmony, that the hammer of judgment had been stayed, and that better days would one day come again. She was at peace, the messenger was saying, and if she was at peace, so should he be. A lone tear finally overpowered him and broke through.

"Well," Robert said energetically, "so much for that. I'll have to be going in a minute. Officially, I'm here to tell you that you have the admiration and the utmost respect of practically everyone at the highest levels. You performed brilliantly, Jack. Armbrister said you were the best he's ever seen. He said it's a shame that you have to be put out to pasture now, what with your feelings about Odyssey and all. It's too bad that—"

"What did you say?" Calumet's eyes were suddenly alert. They were the same eyes that Robert had first encountered in Jack Calumet six years earlier.

Robert suppressed the grin that was struggling to rise to the surface. "I was talking about your performance. You see, Jack, as I mentioned—"

"No!" Calumet exclaimed. "Don't fence with me, Robert. What do you mean? What's this about a pasture?"

Robert cracked the barest smile. "Oh. That. Well—"

"Just hold on a minute," Calumet ordered. "Just hold the phone a second." Turning his head toward the house, he yelled, "Diane! Diane!"

She came to the door.

"I'll take a glass of that tea, if you don't mind. As a matter of fact, how about making me a sandwich?" Glancing back at Robert, he asked, "You want a sandwich?"

Robert was about to answer, but Calumet cut him off.

"You're not going anywhere, Robert, so don't even think about it." Facing Diane again, he said, "Forget the sandwich. Go to the store and buy some steaks." Back to Robert. "Stay right there, buster."

"Steaks?" Diane was smiling through the tears.

"Steaks!" Calumet commanded. "And get charcoal and lighter fluid and whatever else we need." Turning back to Robert once again, "Robert, you just keep your butt planted right there in that lawn chair. We're going to sit right here and talk about this pasture crap . . ." Calumet kept firing, dispensing the words like a Gatling gun.

Robert winked at Diane and grinned. The old schemer's brilliance had superseded them all.